The Best of Weis and Hickman

Celebrating 20 Years of Dragonlance®

Some of the most beloved stories by the original scribes of the Dragonlance setting.

"Dragonlance came out of the red-hot forge of Tracy's mind and was shaped and refined into novels with Margaret Weis. All Tracy needed was a chance."

—Jeff Grubb

"I believe I've written this elsewhere, but it doesn't hurt to say it again: for all the talents I could praise in Margaret and Tracy, both have an extraordinary gift for friendship. It is the thing about them that I regard most highly and that their readers should know."

—Michael Williams

The DRAGONLANCE Saga

The Best of Tales
Volume 1
Edited by Margaret Weis & Tracy Hickman

The Best of Tales
Volume 2
Edited by Margaret Weis & Tracy Hickman

The Players of Gilean
Edited by Margaret Weis & Tracy Hickman

The Search for Magic
Edited by Margaret Weis

The Search for Power
Edited by Margaret Weis

. . . and more than one hundred other DRAGONLANCE novels and anthologies by dozens of authors.

The Best of Weis & Hickman Anthology

Dragons in the Archives

DRAGONS IN THE ARCHIVES

Distributed in the United States by Holtzbrinck Publishing. Distributed in Canada by Fenn Ltd.

Distributed to the hobby, toy, and comic trade in the United States and Canada by regional distributors.

Distributed worldwide by Wizards of the Coast, Inc. and regional distributors.

Printed in the U.S.A.

Cover art by Michael Komarck
First Printing: November 2004
Library of Congress Catalog Card Number: 2004107061

9 8 7 6 5 4 3 2 1

US ISBN: 0-7869-3669-X
UK ISBN: 0-7869-3677-0
620-96931-001-EN

U.S., CANADA,
ASIA, PACIFIC, & LATIN AMERICA
Wizards of the Coast, Inc.
P.O. Box 707
Renton, WA 98057-0707
+1-800-324-6496

EUROPEAN HEADQUARTERS
Wizards of the Coast, Belgium
T Hofveld 6d
1702 Groot-Bijgaarden
Belgium
+322 467 3360

Visit our web site at www.wizards.com

TABLE OF CONTENTS

Introduction

Back in 1984, when we were first working on the Dragonlance project, neither Tracy nor I could have ever predicted that in 2004, we would be celebrating the twentieth anniversary of the Dragonlance Chronicles. As Tracy says, "It's been a wonderful ride!"

Gathered together in this book are some of the short stories and novellas that Tracy and I have written together and with other collaborators. Some of the stories have been published separately in other anthologies. Some stories were published only in Dragon magazine. For the first time, they've been brought together in a single volume.

Two of my favorites are the stories involving Lady Nikol and Brother Michael. These stories were written by Tracy and myself in honor of two very close friends of ours: Nicole Harsch and Mike Sakuta, a.k.a. the Crossed Swords. Mike and Nicole are professional sword-fighters, who have traveled all over the world with their exciting routine. Artist Larry Elmore portrayed them as themselves on the original covers of the Dragonlance Tales II books *The Reign of Istar*

(Volume One) and *The Cataclysm* (Volume Two).

Another of my favorite stories I wrote with Aron Eisenberg, who portrayed Nog on the Star Trek series, *Deep Space Nine*. Tracy and I had a "fan-boy" moment when Aron came up to the booth to ask for *our* autographs, while we were clamoring around trying to find something on which to get his autograph! Aron's idea for the Traveling Players of Gilean gave birth to a group of mysterious players who travel the world giving performances that not only teach the audience something about themselves, but teach the actors, as well.

In addition to the stories, we have brought together in this book reminiscences from early members of the DRAGONLANCE creative team, including artist Larry Elmore, game designers and novelists Jeff Grubb and Douglas Niles, poet and novelist Michael Williams, and our editor, Jean Black. In addition, Jamie Chambers writes about DRAGONLANCE, past and future, from a reader's perspective. Finally, there is an interview with Tracy and myself, talking about the many aspects of Dragonlance and how it has affected our lives.

Tracy and I have enjoyed the "ride" the past twenty years. We hope you have, as well.

May dragons fly forever in your dreams.

—Margaret Weis

The Best

by Margaret Weis

Originally published in *The Dragons of Krynn*

A story from the ancient times . . .

I knew the four would come. My urgent plea had brought them. Whatever their motives—and, among this diverse group, I knew these motives were mixed—they were here.

The best. The very best.

I stood in the door of the Bitter Ale Inn and, surveying them, my heart was easier than it had been in many, many days.

The four did not sit together. Of course, they didn't know each other, except perhaps by reputation. Each sat at his or her own table, eating, drinking quietly. Not making a show of themselves. They didn't need to. They were the best. But though they said nothing with their mouths—using them for the bitter ale so famous in these parts—they were putting their eyes to work: sizing each other up, taking each other's measure. I was thankful to see that each seemed to like what he or she saw. I wanted no bad blood between members of this group.

Sitting at the very front of the inn, short in stature, but large in courage—was Orin. The dwarf was renowned through these parts for his skill with his axe, but then so were most dwarves. His blade—Splithair—lay on the table before him, where he could keep both an eye and a loving hand on it. Orin's true talent lay beneath a mountain, as the saying went. He had traversed more dragon caves than any other dwarf who had ever lived. And he had never once lost his way, either there or (more important) back out again. Many a treasure-hunter owed his life—and about a third of the treasure—to his guide, Orin Dark-seer.

Seated near the dwarf, at the best table the Bitter Ale had to offer, was a woman of incredible beauty. Her hair was long and black as a moonless night; her eyes drank in men's souls the way the dwarf drank ale. The tavern's regulars—a sorry lot of ne'er-do-wells—would have been nosing around her, their tongues hanging out, but for the marks on her clothes.

She was well dressed, don't mistake me. The cloth she wore was the finest, most expensive velvet in all the land. Its blue color gleamed in the firelight. It was the silver embroidery on the cuffs of her robes and around the hemline that warned off the cheek-pinchers and kiss-snatchers. Pentagrams and stars and intertwined circles and suchlike. Cabalistic marks. Her beautiful eyes met mine, and I bowed to Ulanda the sorceress, come all the way from her fabled castle hidden in the Blue Mist Forest.

Seated near the door—as near the door as he could get and still remain in the inn—was the one member of the four I knew well. I knew him because I was the one who had turned the key in his prison cell and set him free. He was thin and quick, with a mop of red hair and green roguish eyes that could charm a widow out of her life savings and leave her loving him for it. Those slender fingers of his could slide in and out of a pocket as fast as his knife could cut a purse from a belt. He was good, so good he wasn't often caught. Reynard Deft-hand had made one small mistake. He'd tried to lift a purse from me.

Directly across the room from Reynard—dark balancing light in the scales of creation—was a man of noble bearing and stern countenance. The regulars left him alone, too, out of respect for his long and shining sword and the white surcoat he wore, marked with the silver rose. Eric of Truestone, Knight of the Rose, a holy paladin. I was as amazed to see him as I was pleased. I had sent my messengers to the High Clerist's Tower, begging the knights for aid. I knew they would respond—they were honor-bound. But they had responded by sending me their best.

All four the best, the very best. I looked at them and I felt awed, humbled.

"You should be closing down for the night, Marian," I said, turning to the pretty lass who tended bar.

The four dragon-hunters looked at me, and not one of them moved. The regulars, on the other hand, took the hint. They quaffed their ale and left without a murmur. I hadn't been in these parts long—newly come to my job—and, of course, they'd put me to the test. I'd been forced to teach them to respect me. That had been a week ago and one, so I heard, was still laid up. Several of the others winced and rubbed their cracked heads as they hurried past me, all politely wishing me good-night.

"I'll lock the door," I said to Marian.

She, too, left, also wishing me—with a saucy smile—a good night. I knew well she'd like to make my good night a better one, but I had business.

When she was gone, I shut and bolted the door. This clearly made Reynard nervous (he was already looking for another escape route), so I came quickly to the point.

"No need to ask why you're here. You've each come in response to my plea for help. I am Gondar, King Frederick's seneschal. I am the one who sent you the message. I thank you for your quick response, and I welcome you, well, most of you"—I cast a stern glance at Reynard, who grinned—"to Fredericksborough."

Sir Eric rose and made me a courteous bow. Ulanda looked me over with her wonderful eyes. Orin grunted. Reynard was jingling coins in his pocket. The regulars would find themselves without ale money tomorrow, I guessed.

"You all know why I sent for you," I continued. "At least, you know part of the reason. The part I would make public."

"Please be seated, Seneschal," said Ulanda, with a graceful gesture. "And tell us the part you couldn't make public."

The knight joined us, as did the dwarf. Reynard was going to, but Ulanda warned him off with a look. Not the least bit offended, he grinned again and leaned against the bar.

The four waited politely for me to continue.

"I tell you this in absolute confidentiality," I said, lowering my voice. "As you know, our good king, Frederick, has journeyed to the north on invitation from his half brother, the Duke of Northampton. There were many on the court who advised His Majesty not to go. None of us trust the twisted, covetous duke. But His Majesty was ever a loving sibling and north he went. Now, our worst fears have been realized. The duke is holding the king hostage, demanding in ransom seven coffers filled with gold, nine coffers filled with silver, and twelve coffers filled with precious jewels."

"By the eye of Paladine, we should burn this duke's castle to the ground," said Eric of the Rose. His hand clenched over his sword's hilt.

"We would never see His Majesty alive again," I shook my head.

"This is not why you brought us here," growled Orin. "Not to rescue your king. He may be a good king, for all I know, but . . ." The dwarf shrugged.

"Yes, but you don't care whether a human king lives or dies, do you, Orin?" I said with a smile. "No reason you should. The dwarves have their own king."

"And there are some of us," said Ulanda softly, "who have no king at all."

I wondered if the rumors I'd heard about her were true, that she lured young men to her castle and kept them until she tired of them, then changed them into wolves, forced to guard her dwelling place. At night, it was said, you could hear their howls of anguish. Looking into those lovely eyes, I found myself thinking it might just be worth it!

"I have not told you the worst," I said. "I collected the ransom. This is a wealthy kingdom. The nobles dipped into their treasuries. Their lady wives sacrificed their jewels. The treasure was loaded into a wagon, ready to be sent north when . . ."

I cleared my throat, wished I had drawn myself a mug of ale. "A huge red dragon swept out of the sky, attacked the treasure caravan. I tried to stand and fight, but"—my face burned in shame—"I've never known such paralyzing fear. The next thing I knew, I was facefirst on the ground, shivering in terror. The guard fled in panic.

"The great dragon settled down on the King's Highway. It leisurely devoured the horse, then, lifting the wagon containing the treasure in its claws, the cursed beast flew away."

"Dragonfear," said Orin, as one long experienced in such things.

"Though it has never happened to me, I've heard the dragonfear can be devastating." Sir Eric rested his hand pityingly on mine. "It was foul magic that unmanned you, Seneschal. No need for shame."

"Foul magic," repeated Ulanda, casting the knight a dark look. I could see she was thinking what an excellent wolf he would make.

"I saw the treasure." Reynard heaved a gusty sigh. "It was a beautiful sight. And there must be more, lots more, in that dragon's lair."

"There is," said Orin. "Do you think yours is the only kingdom this dragon has robbed, Seneschal? My people were hauling a shipment of golden nuggets from our mines in the south when a red dragon—pull out my beard if it's not the same one—swooped out of the skies and made off with it!"

"Golden nuggets!" Reynard licked his lips. "How much were they worth, all told?"

Orin cast him a baleful glance. "Never you mind, Lightfinger."

"The name is Deft-hand," Reynard said, but the rest ignored him.

"I have received word from my sisters in the east," Ulanda was saying, "that this same dragon is responsible for the theft of several of our coven's most powerful arcane artifacts. I would describe them to you, but they are very secret. And very dangerous, to the inexperienced," she added pointedly, for Reynard's sake.

"We, too, have suffered by this wyrm," said Eric grimly. "Our brethren to the west sent us as a gift a holy relic—a finger bone of Vinus Solamnus. The dragon attacked the escort, slaughtered them to a man, carried away our artifact."

Ulanda laughed, made a face. "I don't believe it! What would the dragon want with a moldy old finger bone?"

The knight's face hardened. "The finger bone was encased in a diamond, big around as an apple. The diamond was carried in a chalice made of gold, encrusted with rubies and emeralds. The chalice was carried on a platter made of silver, set with a hundred sapphires."

"I thought you holy knights took vows of poverty," Reynard insinuated slyly. "Maybe I should start going to church again."

Eric rose majestically to his feet. Glaring at the thief, the knight drew his sword. Reynard sidled over behind me.

"Hold, Sir Knight," I said, standing. "The route to the dragon's lair leads up a sheer cliff with nary a hand or foothold in sight."

The knight eyes Reynard's slender fingers and wiry body. Sheathing his sword, the knight sat back down.

"You've discovered the lair!" Reynard cried. He was trembling, so excited, I fear he might hug me.

"Is this true, Seneschal?" Ulanda leaned near me. I could smell musk and spice. Her fingertips were cool on my hand. "Have you found the dragon's lair?"

"I pray to Paladine you have! Gladly would I leave this life, spend eternity in the blessed realm of Paladine, if I could have a chance to fight this wyrm!" Eric vowed. Lifting a sacred medallion he wore around his neck to his lips, he kissed it to seal his holy oath.

"I lost my king's ransom," I said. "I took a vow neither to eat nor sleep until I had tracked the beast to its lair. Many weary days and nights I followed the trail—a shining coin fallen to the ground, a jewel spilled from the wagon. The trail led straight to a peak known as Black Mountain. A day I waited, patient, watching. I was rewarded. I saw the dragon leave its lair. I know how to get inside."

Reynard began to dance around the tavern, singing and snapping his long fingers. Eric of the Rose actually smiled. Orin Dark-seer ran this thumb lovingly over his axe-blade. Ulanda kissed my cheek.

"You must come visit me some night, Seneschal, when this adventure is ended," she whispered.

The four of them and I spent the night in the inn, were up well before dawn to begin our journey.

****

The Black Mountain loomed before us, its peak hidden by a perpetual cloud of gray smoke. The mountain is named for its shining black rock, belched up from the very bowels of the world. Sometimes the mountain still rumbles, just to remind us that it is alive, but none living could remember the last time it spewed flame.

We reached it by late afternoon. The sun's rays shone red on the cliff face we would have to climb. By craning my neck, I could see the gaping dark hole that was the entrance to the dragon's lair.

"Not a handhold in sight. By Paladine, you weren't exaggerating, Seneschal," said Eric, frowning as he ran his hand over the smooth black rock.

Reynard laughed. "Bah! I've climbed castle walls that were as smooth as milady's—Well, let's just say they were smooth."

The thief looped a long length of rope over his shoulder. He started to add a bag full of spikes and a hammer, but I stopped him.

"The dragon might have returned. If so, the beast would hear you driving the spikes into the rock," I glanced upward. "The way is not far, just difficult. Once you make it, lower the rope down to us. We can climb it."

Reynard agreed. He studied the cliff face a moment, all seriousness now, no sign of a grin. Then, to the amazement of all of us watching, he attached himself to the rock like a spider and began to climb.

I had known Reynard was good, but I must admit, I had not known how good. I watched him crawl up that sheer cliff face, digging his fingers into minute cracks, his feet scrabbling for purchase, hanging on, sometimes, by effort of will alone. I was impressed. He was the best. No other man living could have made it up that cliff.

"The gods are with us in our holy cause," said Eric reverently, watching Reynard crawl up the black rock like a lizard. Ulanda stifled a yawn, covered her mouth with a dainty hand. Orin stomped around the foot of the cliff in impatience. I continued to watch Reynard, admiring his work. He had reached the entrance to the cavern, disappeared inside. In a moment, he came back out, indicated with a wave of his hand that all was safe.

Reynard lowered the rope down to us. Unfortunately, the rope he's brought was far too short. We couldn't reach it. Orin began to curse loudly. Ulanda laughed, snapped her fingers, spoke a word. The rope quivered, and suddenly it was exactly the right length.

Eric eyed the magiced rope dubiously, but it was his only way up. He grabbed hold of it, then—appearing to think of something—he turned to the sorceress.

"My lady, I fear your delicate hands are not meant for climbing ropes, nor are you dressed for scaling mountains. If you will forgive me the liberty, I will carry you up the cliff."

"Carry me!" Ulanda stared at him, then she laughed again.

Eric stiffened; his face went rigid and cold. "Your pardon, my lady—"

"Forgive me, Sir Knight," Ulanda said smoothly. "But I am not a weak and helpless damsel. And it would be best if you remembered that. All of you."

So saying, Ulanda drew a lacy, silken handkerchief from her pocket and spread it upon the ground. Placing her feet upon the handkerchief, she spoke words that were like the sound of tinkling chimes. The handkerchief became hard as steel. It began to rise slowly into the air, bearing the sorceress with it.

Sir Eric's eyes widened. He made the sign against evil.

Ulanda floated calmly up the cliff face. Reynard was on hand to assist her with the landing at the mouth of the cave. The thief's eyes nearly bugged out of his head. He was practically drooling. We could all hear his words.

"What a second-story man you'd make! Lady, I'll give you half—well, a fourth of my treasure for that scrap of cloth."

Ulanda picked up the steel platform, snapped it once in the air. Once again, the handkerchief was silk and lace. She placed it carefully in a pocket of her robes. The thief's eyes followed it all the way.

"It is not for sale," Ulanda said, and she shrugged. "You wouldn't find it of much value anyway. If anyone touches it, other than myself, the handkerchief will wrap itself around the unfortunate person's nose and mouth. It will smother him to death."

She smiled at Reynard sweetly. He eyed her, decided she was telling the truth, gulped, and turned hastily away.

"May Paladine preserve me," Eric said dourly. Laying his hand upon the rope, he started to climb.

He was strong, that knight. Encased in heavy plate armor and chain mail, his sword hanging from his side, he pulled himself up the cliff with ease. The dwarf was quick to follow, running up the rope nimbly. I took my time. It was nearly evening now, but the afternoon sun had warmed the rock. Hauling myself up that rope was hot work. I slipped once, giving myself the scare of a lifetime. But I managed to hang on, heaved a sigh of relief when Eric pulled me up over the ledge and into the cool shadows of the cavern.

"Where's the dwarf?" I asked, noticing only three of my companions were around.

"He went ahead to scout the way," said Eric.

I nodded, glad for the chance to rest. Reynard drew up the rope, hid it beneath a rock for use on the way back. I glanced around. All along the sides of the cavern, I could see marks left by the dragon's massive body scraping against the rock. We were examining these when Orin returned, his bearded face split in a wide smile.

"You are right, Seneschal. This is the way to the dragon's lair. And this proves it."

Orin held his find up to the light. It was a golden nugget. Reynard eyed it covetously, and I knew then and there it was going to cause trouble.

"This proves it!" Orin repeated, his eyes shining bright as the gold. "This is the beast's hole. We've got him! Got him now!"

Eric of the Rose, a grim look on his face, drew his sword and started for a huge tunnel leading off the cavern's entrance. Shocked, Orin caught hold of the knight, pulled him back.

"Are you daft, man?" the dwarf demanded. "Will you go walking in the dragon's front door? Why don't you just ring the bell, let him know we're here?"

"What other way is there?" Eric asked, nettled at Orin's superior tone.

"The back way," said the dwarf cunningly. "The secret way. All dragons keep a back exit, just in case. We'll use that."

"You're saying we have to climb round to the other side of this bloody mountain?" Reynard protested. "After all the work it took to get here?"

"Naw, Light-finger!" Orin scoffed. "We'll go *through* the mountain. Safer, easier. Follow me."

He headed for what looked to me like nothing more than a crack in the wall. But, once we had all squeezed inside, we discovered a tunnel that led even deeper into the mountain.

"This place is blacker than the Dark Queen's heart," muttered Eric, as we took our first few tentative steps inside. Although he had spoken in a low voice, his words echoed alarmingly.

"Hush!" the dwarf growled. "What do you mean dark? I can see perfectly."

"But we humans can't! Do we dare risk a light?" I whispered.

"We won't get far without one," Eric grumbled. He'd already nearly brained himself on a low-hanging rock. "What about a torch?"

"Torches smoke. And it's rumored there're other things living in this mountain besides the dragon!" Reynard said ominously.

"Will this do?" asked Ulanda.

Removing a jeweled wand from her belt, she held it up. She spoke no word, but—as if offended by the darkness—the wand began to shine with a soft white light.

Orin shook his head over the frailty of humans and stumped off down the tunnel. We followed after.

The path led down and around and over and under and into and out of and up and sideways and across . . . a veritable maze. How Orin kept from getting lost or mixed up was beyond me. All of us had doubts (Reynard expressed his loudly), but Orin never wavered.

We soon lost track of time, wandering in the darkness beneath the mountain, but I would guess that we ended up walking most of the night. If we had not found the coin, we still would have guessed the dragon's presence, just by the smell. It wasn't heavy or rank, didn't set us gagging or choking. It was a scent, a breath, a hint of blood and sulphur, gold and iron. It wasn't pervasive, but drifted through the narrow corridors like the dust, teasing, taunting.

Ulanda wrinkled her nose in disgust. She'd just complained breathlessly that she couldn't stand another moment in this "stuffy hole" when Orin brought us to a halt. Grinning slyly, he looked round at us.

"This is it," he said.

"This is what?" Eric asked dubiously, staring at yet another crack in the wall. (We'd seen a lot of cracks!)

"It leads to the dragon's other entrance," said the dwarf.

Squeezing through the crack, we found ourselves in another tunnel, this one far larger than any we'd found yet. We couldn't see daylight, but we could smell fresh air, so we knew the tunnel connected to the outside. Ulanda held her wand up to the wall, and there again were the marks made by the dragon's body. To clinch the matter, a few red scales glittered on the ground.

Orin Dark-seer had done the impossible. He'd taken us clean through the mountain. The dwarf was pretty pleased with himself, but his pleasure was short-lived.

We stopped for a rest, to drink some water and eat a bite of food to keep up our energy. Ulanda was sitting beside me, telling me in a low voice of the wonders of her castle, when suddenly Orin sprang to his feet.

"Thief!" The dwarf howled. He leapt at Reynard. "Give it back!"

I was standing; so was Reynard, who managed to put me in between himself and the enraged dwarf.

"My gold nugget!" Orin shrieked.

"Share and share alike," Reynard said, bobbing this way and that to avoid the dwarf. "Finders keepers."

Orin began swinging that damn axe of his a bit too near my knees for comfort.

"Shut them up, Seneschal!" Eric ordered me, as if I were one of his foot soldiers. "They'll bring the dragon down on us!"

"Fools! I'll put an end to this!" Ulanda reached her hand into a silken pouch she wore on her belt.

I think we may as well have lost both thief and guide at that moment, but we suddenly had far greater problems.

"Orin! Behind you!" I shouted.

Seeing by the expression of sheer terror on my face that this was no trick, Orin whirled around.

A knight—or what had once been a knight—was walking toward us. His armor covered bone, not flesh. His helm rattled on a bare and bloodstained skull. He held a sword in his skeletal hand. Behind him, I saw what seemed an army of these horrors, though there were—in reality—only six or seven.

"I've heard tell of this!" Eric said, awed. "These were once living men, who dared attack this dragon. The wyrm killed them and now forces their rotting corpses to serve him!"

"I'll put it out of its misery," Orin cried. Bounding forward, the dwarf struck at the undead warrior with his axe. The blade severed the knight's knees at the joint. The skeleton toppled. The dwarf laughed.

"No need to trouble yourselves over this lot," he told us. "Stand back."

The dwarf went after the second. But at that moment, the first skeleton picked up its bones, began putting itself back together! Within moments, it was whole again. The skeleton brought its sword down on the dwarf's head. Fortunately for Orin, he was wearing a heavy steel helm. The sword did no damage, but the blow sent the dwarf reeling.

Ulanda already had her hand in her pouch. She drew out a noxious powder, tossed it onto the undead warrior nearest her. The skeleton went up in a whoosh of flame that nearly incinerated the thief, who had been attempting to lift a jeweled dagger from the undead warriors belt. After that, Reynard very wisely took himself out of the way, watched the fight from a corner.

Eric of the Rose drew his sword, but he did not attack. Holding his blade by the hilt, he raised it in front of one of the walking skeletons. "I call on Paladine to free these noble knights of the curse that binds them to this wretched life."

The undead warrior kept coming, its bony hand clutching a rusting sword. Eric held his ground, stood fast, repeating his prayer in sonorous Solamnic. The skeletal warrior raised its sword for the deathblow. Eric gazed at it steadfastly, never wavering in his faith.

I watched with that terrible fascination that freezes a man in his tracks until the end.

"Paladine!" Eric gave a great shout, raised his sword to the heavens.

The skeletal knight dropped down in a pile of dust at the knight's feet.

Orin, who had been exchanging blows with two corpses for some time and was now getting the worse of the battle, beat a strategic retreat. Ulanda with her magic and Eric with his faith took care of the remainder of the skeletal warriors.

I had drawn my sword, but, seeing that my help wasn't needed, I watched in admiration. When the warriors were either reduced to dust or smoldering ash, the two returned. Ulanda's hair wasn't even mussed. Eric hadn't broken into a sweat.

"There are not two in this land who could have done what you did," I said to them, and I meant it.

"I am good at anything I undertake," Ulanda said. She wiped dust from her hands. "Very good," she added with a charming smile and a glance at me from beneath her long eyelashes.

"My god Paladine was with me," Eric said humbly.

The battered dwarf glowered. "Meaning to say my god Reorx wasn't?"

"The good knight means nothing of the sort." I was quick to end the argument. "Without you, Orin Dark-seer, we would be food for the dragon right now. Why do you think the skeleton men attacked us? Because we are drawing too near the dragon's lair, and that is due entirely to your expertise. No one else in this land could have brought us this far safely, and we all know it."

At this, I glanced pointedly at Eric, who took the hint and bowed courteously, if a bit stiffly, to the dwarf. Ulanda rolled her lovely eyes, but muttered something gracious.

I gave Reynard a swift kick in the pants, and the thief reluctantly handed over the golden nugget, which seemed to mean more to the dwarf than our words of praise. Orin thanked us all, of course, but his attention was on the gold. He examined it suspiciously, as if worried that Reynard might have tried to switch the real nugget with a fake. The dwarf bit down it, polished it on his doublet. Finally certain the gold was real, Orin thrust it beneath his leather armor for safekeeping.

So absorbed was the dwarf in his gold that he didn't notice Reynard lifting his purse from behind. I did, but I took care not to mention it.

As I said, we were close to the dragon's lair.

We moved ahead, doubly cautious, keeping sharp watch for any foe. We were deep inside the mountain now. It was silent. Too silent.

"You'd think we'd hear something," Eric whispered to me. "The dragon breathing, if nothing else. A beast that large would sound like a bellows down here."

"Perhaps this means he's not home," Reynard said.

"Or perhaps it means we've come to a dead end," said Ulanda icily.

Rounding a corner of the tunnel, we all stopped and stared. The sorceress was right. Ahead of us, blocking our path, was a solid rock wall.

The darkness grew darker at that moment. All hint of outside air had long since been left behind. The scent of blood and sulphur, now enhanced by a dank, chill, musty smell, was strong. And so was the scent of gold. I could smell it and so, I knew, could my companions. Our imaginations, I suppose, or perhaps wishful thinking. But maybe not. Gold has a smell—its own metal smell and, added to that, the stink of the sweat from all the hands that have touched it and coveted it and grasped it and lost it. That was the smell, and it was sweet perfume to everyone in that cave. Sweet and frustrating, for—seemingly—we had no way to reach it.

Orin's cheeks flushed. He tugged on his beard, cast us all a sidelong glance. "This must be the way," he muttered, kicking disconsolately at the rock.

"We'll have to go back," Eric said grimly. "Paladine is teaching me a lesson. I should have faced the wyrm in honorable battle. None of this skulking around like a—"

"Thief?" Reynard said brightly. "Very well, Sir Knight, you can go back to the front door, if you want. I will sneak in by the window."

With this, Reynard closed his eyes, and flattening himself against the rock wall, he seemed—to all appearances—to be making love to it. His hands crawled over it, his fingers poking and prodding. He even whispered what sounded like cooing and coaxing words. Suddenly, with a triumphant grin, he placed his feet in two indentations in the bottom of the wall, put his hands in two cracks and the top, and pressed.

The rock wall shivered, then it began to slide to one side! A shaft of reddish light beamed out. The thief jumped off the wall, waved his hand at the opening he'd created.

"A secret door," Orin said. "I knew it all along."

"You want to go around to the front now?" Reynard asked the knight slyly.

Eric glared at the thief, but he appeared to be having second thoughts about meeting the dragon face-to-face in an honorable fight. He drew his sword, waited for the wall to open completely so that we could see inside.

The light pouring out from the doorway was extremely bright. All of us blinked and rubbed our eyes, trying to adjust them to the sudden brilliance after the darkness of the tunnels. We waited, listening for the dragon. None of us had a doubt but that we had discovered the beast's dwelling place.

We heard nothing. All was deathly quiet.

"The dragon's not home!" Reynard rubbed his hands. "Hiddukel the Trickster is with me today!" He made a dash for the entrance, but Sir Eric's hand fell, like doom, on his shoulder.

"I will lead," he said. "It is my right."

Sword in hand, a prayer on his lips, the holy paladin walked into the dragon's lair.

Reynard crept right behind him. Orin, moving more cautiously, followed the thief. Ulanda had taken a curious-looking scroll from her belt. Holding it fast, she entered the lair after the dwarf. I drew my dagger. Keeping watch behind me, I entered last.

The door began to rumble shut.

I halted. "We're going to be trapped in here!" I called out as loudly as I dared.

The others paid no attention to me. They had discovered the dragon's treasure room.

The bright light's source was a pit of molten rock bubbling in a corner of the gigantic underground chamber. The floor of the cavern had been worn smooth, probably by the rubbing of the dragon's enormous body. A great, glittering heap, tall as His Majesty's castle, was piled together on the cavern floor.

Gathered here was every beautiful, valuable, and precious object in the kingdom. Gold shone red in the firelight, jewels of every color of the rainbow winked and sparkled. The silver reflected the smiles of the dragon-hunters. And, best of all, the cavern was uninhabited.

Sir Eric fell on his knees and began to pray.

Ulanda stared, openmouthed.

Orin was weeping into his beard with joy.

But by now, the secret door had slammed shut.

Not one of them noticed.

"The dragon's not home!" Reynard shrieked, and he made a dive for the treasure pile.

The thief began pawing through the gold.

My gold.

I walked up behind him.

"Never jump to conclusions," I said.

With my dagger, I gave him the death a thief deserves.

I stabbed him in the back.

"I thought you should at least have a look," I said to him kindly, gesturing to my hoard. "Since you're the best."

Reynard died then—the most astonished looking corpse I'd ever seen. I still don't think he'd quite figured things out.

But Ulanda had. She was smart, that sorceress. She guessed the truth immediately, if a bit late—even before I took off my ring of shapechanging.

Now, at last, after weeks of being cramped into that tiny form, I could stretch out. My body grew, slowly taking on its original, immense shape, almost filling the cavern. I held the ring up in front of her eyes.

"You were right," I told her, the jewel sparkling in what was now a claw. "Your coven did possess many powerful arcane objects. This is just one of them."

Ulanda stared at me in terror. She tried to use her scroll, but the dragonfear was too much for her. The words of magic wouldn't come to her parched, pale lips.

She'd been sweet enough to invite me to spend the night, so I did her a favor. I let her see, before she died, a demonstration of the magic now in my possession. Appropriately, it was one of my most prized artifacts—a necklace made out of magical wolves' teeth—that encircled her lovely neck and tore out her throat.

All this time, Orin Dark-seer had been hacking at my hind leg with his axe. I let him get in a few licks. The dwarf hadn't been a bad sort, after all, and he'd done me a favor by showing me the weakness in my defenses. When he seemed likely to draw blood, however, I tired of the contest. Picking him up, I tossed him in the pool of molten lava. Eventually, he'd become part of the mountain—a fitting end for a dwarf. I trust he appreciated it.

That left Sir Eric, who had wanted, all along, to meet me in honorable battle. I granted him his wish.

He faced me bravely, calling on Paladine to fight at his side.

Paladine must have been busy with something else just then, for he didn't make an appearance.

Eric died in a blaze of glory.

Well, he died in a blaze.

I trust his soul went straight to the Dome of Creation, where it's my guess his god must have had some pretty fancy explaining to do.

They were dead now. All four.

I put out the fire, swept up the knight's ashes. Then I shoved the other two corpses out the secret door. The thief and the sorceress would take the place of the skeletal warriors I'd been forced to sacrifice to keep up appearances.

Crawling back to my treasure pile, I tidied up the gold a bit, where the thief had disturbed it. Then I climbed on top, spread myself out, and burrowed deeply and luxuriously into the gold and silver and jewels. I spread my wings protectively over the treasure, even paused to admire the effect of the firelight shining on my red scales. I wrapped my long tail around the golden nuggets of the dwarves, stretched my body comfortably out over the jewels of the knights, laid my head down on the magical treasure of the sorceress's coven.

I was tired, but satisfied. My plan had worked out wonderfully well. I had rid myself of them.

They'd been the best. The very best.

Sooner or later, separately or together, they would have come after me. And they might have caught me napping.

I settled myself onto the treasure more comfortably, closed my eyes. I'd earned my rest.

And I could sleep peacefully . . . now.

Honor and Guile

by Margaret Weis
Originally published in Dragon *Magazine* #243

Located on a well-traveled crossroads, the town of Solace, unlike many towns, welcomed strangers. Solace even offered the parched and weary traveler a choice of drinking and dining establishments. The best known of these was the Inn of the Last Home. Built high among the limbs of one of the enormous vallenwoods, the Inn was renowned all the way to distant Palanthas for its ale, its friendliness, and the proprietor's spiced potatoes. Light beaming through the Inn's stained glass windows was a beacon to the thirsty, the smell of the potatoes a lure to the hungry. Otik's smile, as he greeted arriving guests, was warmer than his own hearth fire.

Not all travelers find that spiced potatoes, warm smiles, or bright lights agree with them, however. Some find the darkness welcome and soothing, never mind that the potatoes are boiled and generally underdone at that. Some prefer the more potent dwarf spirits to foaming nut-brown ale. Thus, some travelers to Solace found that its second tavern, one known as The Trough, more suited to their tastes.

Built on the ground for the primary reason that no person under the influence of dwarf spirits should be climbing trees, The Trough lived up to its name and its signboard, which featured a pig wallowing in swill. The tavern even looked like a trough, a V-shaped gray building with a collapsing roof wedged between the boles of two large vallenwoods. The Trough had another advantage. People could reach The Trough from the main road without going into Solace proper. People could meet safely in The Trough, where they could meet safely nowhere else.

Three such people sat this night, eating the watery potatoes and the stringy beef and drinking beer, not dwarf spirits, since the three were discussing business. They kept their voices low, although it was well-known that the barmaids in The Trough were deaf, the tavern keeper mute, and all of them blind—handicaps purchased with good steel coins. "This is a rich town," said one with a knowing wink and a cunning leer. "I tell you, Cutthroat. I've lived here three months, and there's money for the taking. Why, the amount raked in by that fat old innkeeper Otik alone would set us up for a year in Sanction!

"And I say that I've seen no sign of it," argued another, glaring down at his potatoes with a scowl they richly deserved.

"That's because you have no imagination, Cutpurse," said his brother. The two thieves, in a fit of cleverness from which they had never fully recovered, called themselves Cutpurse and Cutthroat. "Go on, Jack Ladyfinger. What else have you found out?"

"There's a wife of a Solamnic knight living here. You know that she's just dripping with jewels, for all she pretends to be so poor! And a dwarven metal-smith. His house must be loaded with silver and steel."

"Well and what if they are?" groused Cutpurse. He was in a bad mood, the beef was doing strange things to his insides. "We can't rob them all in one night! And after the first heist, the whole damn place will be up in arms. Ogres take them! This stuff is swill!" He flung his plate to the floor, spilling the potatoes and scattering the beef.

The tavern dog—a lean and perpetually starved animal—dashed up, sniffed at the beef, wisely ignored it, and ate the potatoes. The barmaid let the dog do her cleaning for her, then picked up the plate. She kicked the beef under the table.

"Would I have sent for you if I didn't have a plan? demanded Jack Ladyfinger—so called because of his deft and delicate hands. He bragged that his touch so light he could slide his hand inside a mark's pocket, sort out the steel coins from the pence, take only the steel, with the mark being none the wiser.

"No, of course, you wouldn't, Jack," said Cutthroat, giving his brother a kick in the shins.

"Listen to this, my friends," said Jack. He beckoned the other two to lean their heads closer. "Three weeks ago, the sheriff caught wind that goblins were planning a raid on the town. He called out the militia, and all the warriors in the town left their homes, ready to defend the town. The women and kids holed up in the Inn."

"So?" Cutpurse growled.

"So, I'm not finished yet. The Sheriff told the good citizens to bring all their valuables to him. He and a couple of guards carried them off in a box to stash them away in a safe hiding place." Jack sat back, looking pleased. What do you think of that? It will be the easiest job we ever pulled."

"I get it. We rob the houses while the men are away!" said Cutpurse.

"No, you booby!" His brother kicked him again. "What's the use of robbing the houses if the owners have hauled off all the steel and the jewels?"

"Well, then, I don't understand," said Cutpurse sourly.

"We rob the place where they're hiding the valuables!" Cutthroat explained.

"Oh," said Cutpurse, considering. "Yeah, that's a good plan. Well done, Jack." He belched. "Where is this hiding place?"

"I don't know," said Jack, shrugging.

"What?" Cutpurse demanded. His hand went to the knife he carried hidden in his boot. "I don't like games, Jack Ladyfinger."

"How could I find out?" Jack protested. "You think they'd tell me?

"Hell, most of them don't know. The sheriff uses a different hiding place each time. The only ones who know the hiding place are those who help to carry the loot there and those who stay behind to guard it."

"So we follow them to the hiding place?"

"Naw. I tried that last time. They keep a close lookout. Nearly tossed me in the lock-up, but I pretended like I was drunk, and so they let me go."

"What good does this do us then?" Cutthroat frowned. He was starting to agree with his brother. "You've brought us here on a wild kender chase, Jack Ladyfinger, that's what I think."

"You should do less thinking," suggested Jack. "It obviously hurts." He motioned them all closer. "Now, here's my plan . . ."

****

The horn blast split the quiet night wide open and woke the twins out of a sound sleep.

"Not again!" Raistlin complained. Pulling the blankets up around his chin, he rolled over and clamped his pillow over his head to shut out the raucous noise.

Caramon was out of bed, pulling on his breeches. "C'mon, Raist! You've got to come. We're part of the militia. You know the law. All able-bodied men sixteen and older—"

"I am not able-bodied," said his brother, his voice muffled by the blanket. "Tell them that, and leave me in peace."

"I did tell them last time, Raist," said Caramon earnestly. "But the sheriff said that even if you couldn't fight you could be useful gathering up spent arrows or carrying water—"

"No," said Raistlin, snuggling deeper into his warm bed.

The horn brayed. Torch lights flared. Voices shouted, spreading the alarm. Children wailed. Booted feet clumped past, running along the boardwalk.

Raistlin sighed and threw off the blanket. He sat up in bed.

"You might be able to use your magic," Caramon suggested, hoping to cheer his disgruntled twin.

"And do what?" Raistlin snapped. "Pull coins from their ears? Pluck silk scarves from their navels? Don't be an ass, Caramon. You know very well that I have no spells in my spellbook! Not yet. I am only a student. Well, don't just stand there gawking at me! Go on! Answer the call! Go protect us from the forces of evil!"

"Aren't you coming?" Caramon asked, worried.

"I suppose I must," Raistlin said crossly. "I might as well. I'm not going to get any more sleep tonight. That much is obvious. Besides, I look forward to plucking bloody arrows from mangled corpses."

"Do you, Raist?" Caramon was pleased. "I'll tell the Sheriff."

Raistlin didn't bother to respond. Sarcasm was wasted on Caramon.

Caramon dashed out, grabbing hold of his father's woodchopping axe, Gilon's one legacy to his children, which stood beside the door. Merging with the throng of people clattering along the boardwalk, Caramon hurried off to the blacksmith shop, the gathering point for the militia. Women and children, the elderly, and the infirm hastened to the Inn of the Last Home, where they would take refuge.

Pulling on his white robes—robes that he wore to honor his mentor, an archmagus of the White—Raistlin stood in the doorway. Men and women, armed with sword or bow, hurried past, ready to do their part to defend their town. Watching them, Raistlin contemplated his own uselessness. Although he and his brother were twins, they were nothing alike. Caramon at sixteen was taller than most of the men in Solace, with well-developed muscles from laboring on a nearby farm. Genial and cheerful, he was everybody's friend.

Raistlin, by contrast, was thin with spindly arms and legs. Often sick, he was easily and quickly fatigued. He could not so much as lift his father's axe, which Caramon hefted with ease. To compensate for his weakness, Raistlin sharpened his wit instead of steel. Brains would win him his way in the world, not brawn. Brains and his skill as a mage. That skill was not much in evidence at the moment, however. Raistlin was still a student, permitted to learn only a very few minor spells, and then he was ordered not to use them.

Standing in the doorway of the home he shared with his brother, he wondered bitterly if he should go to the Inn with the women and children. At least there he could sit beside a roaring fire; no standing about on the frost-riven ground in the dead of night, waiting to be attacked by goblins. Otik would undoubtedly be serving hot cider. Just as he was considering this pleasant possibility, he remembered that the Inn would be crowded with mewling infants and bawling toddlers. Upon consideration, Raistlin decided to take his chances on the goblins.

It occurred to him then that he could be of some use in a battle—and not picking up arrows. His studies in herb lore had gained him a reputation as a healer, an occupation much in demand in these days when the clerics had disappeared with the Cataclysm. Hastily Raistlin gathered some of his unguents and salves known to help ease the pain of burns and prevent wounds from becoming infected. He added to this strips of cloth for bandages, of which he kept a supply. Armed with these, he hastened out to join his brother and the rest of Solace's defenders.

"Hurry up there, lad," grumbled one of the town guards. "We're about to hoist up this ladder."

Raistlin descended the ladder that led from the boardwalk to the ground below and that could be pulled up as part of Solace's defense. No enemy without wings could launch a truly effective attack against the tree-top town. Fire was the biggest danger. The vallenwood trees did not burn easily, but they would burn, as would the houses within the trees. Buckets of water were being drawn from the wells, swung up on ropes, placed at strategic locations.

Raistlin searched through the large crowd which had gathered in a semi-circle around the Sheriff, looking for his brother, whom he found standing next to Sturm. The flaring brands lit the area as bright as day, filled the air with smoke. Raistlin began coughing.

"Are you all right, Raist?" Caramon asked anxiously.

"No, he isn't," said Sturm, casting Raistlin a disapproving glance. "What's more, the night air is chill, and there is liable to be fighting. He should not stay."

Sturm Brightblade, two years older than the twins, was the son of a knight of Solamnia and, as such, had little use for mages. He and Raistlin had known each other for about ten years and had disliked each other for at least that long.

"Perhaps you should go to the Inn, Raistlin. At least there you will be out of the—" Sturm paused, amended his statement. "You will be safe."

"Perhaps you should go soak your head in a bucket, Sturm Brightblade," Raistlin returned caustically. "If you're lucky, people might mistake the bucket for a helm and so mistake you for a knight."

"Suit yourself," Sturm retorted, coldly angry. "But keep out of my way. I shall not have time to look after you." He moved several paces away.

"Hush, you two," said Caramon, unhappy at the quarrel. "The Sheriff is talking."

"We have word that the same roving band of goblins we heard about three weeks ago is still in the area and planning an attack on our town." The Sheriff pointed to a tall, thin, shabbily dressed man. "This man claims to have seen them while he was out hunting. He overheard their plans."

"I speak a little Goblin," said the shabby man modestly.

"Humpf!" Raistlin snorted. "And I speak gully dwarf."

"Be quiet!" Sturm said, glaring at Raistlin severely.

"You all know the drill," the Sheriff continued. "You know where you're supposed to be. You know your duties. Bowmen up above in the trees, those with swords and axes on the ground below."

"I saw a goblin once!" cried a shrill voice. A small hand could be seen waving from the depths of the crowd. "Back in Kendermore. Or was it the Ruins? Maybe it was Palanthas. I can show you the place. I have a map. Anyway this goblin was a big, ugly brute with squinty eyes and he said to me, he said—"

"It's that kender," whispered Caramon under his breath. "The one who lives with the dwarf."

At the sound of the kender's voice, every person in the crowd—including the Sheriff—checked to make certain they were still in possession of purses, pouches, weapons and any other articles likely to fall victim to a kender's curiosity. Raistlin took a hasty inventory of his bag of unguents and salves, made certain it was still tied securely to his belt.

The kender's speech was interrupted by the sounds of a scuffle.

After one indignant "ouch!" the kender's voice was silenced, replaced by a gruffer, deeper voice.

"Beg pardon, Sheriff. He won't interrupt you again."

A muffled shriek could be heard, a shriek which might have come from a kender with a hand over his mouth.

"You do that, Fireforge," said the Sheriff, frowning. "And make certain he stays away from our belongings."

"I'll keep an eye on him," said a tall, soft-spoken man, a half-elf.

"Thank you, Tanis. Now, speaking of our belongings, those who have brought valuables to be taken into hiding, bring them forward."

People took turns trooping forward, depositing bags of coins, family jewels, and other precious objects and heirlooms into a large metal box. The Sheriff noted down the contents on a board, which was to be taken to the Inn for safe-keeping. When the last person had made a deposit, the box was closed and padlocked.

"I need volunteers to help carry it," called the Sheriff.

The shabby man raised his hand with alacrity.

The Sheriff gave him a dubious glance and passed over him. His gaze rested on the stalwart Caramon and upon Sturm, standing at his side.

"You two young men." The Sheriff beckoned. "Bring the box and come with me. I'll show you where to stash it. You men"—he singled out two of the town guards—"follow along behind and keep a close look-out."

The Sheriff gave Caramon and Sturm each a piercing glance. "You promise never to reveal the location of the box."

"I swear on my honor as the son of a Knight of Solamnia," said Sturm solemnly. Lifting his sword, he kissed the hilt. "Death will take me before I break my oath."

"Yes, well. I don't hold with oaths, young man," said the Sheriff, looking displeased. "Just a promise will do. What about you, Caramon Majere?"

"I won't tell a soul," Caramon promised, adding eagerly, "I'll even close my eyes so that I won't see where it is!"

"Fine, you do that," muttered the Sheriff, rolling his eyes. He was probably regretting his choices. "Come with me. The rest of you, take up your positions."

****

The night wore away with no sign, no sight, no sound, no smell of a goblin. Raistlin sat yawning and shivering beneath a tree near the smithy's, waiting for something to happen. He was regretting having ever left his bed and was seriously considering returning to it, when one of the town guard who had been detailed to accompany the sheriff and the box ran into the clearing.

"Majere! Come with me!" he cried, spotting Raistlin. "There's been an accident! It's your brother!"

"What's Caramon done now?" Raistlin demanded, a

sliver of fear piercing his heart. Caramon might be a dolt, an idiot, an oaf, but he was Raistlin's twin and the only family he had left now that both parents were dead.

"Smashed into a tree. Knocked himself out cold." The guardsman grinned. "He was walking with his eyes closed."

As Raistlin checked to make certain once again that he had everything he needed, he noted, out of the corner of his eye, the shabby man looking his way with interested attention.

"What business is it of yours?" Raistlin demanded irritably.

"Only the concern of a friend," said the shabby man humbly. "I hope your brother has taken no serious harm."

"If the injury is to his head, you may count upon it," Raistlin returned.

****

Caramon was already conscious by the time his brother arrived, which was a good sign. He recognized those standing anxiously around him.

"Hullo, Sturm. Gee, my head hurts. What happened? Hi, Raist? What are you doing here? Say, I know where they hid that box. In a boat—"

"Shut up!" cried Sturm, the Sheriff and the two guards simultaneously.

"What's your name?" Raistlin interrupted, gently examining the egg-size bump on his brothers forehead.

Caramon thought a moment, then, brightening, he said, "I'm the Kingpriest of Istar."

Raistlin sighed and turned to the Sheriff.

"The injury isn't serious, sir, but, as you see, he needs attention. Could some of your men take him to the Inn? He must be kept warm, made to lie still, and watched to make certain that he does not fall asleep."

"I'll see to it. He won't keep blabbing about the hiding place, will he?" the Sheriff asked.

"If he does, tell him he's wrong, its at the bottom of the Blood Sea. I must go to Weird Meggin's to fetch a few things I need to make a poultice for him, and then I will join you at the Inn."

"But you shouldn't be wandering around here alone, son," said the Sheriff. "Not with goblins about."

Raistlin bit off a caustic remark about just what he thought of this supposed goblin attack. "I must tend to Caramon immediately, sir. Otherwise he might think he's the Kingpriest for the rest of his life."

"That would indeed be a pity," said Sturm. "One was more than enough." He added magnanimously, "I will go with Raistlin, Sheriff."

Raistlin frowned, annoyed, but there was no time to waste arguing.

"Very well. If you insist! Come along, Brightblade."

The guardsmen lifted the groggy Caramon and, groaning under the strain, hauled him off in the direction of the Inn. His last words, as they carried him away, were, "Burn the heretics!" The Sheriff left to inspect the town's defenses.

Raistlin and Sturm headed in the opposite direction, taking a short cut through the trees. Weird Meggin's house was located in the same disreputable part of town as The Trough. Soon, the two left the sound of voices and the flare of torches behind. The boardwalks under which they walked were empty.

Solace had long ago abandoned this portion of itself. The boardwalks were falling into disrepair, the rope bridges sagged. Those houses which were still standing were uninhabited. The two young men walked in silence, neither having much of anything to say to the other.

"You are certain Caramon will be all right?" Sturm asked at one point. "Perhaps someone else should examine him. Someone more experienced in the healing arts."

Raistlin saw no reason to respond to this insult, and that ended all attempts at conversation. They continued walking among the thick trunks of the trees, Sturm holding a torch high so that they could find the path which led through the tangled undergrowth. The two moons, silver Solinari and red Lunitari, had risen and set long ago. Raistlin guessed that it must be long past midnight.

"Are we clo—" Sturm began, but his question was never finished.

Raistlin heard the rustling in the brush. He had no time to react.

A heavy weight struck him from behind, a hand clamped firmly over his mouth. Cold steel pressed against his neck.

"Breathe a sound and I'll slice you ear-to-ear," said a voice.

Raistlin nodded to show he understood and would keep silent. The man pricked Raistlin's skin, just to show he meant what he said. Raistlin held perfectly still, tried to see what had become of Sturm, for he could hear the clash of steel and the sounds of panting, grunting and scuffling feet. The torch lay upon the ground, its light extinguished, and Raistlin's eyes had not yet adjusted to the darkness. A groan, a thud. The sound of heavy breathing indicated that the fight was over.

"You haven't killed him, have you Cutthroat?" asked another man, emerging from the forest.

"Naw, Jack. Just rapped him on the head to teach him some manners."

Cutthroat rubbed his jaw, glared down at Sturm. "He'll pay for this, the bastard."

"All in good time. Tie his arms with bow strings and get him on his feet. And show a light. I want to see their faces. If either of them so much as squeaks, stick them."

"A light? What if someone sees us?"

"They'll think we're part of the militia."

One of the men lit a lantern. The other trussed up Sturm and dragged him to his feet, bleeding from a cut on his forehead, but otherwise unharmed. The man named Cutthroat grabbed Sturm's short sword, tossed it into the trees. Sturm stood rigidly straight and glared at the men in defiance, particularly at the shabbily dressed man named Jack.

Raistlin recognized him—the man who had claimed to have overheard goblins talking about attacking Solace. Raistlin saw the thieves' scheme with sudden, sickening clarity.

"There are no goblins, are there?" Raistlin said, as they bound his wrists with a rope.

"Oh, sure there are. Lots of goblins." Jack winked. "About a hundred miles from here."

"It was a ruse," Raistlin explained to the glowering Sturm. "A ruse to trick us into gathering all our valuables together and depositing them in one place."

"And you're going to tell us where they're hid, boy," said Jack, walking over to stand in front of Sturm. "And don't tell me you don't know. I saw you go off with the box."

"I will die before I tell you," said Sturm calmly.

"We're not going to kill you," Jack returned, leering. "You're of no use to us dead." His voice hardened. "But we can make you wish you were dead. Cutthroat here as a way with people. First he slices off a finger or two. Then he gouges out an eye—"

"Do your damnedest," said Sturm coldly. "I will not break my trust."

No, you will let them chop you into pieces, you great fool, Raistlin thought.

Seeing that the thieves were paying no attention to him—their eyes were fixed on Sturm—Raistlin twisted his wrists in their bindings, testing to see whether he might be able to work the knots loose. He might be able to, but it was going to take time. Time he didn't have.

"Maybe he don't mind dying," Cutthroat was saying. "But what about watching his friend die? That might change his tune."

Not likely, Raistlin thought and decided to avoid hearing Sturm's answer.

"I'll tell you where to find the treasure!" Raistlin offered, cringing. "Just don't hurt me. I'll tell you everything!"

"He knows nothing," said Sturm scornfully.

Raistlin ignored him, kept his gaze fixed upon the thieves.

"That's right. You don't know," said Jack, coming around to eye Raistlin. "You weren't with them. You were at the smith's shop with me."

"My brother told me," Raistlin said.

"Your brother? The big lout? The one who knocked himself silly?" Jack was dubious.

"That's him. He told me when I leaned down to examine him."

"He's right, Jack," said Cutthroat. "I heard the big guy say something about a boat. Then the others shut him up."

"A boat, huh?" Jack eyed Raistlin with interest.

"I know which one. I'll take you there. Just don't hurt me!" Raistlin pleaded.

"You coward!" Sturm struggled furiously against his bonds. "I'll—"

"Gag him!" Jack ordered. "You, boy. You lead the way. And remember, if you're tricking us, your friend here dies first while you watch. Then it'll be your turn. March."

Raistlin marched. He knew where he needed to go. He'd been there many times before, gathering herbs with Weird Meggin. But he'd never had to find the place in the darkness before, never had to find it with a killer walking behind him, prodding him in the back with a dagger. He dared not show any hesitation or they would cease to believe him. And then they would kill him.

Raistlin slogged through the undergrowth, searching frantically for landmarks, for something which would tell him he was on the right trail. At least he could be thankful for one thing—they'd tied a gag around Sturm's mouth. It would be just like the would-be knight to blurt out the truth in a fit of misguided honor.

"Hey, it can't be this far," Jack said, growing suspicious. "The men weren't gone that long."

"It's just up ahead," said Raistlin and hoped to the gods—if the gods did truly exist—that he was right. He was near exhaustion, panting for breath, shivering with the cold and his fear.

Just when he knew he had failed utterly, knew that he'd come the wrong way, he caught the whiff of decay, saw a glimmer of starlight reflected off water. This was the place. He could never forget that smell.

"We're here." Raistlin breathed a heartfelt sigh of relief.

"Where?" The thieves flashed their lantern about.

The light flashed on the still surface of a large pond, where farmers watered their herds. A small skiff, tied to a tree, floated on the smooth water.

"A boat!" cried one.

"It's in there," Raistlin said. Seemingly exhausted, he slumped against a tree.

Raistlin cast Sturm a warning glance. Sturm either caught the warning or he had guessed Raistlin's intent. He came to a halt.

"I'll go fetch the treasure," Jack said. "You two stay with the prisoners."

"Yeah, and let you sail off with the loot. I wasn't born yesterday, Jack Ladyfinger. I'm going with you," said Cutthroat. "Cutpurse can stay with the prisoners."

"And let you two split it two ways instead of three? Not bloody likely!"

The three thieves plunged on ahead, running for the boat over the leaf-covered ground. In their haste and excitement, they did not see the sticks, painted red, which had been placed there to warn the unwary to keep away from this place.

Their excited cries suddenly gave way to curses and splashing. The lantern light vanished. The curses changed to panicked shrieks and yells for help. They were caught in the sucking mud of a deadly bog.

Raistlin slid his thin wrists from out of the loosened bindings, rubbed them a moment to ease the burning where the ropes had cut into his flesh. Then Raistlin removed the gag from the young man's mouth and used his knife to cut through the ropes on his arms.

The thieves' cries were piteous, blubbering, begging for help. Raistlin turned away.

"Where are you going?" Sturm demanded. He was unlacing his leather vest. "You can't leave them to die!"

"Oh, yes, I can," Raistlin returned. "What do you think they were going to do us?"

Sturm made no reply. Calmly, he stripped off his shirt.

"Go in there and the bog will suck you down, too," Raistlin said grimly.

"That's a chance I will have to take." Sturm peered around, trying to see by the lambent light of the stars. "We need to find a large tree branch. Hurry up. They can't last much longer."

"They're thieves, Sturm!" Raistlin said. "They're murderers!"

Sturm found his branch. Hefting it, he began dragging it toward the bog.

"They are Paladine's children," said Sturm, wading carefully out into the mire. "Come here, Raistlin," he added in a commanding tone. "I require your help."

"You can go to the Abyss," Raistlin told him. "You and Paladine's children."

Sturm said nothing. He continued on.

Raistlin's hesitated a moment, fuming, then, seeing that Sturm was not going to listen to reason, Raistlin tucked the hem of his white robes into his belt and followed the would-be knight into the muck of the stinking, oozing bog.

****

Sturm and Raistlin returned to the Inn of the Last Home, where Sturm handed over the muddy, sodden and sullen children of Paladine and explained the plot to steal the treasure. The Sheriff eyed his charges gloomily. Not only would there be the bother and expense of a trial, but he would have tell the good citizens of Solace that he'd been duped. "You should have let the bog have them," the Sheriff grumbled.

"That way no one would have known the difference."

"I would have known, sir," Sturm replied stiffly.

Shaking his head, the Sheriff marched his prisoners off to jail.

Raistlin's robes were soaked through. His shoes were wet. He shivered uncontrollably, could already feel the pain in his chest and the fever start to burn in his blood. He would be sick for days after this.

After checking on his brother, finding Caramon much improved—he no longer thought he was the Kingpriest—Raistlin sat huddled near the fire, drinking a honey posset to soothe his throat.

"May I join you?" Sturm walked over to stand beside the fire.

"Sure, Sturm!" Caramon shoved over a chair. "Sit down and have a drink."

"I cannot stay long. My mother will be worried. I only came by because I owe Raistlin an apology."

Raistlin glanced up. "For what?"

"I misjudged you tonight," Sturm replied. "I thought . . ." He paused.

Raistlin filled in the blank. "You thought I was a coward who would betray my friends to save my own skin."

"I made a mistake," Sturm admitted. "What you did took quick thinking and courage. I admire you for it."

"Thank you," said Raistlin.

Sturm made a bow and started to leave.

"Sir Knight," Raistlin called.

Sturm looked back, frowning, fearing Raistlin was mocking him.

"Yes, what is it?"

"Risking your life to save those miserable wretches was stupid and foolish," Raistlin said. "Stupid and foolish and noble. I admire you for not leaving those men, who would have taken your life, to die."

Sturm smiled, a rare thing for him.

"Thank you," he said.

"We make a good team," Caramon chimed in enthusiastically. "We should go adventuring together someday."

The two young men nodded politely, glanced at each other.

"Heaven forefend!" Raistlin muttered.

"Paladine forbid it!" Sturm prayed.

Remembering Dragonlance

A flashback by Jeff Grubb

1. Meeting Tracy

"This is HP 2500-series Computer. It will be your friend." So drawled Tracy Hickman to me, the first time I met him. The place was the old Hotel Claire in downtown Lake Geneva, Wisconsin. You go to Lake Geneva now, and the hotel is a stylish renovated brick building with a chocolate shop on the first floor. At the time of the conversation it was before the renovation. The Dungeon Hobby Shop occupied the first floor. The Art and Design departments of TSR occupied the second and third floors, respectively. To call the building dilapidated would be rounding up. Tracy informed me at the time we could not hold a departmental meeting in the largest room because the added weight would cause the building to topple. Tracy told me a lot in that first meeting.

TSR at the time was bringing people on without thinking about equipment, or even where exactly they were going to put them. The building had a handful of monitors hooked up to a rather temperamental mainframe. Tracy had one of the monitors. I did my first work on a typewriter across the hall. But that first day, he showed me how the computer worked, how to transfer files, and many of the other ins and outs of the jury-rigged system we had at that point. From the discussion I quickly tweaked to the fact that Tracy loved the leading edge of tech, which at that point was the then-nascent Internet. He also told me about the unevenness of the floor, and the fact there was a fourth floor above us that had been a ballroom, but they had ripped up the floorboards years ago.

I listened and learned. About half of what he said sunk in, and when I had a question later in the day, I came over to his office, and he was out. I mentioned to the other guy in the office that I had a tech question and was looking for Trace since he was obviously the pro who had been working there for a while. The "other guy" was veteran designer Dave Cook. He just laughed. "He's been here about two months. He just picks stuff up fast."

Indeed he does.

2. Meeting Margaret

The first time I met Margaret Weis I lied to her. Not intentionally, mind you, but I lied to her nonetheless. It was Margaret's first week on the job, and by that time we had moved the creative department to the new building, into a windowless area above the warehouse known as "the Vault." We all had monitors by now but still didn't have personal phones (the department phone was at the end of the aisle). Margaret had just come on, and one of her early jobs was to come up with an art order for a Heartquest (a Romance Pick-a-Path) book that my wife had written. The art order was due immediately, and Kate was out horseback riding with a visiting friend. No time to wait for her to come back.

So Margaret came to me. This is as far as I know the only misstep she made in an otherwise sterling career. I knew little of the details of Kate's book but did not want to disappoint a co-worker (nor admit I had not read my wife's work). I knew it was about young woman, her horse, and couple of potential suitors. How tough could it be? So I worked out an art order with Margaret.

I think I got every single detail wrong in that art order—color of the heroine's eyes, color of her hair, breed of her horse, background, weather, time of day. I got the fact there was a young woman and horse right, but everything else was downhill. By the time I got home and told Kate about it and she informed me how much I had gone wrong, it was up to Margaret to try to bring it back on-line. She did a pretty good job. To be honest, we should have waited, but she was in her first week, and I was still new and wanted to help.

I think Margaret has forgiven me for giving her a totally bogus art order. I'm not quite sure Kate has.

3. The Secret Origins of the Dragonlance Setting

It started with a couple of management decisions—or rather, one of its roots was in one management decision, and it blossomed under another. At the time TSR had assembled its talent and wanted to direct it into producing modules for its RPG Games, including D&D. So the designers and editors were asked to pitch module ideas. Lots of module ideas. Three low level, three mid level, three high level, three very high level, three Basic D&D, three Expert D&D, three Boot Hill, three Star Frontiers, three Gangbusters. Trilogies for each and every role-playing line we did.

The concepts varied from okay to . . . well, horrible, and some even made it into print. The resulting paper landslide succeeded in burying management for a while, so we could get on with the job of designing (a tactic we would use in future encounters). But in the midst of this, Tracy Hickman pitched an idea he had been playing with—three adventures about dragons (hey, it was Dungeons & DRAGONS, wasn't it?).

Three modules. One using good dragons. One using neutral dragons. One using evil dragons. Then-manager Harold Johnson liked the idea and encouraged Tracy to develop it further. It soon became a larger series, one module for each color of dragon. That would be ten at the time—five chromatics and five metallics. We had never done ten anythings before. Could we sell the idea to the Upper Brass?

Then management handed down another edict: We would not work on any projects until Upper Management gave the go-ahead. This gave us a few weeks (actually, it felt like months) of downtime while the Brass figured out what we should be doing. During that time I ended up turning a scratchbuilt home system into what became Marvel Super Heroes. Tracy used the time to draw maps, build timelines, and create the plot for what would become the Dragonlance Campaign Setting. I got sucked in—in part because Tracy and I were commuting together at the time (Tracy had bought a used car from Harold, which literally self-destructed in front of the Old Hotel one afternoon, leaving him vehicle-less; but that's another story). So we talked.

And bits of my D&D adventures moved over into Project Overlord. And my engineers became gnomes. And my gods moved over after adventures involving the Platinum Dragon and the Chromatic Dragon were added, swelling the number of original adventures to twelve in all. And editor Carl Smith was added to the team—because we had become a team by then. And Tracy began talking to the artists—Larry Elmore in particular. And we got Larry to do four pieces of pitch art for our presentation to upper management.

And we made the pitch. We broke it into four trilogies, since we knew the upper management understood that. We showed them the art, with early drafts of Tanis and Raistlin and Flint and Riverwind and Goldmoon. We talked about a long plotline and modules and, yes, the potential for toys. (Minotaur action figures! A Percheron play set!) We got the go-ahead. Each of the four initial pitchmen got one of the art pieces. Mine was from the third trilogy and showed

Caramon and Raistlin and a prototype of Lord Toede, which was later used as an art piece for a Margaret Weis short story in Dragon Magazine and is now hanging downstairs. I know Trace still has his, but I don't know about Carl's and Harold's. Those have become pieces of history.

Dragonlance came out of the red-hot forge of Tracy's mind and was shaped and refined into novels with Margaret Weis. While I am proud of my contributions to the tale, I always remember it was a couple of management decisions that gave us the chance to tell the tale. But all Tracy needed was a chance.

Jeff Grubb, one of the original Dragonlance creative team, has written fifteen novels, but only one of them set in the world of Krynn (*Lord Toede*). He continues to work with new worlds, and has recently completed short stories for Dragonlance, Thieves' World, and Monte Cook's Diamond Throne.

The Silken Threads

Margaret Weis and Tracy Hickman
Originally published in *Tales II, Volume One: The Reign of Istar*

Part I

The tower of high sorcery at Wayreth is, at the best of times—such as now, with the war's end—difficult to find. Guided by the powerful wizards of the Conclave, the tower roams its enchanted forest, the wildest of the wild creatures within its boundaries. One often sees young mages standing, hovering, on the outskirts of Wayreth Forest, their breath coming fast, their skin pale, their hands nervously clenching. They stand hesitating on the outskirts of their destiny. If they are bold and enter, the forest will permit them. The tower will find them. Their fate will be determined.

That is now. But then, long ago, before the Cataclysm, few found the Tower of High Sorcery at Wayreth. It prowled the forest only in the shadows of night, hiding from the light of day. Wary of interlopers, the tower watched all who ventured within (and there were few) with restive, suspicious eyes, prepared to pounce and destroy.

In the days right before the Cataclysm, the wizards of Ansalon were reviled and persecuted, their lives forfeit to the holy zeal of the Kingpriest of Istar, who feared their power, claimed it was not spiritual in nature.

And he was right to fear them. Long and bitter were the arguments within the Conclave, the governing body of magic-users. The wizards could fight back, but in so doing, they were afraid they would destroy the world. No, they reasoned, it was better to withdraw, hide in the blessed shadows of their magic, and wait.

Wait.

****

It was Yule, a strange Yule, the hottest Yule anyone in Ansalon could remember. Now we know the heat was the wrath of the gods, beating down upon an unhallowed world. The people thought it was merely an odd phenomenon; some blamed it on the gnomes.

On one particular night, the wind was still, as if the world had ceased to breath. Sparks jumped from the black fur of the cat to the black robe of its master. The smell of doom was in the air, like the smell of thunder. On that night, a man entered Wayreth Forest and began to walk, with unerring step, toward the Tower of High Sorcery.

No enchantment stopped him. The trees that would attack any other intruder shrank back, bowed low in reverent homage. The birds hushed their teasing songs. The fierce predator slunk furtively away. The man ignored it all, said no word, did not pause. Arriving at the tower, he passed through the rune-covered walls as if they did not exist, alerted no guard, roused no one's interest. He walked unhindered across the courtyard.

Several white and red-robed wizards walked here, discussing, in low voices, the troubles afflicting the outside world. The man strolled up to them, pushed his way between them. They did not see him.

He entered the tower and began to climb the stairs that led to the large rooms at the very top. Guest rooms and rooms for apprentice mages were located at the bottom.

These were empty this night. No guests had been permitted in the tower for a long, long time. No apprentices studied the arcane art. It was far too dangerous. Many apprentices had paid for their devotion with their lives.

The rooms at the top of the tower were inhabited by the most powerful wizards, the members of the Conclave. Seven black-robed mages ruled the evil magic of night, seven white-robed mages ruled the good magic of day, and seven red-robed mages ruled the in-between magic of twilight. The man went straight to one room, located at the very top of the tower, and entered.

The room was elegantly furnished, neat, and ordered, for the wizard was rigid in his habits. Spellbooks, bound in black, were arranged in alphabetical order. Each stood in its correct place on the bookshelves, and each was dusted daily. Scrolls, in their polished cases, glistened in honeycomb compartments. Magical items—rings and wands and such—were stowed away in black-lacquered boxes, every one labeled clearly as to its contents.

The wizard sat at work at a desk of ebony, its finish reflecting the warm yellow glow of an oil lamp suspended from the ceiling above his head. He was at work upon a scroll, his brow furrowed with concentration, his lips silently forming the magical words his pen, dipped in lamb's blood, traced upon the parchment. He did not hear his guest's arrival.

The doors to the wizards' rooms in the tower have no locks upon them. Every wizard is respectful of another's privacy, respectful of personal possessions. Thus the visitor could enter unimpeded, had no need to wait until a bolt was thrown, a lock unlocked—not that there existed any lock that could have stopped him. He stood on the threshold, gazing at the wizard in silence, waiting, respectfully, until the mage completely his work upon the scroll.

At last the wizard sighed, passed a hand that trembled from the reaction to his concentrated effort through his long, iron-gray hair, and lifted his head. His eyes widened;

his head sank nervelessly to the tabletop. He stared, then blinked, thinking the apparition might vanish.

It did not. The man, clad all in black, from the satin-lined cowl to the velvet hem that trailed the stone floor, remained standing in the doorway.

The wizard rose, slowly, to his feet.

"Approach, Akar," said the man in the doorway.

The wizard did so, limbs weak, heart fluttering, though Akar had never before known fear of anything on Krynn. He was in his forties, tall and well built. The iron-gray hair, long and luxuriant, framed a face tight-lipped, resolute, unforgiving, unyielding. He went down on his knees awkwardly; never in his life had Akar bowed to any man.

"Master," he said humbly, spreading wide his hands to indicate he was open to receive any command, obey any summons. He kept his head lowered, and did not look up. He tried to, but his heart failed him. "I am honored."

The man standing before him made a gentle motion with his hand and the door shut behind him. Another motion, a whispered word, and the door disappeared. A solid wall stood in its place. The wizard saw this obliquely, out of the corner of his eye, and a chill shook him. The two were locked in this room together, with no way out, except death.

"Akar," said the man. "Look at me."

Akar raised his head, slowly, reluctantly. His stomach clenched, his lungs felt paralyzed, and sweat was cold on his body. He gritted his teeth against the cry that welled up in his throat.

A white face, disembodied within the shadows of the black cowl, hung over Akar. The face was round, with heavy lidded eyes and full lips, and it was cold, as cold as stone that hangs suspended in the vast void of space, far from the warmth of any sun.

"Speak my name, Akar," commanded the man. "Speak it as you speak it when you summon my power to enhance yours."

"Nuitari!" gasped Akar. "Nuitari! God of the black moon!"

The pallid face glowed with a ghastly, unholy light. A pale, translucent hand reached out of the darkness.

"Give me your left palm."

Akar raised his left hand, wondering, as he did so, that he had the power to move it.

Nuitari clasped hold of Akar, the god's pale, delicate fingers closing over the human's tanned, strong hand.

Akar could no longer swallow his screams. Pain wrenched strangled cries from him. The chill that flowed through his body was like the burning of ice on wet flesh. Yet his hand did not move, he did not wrench it from the dread touch, much as he longed to do so. He remained on his knees, gazing up at the god, though his limbs twisted with the agony.

The heavy-lidded eyes flashed; the full lips smiled. Nuitari let loose his grasp suddenly. Akar clutched his chilling, burning hand, saw five livid marks—the fingers of the god—upon his skin.

"My mark will be the sign and symbol of our discussion," said Nuitari. "That you may know, should you by chance ever doubt, that I have spoken to you."

"If I would ever know doubt, it would only be to doubt my own worthiness of such an honor," said Akar, staring at the imprints on his flesh. He looked again at Nuitari. "How may I serve my lord?"

"Rise, be seated. We have much to discuss and we should be comfortable."

Akar rose to his feet, stiffly, awkwardly, and returned to his desk, trying to keep from wringing his wounded hand. He knew what was expected of him, despite his suffering, and conjured up a chair for his guest, a chair that was made of night, held together by stars. This done, he stood humbly until his guest had seated himself, then Akar sank behind the desk, glad to be able to sit before he fell. He kept his hand hidden in the folds of his robes, bit his lips now and then as sharp flames of ice flickered over his skin.

"The gods are angry, Akar," said Nuitari, the heavy-lidded eyes watching the flickering light of the oil lamp hanging above him. "The scales of balance have tipped, threatening the world and all who live upon it. Krynn's destruction has been foreseen. In order to prevent that end, the gods have determined to take drastic measures to restore the balance. Within a fortnight, Akar, the gods will cast down from the heavens a mountain of fire. It will strike Ansalon and split it asunder. The mountain will fall upon the Temple of the Kingpriest and drive it far, far beneath the ground. Rivers of blood will wash over the temple, and the waters of the sea will drown it forever. This doom the gods intend, unless mankind repents, which, between you and me, Akar"—Nuitari smiled—"I do not see him doing."

Akar no longer felt the pain in his hand. "I thank you for the warning, Master, and I will carry it to the other members of the Conclave. We will take such steps as are necessary to protect ourselves—"

Nuitari raised his pallid hand, made a gesture as if to brush away the inconsequential. "Such is not your concern, Akar. My brother, Solinari, and my sister, Lunitari, both walk the halls of magic, bearing the same message. You have no need to fear. Nor," he added softly, "do you have any need to become involved. I have another, more important task for you."

"Yes, Master!" Akar sat forward eagerly.

"Tomorrow night, the gods will come to Ansalon to remove those clerics who have remained true to their faith, those who have not been swayed by the corrupt tenets of the Kingpriest. At this time, the Lost Citadel will reappear, the true clerics will enter, and a bridge will form, leading from this world into worlds beyond. All true clerics may cross the bridge and will be sent to other realms far from this. Do you understand, Akar?"

"I do, Master," said Akar, somewhat hesitantly, "but what has this to do with me? I have little use for clerics, especially those who serve the god Paladine and his ilk. And there are none left alive who serve Her Dark Majesty. The Kingpriest saw to that with his edicts. The dark clerics were among the first to face his inquisitors, the first to feel the hot fires of the so-called 'purging' flames."

"None left alive. Did you ever wonder about that, Akar?"

Akar shrugged. "As I said, Master, I have little use for clerics. Takhisis, Queen of Darkness, was long since banished from the world. I could only assume that she was unable to come to the aid of those who called out her name to save them from fiery death."

"My mother remembers those who serve her, Akar," said Nuitari. "Likewise, Akar, she remembers those who fail her."

Akar flinched as the pain in his hand flared through his blood. He gnawed his lip and cast down his eyes.

"I beg forgiveness, Master. How may I serve our queen?"

"On the night when the bridge forms, good and true clerics will cross from this plane to the next. It will be possible, at that particular moment, for the souls of the dark clerics who wait in the Abyss to cross as well."

"Those who have perished serving the Dark Queen in this world will be able to return to it?"

"As all good and true clerics leave it. And thus, after the fall of the fiery mountain, there will be no clerics left in Krynn except those belonging to Her Dark Majesty."

Akar raised his eyebrows. "Truly an interesting plan, Master, and one that surely will aid Takhisis in her return to this world. But what has this to do with me? Forgive my speaking plainly, but it is the son I serve, not the mother. My loyalties lie to magic alone, as do yours."

Nuitari appeared flattered by this answer. His smile widened, and he inclined his head. "I am doing a favor for my mother. And the wizard who serves the mother will find rich reward from the son."

"Ah!" Akar breathed softly, settled back in his chair. "What reward, Master?"

"Power. You will become the most powerful wizard on

Krynn, now and in the future. Even the great Fistandantilus—"

"My teacher," Akar muttered, paling at the name.

"The great Fistandantilus will be forced to bow to your might."

"Fistandantilus?" Akar stared. "I will be his master? How is that possible?"

"With the gods, all things are possible."

Akar continued to look dubious. "I know the tremendous power of this mighty wizard. It is a power that might well rival that of a god."

Nuitari frowned, and the black robes stirred. "So he fancies himself. This Fistandantilus has displeased my mother. Even now he is in the Temple of the Kingpriest seeking to usurp the Dark Queen. He aspires to heights far above him. He must be stopped."

"What must I do, Master?"

"If the blood of a good and true person is spilled in anger upon the bridge, the door to the Abyss will open and the dark clerics may return."

"How am I to find the Lost Citadel, Master? None know its location. It exists only in the planes of magic. None have seen it since the beginning of time!"

Nuitari pointed. "The lines upon your hand."

Akar's hand pulsed and throbbed; skin writhed, and bones shifted. The pain was, for an instant, almost unendurable. He gasped, pressed his lips over a cry. Lifting his hand, he stared at it in silence. At length, drawing a shuddering breath, he was able to speak. "I see. A map. Very well. Have you further instructions, my lord?"

"Steel must draw the blood."

Akar shook his head. "That makes matters more difficult. The only steel weapon we mages are permitted to carry is a dagger."

"You may find another to perform the deed. It doesn't have to be yourself."

"I understand. But what about guards, my lord? Won't the gods be guarding the bridge?"

"One of the gods of neutrality will stand guard. Zivilyn will not interfere, as long as you or whoever you find to serve chooses to do this deed of his own free will."

Akar smiled grimly. "I see no difficulty. I will undertake this task, Master. Thank you for the opportunity."

Nuitari rose to his feet. "I have long watched and been impressed by you, Akar. I believe I have chosen wisely. The blessing of the god of the black moon on you, my servant."

Akar bowed his head in reverence. When he lifted it again, he was alone. The chair was gone, the wall was gone, and the door was back. He held the pen in his hand; the newly completed scroll lay on the table before him. All was exactly as it had been before. He might have thought he'd dreamed it, but for the pain.

He lifted his hand to the light, saw upon it the marks of the god's fingers. The marks formed roads that led up to the hills of his knuckles and over and around to the crisscrossed valley of his palm. He studied his hand, attempting to decipher the map.

Outside the door, he heard shuffling footfalls pass, robes brush against the stone floor. Someone coughed, softly.

A visitor now, of all times.

"Go away!" Akar called. "I'm not to be disturbed!"

He brought out a sheet of parchment, began to copy the lines on his hand onto his scroll.

The person standing outside his door coughed again, a smothered sound, as if he were trying to stifle it.

Irritated, Akar raised his head. "To the Abyss with you and that coughing! Be off, whoever you are!"

A moment's silence, then the footfalls, the whisper of the robes, continued past the door and down the echoing hall.

Akar paid it no further attention.

PART II

The high cleric frowned, and the lines of his frown extended down his mouth, creasing the numerous chins that rolled over his breast, above the mound—enveloped in rich cloth of gold—that was his belly.

"And this is your final word on the subject, Sir Knight?"

The knight to whom these words were spoken looked troubled, lowered his head to stare unseeing at the still-full chalice he held in his hand. He was a young man. He "rattled in his armor" as the saying among the knights went, referring to the fact that the youthful body didn't quite fill out the breadth and width of the breastplate that had been his father's. The young man had been accepted into the knighthood early, to take over the responsibilities of his father, who had left this world and its many burdens to his son.

The burdens were heavy ones, to judge by the careworn expression that prematurely aged the young face. But he was not bowed down or crushed beneath them. He raised his eyes, faced the high cleric steadfastly.

"I am sorry, Revered Son, but that is my final word. My father donated generously to the building of the temple in Istar, more generously than he ought, perhaps, but he could not have foreseen the bad times to come."

A young woman, who had been standing behind the knight's chair, suddenly stepped forward, faced the priest.

"Nor could my father have foreseen that the time would come when the Kingpriest would go back on his sworn word to those who placed him in power!"

The woman's features were so like those of the young knight that many people meeting the two for the first time thought they met twin brothers. Both were of equal height and nearly similar in build and weight, for the twins were each other's companion in everything they did, including swordsmanship.

The one marked difference between the two was the woman's sheaf of long, wheat-colored hair that, when she let it down from its tight braid around her head, fell in shining cascades almost to her knees. Her brother's hair, the same color, was kept short, falling to his shoulders.

The sister's beautiful hair and the beginnings of the long moustache of a Solamnic Knight growing upon the brother's upper lip marked the difference in their sexes, but in all else they were alike—moved alike, spoke alike, thought alike.

"Peace, Nikol," said her brother, reaching out to take hold of his sister's hand.

But she would not be placated. "'Give to the temple,' you say. 'Increase the glory of Paladine!' It isn't Paladine's glory you've increased, but your own!"

"Take care how you talk, Daughter," said the high cleric, glaring at her. "You will bring down the wrath of the gods."

"Daughter!" Nikol's skin flushed in anger; her hands clenched. She took another step toward the priest. "Don't you dare call me daughter! The two people who had to right to speak that dear word to me are dead, my father in the service of your lying Kingpriest, my mother of hardship and overwork."

The high cleric looked rather alarmed at the sight of the impassioned young woman advancing on him. He glanced uneasily behind him at his two bodyguards, wearing the military insignia of Istar, who stood stalwartly near the door. Reassured and, perhaps reminding himself that he was, after all, a guest in the castle of the Knight of Solamnia, the high cleric turned back to the brother.

"I do not blame you for this unseemly outburst, Sir Knight. If your sister has not learned to speak respectfully to men of the cloth, it is not your fault, but, rather, the fault of the one who has her religious training in her care."

The high cleric's narrow-eyed gaze shifted to another man in the hall, a man clad in the humble clerical garb of a family healer. He was young, near the same age as the brother and sister, yet the gravity of his expression made him seem older. His robes were not fine, as were those of the visiting clerics of Istar. He wore no jewels on his fingers.

His only emblem was a holy symbol, shining with a soft blue light, that hung from a leather thong around his neck. He looked troubled by the high cleric's accusation, but made no comment and bowed his head in silent acknowledgment of the rebuke.

Nikol flushed, glanced at the young healer. "Do not blame Brother Michael for my sharp tongue, Revered Son of Paladine," she said, her voice low. "Forgive my outspokenness, but it is hard to see those left in our care suffer and know that there is little we can do to help them."

"There is something you can do, Sir Knight," said the high cleric, talking to the brother, ignoring the sister. "Turn your lands and estates over to the church. Release your men-at-arms from their service. The time of warring is past. Peace is at hand. All evil has been—or soon will be—eradicated from Ansalon.

"Face reality, Sir Knight. Once the knighthood was necessary. Once we relied upon you and those like you to keep the peace, protect the innocent. But that age is ended. A new age is dawning. The knighthood is outdated, its virtues admirable but strict, rigid, old-fashioned." The high cleric smiled, and his chins waggled. "People prefer more modern ways.

"Give your lands to the church. We will take over control, send priests well qualified"—the high cleric cast a scathing glance at Brother Michael—"to collect the rents and maintain order. You will, of course, be permitted to live in your ancestral manor as caretaker—"

"Caretaker!" The knight rose to his feet. His face was pale, and his hand trembled on the hilt of the word he wore at his side. "Caretaker of my father's house! Caretaker of a noble estate that has been handed down in honor from father to son for generations! Get out! Get out or, by Paladine I will—" He drew the sword halfway from its scabbard.

The high cleric's fat face mottled over with red and white splotches; his eyes bulged. He heaved himself up out of his chair. His guards drew their weapons, and steel rang in the hall.

"Revered Son, allow me to escort you to your carriage." Brother Michael strode forward, taking care to place his body between that of the outraged knight and the offended priest.

Nicholas, with an effort, restrained himself, slid his sword back into its scabbard. His twin sister stood at his side, her hands clasped over his arm. Brother Michael, talking smoothly, politely, was hastily ushering the priest from the hall. At the door, the high cleric of Istar paused, looked back, his gaze hard and stern.

"You dare threaten a man of the cloth in the name of Paladine? Beware, Sir Knight, lest the wrath of the gods descend upon you!"

"This way, Your Reverence," said Brother Michael, clamping his hand over the high cleric's fleshy arm.

The healer steered his superior out of the hall, into the corridor that was devoid of furnishings. Only the Yule branches, drooping in the heat, and a few relics of a bygone era—an ancient suit of armor, faded tapestries, a torn and blood-stained standard—decorated it. The high cleric sniffed, glanced around in disdain.

"You see, Brother Michael, how run-down this fine manor has become. The walls crumbling about their ears. It is a shame, a waste. It will not be tolerated. I trust, Brother, that you will counsel these two prideful young persons, make them see the error of their ways."

Brother Michael folded his hands in the sleeves of his shabby robes, did not answer. His gaze went to the numerous sparkling rings worn on the high cleric's fat fingers. The healer's lips tightened, keeping back words that would have done no good, maybe much harm.

The high cleric leaned near him. "It would be a pity if the inquisitor was forced to pay a visit to this knight and his sister. Don't you agree, Brother Michael?"

The healer lifted his eyes. "But they are devout followers—"

The high cleric snorted. "The church wants these lands,

Brother. If the knight truly was a worshiper of Paladine, he would not hesitate to grant all he owns to the Kingpriest. Therefore, since this knight and his foul-tongued witch of a sister thwart the wishes of the church, they must be in league with the powers of darkness. Bring them back to the paths of righteousness, Brother Michael. Bring them back, or I will begin to wonder about *you.*"

The high cleric waddled out the door, accompanied by his heavily armed bodyguards. He rolled to his carriage, waving his hand in lethargic blessings to several peasants, who humbly doffed their caps and bowed their heads. When the priest disappeared inside the carriage, the peasants stared after his rich equipage with grim and angry faces in which could be seen the cruel pinch of hunger and want.

Brother Michael stood a long time in the doorway, watching the cloud of dust raised by the carriage wheels. His hand clasped the holy symbol around his neck.

"Grant me understanding, Mishakal," he prayed to the gentle goddess. "You are the only light in this terrible darkness."

Brother and sister, within the hall, heard the carriage wheels rattle over the flagstone of the courtyard and each breathed a sigh. The knight drew his sword, stared at it ruefully.

"What have I done? Drawn steel against a holy father!"

"He deserved it," said Nikol stoutly. "I wish I'd had mine. I'd have relieved him of a few chins!"

Both turned at the sound of footsteps entering the hall. The family healer paused in the doorway.

"Come in, Brother Michael. As always, you are one of us," said Nikol, mistaking his hesitation for a reluctance to intrude on their private conversation.

Michael was, in reality, wondering how he would tell them, wondering whether or not to impart the terrible threat. They were so young, already struggling with the burdens of a manor and its poverty-stricken people. There was little Nicholas could do for his tenants. He had trouble enough supporting the men-at-arms, who kept marauding goblins from plundering what meager stores the people had remaining.

Michael looked at the young knight, the healer's eyes dimmed with tears. Nicholas should have been riding to tourneys in his shining armor, wearing the favors of his lady. He should have been winning renown in gallant contest, but the only contest this knight fought was an inglorious battle against hunger and deprivation. The only horse he rode was a plow horse. The healer closed his eyes and bowed his head.

He heard a rustle of skirts, felt gently fingers on his hand.

"Brother Michael, are you in trouble with the Revered Son? It's all my fault. My tongue's sharper than my sword. I'll send a note of apology if you think it will help."

Michael opened his eyes, stared at her dumbly. As always, she took his breath away. His love for her and his longing, his admiration, pity and compassion, surged inside him, tangled up his voice. Gently, he removed her hand from his, took a step away from her. She was the daughter of a knight; he, a cleric of the lowest standing, with no money to pay the temple to rise higher.

"Brother Michael, what is it? What's wrong? What did that man say to you?" Nicholas strode across the room.

Michael could not bear to look at either of them. He lowered his gaze to the floor. "He threatens to send for the inquisitor, my lord."

"If we don't give up the lands to church?"

"Yes, my lord. I'm deeply sorry that one of my own kind—"

"Your kind!" Nikol cried. "That man is not like you, Michael, not in the slightest! You work tirelessly among the people. You share our poverty. You take nothing, not even what rightfully belongs to you. Oh, I've seen you, Brother! I've seen you slip the salary we pay you for your services back into my purse when you think I'm not looking."

She laughed at the foolish expression on his face, though there was a catch in her laughter, as if she might weep.

"M-my lady," Michael stammered, face burning, "you make too much of it. I need nothing. You feed me, honor me. I—" He could not go on.

"Come, Nikol," said her brother briskly. "You'll unman us all if you keep this up. And we have urgent matters to discuss. Will the high cleric make good his threat? Will he send this inquisitor?"

"I fear so," said Michael reluctantly, though he was thankful to Nicholas for changing the subject. "It has been done to others in the past."

"Surely only evil men," protested Nikol, "clerics of the Dark Queen, wizards, and those of their ilk. What have we to fear if they do send an inquisitor to us? We have always worshipped Paladine faithfully."

"There used to be nothing for the faithful to fear, my lady," said Michael. "In the beginning, the Kingpriest truly meant to try to rid the world of darkness. He did not realize, however, that to banish darkness he would have to banish us all, for there is a touch of darkness in each of us. We are none of us perfect, not even the Kingpriest. Only by recognizing that darkness and constantly striving against it do we keep from being overwhelmed by it."

Michael had his own darkness, or so he considered it. His love for this young woman was not pure, not holy, as he wanted it to be. It was tinged with burning desire. He wanted to take her in his arms, press his lips to hers. He wanted to undo her crown of hair and feel it cascade down around them both.

"I understand," said Nikol softly. "I long for a beautiful new dress. Isn't that terrible of me, when people are starving? Yet, I'm so tired to wearing this one poor gown." Her hands smoothed the well-worn, oft-mended fabric. She sighed, turned to her brother. "Maybe we are wrong, Nicholas. Maybe it is proud and sinful of us to want to keep these lands. Maybe we should give them to the church. After all, if it is the will of Paladine—"

"No," said Nicholas firmly. "I cannot believe it is Paladine's will. It is the will of the Kingpriest and his Revered Sons."

"How can you be sure?"

"Because, my lady," answered Michael steadily, "the Kingpriest claims to know the minds of the gods. How can any mortal claim such a thing?"

"You serve Mishakal."

"I follow the laws of the goddess. I obey her commands. I would never presume to speak for her, my lady."

"But is it wrong to want to rid the world of evil?"

Michael hesitated before answering. This was a question he himself had long argued internally, and it was not easy to utter his innermost thoughts and feelings.

"How do you define evil, my lady? Too often, we define it as that which is different from ourselves, or that which we do not understand. You said before that we should rid the world of wizards, but it was a wizard, one Magius, who fought at the side of the great Huma and who was knight's dearest friend.

"In the lands of my birth, near Xak Tsaroth, there live a band of nomads called the Plainsmen. They are barbarians, according to the Kingpriest. Yet a more generous, loving people never lived. They worship all the gods, even the dark ones, who are supposedly banished from this world. When one of their people falls ill, for example, the Plainsmen pray to Mishakal for healing, but they pray also to Morgion, evil god of disease, to withdraw his foul hand."

"What is their reasoning?" Nicholas's brow furrowed. "Morgion, along with the Dark Queen, was driven from the world long ago."

"Was he?" asked Michael gently. "Have plagues and illness left the world? No. What do we say, then? We say that it is the unworthy who suffer. Was your mother unworthy?"

Brother and sister were silent, absorbing this thought. Then Nicholas frowned and stirred. "What is your counsel, then, Brother Michael? Do we defy the Kingpriest? Think well before you answer." The knight smiled wanly. "As the one in charge of our spiritual guidance, you will be in as much danger from the inquisitor as my sister and I."

Michael did not respond immediately. He rose to his feet, paced thoughtfully about the hall, hands clasped behind his back, as if wondering what to say, how to say it.

Brother and sister drew near each other, held hands. At last, Michael turned to face them.

"Do nothing. Not yet. I . . . I cannot explain, but I have had strange dreams of late. Last night, Mishakal came to me as I slept. I saw her clearly. Her face was grieved, her eyes sad. She started to say something to me, to tell me something. She reached out her hand to me, but, at the last moment, she faded away. I will pray for her return tonight, pray that she will speak to me. And then, hopefully, I will be able to guide you."

Nicholas looked relieved; the burden listed, for a time, from his shoulders. Nikol smiled tremulously at Michael. Reaching out her hand, she took hold of his, pressed it warmly.

"Thank you, Brother. We have faith in you."

Michael's hand tightened on hers. He couldn't help himself. She was so lovely, so caring. Nikol, looking into his eyes, flushed, removing her hand from his grasp.

"Nicholas," she said, "it is time for our sword work. I, for one, could use the exercise."

Her brother went to the weapons rack, lifted a sword. "Yes, and I feel the need to sweat the touch of that fat priest out of my pores."

He tossed the weapon to her. She caught it expertly. "I'll change my clothes first. It wouldn't do to put any more rents in this poor dress of mine." Teasing, she glanced demurely at Michael. "You need not come with us, Brother. I know how fighting, even in practice, disturbs you."

She didn't love him. Liked and respected him, but she didn't love him. How could he expect her to? What was he?

A healer, not a warrior. How often he had seen her eyes shine when she listened to tales of courage and valor on the battlefield. Her dreams were of a bold knight, not a humble cleric.

The twins ran off, laughing and jesting, leaving him behind, empty, lonely, and afraid. Sighing, he went to the family chapel to say his prayers.

Part III

"You know what you must do?"

"I know," growled the goblin chief. He was some part human, and thus smarter and more dangerous than most of his kind. "Give me the money."

"Half now. Half when you deliver the knight. Alive!"

"You didn't say anything about that!" The goblin glowered, his face hideous in the bright light of the red moon, Lunitari. "You just said bring you the knight. You didn't say you wanted him alive."

"And what would I do with him dead?" Akar demanded testily.

"I don't know what wizards do. And I don't care." The goblin sneered. "Alive will cost you extra."

"Very well." Akar gave in with an ill grace. Reaching into a black velvet pouch, he carefully counted out a few gold pieces.

"The goblin stared at them with deep suspicion.

"They're real," snapped Akar. "What do you expect them to do? Disappear?"

"It wouldn't surprise me. If they do, so do I. Remember that, wizard." The goblin chief thrust the coins into a hairy pouch at his belt. "Tomorrow night. Here."

"Tomorrow night. Here," repeated Akar.

The two parted, both skulking back into the dark shadows that bred and sheltered them.

****

It was the hour before dawn. Brother Michael's sleep had been restive. He woke often, thinking he heard a voice calling him. He sat upright, holding his breath, staring into the darkness of his small, windowless room.

"Who? Who's there?"

No answer.

"Am I needed? Is someone ill?"

No response.

He lay back down again, telling himself he'd imagined it, and drifted into sleep, only to be roused again by the same call.

"Michael . . . Michael . . ."

He sat up, weary, sleep-dazed. "What now—" He began, then stopped and stared.

The image of a beautiful woman, surrounded by a radiant blue light, glimmered and the foot of his bed. He had seen her image before, but never this clearly, never this close. He knew, now, that she would speak to him, that she had come to comfort and guide him. His prayers had been answered.

Michael had no care for his nakedness, for the goddess sees all men naked, when they come into the world, sees the nakedness of their souls, their hearts. He slid from his bed and fell to his knees upon the cold stone floor.

"Mishakal. I am your servant. Command me. What is your bidding?"

The goddess's voice was lovely, like the song of myriad birds, like his mother's whisper, like silver bells on a bright new morning. "Truly you are my servant, Michael. One of my faithful servants. I need you. Come with me."

"Yes, of course, Holy One." Michael rose swiftly, began dressing himself, hardly knowing what he was doing. The blue light surrounding him was blinding, filled his heart with uplifting joy. "Is someone sick? Someone in the village, perhaps?"

"Put aside the cares of this world, Brother Michael. They are no longer yours." The goddess held out a hand of surpassing beauty and wondrous softness. "Come."

Michael heard horns blowing the call to battle. He heard shouts and voices, the rattle of armor and of sword. He heard feet pounding on the battlements. He paused, looking behind him, looking toward the door that led to the family chapel.

"Yes, Lady, but there is fighting! They will need me—"

"Not for long," said the goddess. "Paladine has them in his keeping. He will gather their souls to him, remove them from a world that soon will erupt in fire. Lay down your burden, Michael, and walk with me."

"And I will see them again? Nicholas, Nikol?"

"On the other side. You will wait for them. It will not be long."

"Then I will come." He was glad to leave, glad to give up the pain of living, the pain of his desires. Soon, he would be able to love her purely. He reached out his hand to take the hand of the goddess. . . .

A scream shattered the dawning. Fists pounded on his door.

"Michael! Brother Michael! You must come! It's Nicholas! He's hurt! He needs you!"

"Nikol's voice!" Michael trembled; his hand shook.

"There is nothing you can do, Brother," the goddess told him sadly. "True, the valiant knight is wounded, but, even as his sister stands here, pleading for your aid, the knight is being carried away by his attackers. You will arrive too late to save him."

"But if Nicholas has taken ill, who will lead the men? The manor will fall—"

"Brother Michael! Please!" Nikol's voice was raw with shouting.

The goddess gazed at him with cool eyes. "What will happen, will happen. You can do nothing to prevent it. Have faith in us, believe that all is for the best, though you do not understand. You said yourself, 'What mortal can know the mind of a god?' If you refuse, if you lack faith, if you stay and interfere, you run the risk of dooming yourself, the woman, and the world to a terrible fate!"

"Michael! I need you!" Nikol cried. Fists pounded on the wood.

"Then so be it, Lady," he said heavily, "for I cannot leave them." His hand dropped to his side. He could no longer look on the radiance of the goddess. It hurt his eyes. "I love her. I love them both. I can't believe that their deaths would be for the best! Forgive me, Mishakal."

He started toward the door. His hand was on the handle. His heart ached. He longed to go with the goddess. Yet, outside, he heard Nikol crying. He placed his hand upon the door. The light around him seemed to soften. He glanced back.

"Tomorrow night, the Night of Doom, the bridge at the Lost Citadel will open to all true clerics. Only those who have faith may pass."

The blue light glimmered and died. Michael yanked open the door.

Nikol clutched at him. "Where have you been? What have you been doing? Didn't you hear me call?"

"I was . . . at my prayers," Michael said lamely.

Her eyes flashed. Daughter of a knight, she could not understand the soft cleric who fell to his knees and prayed to his goddess to save him, when other men were grabbing shield and sword. Catching hold of his hand, she began running down the hallway. He stumbled to keep up with her. She was clad in her nightclothes. Her long gown whipped around her ankles, nearly tripping her. Blood stained the white cloth. Michael had no need to ask whose it was.

"They carried him inside," Nikol was walking feverishly, as they ran. "We stripped off the armor. His wound is deep, but not mortal. We have to hurry. He's lost so much blood. I left old Giles with him . . . ."

No, we don't need to hurry! Michael cried silently. Too late. We will be too late! But he found himself running all the faster, as if he could outrun destiny.

They reached a room on the ground level, near the entrance. They had not carried the wounded man far.

"Giles!" Nikol cried, pushing on the door. "I've brought the healer. I—Nicholas? Where are you? Giles! Oh god, no! Paladine, no!"

Her heartbroken cry went through Michael like iron. Nikol caught up the body of the elderly servant, lifted him gently from the floor.

"Giles! What happened? Where's Nicolas?"

Michael knelt beside the old man. A goblin arrow stuck out of his chest, the shaft buried deep.

"Mishakal, heal . . ." Michael's voice cracked. The holy medallion of Mishakal he wore around his neck, the symbol of his faith that gleaming blue with the radiance of the goddess, was dark, its light gone. He stammered, his words halted.

The old man gasped. "They . . . took him!"

"Who took him? Giles, answer me!" Nikol cried.

"Goblins . . ."

The old man stared at her, but his eyes no longer saw her. His head lolled in her arms. She laid him on the floor, her face expressionless, shocked past hut and sorrow.

Michael stood, looked around the room. Broken glass littered the floor; the window swung crazily on its hinges. It had been smashed open with a heavy object, probably a club or mace. Blood smeared the windowsill.

"They carried him out this way," he said.

"But why?" Nikol stared at the empty bed, the bloodstained, rumpled sheets. Her face was whiter than the linen. "Why would they take him? Goblins butcher and kill. They never take prisoners. . . . Oh, Nicholas!"

A shudder swept over her. She buried her face in the still-warm bedclothes, twisted the cloth in her fingers. Michael ached to comfort her. He drew near, reaching out to her. His hand touched her shoulder.

"My lady—"

Nikol rounded on him with a savage cry. "You! This is your fault! If you had been here, instead of hiding behind the skirts of your goddess, my brother would be well! He would be alive! He could have fought them—"

A bowman, bloodied and disheveled, appeared in the doorway.

"Where's my lord?" he demanded harshly. "The enemy is assaulting in force. What are his orders?"

Michael straightened, was about to give the man the terrible news that his lord was gone.

Sharp nails dug into his skin. Nikol pushed past him.

"My lord will be with you presently," she told him, her voice cols and level. "We are binding his wound."

"Pray Paladine he comes swiftly," said the bowman, and dashed off.

"Katherine!" Nikol cried, "Katherine—there you are."

The woman who had been nursemaid and nanny to the girl, lady-in-waiting to the young woman, hastened into the room at her mistress's call.

"Fetch me the men's clothing I use when I practice with Nicholas! Be quick about it! Hurry!"

Katherine stared at her, confused and upset. "Oh, my lady, there is no time! We must flee—"

"Go!" Nikol shouted at her. "Do as I command!"

Katherine cast a frightened look at Michael, who shook his head, bewildered. The woman fled, her wooden clogs clattering over the stone floor.

Nikol glanced about the room, found what she sought. Catching hold of her brother's leather belt, she drew a sharp knife from its sheath and held it out to Michael. He stared at it, then at her.

"My vows forbid me to carry sharp weapons, my lady—"

"You weakling! I'm not asking you to fight with it!"

Nikol thrust the knife into his limp hand. Lifting the heavy braid of long, golden hair, she twitched it around, held it out to him.

"Cut it. Cut it to match the length of my brother's hair."

Michael understood suddenly what she intended. He stared at her, aghast. "Nikol, you can't be serious! You're not thinking—"

"No, it's you who's not thinking!" She turned, faced him. "This is my only chance to save Nicholas. Don't you understand? They've taken him away. Now they're launching an assault to cover their escape. We must drive them back, then I can lead a party to go rescue my brother."

"But you're a woman. The men won't follow you."

"They won't know they're following me," Nikol said calmly, turning around again. 'They'll think they're following my brother. We look enough alike that I can fool them, beneath the armor. And don't worry, Brother," she added bitterly. "You can stay here in safety and pray for me. Now, cut."

Her sarcasm was sharper than the blade. He realized now how wide was the gulf that separated them. He had sometimes dared to hope that she was fond of him. He had sometimes fancied that she had responded warmly to his touch.

If I were noble or if she were common, might we not love?

But now he knew the truth, he saw it in her eyes. She despised him, despised his weakness.

Michael grasped the knife awkwardly. Lifting the heavy braid of hair in his hand, he felt its silk beneath his fingers.

How many times have I dreamed of this moment, he thought to himself bitterly. The grace, the privilege of touching her beautiful hair.

He heard frantic shouting outside. A spent arrow whistled in through the window. Gritting his teeth, Michael hacked away at the shining, twisted strands.

****

"My lord!" A grizzled sergeant caught hold of the knight's arm. Blood streamed from a cut on the sergeant's hand. He limped from either a new wound or an old. "My lord! It's hopeless. There are far too many of the fiends! Sound the retreat!"

"No!" The knight shook him off furiously. "They're falling back. Rally the men for another charge!"

"My lord, they're regrouping, making ready for the killing blow, that's all," said the sergeant gently.

Michael realized then that the sergeant knew the truth. He knew he wasn't following his lord, but his lady.

The cleric edged closer, to listen to the conversation. The battle had been brief and brutal. He had done what he could to ease the pain of the dying, but that hadn't been much. The situation had been too dire, too confused, for anyone to notice that their cleric had tucked his medallion of faith inside his robes, that no prayers passed his lips. Merciful death came to most swiftly. Michael's one panic-stricken thought was that Nikol would fall, wounded. And then what could he do for her?

"What are your orders, my lord?" the sergeant asked respectfully.

Nikol did not immediately answer. Exhaustion had taken its toll. The ragged blond hair that fell to the metal-armored shoulders was wet with sweat. Any other knight would have removed the heavy helm, wiped his face. The knight kept her helm on.

Michael joined them, stared out over the battlements into the woods beyond. Day had dawned. The vast numbers of the enemy could be counted easily; they made no secret of their strength. The knight glanced around at the pitiful number of men who remained.

"Release the men from duty," said Nikol, in a low toneless voice. "If they leave now, they can make good their escape. The goblins will be too busy looting and burning to chase them."

"Very good, my lord," said the sergeant, bowing.

"Give them my thanks. They fought well."

"Yes, my lord." The old sergeant's voice was choked. "My lord will be coming with us?"

Nikol made no response. Michael stepped forward, prepared to argue, prepared to tell everyone the truth if necessary. Anything to save her. He caught the flash of blue eyes from behind the helm. Nikol's gaze held his a moment, warned him to keep silent.

"No, not immediately," she replied. "And don't wait for me. I will try to save what little of value remains."

"My lord—"

"Go, Jeoffrey, Take my thanks and my blessing."

The knight held out a gauntleted hand. The old man caught hold of it, pressed it to his lips.

"Never did a noble knight fight with such courage as you have fought this day, my lord! May Paladine walk always at your side."

The sergeant bowed his head. Tears streamed down the weathered cheeks. Then he was gone, running through the smoke, shouting orders.

Michael stepped forward, out of the shadows. "You should go with them, my lady."

Nikol did not even glance at him. She stood staring out into the woods, crawling with evil creatures. "Your prayers did little good, Brother."

Michael's face burned with shame. Did she know the truth? Suspect? He turned away in unhappy silence.

"Don't go, Michael," she said softly, remorsefully. "Forgive me . . . and ask the gods to forgive me. It's just . . . so hopeless!"

She leaned against him, thankful for his support. He couldn't very well take an armored knight in his arms. He made do by squeezing her hand tightly. "We must get away, my lady."

"Yes," Nikol murmured. She talked as if she were in a daze. "There is a cave, not far from the castle. Nicholas and I used to play there, when we were little. It is well hidden. We will be safe."

"Is there anything you want to take with you?" Michael asked, feeling helpless. He looked at the castle walls. Even now, they appeared stalwart, impregnable. It was difficult to imagine that they could no longer offer the shelter they promised. "What about the servants?" he asked.

"I sent them away long ago," said Nikol. They were alone

now. The men had fled. She removed her helm. Her face was ashen, grimy with dirt and blood and sweat. "Most of them have family in these parts. They'll warn them, hopefully in time to get away safely. As for the jewels, we sold them years ago. I have with me what matters to me most."

Her gaze went fondly, sadly to the sword in her hand—her brother's sword, which once had been her father's and his father's before him.

"But we'll need food, water skins . . ."

A hideous yell went up from the goblins in the woods. A black wave started to roll across the torn and trampled grasslands in front of the castle. The gate was shut. It would take them some time to storm the walls, even though they were no longer defended.

Nikol's lips tightened. She replaced the helm over her head, gripped the sword. "Stay behind me and keep clear of my sword arm. I may need to fight our way out."

"Yes, my lady."

They hastened to stairs, leading downward. Nikol paused, turned to him, grasped his hand.

"We'll find Nicholas, and you will heal him," she said.

"Yes, my lady," Michael replied. What could he say?

She nodded abruptly and disappeared into the darkness of the spiral staircase. Michael followed after her, his heart aching, heavy.

"It's hopeless!" he wanted to shout. "Hopeless! Even if we did find him, I can't heal him! Don't you see? Don't you understand?"

Grasping the blue holy symbol of Mishakal, he drew it forth from beneath his robes. Once it would have lit the darkness. Once it would have glowed brightly, radiantly. Now he could barely see it for the thick shadows surrounding him.

He let the medallion fall heavily to his chest. "You will see, soon enough. Now you despise me. Then you will hate me."

He stumbled after her through the darkness.

Part IV

Night crept over the land. Nikol stood at the entrance to the cave and watched the lurid red glow of flame lighting the dark sky, at first brilliantly, then gradually growing dim. The smoke of the burning stung the eyes, bit into the nostrils. Occasionally, raucous shouts and wild laughter could be heard, carried on the wind.

"You should rest, my lady," said Michael gently.

"You sleep, Brother," she told him. "I'll keep watch."

Her spirit was strong, but it could not lend its strength to her muscle and bone and sinew. Even as she spoke, her knees buckled beneath her. Michael caught her in his arms, eased her to the cavern floor. He pried her fingers from the sword she still held, fingers gummed black with goblin blood. He washed her hands, bathed her face with cool water.

"Wake me before the dawn," she murmured. "We will follow them . . . find Nicholas." She slept.

Michael sat back, closed his eyes. Tears of weariness and despair filled his eyes; a lump grew in his throat, choke him. He loved her so, and he must fail her. Even if they found Nicholas and saved him—and how could they do that, against a goblin army?—Michael could not heal him.

Tomorrow night, the Night of Doom, the bridge at the Lost Citadel will open to all true clerics. Only those who have faith may pass. Mishakal's voice came to him. The goddess had given him a chance to redeem himself.

Tomorrow night. The cleric had until tomorrow night to find the bridge, the Lost Citadel, a place remembered only in legend, from the beginnings of the world. He would cross the bridge. The light of the goddess once more would shine on him, envelop him, end the pain of this hopeless love, this useless existence. Once he was there, he would rediscover his lost faith.

"Good-bye, Nikol. Tomorrow, when you wake, I will be gone," he told her. Reaching out his hand, he touched the rough-cut hair. "Don't be angry with me. You don't need me.

I would be a liability to you, a weak man who cannot even call upon the power of the goddess to aid you. You will travel faster alone."

He propped himself up against the cavern wall, fully intending to stay awake, watch for the gray light of dawn, when he would sneak away. But easeful slumber stole over him. His head drooped; his body slumped to the ground. He did not see it, but in the darkness, the holy medallion he wore began to glow a soft blue, and no harm came to them during the night, though many evil creatures skulked about their hiding place.

With the dawn, however, the medallion's soft light faded.

****

The black-robed wizard squatted on a cleared patch of ground in the middle of the forest. It was midmorning. The sun shone through a haze of smoke that drifted among the treetops. Akar sneezed, glanced up at the smoke irritably, then turned his attention back to the divining rocks he had tossed on the ground. Leaning over them, he studied them carefully.

"This is it, the Night of Doom. The true clerics will depart Ansalom. I have one night to find the Lost Citadel. Where are those blasted goblins anyway?" Akar looked once again, grimly, at the smoke. "Enjoying themselves, I fancy. We'll see how long they do if they fail me—"

The rustling of tree branches interrupted him. Akar gathered up the stones in one swift movement of this hand, thrust them into a black leather pouch. The words of a deadly spell on his lips, he crept back swiftly into the protection of the trees and waited.

A group of four goblins burst into the cleared space. They moved loudly, with the confidence of those engorged on victory. They bore between them a litter on which lay the body of a human male. The wizard, seeing the litter, cursed.

The goblin chief shoved past his men, looked around

the forest. "Wizard? Show yourself! Make haste! I want my money!"

Akar stalked out of the woods. Ignoring the chief, he strode over to the litter, which the goblins had dropped on the ground. The young man on the litter groaned in pain. He was conscious, though he seemed to have little idea what was happening to him. He looked up at the wizard with dazed puzzlement.

Akar regarded him coldly.

"What's this?" he demanded. "What have you brought me?"

"A Knight of Solamnia. They stripped him of his armor." The goblin sounded bitter. He could have used that armor.

"Bah! He's too young to be a knight. Even if I believed you, the man is wounded, near dying! What use is he to me in this state?"

"Lucky you are to have him in any state!" hissed the goblin. "Did you expect us to take a Knight of Solamnia without a fight?"

Akar bent over the young man. Roughly, he lifted the blood-soaked bandages wrapped tightly around the abdomen, peered at the wound. The man cried out in agony, clenched his fists. A ring flashed in the light. Akar grasped it, stared at it, grunted in satisfaction.

"Well, well. You are a knight."

"What do you want of me?" the wounded man managed to gasp.

Akar ignored him. He felt for the lifebeat in the neck, noted the fever burning the blood. The wizard sat back on his haunches.

"He won't last another hour."

"I suggest you do what you must do with him quickly, then," advised the chief.

"Impossible. I need him alive all night."

"Oh? I supposed now you'll want us to go out and capture you a cleric?" The goblin chief sneered.

"It would do no good. No cleric you would find this night

on Krynn could heal him."

The goblin chief gestured. "Then you take care of him. You're a wizard, after all. I supposed your magic's good for something. Pay us what you owe us and let us be gone. We plan to make something out of this deal. The castle was picked clean before we got there. Not a woman to be had."

The knight cried out, struggled to rise. His hand went for his sword, but it was no longer at his side.

"Save your strength." Akar shoved the knight back down. The wizard stood up. He was in a better mood, almost smiling. "Here's your pay." He tossed a few gold coins at the goblin chief.

The chief found this sudden change in the wizard suspicious, apparently, for he eyes the money dubiously. "You pick it up," he ordered one of his cohorts, who did as he was told.

The goblins slunk back to their looting, their chief keeping a careful eye on his man who held the wizard's money.

Akar turned to the knight, who lay still and silent, fighting against the pain, refusing to show weakness.

"What do you want of me?" he repeated hoarsely.

"This night, I must spill the blood of a good and true person on the bridge of the Lost Citadel. You have the misfortune to be, Sir Knight, a good and true person. At least that's what your people say of you. Something of a rarity these days, I must admit. Don't trouble yourself over the how and why, but, with your murder, the clerics of Her Dark Majesty will at last be able to return to this world."

The knight smiled. "I am dying. I will not live long enough to be of use to you, thanks to Paladine."

"Ah, now. Don't give up hope. My magic is good for something. I cannot heal you, Sir Knight. Nor do I necessarily want you healed. You would, I fancy, prove a most troublesome captive. Yet you will remain alive until I can transport you to the Lost Citadel.

"A wish spell will accomplish what I want. Yes, a wish will do nicely. The spell will cost me a year of my life." The wizard shrugged. "But what is that? When I have the power of the great Fistandantilus, I will gain that year back, with interest!"

Akar lifted his hands, gazed up at the sky, to the black moon, Nuitari, the moon that only those with the vision of darkness can see.

"My wish is thus: Let the knight remain alive until he meets death at the point of a dagger." Akar removed the dagger from its sheath at his belt, held it up to the sky. The metal darkened, as if a shadow fell across it, then it flashed with a terrible, unholy light.

"My wish is granted!" Akar said in satisfaction.

"No! Paladine, forfend! Take my life! Kill me now!"

The young knight struggled to his feet. Ripping the bandages from his wound, starting the blood flowing freely, he lurched across the clearing, heading toward the forest.

Akar made no move, watched calmly.

Nicholas fell to his knees. His lifeblood flowed from him. He stared at it, watching it soak into the ground. The pain was intense, excruciating. He doubled over, cried out to die.

Death did not come. Nicholas lay in his own blood, writhing in agony.

Akar whistled. A horse as black as goblin's blood—which was, indeed, the steed's name—cantered into the clearing, drawing behind it a small wooden cart. The wizard grasped hold of the knight by the shoulders, dragged him across the bloody grass to the cart, and heaved him up into it. Removing a length of rope from the cart, Akar bound the suffering knight's hands and feet securely.

"Not that I think you're in any shape to do me harm," said Akar. "But you're a tough breed, you knights. I'm sorry I can do nothing to ease the pain. But, look at it this way. After a few hours of agony, you'll be more than ready to die. Try not to groan too loudly. Foul creatures roam the countryside these days. And now, to find the Lost Citadel."

Akar mounted the cart, lifted the reins in his hands. Once again he gazed up at the sky. As he watched, a shadow crossed the sun, like the moon eclipsing it, but it was a shadow only he could see. He stared at it, squinting against the sunlight, until he found what he sought.

The shadow extended downward from the sun, formed a shaft of darkness that pierced the daylight. Whatever that shadow touched instantly burst into flame. Fire roared through the forest. Smoke, foul and poisonous, hung in the air. Akar sniffed its perfume. Behind him, he heard the knight choke and retch,

When the smoke dissipated, blown aside by a death-cold wind, Akar saw that a trail had been burned among the charred trees, a trail of blackness, a trail of night in day,

"Nuitari be blessed," said Akar.

Slapping the reins on the horse's back, he drove the cart onto the shadow-shrouded path.

Part V

The goblins' trail was easy for Michael and Nikol to follow . . . too easy. The army had cut a swath of destruction through the forest surrounding the burned and gutted castle. Their numbers were strong; they had no need to hide or conceal the path that led back to their lair in the mountains. They feared no retribution. Neighboring knights, in neighboring manors, had their own lands and people to consider.

Michael stared in dismay at the broken trees, the trampled brush, the bodies of dead goblins, who, wounded, had been left behind by their loutish comrades. Nikol roamed the path, her gaze fixed on the ground, searching for any clue of her brother.

"My lady, if they did take him, what chance do you have to rescuing him? There must be . . . hundreds of them!" Michael waved his hand at the destruction.

"Then at least I will have the comfort of dying with him," Nikol returned. Straightening, she brushed her hair back out of her eyes. "You knew what we faced. I warned you this morning."

Michael didn't want to be reminded of the morning. The two had awakened, clasped in each other's arms. Confused and embarrassed, each of them kept the other well at a distance. He meant to tell her, then, that he was leaving her, but somehow he couldn't find the words.

The silence between them grew uncomfortable. Undoubtedly she was thinking of the morning as well.

"Nikol," he began, longing to say what was in his heart.

She turned away from him hurriedly, began looking with self-conscious intensity back at the ground.

"Have you ever known goblins to take hostages, Brother?" she asked him abruptly, putting, he thought, a heavy emphasis on his title.

Michael sighed, shook his head tiredly. "No, I haven't. It takes a subtle mind to plot exchanging hostages for ransom. Goblins think only of looting and killing."

"Precisely. And yet they took Nicholas, stole him deliberately. They took him alone. They didn't want anyone else. They killed poor old Giles. Why? Unless they were under orders to capture Nicholas . . ."

Her face was flushed with her new idea. She forgot the strained formality. "That's it, Michael! The attack on the castle was a diversion to cover their real intent: capturing Nicholas. Which means that someone wants him and that someone must want him alive!"

"Yes, my lady." Michael agreed.

No need to tell her that her twin, if he was still alive, might well have good reason to wish himself dead. A few hours fruitless searching and Nikol would be forced to admit defeat. Then, perhaps, he could persuade her to take refuge in some neighboring manor, while he himself prepared to leave. . . .

"Michael!"

Her excited voice rang like silver in the still air. He hastened through the brush toward her.

"Look! Look at this!" Nikol pointed to a splotch in the trampled grass. Blood. Red blood. Human blood.

Before Michael could say a word, Nikol had dashed off, following a trail that broke from the main one. He hurried after her, not knowing whether to give thanks or curse the gods that had put this sign in her way.

They came upon the clearing. Both stopped. Although the sun shone brightly, the evil that lingered in the place covered it with a dark cloud. Nikol put her hand to the hilt of her sword, but nerveless fingers slipped from it. Unconsciously, she reached out to Michael. His hand closed over hers, and they drew close together, shivering in the chill, sunlit darkness.

"Oh, Michael," Nikol whispered brokenly, "where is he? What have they done to him? I—"

She gave a cry. The large puddle of red blood glistened in the light. Near it lay the bandage she had wrapped with her own hands around her brother's wound. Nikol covered her face with her hands, slumped against Michael's chest. He put his arms around her, held her shivering body close.

"My lady, we must go away from here." Michael's love for her, his pity, was agony. "Let me take you to Sir Thomas's manor. You will be safe—"

"No!" Hastily, Nikol wiped her eyes, pushed herself away from his comforting embrace. "I was weak for a moment. This dreadful place . . ." She looked around, shuddered. "But Nicholas isn't here. His body isn't here," she continued, her tone grim, resolute. "They've taken him off somewhere. He's still alive. I know he's alive!"

She began searching the clearing. It did not take long to find the tracks left by the wheels of the cart, or the spoor of blood that led to it. She followed the signs; Michael followed her. Both found the opening burned into the forest, the opening of darkness. They stopped, stared at it, blood chilling in their veins.

"I think this is what it must be like to gaze into the Abyss," said Michael in awe.

Nikol's face was ashen, her eyes wide and terrified. She stood close to him, and he could feel her body tremble beneath the armor. "I can't go in there. . . ."

Wind moaned in the tops of the blacked trees, a cry of pain, as if the trees were screaming. And then Michael realized, with a thrill of horror, that the cry came from a human throat. He hoped against hope that Nikol had not heard.

"Come, my lady, let us go away from this evil place—"

"Nicholas!" Nikol called out in anguish. "I hear you! We're coming!" She took a step forward, into the noisome shadows.

Michael caught hold of her. "Nikol, you can't!"

She struck at him, hard, shoved him back. "I'm going. And so are you, you coward!" Her hand closed over his wrist with a grip of iron. "You will heal him—"

"I can't!" Michael cried savagely. "Look! Look!" He yanked the holy symbol from its hiding place beneath his robes, held it up for Nikol to see. "It's dark, as dark as that path before us. Do you know what that means? The goddess has turned away from me. She won't answer my prayers. Even if we did find Nicholas, I could do nothing for him."

Nikol stared at him, not comprehending. "But . . . how? How could the goddess abandon you?"

Because I abandoned the goddess! I did it for you, for you and Nicholas! Michael wanted to shout at her, vent his frustration, his fear and anger—anger at her, anger at the gods. . . .

He shivered suddenly. He shouldn't be angry. That was wrong. The faithful were never angry, never questioned. Again, he'd been found lacking.

"I can't explain," Michael said tiredly. "The matter is between myself and my god. But, now, you must come away from this place. As you see, there's nothing we can do. . . ."

Nikol let go of him, as she might have tossed away a piece of rubbish.

"Thank you for accompanying me this far." Her voice was cold, bitter with disappointment. "You needn't go on with me. This place holds far more danger for you than for me, for now it appears that you are defenseless against its evil. Farewell, Brother—I mean, Michael."

She turned and walked, with firm step, into the fearsome, fire-ravaged forest. The shadows surrounded her instantly. He lost sight of her, could not even see a glint of her armor.

Michael stood shivering on the outskirts of the blacked woods. Mishakal's words, forgotten until now, came back to him suddenly, as if spoken for this very time, this very place. *If you lack faith, if you stay and interfere, you run the risk of dooming yourself, the woman, and the world to a terrible fate!*

He had stayed. He had interfered. He had helped bring this evil upon her, upon himself, perhaps upon the world!

"I should have faith," he counseled himself. "If I did, I'd let her go. Paladine is with her. Love armors her. She will only lose her life. I might have lost my soul! I should turn away, seek the Lost Citadel, beg the goddess to forgive me. I have only until tonight to find it, to retrieve my faith. . . ."

He did turn away. He turned his back on the dark and fearsome woods into which she had vanished. He took a step away from her and then another. And then, he stopped.

He could not leave her. He could not leave her to die alone, in pain and in terror. Although it would cost him his soul, he would go with her, be with her until the end.

Until the doom fell upon them . . . and the world.

Part VI

Michael was blind. Darkness, thick and suffocating, fell over his sight the moment he entered the fearsome woods. His loss of vision was utter and instantaneous. He could see nothing—not vague shadowy outlines, not movement. He could see neither the shine of Nikol's armor nor the sheen of her golden hair. So strange and terrifying was his sudden blindness that he involuntarily put his hand to his eyes. It seemed to him that they must have been plucked out.

"Michael?" Nikol was frightened. "Michael . . . is that you? Michael, I can't see!"

"I'm here," he said.

He tried to sound reassuring, but he choked on the words. Yes, he was here. A lot of good it would do her, do either of them. A lot of good it would do her, do either of them. He reached out with groping hands toward the sound of her voice, the silvery jingle of the buckles on her armor. "I . . . can't see either, my lady."

He paused, blinked. Suddenly, he could see. He could see the way out, the way back. He could see the hot sunlight shining in the clearing, see the ruts left by the wagon wheels leading into these woods. He gasped aloud in thankfulness. He had feared, for a moment, that his sight had been stolen from him forever.

"What is it, Michael?" Nikol heard him, caught hold of his hand.

"Turn around, my lady," he said, guiding her.

She did so, slowly, feet shuffling in the charred undergrowth and ashes. Her eyes widened, she clasped his hand tightly.

"I was so afraid!" She breathed, shifted to look at him. Her smile slowly faded. "I can't see you!" She moved her head around. "I can't see anything ahead of me. . . ."

"We can see the way out—"

"But I don't want to go out!" she cried angrily. "I—"

The sound of the scream came again, but it sounded farther away, came from deeper within the wood. They could hear a horse's hooves and the rattle of a cart being driven at a slow pace over uneven ground. Letting go of Michael's hand, Nikol ran forward.

"Nikol! Come back—"

He heard her running footsteps, then heard her stumble, fall, heard the sound of angry, frustrated sobbing. He made his way to her, fumbling through the terrifying darkness that seemed to become darker the farther into it he ventured. He almost fell over her, knelt beside her.

"Are you hurt?"

"Leave me alone!" Nikol started to get to her feet. "I'm going after him."

He lost patience. "Nikol, be reasonable. It's hopeless! Even if you could see, could you keep up with a cart on foot? You can't find the trail! You can't see what obstacles or dangers lie in your path. You could step off a cliff, fall into a chasm—"

"I will not abandon him. I will go after him if I have to crawl!"

He felt her, so near him, turn. He knew she was looking back to the way they'd come. He turned as well. Never had sunlight looked so bright or so beautiful. The clearing, which had seemed a place of terror before, was now a haven of peace and safety.

Thus, do we take our blessings for granted, until they are gone, he thought in bitter sadness, putting his hand to the symbol of Mishakal that lay, a heavy burden, on his chest.

"What is causing this?" Nikol demanded in frustration, "What evil has created this darkness?"

"Nuitari," answered a soft and whispering voice, "god of the unseen. You walk in the light of the dark moon."

"Who is it?" Nikol was on her feet. Michael heard the ring of steel. She had drawn her sword. "Who is there?"

"Your weapon is useless, Sir Knight." The voice was heavily ironic. "I've been sitting here, watching you two bumble about for the last ten minutes. I could have slain you both twice over before now."

Michael stood, grasped Nikol's sword arm. He could feel her trembling in frustration and fear. She shoved him away, swung the sword in front of her wildly, more to relieve her own sense of helplessness than in hope in hitting anything. He heard the blade whistle harmlessly through the air.

The unseen watcher began to laugh, a laugh that caught suddenly in his throat, clanged to a racking cough. After a long moment, the coughing spasm ceased. Michael heard a ragged, indrawn breath.

"My lady," Michael counseled, reaching for her, finding her arm, holding it firmly. "If this person has watched us, as he claims, then he must be able to see."

"That is true," said Nikol, lowering her sword. "Can you see?"

"I can," answered the voice calmly. "To those of us who walk in Nuitari's night, this wood is lit as brightly as the day. For you, it will grow ever darker with each step you take. But, perhaps, you have wandered in here by accident. I suggest you leave, while you can still find the way out."

"If you have been watching us, as you say, you know that we did not enter the wood by accident," said Nikol coolly. She had turned in the direction of the voice, her sword still in her hand, her guard raised. "Someone has been taken into this wood, someone dear to us. We have reason to believe he is being held captive by goblins."

"A young man?" asked the voice. "Comely, well made, with a grievous wound in his side? He is wrapped in bloody bandages. . . ."

"Yes," said Nikol softly, her hand closing over Michael's, holding him tightly for support. "Yes! That is my brother. You've seen him?"

"I have. And I offer you this counsel. Turn back. There is nothing you can do for him. He is a dead man. You will die yourselves. Nothing you can do will save him. Isn't that true, Revered Son of Mishakal?" The voice seemed to sneer.

"I am not a Revered Son," answered Michael quietly, "only a humble brother."

"Not even that, seemingly," said the voice.

Michael felt eyes staring at him, strange eyes that he swore he could almost see, eyes like hourglasses. Self-consciously, the healer put his hand over the medallion on his chest, thrust it hastily beneath his robes.

"Let him alone," Nikol retorted angrily. "He has no

reason to be here, not as I do. He comes with me not out of love, but out of loyalty."

"Is that so?"

Michael could see the hourglass eyes laughing at him.

"So you come in here for your brother, Sir Knight?" the voice continued, soft, hissing. "Give him up. You can do nothing for him except die with him."

Nikol spoke steadily. "Then I will do so. I could not live without him. We are twins, you see—"

"Twins?" The voice was altered, low and dark, darker than the woods. "Twins," it repeated.

"Yes," said Nikol, hesitant, uncertain at the sudden change she sensed in the speaker. Did it bode good? Or ill? "We are twins. And if you know anything of twins, you know that we are close, closer than most siblings."

"I know . . . something of twins," said the voice.

The words were spoken so softly that the two might not have heard them, but both were straining every sense to make up for the loss of their eyesight.

"Then you know that I will not abandon him," said Nikol. "I will go after him, to save him if I can, die with him if I cannot."

"You cannot save him," said the voice, after a moment's pause. "Your brother has been captured by a powerful wizard of the Black Robes, a man named Akar. He needed a virtuous person. Is your brother, by chance, a knight as well?"

"My brother is a knight," answered Nikol. "I am not. I am a woman, as you well know, for I can feel your eyes on me, though I cannot see them."

"One twin born to a body fragile and frail, one twin strong and powerful. Did you never resent him?"

"Of course not!" Nikol answered too fast, too angrily. "I love him! What are you talking about?"

"Nothing important." The voice seemed to start to sigh, but the sigh was broken by a cough that seemed likely to rend the man apart.

Involuntarily, forgetting that he was powerless, Michael reached with a hand toward the stranger. He heard a hissing laugh.

"There is nothing you could do for me, healer! Even if you retained the favor of your goddess. It is the wrath of heaven that batters this poor body of mine, the anger of the gods that will soon cleanse this world in fire!"

The voice changed, abruptly, becoming cool and business-minded. "Do you speak truly, Lady? Will you follow your brother, though the way be dark and terrifying, the end hopeless?"

"I will."

"How can we go anywhere?" Michael demanded. "We cannot see the way."

"I can," said the voice, "and I will be your eyes."

Michael heard a rustle of cloth, as of long robes brushing across the ground. He heard odd sounds, objects hanging from a belt, perhaps, clicking and rubbing together. He heard a soft thud that accompanied whispering footfalls—a staff, helping the speaker walk. Michael sniffed, his nose wrinkled. He smelled the sweetness of rose petals, and a more horrible sweetness—that of decay. He sensed an arm moving toward them.

"Wait a moment," Michael said, halting Nikol, who had sheathed her sword and was reaching out to the stranger. "If you can see in the light of Nuitari, then you, too, must be a mage of evil, a wizard of the Black Robes. Why should we trust you?"

"You shouldn't, of course," said the voice.

"Then why are you helping us? What is your reason? Is this a trap?"

"It could be. What choice do you have?"

"None," said Nikol, her voice suddenly gentle. "Yet I believe you. I trust you."

"And why should you do that, Lady?" The voice was bitter, mocking.

"Because of what you said about the twins. One weak, the other strong . . ."

The stranger was silent a long moment. Michael might have thought the man had left them, but for the rasping breathing of sickness-racked lungs.

"My reason for helping you is one you would not understand. Let us say simply that Akar has been promised that which is rightfully mine. I intend to see he does not acquire it. Will you come or not? You must hurry! The Night of Doom approaches. You have very little time."

"I will go," said Nikol. "I will follow where you lead, though it cost me my life!"

"And you, Brother?" said the wizard softly. "Will you walk with me? The woman has pledged her life. For you, as you surmise, the cost will be greater. Will you pledge your soul?"

"No, Michael, don't!" Nikol said, interrupting the cleric's answer. "Go back. This is not your battle. It is mine. I would not have you sacrifice yourself for us."

"What's the matter, my lady?" snapped Michael, suddenly, irrationally angry. "Don't you think I love Nicholas as well as you? Or perhaps you think I don't have a right to love him or anyone else in your family? Well, my lady, I do love! And I choose to go with you."

He heard her sharp intake of breath, the jingle of armor, her body stiffening.

"The decision is yours, of course, Brother," she said in a low voice. She reached out to hold the mage's arm.

The wizard made a raspy sound that might have been a laugh. "Truly, you *are* blind!"

Michael reached out, and his hand closed over the wizard's arm—as thin, frail and fragile as the bones of a bird. Fever burned in the skin; the sensation of touching the mage was an unpleasant one.

"What is your name, sir?" Michael asked coldly.

The wizard did not immediately answer. Michael was startled to feel the arm he held flinch, as if the question was a painful one.

"I am . . . Raistlin."

The name meant nothing to Michael. He assumed, from the wizard's hesitation, that he'd given them a false one.

The mage led them forward into a darkness that grew impossibly darker, as he had warned. They walked as fast as they dared, not entirely trusting him, yet holding tightly to his guiding arm, listening to the rustle of his robes, the soft tapping sound of his staff.

In their nostrils was the smell of roses and of death.

Part VII

No harm befell them. They began to trust Raistlin and, as their trust increased, they started to move with incredible speed. Michael's feet barely skimmed the ground. A chill wind blasted in his face, stung his blind eyes. Branches scratched his cheek, tore his hair. Thorns and brambles caught at his robes. He pictured vividly what it would be like to smash headlong, at this speed, into tree or rock, or hurtle into some boulder-strewn chasm. He grasped harder the mage's frail-boned body.

Michael had no idea how long they traveled through the darkness. It might have been the span of a heartbeat or it might have been eons. He wondered how much longer he could keep going, for though it didn't seem that he exerted himself, his body was growing more and more fatigued. He was forced to lean heavily on the mage's shoulder, wondered that such a frail body could support his own. His limbs were stones; he could barely move them. His feet stumbled. He tripped, lost his grip on Raistlin, and fell.

Sobbing for breath, Michael started to try to regain his footing. He lifted his head and stared.

Before him stood a building, a structure of beauty and simplicity and elegance. Columns of black, white, and red marble supported a domed roof whose shining exterior was a mirror for the night sky. Reflected in it, the constellations wheeled about its center. The two dragons, Paladine and the

Queen of Darkness, each kept careful watch upon the other; in the middle, Gilean, the book of life, turned; around them wheeled the rest of the gods—good, neutral, evil.

A bridge of shining starlight burst, gleaming, from beneath the dome. The bridge spanned up and over the temple, extended to the night sky. An open door appeared in the starlit blackness. Beyond it, strange suns burned fiery red and yellow against deep blackness. Strange planets circled around them.

The beauty of the vision made Michael weep, and only when he felt the tears cold on his cheek did it occur to him that he could see again, that his sight was restored.

When he realized he could see, he noticed a dark shape mar the radiance of the temple.

A mage in black robes, tall and powerfully built, was untying the hands and feet of another man, lying in a horse-drawn cart. They stood in deep shadow. The black-robed mage could barely be seen, a shape of darkness against night, but the light of the temple fell on the face of the man in the cart. The young face was pale, drawn with pain and suffering. Sweat glistened on the pallid skin.

Michael could see Raistlin now as well, and the healer was considerably astonished to note how young the wizard appeared. Young and weak and ill. The thin face was blanched; feverish spots burned in the cheeks. His breathing was shallow and raspy. He leaned on a wooden staff, the top of which was adorned by a dragon's claw clutching a faceted crystal. Soft, pale light shone from the crystal, glittered in the mage's cold brown eyes.

Odd, thought Michael. I could have sworn they were the shape of hourglasses.

"Nicholas!" cried Nikol.

She would have run to him, but Raistlin grasped her tightly by the wrist and held her fast.

Nikol had been her brother's partner and equal in all his sports and training. She was as tall as Raistlin and was far stronger physically. Michael expected her to break the wizard's weak hold easily, and the cleric steeled himself to try to stop her impetuous rush to what undoubtedly would be her death.

Already, the other wizard, the one called Akar, had paused in his work and was peering about in alarm.

"What was that? Who is there?" he called in a deep, harsh bellow.

The thin, frail hand of Raistlin remained closed over the woman's wrist. Nikol gasped in pain. She seemed to shrink in his grasp.

"Make no sound!" he breathed. 'If he knows we are here, all is lost!"

Raistlin dragged the young woman back into the shadows of the blacked, burned trees. Michael accompanied them reluctantly, unable to wrench his rapt gaze from the radiant splendor of the shining temple and the wonderful bridge that soon would take him away from pain and suffering, despair and fear.

"You're hurting me," Nikol whispered, trying ineffectually to pull away. "Let me go!"

"You would be hurt far worse than this if I did," said Raistlin grimly. "Akar is powerful and will not hesitate to destroy you if you interfere in his plans.

Nikol cast a stricken glance at her brother. Akar, apparently deciding he'd been hearing things, had returned to his work. He took rough hold of the young man, pulled him from the cart, and dumped the knight on the ground. Nicholas cried out in agony.

"Soon your torment will be ended, Sir Knight," said Akar, rubbing his hands on his robes to cleanse them of blood.

Akar removed an object from his belt, held it up to the light. Steel glinted, bright and sharp. He inspected the dagger and thrust it back into his belt with a grunt of satisfaction. He bent down, started to lift the knight by the ankles, intending to once again haul him over the ground.

Nicholas struck out; his feet knocked the wizard backward. Caught off guard, astonished that his feeble victim should have fight left in him. Akar stumbled, off balance. He tripped on the hem of his robe and fell heavily.

Nicholas began, pitifully, to try to crawl away, to lose himself in the hideous darkness from which he had come.

"I'm going to him. You can't stop me." Nikol, her right hand still held fast in Raistlin's grasp, reached for her sword with her left.

Sparks jumped from the hilt. She snatched her hand back, wringing it in pain. Again she tried; again the sparks. She glared at the mage.

"You foul wizards are in league! I should have known! I never should have trusted—"

"Silence!" ordered Raistlin.

His gaze was intent on Akar. His entire being seemed concentrated on his counterpart. He had even ceased, for the moment, to cough. A faint tinge of color burned in the thin cheeks. He didn't seem to notice the woman struggling in his grasp, though his hold on her never loosened.

Nikol twisted around to face Michael.

"Why are you standing there? Go to Nicholas! Save him! This wicked man has no hold on you! He cannot fight us both!"

Michael started forward, reluctant to turn away from the shining bridge, yet his heart ached for the gallant young knight and for the sister who suffered with him. The voice of Raistlin stopped him, held the cleric as completely as the mage's hand held Nikol.

"Far more is at stake here than the life of one brave knight. The fate of the world hangs in the balance on Gilean's scales." Raistlin glanced at Michael. "What do you see, healer?"

"I see . . . a sight more beautiful than anything I've ever seen in my life. A temple stands before me, its columns of black and white and red marble. Its dome is the heavens, its roof the constellations. A bridge of starlight extends from this world to worlds beyond. People walk across that bridge—men, women, human, elven. They look back at this world with regret, their faces sad. But Paladine is with them, and he reassures them, and they turn to the door with hope."

"What have you done?" Nikol demanded of Raistlin. "You've bewitched him!"

Michael himself took a step forward, as if he would follow. An outraged cry jolted him back to this world. Akar had regained his feet. He glared at the knight in anger.

"Truly, as I said, a tough breed. Come, Sir Knight, I am losing patience. Time grows too short for more games."

Akar kicked Nicholas in the face. The knight fell back without a sound and lay still and unmoving. Akar gasped Nicholas, this time by the shoulders, and began hauling the limp body across the ground.

"He's taking him to the temple! What does he plan to do?" Michael asked Raistlin, who watched all with an expression grim and stern.

"He plans to murder him!" Nikol cried, trying again to free herself.

"My lady, please—" Michael began gently.

"Leave me be!" Nikol's eyes flared. "You're ensorcelled. The wizard's cast some sort of spell on you! Bridge of starlight! Radiant temple! It's a broken ruins, probably an altar of evil, consecrated to the Dark Queen!"

Michael stared at her. "Can't you see? . . ."

"No, she cannot," said Raistlin. "She sees a ruined citadel, nothing more. You alone, cleric, see the truth. You alone can stop Her Dark Majesty in her efforts to return to this world."

Michael didn't believe the wizard. How could Nikol not see what was so obvious and beautiful to him? And yet Nikol was staring at him angrily, fearfully, as if he were indeed a person acting under a spell.

"What must I do?" he asked in a low voice.

"The lady is right. Akar intends to murder the knight, but the mage must commit the crime within the precinct of the ruins or, as you see it, on the bridge of starlight. If the blood of the good and virtuous is spilled on the sacred bridge, the dark clerics, long held prisoner in the Abyss, will be free to return to Krynn."

"Will you help me?" Michael demanded.

"Don't trust him!" Nikol cried, twisting in the mage's grasp. 'His robes are cut from the same black cloth!"

"I brought you here," said Raistlin softly. "And without my help, you will not succeed. Your brother will die, and all of Krynn will fall into the hand of the Dark Queen."

"What must we do?" Michael asked.

"When Akar drops the dagger, pick it up swiftly and do not allow him to retake it. He has foolishly bound the knight's life in the weapon."

"I will seize it," said Nikol.

"No!"

Perhaps it was a trick of the light shining from the temple, but the wizard's brown eyes, staring at Michael, gleamed suddenly golden, as if that were their true color, the other, only a disguise.

"The cleric alone must take the dagger, else the spell cannot be broken."

"What do I do then?" Michael's gaze shifted back to the black-robed wizard, laboriously dragging the body of the dying knight across the grass.

"I do not know," said Raistlin. "I cannot hear the voice of the gods. You can. You must listen to what they say.

"And you, my lady"—the wizard released Nikol's hand—"must listen to your heart."

Nikol sprang away from Raistlin, drawing her sword in the same motion. She held it, blade toward the wizard, as she began backing up. "I don't need either of you. I don't need your gods or your magic. I will save my brother."

She ran off, sword flashing in the temple light, a light that, to her, was darkness.

Michael took a step after her, fear for her and for himself and for them all constricting his heart. Then he paused, turned to look at the wizard.

Raistlin stood leaning on his staff, regarding the cleric intently.

"I don't trust you," said Michael.

"Is it me you do not trust?" asked the wizard, his thin lips twisted in a smile. "Or yourself?"

Michael turned without responding, ran after Nikol. There came to him the words, "Remember, when the dagger falls, pick it up."

Part VIII

Sweating and straining, stumbling over the hem of his black robes, Akar dragged the unconscious knight across rough and uneven ground. The mage, though strong, was more accustomed to spending his time studying his spells. Akar was forced to pause a moment in his exertions, rest aching muscles. He glanced over his shoulder to judge the distance to his destination.

He could see, by Nuitari's dark light, a ruined citadel, its stone walls crumbling into dust. A bridge extended outward from the broken floor, a bridge that glimmered with a ghostly, wraithlike glow. On the far side of the bridge, shadowy figures reached out eager hands to him. Hollow voices shouted for him to free them, release the legions of darkness.

"A few moments more, Knight, and you will be free of this life and I will be free of you, for which we both will be grateful," Akar grunted, bending once again to his task.

Nicholas had regained consciousness, pushed back the shadows that would have brought him blessed relief from the agony he suffered. But worse than the pain of his wounds was the bitter knowledge that he would be, however innocently, responsible for the resurgence of evil in the world. He kept his gaze focused on the face of his enemy.

"Why do you stare at me so?" Akar demanded, somewhat disconcerted by that burning-eyed gaze that never left him. "If you are afraid you will not recognize me when our souls meet on the other side, save yourself the trouble. I will be more than happy to introduce myself."

It took all the knight's will to release each indrawn breath in a sigh and not a scream. Nicholas managed a smile, through lips caked with blood, parched and cracked from thirst. "I watch you as I would watch any opponent," he whispered hoarsely. "I wait for you to slip, to lower your guard, to make a mistake."

Akar laughed. "And then what will you do, Sir Knight? Drool on me? Or do you have the strength to do that much?"

"Paladine is with me," said Nicholas calmly. "He will give me the strength I need."

"He had better hurry, then," said Akar, grinning.

Perhaps it was the urging of the dark voices, but Akar found himself suddenly anxious to have this task done. He allowed himself no more rest, but manhandled the knight up the broken stairs of the citadel, listened to the cries of agony wrenched from the man with a certain satisfaction.

"I do not think Paladine hears your cries"—Akar sneered—"for here we are at the bridge. And here, Sir Knight, your life ends."

Dreadful moonlight shone upon the knight's face and bandaged, bloodied body. The unholy radiance washed out all color, turned red blood black, reduced waxen flesh to bone, glistened in the eyes like unshed tears. The light blinded Nicholas with its vast and terrible darkness. He cried out, clutched at nothing with groping hands.

"Know despair!" breathed Akar, drawing the dagger from his belt. "Know defeat. Know that your god has forsaken you and the world—!"

"Halt, foul servant of evil! Stay your hand or I swear by Paladine, I will cut it from your arm!"

Akar stopped, peered out into the darkness. He was not arrested in his movement by the living voice, though it was stern and commanding, as he was halted by frantic, whispered warnings coming from the shadow voices on the other side of the bridge. What threat did they see?

The wizard's gaze flickered over the figure of a knight in armor, sword in hand, who ran forward to challenge battle. Strong enchantment surrounded the Lost Citadel. Akar doubted if the knight could break through it. As he expected, the armored figure came up against a barrier that was like an explosion of stars, was thrown suddenly and heavily backward.

"Nikol!" cried the knight, straining to reach her, but he only managed to fall forward on his bloodied breast.

The woman hurled herself once again into the barrier, cried out in pain and frustration when she could not get through, and she began to hack at it with her sword. A cleric in nondescript blue robes appeared to be trying to remonstrate with her. Akar paid them scant attention. He saw, by Nuitari's dark light, something far more disquieting.

A mage clad in black robes stood leaning heavily on a staff that had at its top a crystal clasped in the claw of a dragon. Akar recognized the staff the Staff of Magius, a powerful magical artifact that was, the last he had heard, in safekeeping in the Tower of Wayreth. Akar recognized the staff, but not the mage who held it, and that disturbed him, for he knew all who wore the black robes.

"So you would try to usurp me, would you, Akar?" said the mage. Raistlin strode closer.

Who was this stranger wizard? His voice sounded familiar, yet Akar could swear he had never before seen him. The words of a killing spell were on Akar's lips. He shifted the dagger to his left hand; the fingers of his right slid into his pouch, gathering components. The voices from the darkness shouted cries and warnings, urged him to destroy the silent onlooker, but Akar dared not kill the stranger without first ascertaining who he was, what his purpose. To do so would be against all the laws of the Conclave. In a world in which magic is mistrusted and reviled, all magi are loyal to one another for the sake of the magic.

"You have the advantage of me, Brother Black Robe," shouted Akar, trying in vain to see more clearly beneath the shadows of the hood that covered the mage's face. "I do not recognize you, as you seem to recognize me. I would be glad to renew old acquaintance but, as you see, I am somewhat busy at the moment. Allow me to dispatch this knight and complete the spell and then I will be happy to discuss whatever grievance you think you have against me."

"You don't recognize me, Akar?" came the soft, whispering voice. "Are you sure?"

"How can I if you do not remove your hood and let me see your face?" demanded Akar impatiently. "Be swift. My time is short."

"My face is not known to you. But this, I believe, is."

The strange mage lifted an object in his hand and held it forth to be illuminated by Nuitari's dark light. Akar saw it, recognized it, felt the chill hand of fear close around his heart.

In a thin and wasted hand—a hand that seemed, to Akar, to gleam with a golden light, as if the skin had a strange gold cast to it—the mage held a silver pendant, a bloodstone.

Akar knew that pendant. Often he'd seen it hanging around the neck of his teacher, one of the greatest, most powerful wizards who had ever lived—and one of the most evil. Akar had heard the whispered rumors about that bloodstone, how the ancient wizard used it to suck life out of an apprentice, infuse his own powerful life into a new, younger body. Akar had never believed the rumors, never believed them until now.

"Fistandantilus!" he cried in recognition, and fumbled for the spell components with fingers gone numb while his brain fumbled for words that eluded his grasp.

A jagged bolt of lightning streaked through the night, struck Akar's left hand. The jolt knocked the dagger from the wizard's grasp, flung him backward, momentarily dazed.

Nicholas made a feeble effort to try to escape. Crawling on his hands and knees, he dragged his suffering, tortured body out of the ghastly light. He reached the edge of the stairs, tried to crawl down, slipped in a pool of his own blood, and plummeted down the steps. His death-shadowed eyes sought and found his sister. He stretched his hand out to her.

She dropped her sword, tried to clasp him, but the magical barrier kept them apart.

From behind them, out of the darkness, came the urgent command, "Pick up the dagger!"

Part IX

Michael heard Raistlin's command, remembered the mage's instructions.

When the dagger falls, pick it up!

"But how can I?" Michael cried. "How can I cross the barrier?"

The cleric had been attempting to keep Nikol from injuring herself, flinging herself again and again into the magical wall that kept her from her brother. Her hands were burned and blistered, yet, even now, she ignored the pain, trying her best to reach Nicholas, though every time she did so, a cascade of sparks burst around her.

Michael looked past her, looked past the tortured Nicholas, and saw the dagger that lay gleaming on the citadel steps, near the bridge. The black-robed wizard who had wielded it, who sought to bring into the world the dark clerics that shouted and gibbered from the other side, was recovering from his shock, was starting to look around and take stock of his situation. He was much closer to the dagger than Michael.

"You can enter, fool cleric!" Raistlin cried. The words were his last, however, tearing the breath from his body. The spell he had cast had weakened him. A violent fit of coughing brought him to his knees, near where Nikol stood.

Akar saw his enemy falter. His eyes glinted. He lurched to his feet.

Michael grasped his holy medallion, the medallion that was dark and lifeless, and plunged forward, gritting his teeth against what he knew must be a surge of magic that would most likely kill him.

To his amazement, nothing happened. The barrier parted. He ran up the stairs and plunged forward to snatch the dagger from beneath Akar's clutching fingertips. The mage's chill touch brushed the cleric's skin. Michael shrank from the horrible feel and the sight of the burning enmity in the black eyes, but he had the dagger.

Clasping the weapon in his hand, hardly knowing what he was doing, only wanting to escape the wizard, Michael stumbled back down the stairs.

At the bottom lay Nicholas. Michael looked down at the pain-twisted face, lost his fear in his compassion for the young man's suffering, his admiration for his courage. He knelt, lifted Nicholas's hand in his, held it fast. The dying knight managed a pain-filled, weary smile.

"Paladine, help me!" Nicholas said, gasping for breath.

A blue light bathed Michael, bathed the knight, washed the dreadful lines of pain from the gaunt face, as if he had been immersed in a lake of placid water. Time ceased its flow. Every person was arrested in motion, from Nikol, striving desperately to reach her brother, to the evil wizard, still trying to achieve his heinous goal. Michael, his heart filled with thankfulness, raised his eyes to the radiant blue goddess who stood at the entrance to the shining bridge.

"Mishakal," Michael prayed, "grant me the power to heal this man, Paladine's faithful servant."

The blue light dimmed. The goddess's face was sorrowful.

"I have no power here. The knight's life is bound by the magician's cursed wish to the dagger you hold. Only the dagger and the one who wields it, for good or evil, will bring this young man ease."

Michael stared at the dagger in his hand with horror and the sudden, sickening realization of what he was being asked to do.

"You can't mean this, Lady! What dread task is this you give me? I am a healer, not a killer!"

"I give you no task. I tell you how the knight's pain may be forever ended. The choice is up to you. You can see the bridge, can you not?"

"Yes," said Michael, looking with longing at the radiant, shining span and the peaceful, serene features of those ethereal figures who walked it. "I see it clearly."

"Then you may cross it. Throw aside the dagger. The concerns of this world are no longer yours."

Michael looked down at Nicholas, who lay still, eyes closed, in peaceful sleep . . . as long as the light of the goddess shone on him. When it was withdrawn, the terrible spell that bound him to his cruel suffering would be empowered once more. Nikol had ceased her bitter struggle and was on her knees, as near her brother as was possible for the magical barrier that barred her way.

"You can heal him, Michael," she was saying.

Near her, the strange, black-robed mage, Raistlin, who had fought one of his own kind, watched Michael with glittering eyes that reflected back the goddess's light, seemed to see and know all that was passing.

Who was Raistlin? What was his purpose? Michael didn't know, didn't understand. He didn't fathom any of this, knew himself suddenly to be nothing more than a frayed thread in a tangled skein.

Anger stirred in him again. What was his life or any of their lives worth to the gods, who live forever? How could he be expected to know what was right and what was wrong if he stumbled through life as blind as he'd been in that enchanted forest?

"While I am in this world, its concerns are mine," cried Michael. "When I took your vows, Lady, I accepted responsibility for the world and its people. Those will be mine, as long as I live. How can you ask me to break them?"

"But by killing this man, Michael, you do break my vows."

"So be it," said the cleric harshly. He gripped the dagger with hands that trembled. "Must . . . must I stab him?"

"No," said the goddess gently. "Draw blood only. That will break the spell."

"And my vows?" Michael looked up at her again, calmly, not pleading, but in deep sadness. "Will I lose your favor?"

The goddess did not reply.

Michael bowed his head. The blue light faded. Time began its ticking, like the beating of a heart. He heard, behind him, Akar's trampling footfalls, the rasping of his breath. He saw, before him, Nikol regarding him hopefully, expectantly. He felt the knight's hand, still clasped in his own, stiffen in agony, saw the young man's face twist.

"Strike now!" ordered Raistlin, so weak with coughing that he could not stand. "Or else all is lost!"

"Strike? What do you mean?" Nikol sprang to her feet. She saw the dagger in Michael's hand, suddenly understood his intent. "What are you doing? False cleric! You have betrayed me!" She turned to Raistlin. "Help me! You understand what I feel! Don't let him kill my brother!"

She wasn't watching. Michael must strike now, while she wasn't watching. Barely able to see for the tears in his eyes, Michael rested the dagger's tip on the knight's sweat-covered brow and pressed the point into the flesh. A thin trickle of blood oozed from the scratch.

Akar cursed bitterly.

Nicholas opened his eyes, turned his head. The light of the bridge shone on his face.

"Paladine is merciful," he said. "He gave me the strength."

At the sound of his voice, Nikol turned swiftly. "Nicholas!"

His eyes closed. His breath left him in a sigh. The lines of pain and suffering were smoothed away, as if by some immortal, soothing hand.

She saw Michael lay the dagger reverently on the knight's bare breast.

"Nicholas!"

Nikol's voice, ragged with grief, pierced Michael more deeply than the dagger had pierced her brother's flesh. The barrier was lifted. She fell upon the lifeless body. The hair that she had shorn for his sake mingled with the hair that was so like it that it was impossible to tell them apart.

Suddenly, she raised her head, stared at Michael and Akar.

"The cleric killed your brother!" Akar cried. "It was my spell that kept him alive. The cleric broke it!"

Michael could say nothing, couldn't explain, if she didn't understand.

She stared at him, eyes empty of all feeling.

Rough hands grabbed hold of Michael from behind, jerked him to his feet. A black-robed arm wrapped around his neck.

"Here, cleric!" Akar said. "Come up here to the temple. Away from that evil wizard, Fistandantilus. You don't know him. He's dangerous!"

Michael started to cry out a warning. Akar's hand covered the cleric's mouth.

"Yes, I've captured you. The good and virtuous!" Akar laughed beneath his breath. "I saw the goddess speak to you! You are in her favor. Your blood will do as well as the knight's!"

Michael tensed, prepared for a struggle.

"I wouldn't try it," breathed the wizard, "unless you want to see the young woman die in flames! There, that's better. Come quietly. And you, Fistandantilus!" Akar sneered, all the while dragging Michael backward, up the stairs. "You are too weak to stop me!"

Raistlin was on his knees, clutching the staff to keep from falling. Blood flecked his lips. He could not speak, yet he smiled and pointed.

Michael clasped close against the mage, heard Akar draw in a sucking breath.

The dagger. The dagger lay shining on the knight's lifeless breast.

Steel must draw the blood.

Akar halted, ground his teeth in frustration. Michael saw the bridge beneath his feet. And now that he was this near to the other side, he could hear cold voices calling for his death, see shadowed shaped writhing in eagerness to be free.

Michael had, at first, thought it was his fevered imagination, but now he was sure of it—the light of the bridge was growing gradually dimmer, the clamoring shouts of the dead growing louder, more frantic. The Night of Doom was ending.

"Girl!" Akar's voice was suddenly soft, sweet and thick and warm. "Girl, bring me the dagger."

Nikol shifted her gaze to him, blinked. Slowly, she lowered her eyes to the dagger that rested on her brother's body.

"The false cleric killed him, this knight that was dear to you. Bring me the dagger, girl, and you will have your revenge."

Nikol reached out with her hand, lifted the dagger in fingers that trembled. She stared at it, looked from it to the wizard, from the wizard to Michael. Her eyes were dark. Slowly, she rose to her feet and began to climb the stairs of the Lost Citadel, coming toward them, the dagger in her hand.

Was she ensorcelled? The wizard had spoken no words of magic, had cast no spell that Michael had heard.

"Come, girl, swiftly!" Akar hissed.

Nikol did as he bade. She walked forward steadily, her eyes as empty as her brother's. Something within her had died with him.

Akar's grip around Michael's throat tightened. "I know what you're thinking! But if you break free, cleric, it will be her blood I spill on the bridge. Make your choice. You or her. It matters little to me."

Nikol was level with them, the dagger held loosely in her limp, outstretched hand. Her left hand. Her sword hand, her right, was free.

The light of the bridge was fading fast. A pale glow in the far distant sky presaged morning, a gray morning, a dawning of unhappiness and fear for those left in a world where man had forsaken the gods.

Akar had seconds only. He made a grab.

Nikol's grasp tightened on the dagger. She stabbed. The blade tore through the wizard's palm, tore though bone and tendon and muscle, thrust out, blood-blackened, on the other side of the hand.

Akar howled in pain and rage. Michael broke free of the mage's weakening grasp, flung himself to the ground. The only help he could offer Nikol was to keep clear of her sword arm.

Nikol's blade, which had been her brother's before that, swept past Michael in a shining silver arc. The wizard screamed. The blade drove deep into his vitals.

Michael rolled over, was on his feet. Akar stood spitted on Nikol's sword, his hands grasping at it, his face distorted with fury and pain.

Nikol jerked the sword free. Blood burst from Akar's mouth. He pitched forward on his face and lay dead on the steps of the Lost Citadel.

Her face pale and set, as rigid as the stones, gray in the morning light, Nikol nudged Akar's body with the toe of her boot.

"I'm sorry if I frightened you," she said to Michael. "I had to play along with him. I feared he'd cast a spell on me before I could slay him."

"Then you do understand!" was all Michael could think to say.

"No," Nikol answered bitterly. "I don't understand any of it. All I know is that this Akar was the one responsible for my brother's death and, by the Oath and the Measure, that death is avenged. As for you"—her lifeless gaze turned to Michael—"you did what you could."

Nikol turned and walked back down the temple steps. Sickened by the terrible death he had just witnessed, shaken by his ordeal, the cleric tried to follow, but his legs gave way. Sweat chilled on his body. He leaned weakly against a crumbling pillar, his wistful gaze going back to shining bridge, that line of peace-filled, serene figures leaving this world of pain and sorrow and suffering.

The bridge was gone. The door amid the stars was closed.

Part X

The morning was deathly quiet.

Quiet.

Michael raised his head. The dread voices of the dark clerics were silenced. Their threat to take over the world, now that all the true clerics of the gods were gone, was ended.

All true clerics gone. Michael sighed. His hand went to the symbol of Mishakal that hung dark and cold about his neck. He had questioned when he should have believed. He had been angry, defiant, when he should have been humble, submissive. He had taken life when he should have acted to save it.

Michael drew a deep breath to dispel the mists that blurred his vision. One more task was left for him to perform, the only task for which he was seemingly worthy now—composing the body of the dead for its final rest. Then he could leave, leave Nikol alone with her bitter grief, remove himself and the knowledge of his failure from her sight. It was poor comfort, but all he could offer. He pushed himself away from the pillar, slowly descended the stairs.

Nikol knelt beside her brother's body, his lifeless hand clasped fast in her own. She did not glance up at Michael, did not acknowledge his presence. Her armor was splattered with the blood of the dead mage. Her skin was ashen. The resemblance between the twins was uncanny. It seemed to Michael that he looked on two corpses, not one. Perhaps he did. Daughter of a knight, Nikol would not long outlive her brother.

A shadow fell across the two, and a gasping cough broke the stillness. Michael had forgotten the black-robed mage who had led them here, was startled to find the man standing quite near him. The smell of rose petals and decay that clung to the soft black robes was unnerving, as was the fevered heat that emanated from the frail body.

"You got what you wanted?" Michael asked abruptly, bitterly.

"I did." Raistlin was calm.

Michael rounded on him. "Who are you, anyway? You gave us one name. Akar gave you another. Who are you? What was your purpose here?"

The mage did not immediately answer. He leaned on his staff, stared at Michael with the brown eyes that glittered gold in the chill light of a sad dawn.

"If I had met you a year ago and asked you the same questions, cleric, you would have answered glibly enough, I suppose. A month ago, a day ago—you knew who you were—or thought you did. And would you have been correct? Would your answer be the same today as it was yesterday? No." Raistlin shook his head. "No, I think not."

"Stop talking in riddles!" Michael said, fear making him angry, frustrated. "You know who you are, why you came. And we served your needs, whatever they were, since you were too weak at the end to stop Akar yourself. I think you own us an explanation!"

"I owe you nothing!" Raistlin snapped, a flush of color mounting in the pale cheeks. "It was I who served your needs, far more than you served mine. I could have dealt with Akar on my own. You were a convenience, that is all."

The mage lifted his right arm. The black sleeve fell away from the thin wrist. A flash of metal gleamed cold in the sunlight. A dagger, held on by a cunning leather thong, slid into Raistlin's hand when the mage flicked his wrist. The movement was so fast that Michael could scarcely follow it.

"If she had tried to murder you," the mage said, turning the dagger, making it flash in the light, "she would not have succeeded."

"You could have slain Akar."

"Bah! What good would that have done? He was never more than a tool for the Dark Queen, He was not needed, only the blood of the good and virtuous, spilled in anger."

"You would have killed Nikol!" Michael stared in disbelief.

"Before she killed you."

"But, then, the curse would have been fulfilled anyway. Her blood would have fallen on the bridge."

"Ah," said Raistlin, with a cunning smile, "but it would no longer have been the blood of a good and virtuous person. It would have been the blood of a murderer."

Michael stared at him, shocked. The calculating coldness of the mage appalled him.

"Go away," he said thickly.

"I intend to. I am needed in Istar," said Raistlin, briskly. "Events will move fast there in these last thirteen days before the Cataclysm, and my presence is essential."

"The Cataclysm? What is that??"

"In thirteen days' time, the gods in their wrath at the folly of men will hurl a fiery mountain down upon Ansalon. The land will be sundered, seas will rise, and mountains topple. Countless numbers will die. Countless more, who will live in the dark and terrible days to follow, will come to wish they had died."

Michael didn't want to believe, but there was no doubting the calm voice or the strange eyes, which seemed to have witnessed these terrifying events, though they had not yet come to pass. He recalled the words of Mishakal. *He will gather their souls to him, remove them from a world that soon will erupt in fire.*

Michael looked back down at the two motionless figures, who seemed to personify the wizard's prediction: one who was dead, one who could not bear the pain of living.

"Is there no hope?" Michael asked.

"You are the only one who can answer that, my friend," the mage responded dryly.

At first it seemed to Michael that there was no hope. Despair would cover the world in a black tide that must drown all in its poisonous waters.

But as he looked at the brother, the cleric saw the peace and serenity on the pallid features, the knowledge of a battle well fought, a victory won. The goddess had not forsaken Michael. The Dark Queen had been defeated in her ceaseless efforts to reenter the world.

Michael, Nikol, Nicholas—three silken threads, stitched together for a time. Raistlin, Akar—two more threads, crossing theirs from opposite directions. None of them could see beyond their own insignificant knots and tangles. But in the eyes of the gods, the individual threads formed—not a tangled skein—but a beautiful tapestry. If the gods chose to rend that fabric, it would no longer be as beautiful. But it might, when it was mended, be far stronger.

Gently, Michael removed her brother's lifeless hand from Nikol's grasp, laid the still hand across the still breast. A soft blue radiance surrounded them. Nicholas opened his eyes. He rose. He was once more clad in knightly armor, the symbol of the crown glittering on his breastplate. All marks of his suffering and pain were gone.

Nikol reached out to him, joy lighting her face. But Nicholas backed a step away from her.

"Nicholas?" Nikol faltered. "Why won't you come with me?"

"Let him go, my lady," Michael told her. "Paladine waits for him."

Nicholas smiled at her reassuringly, then he turned away and began walking toward the stairs, toward the Lost Citadel.

"Nicholas!" Nikol cried in anguish. "Where are you going?"

The knight did not reply, but kept walking.

Nikol ran after him. "Let me come with you!"

The knight paused on the steps of the ruined temple, look back at his sister sadly, pleadingly, as if begging her to understand.

The blue light grew stronger. The radiant figure of the goddess materialized, standing beside the knight.

"For now, you two must part. But take with you the knowledge that someday you once more will be together." Mishakal's gaze went to Michael. The goddess held out her hand to him. "You may come, Brother, if you choose."

The holy light that surrounded them shone from the medallion around Michael's neck. He clasped his hand around it thankfully. He recalled with aching heart the beauty and the wonders of the worlds beyond. The light of his medallion strengthened, shone on Nikol's face. He saw her standing alone in the darkness, bereft and forlorn, not understanding. There would be many, many more like her in the dread days to come.

"I will stay," said Michael.

Mishakal nodded wordlessly. The bridge flashed back into being, the door to the stars opened. The knight set foot upon the shining span, turned for one last look at his sister, one reassuring smile. Then he was gone. The bridge vanished. The blue light faded.

Next to Michael, the mage began to cough.

"Finally!" Raistlin muttered.

He wrapped his black robes closely about his thin body and clasped the magical staff. He spoke a word of magic.

The crystal's light flared, nearly blinding Michael. The cleric held his hand before his eyes to block out the painful glare.

"Wait!" he called. "You claim to know the future! What will happen to us! Tell us what you see!"

The mage's image was starting to fade. For a moment it wavered, and, as it did so, it altered, startlingly. The black robes changed to red, the hair whitened, the skin glistened gold, the eyes had pupils the shape of hourglasses.

"What do I see?" Raistlin repeated softly. "In a world of the faithless, you are the only one who is faithful. And, because of that, you will be reviled, ridiculed, persecuted." The golden eyes shifted to Nikol. "But I see one who loves you, who will risk all to defend you."

"You see this happening to us?" Nikol faltered.

Raistlin's mouth twisted in a bitter smile. "To myself."

He was gone. Nikol and Michael stood in the chill dawn of a gray morning.

They stood alone, together.

Dragons of Ancient History

A flashback by Douglas Niles

I think it was 1983, which is more years ago than I can usually remember. I was a hotshot young game designer at TSR, Inc, and Harold Johnson, the manager of our department, had asked me for a proposal on a really cool project. For the first time, TSR was considering a series of modules for Dungeons & Dragons (the AD&D game, technically) that would actually be about *dragons!* It was an exciting concept, one that any game designer would love to tackle.

Of course, Harold made the same challenge to all the designers on the staff: come up with a knock-'em-dead slam-dunk idea for a series of modules featuring the biggest, baddest monsters in the fantasy pantheon. At the time, the TSR design staff included a seasoned veteran of the games industry, Zeb Cook; the talented and charismatic Mark Acres; the insanely inspired Jeff Grubb; the esteemed and venerable Merle Rasmussen; myself; and a new kid who had just brought his family out to Lake Geneva, Wisconsin, from Utah—a guy named Tracy "Something."

Well, I poured my heart and soul into that proposal for the better part of an afternoon and came up with a nifty little module trilogy that involved red, green, and—really, who cares? As each of us submitted our few pages of proposal, we noticed that the new guy, Tracy, was really taking his time. He finally submitted a concept that was a little bit fatter, a little more detailed, and a little more ambitious than any of the others. When the luminaries of TSR management reviewed these ideas, they looked over a collection of concepts for RPG adventures involving big monsters and big treasures. Each offered villains minor and major, opportunities for bold heroes to vanquish great challenges.

But one of them really stood out. Whereas most of us had proposed a series of three adventure modules, or perhaps four or five, that new guy, "Tracy Something" went the extra mile. His proposal not only called for the unprecedented commitment of a *twelve* module series, but it included one adventure for each of the colors of dragons of the D&D universe! And he had actually invented a whole new world as a setting for this adventure, a world in which the dragons were not just inhabitants, but formed a crucial component of the history and future. In fact, this world *had* a history that went far beyond the realms of any previous gaming world—and indeed beyond most of the popular milieu in fantasy fiction.

Furthermore, Tracy went on to propose books—actual fiction novels!—to go along with these RPG adventures. He got artists involved—talented guys like Larry Elmore, Keith Parkinson, and Jeff Easley, who all sketched up concept material, characters, and settings. Larry even designed some new-fangled lance-and-saddle contraption that would let a knight wield a large lance while riding dragonback through the skies of this richly detailed fantasy world. The series had, from the beginning, a very cool name:

Dragonlance.

To tell the truth, I was a little embarrassed about my own concept after I saw what Tracy proposed. The contest was no contest, really. His idea was so good, so rich, so thoroughly realized that it was clear to all of us where the future of this dragon series was going. By this time, of course, he was no longer the new guy, but one of the most talented and productive designers on a very talented and productive staff. Furthermore, he had a gift for bringing other people on board, and the Dragonlance setting began to grow even beyond the bounds of his first ambitious concept.

The company was just beginning to get into book publishing in the early '80s, mostly with a series of "pick-a-path" stories for young readers. A talented editor and writer named Margaret Weis had recently joined us, and she saw the potential for a series of novels. Perhaps even then she realized that those novels would become the true centerpiece of Krynn's story.

There were pitfalls along the way—the economy tanked, good friends were laid off, and some company managers and executives were reluctant to commit to something so bold, so different. Several times the project came within a hair's breadth of cancellation. But with the game designs really coming together, and the Weis/Hickman writing team hitting its stride, the modules began create a fantasy epic, and the first-ever game related novels made a beeline for the *New York Times* bestseller list.

And the rest is history.

Douglas Niles is completing the first volume of his new DRAGONLANCE trilogy. The paperback edition of his alternative-fiction about World War II, *Fox at the Front* (co-written with Michael Dobson) has just been issued (a Forge Book from Tom Doherty Associates, LLC).

True Knight

Margaret Weis and Tracy Hickman

Originally published in *Tales II, Volume Two: The Cataclysm*

Part I

Nikol and Brother Michael left the Lost Citadel and traveled the forest, now bereft of its enchantment, with the dazed and bewildered expressions of those who have undergone some awful, wondrous experience and who do not, on reflection, believe in it.

They had evidence the events had occurred—the blood of Nikol's twin brother and the blood of the evil wizard who had been responsible for Nicholas's death stained Nikol's hands. The holy medallion of Mishakal, which once had glowed with the blue light of the goddess's favor, hung dark around Brother Michael's neck. All the true clerics had departed, gathered by the gods to serve on other planes. The dark clerics, worshipers of the Queen of the Abyss, had not succeeded in their scheme to fill the void left by the departure of the other gods' faithful. The words of the strange mage, who called himself Raistlin, echoed in their hearts.

In thirteen days' time, the gods in their wrath at the folly of men will hurl a fiery mountain down upon Ansalon. The land will be sundered, seas will rise, and mountains topple.

Countless numbers will die. Countless more, who will live in the dark and terrible days to follow, will come to wish they had died.

Michael and Nikol reached the edge of the forest, came to the clearing where Akar had received his prize—the dying knight, Nicholas—from the goblins who had captured him. The knight's blood still stained the crushed grass. Both paused, without a word spoken. Neither had said a word to each other, following their departure from the Lost Citadel.

Thirteen days. Thirteen days until the destruction of the world.

"Where do you want to go, my lady?" Michael asked.

Nikol glanced around the clearing, slowly darkening with the coming of night. The dazzled bewilderment was fading, a numbness and lethargy that was not so much a weariness of body as it was a weariness of spirit that made her feet seem too heavy to lift, her heart too heavy to bear.

She had only one thought. "Home," she said.

Michael looked grave, opened his mouth, probably to protest. Nikol knew what he was going to say, stopped the words on his mouth with a glance. Her manor castle, which had been in her family for generations and had housed the three of them in far happier days, had probably been attacked and sacked and looted by goblins. She would return to find the castle charred and gutted, a ghastly skeleton. She didn't care. The castle was her home.

"It's where I want to die," she said to Michael.

She started walking.

****

Brother Michael was astonished to discover the castle had been left in relatively good repair, perhaps because the goblins had decided to make it their base while they despoiled the countryside. Noting from a distance that the castle was still standing and was not a burned-out hulk, Michael was more than half convinced that the goblins were still around. A day's watching persuaded him that the goblins had moved on, perhaps in search of richer pickings. The castle was empty.

Inside, he and Nikol found a horrible mess; both gagged from the stench, fled back outside to fresher air. Filth and remnants of dread feasting choked the halls. The heavy oaken furniture had been axed, used for firewood. Curtains had been torn down. The ceremonial armor was gone, probably being worn now by some goblin king. Yule decorations and the tapestries had been desecrated, burned. Vermin roamed the halls now extremely loathe to leave.

The villagers and manor tenants all had fled and had not come back, either out of fear of the goblins or because they had nothing to which to come back. Not a house remained standing. Stock had been slaughtered, granaries raided and burned, wells poisoned. At least most had escaped with their lives, if little else.

Michael gazed at the destruction and said firmly, "My lady, Sir Thomas's manor is a fortnight's journey. Let me take you there. We can travel by night. . . ."

Nikol didn't hear him, walked away form him in mid-speech. Stripping off her armor, she stacked it neatly in a corner of a blacked wall. Beneath the armor she wore the cast-off clothes of her brother that she had worn when the two of them practiced their sword work together. Binding a strip of torn linen, found hanging from a tree limb, around her nose and mouth, she entered the castle and began the thankless task of cleaning.

She was vaguely aware, after a time, that Michael was at her side, attempting, when he could, to take the more onerous tasks upon himself. She straightened from her work, brushed a lock of her ragged-cut hair from her face, and stared at him. "You don't have to stay here. I can manage. Sir Thomas would be glad to have you."

Michael regarded her with an air of exasperation and concern. "Nikol, don't you understand by now? I could no more leave you than I could fly off into the sky. I want to stay. I love you."

He might have been speaking the Elvish tongue, for all she understood him. His words made no sense to her. She was too numb, couldn't feel them.

"I'm so tired," she said. "I can't sleep. It's all hopeless, isn't it? But, at least we'll have a place to die."

He reached for her, tried to take her in his arms. His face was anxious, his expression worried.

"There is always hope. . . ."

Nikol turned away from him, forgot about him, began again to work.

****

They made preparations in order to survive the coming Day of Destruction. That is, Michael made preparations. Nikol, once the castle was clean, sat, talking and laughing in the room where she and her brother used to sit during the long evening hours. She sat, doing nothing, staring at the empty chair across from hers. She was biddable, tractable. If Michael found some slight task for her to do, she did it without comment, without complaint, but then she would return to her chair. She ate and drank only if Michael put the food into her hand.

He was gentle with her at first. Patiently, he tried to coax her back to the life she was fast leaving. When this failed, his fear for her grew. He argued, shouted at her. At one point, he even shook her. Nikol paid no attention to him. When it seemed she thought of him at all, he was a stranger to her. At length, he grew too busy to take time to do more than see to it that she ate something.

Michael was forced to spend his days roaming the countryside, foraging for whatever the goblins had left behind, which wasn't much. He found a stream that had not been fouled and, though he had never been taught the art of fishing, managed to catch enough to serve their needs. He knew nothing about setting traps, nor could he bring himself to snare small animals. He had not eaten animal flesh since he had come to serve the goddess of healing. He was knowledgeable about berries and herbs, wild vegetables and fruits, and these kept them alive. Although the strange, hot wind that blew incessantly day and night was rapidly drying up the land, he set in a store of food that could feed them for a long time, if they ate sparingly.

And he firmly put aside the chilling thought that, unless something happened to shake Nikol out of her dark melancholia, he would have only himself to worry about.

He prayed to Mishakal to help Nikol, to heal the wound that had not touched the flesh but had torn apart the woman's soul. He prayed to Paladine as well, asking the god of the Solamnic Knights to look with favor upon the daughter who had fought evil as valiantly as any son.

And it was, or so it seemed at first, Paladine who answered.

They had no visitors; the countryside around them was deserted. Michael watched for travelers closely, for he desperately wanted to send a message to Sir Thomas, to warn him of the coming destruction and to ask for whatever aide the knight could give them. No one came. The thirteen days dwindled to nine, and Michael had given up looking for help. At twilight, the stillness was broken by the sound of hooves, clattering on the paved courtyard.

"Hail the castle!" shouted a strong, deep voice, speaking Solamnic.

The sound roused Nikol from her dread lethargy. She glanced up with unusual interest. "A guest," she said.

Michael went hurriedly to look out the window. "A knight," he reported. "A Knight of the Rose, by his armor."

"We must make him welcome," said Nikol.

The Measure dictated the treatment of a guest, who was said to be a "jewel upon the pillow of hospitality." The honor of the knighthood bound Nikol to offer shelter, food, whatever comfort her home could provide to the stranger.

She stirred, rose from her chair. Glancing down at her shabby men's clothes, she seemed perplexed.

"I'm not dressed to receive visitors. My father was very

strict about that. We always put on our finest clothes to honor the guest. My father wore his ceremonial sword. . . ."

Looking around, as if she thought a dress might materialize from out of the air, she caught sight of her brother's sword, standing in its place upon the weapons' rack. She buckled the sword about her waist, and went to make the guest welcome—her first voluntary action in days.

Michael followed her, silently thanking this knight, whoever he was, whatever his reason for being here. The man obviously had traveled far; his black horse was coated with dust and sweat.

Nikol entered the courtyard. If the strange knight was shocked at her shabby appearance, he politely gave no indication. In this day and age, perhaps he was used to the sight of impoverished members of the knighthood. He drew his sword, held it to his helm, blade upward in gesture of salute and peace.

"My lord," he said. "I regret that I have no squire to ride forward and give notice of my coming. Forgive my intrusion at this unseemly time of night."

"Welcome to Whitsund Manor, Sir Knight. I am not lord of the manor, but its lady. I am Nikol, daughter to Sir David Whitsund. Dismount your noble steed and give yourself rest and ease this night. I regret I have no groom to lead your horse to stable, but that task I will take upon myself and count it an honor."

The knight, who traveled in full armor, the breastplate decorated with the rose that marked his high standing in the knighthood, removed his helm. Shocked, Michael moved a step nearer to Nikol.

"Forgive me, my lady," the knight was saying. "I can only plead dusk's shadows as an excuse for having mistaken noble lady for noble lord."

Nikol accepted the compliment with a smile and a nod, turned her attention to the man's fine horse.

Michael could not take his eyes from the knight's face. The strong and darkly handsome visage was gaunt and haggard. He looked exhausted to the point of falling. But it was the knight's eyes that arrested Michael, caused the words of thanksgiving that had been on the cleric's lips to die. The black eyes burned with a strange and terrible fire that seemed to be consuming his flesh. So fey was the knight that Michael feared they were dealing with a madman. Nikol had not noticed. Her attention was for the fine horse, which was accepting her overtures at friendship with gracious forbearance.

"My lady," Michael began, licking dry lips, not certain how to proceed. "I think perhaps . . ."

"Now it is I who ask forgiveness," Nikol said, glancing up. "I present our family chaplain, Brother Michael."

The knight bowed.

"I am honored to meet you, Brother Michael. My name is Lord Soth, of Dargaard Keep. Lady Nikol, I thank you for your kind offer of hospitality, but it is an offer that I regretfully must refuse. Urgent need carries me back on the road this night. I will not even dismount, by your leave. I only stopped to ask for water for myself and my horse."

The knight's words were cool and courteous, but they were tinged with the crackling of the flames that burned in the eyes. Nikol gazed up at him in admiration. Perhaps night's shadows blinded her as well.

"Gladly, Lord Soth. I will fetch the water myself."

The daughter of a knight, Nikol recognized the knight's need for haste and did not waste time in further niceties. She left immediately to find water. Michael went to find a bucket and some straw for the horse. He returned to find the knight drinking slowly and sparingly from the iron dipper. Michael placed the bucket before the horse, who drank more deeply than its master.

"I would not have disturbed you at all, my lady," said the night, "but would have stopped at stream or pond. I could find no pure water in these parts, however. Goblins attacked you, I take it." He glanced about the ruined castle with the air of an experienced warrior.

"Yes," said Nikol softly. She stroked the horse's neck. "They fell upon us about a fortnight ago. My brother died, defending the castle and our people."

"He was not the only one who defended it, seemingly," said Lord Soth, the burning eyes fixed upon the sword Nikol wore easily and confidently at her side.

Nikol flushed. "It is my home," she said simply.

"Your home. And a blessed one, despite all," said the knight. The flames in the black eyes blazed higher. The countenance grew grim, scarred by bitterness and regret. He stirred restlessly in the saddle, as if in pain.

"I must be on my way." He handed the dipper back to Nikol.

"I would not hinder you on whatever urgent business takes you out into the night," said Nikol, "but I repeat again, you are welcome in my home, Lord Soth."

"I thank you, Lady Nikol, but I may not rest until my task is complete. I ride to Istar and I must be there in four days' time."

"Istar!" cried Michael, shaken. "But you should not go there! In four days' time—" He paused, uncertain of what he was going to say, not sure how he knew what he knew or how he would explain it.

The knight's burning eyes seared Michael. "You know, then, Brother. You know what terrible fate hangs over this world. Then I leave you with this hope: With the help of the gods, I will prevent it, though it cost me my life."

The knight bowed again to Nikol. Replacing his helm, he turned his horse's head out into the night and soon was lost to their sight.

"Though it cost him his life," said Nikol softly, gazing after him with shining eyes. "He is a true hero. He rides forth to save the world, though it cost him his life. And what I do? What have I done?"

She turned, stared at the castle, perhaps truly seeing it for the first time since they had returned.

"The Measure. The Oath. 'My honor is my life.' I came

near forgetting that, came near failing thee memory of my father, my brother. This knight has reminded me of my duty. Perhaps Paladine sent him for that very reason. I will always honor his name: Lord Soth of Dargaard Keep."

Michael would have added his own fervent blessing on the knight, who had brought Nikol back to life, but a shadow drifted across the cleric's heart, like smoke from a distant fire. The effect was chilling. He could not speak.

Part II

Nikol's melancholia vanished, borne away by the Knight of the Rose. She began to believe, once again, in a future, to find hope in it, and threw herself into preparing for it with her usual energy. It was a future of promise she believed in, a future unscarred by the terrible calamity foreordained by the gods.

Michael, whose fears were growing, not receding, sought to gently temper this newfound hope.

"I have had dark dreams of late, Nikol. I see the Kingpriest confronting the gods. He does not approach them in humility, remembering that he is man and mortal. He makes demands of them. He has come to think of himself as equal to the gods. I feel their wrath. This strange wind . . ."

Nikol interrupted him, placed her hand upon his with a patronizing air. "Brother, be at peace. A Knight of Solamnia rides to Istar to stop this. *He* goes with Paladine's blessing."

He knew she did not mean to hurt him by adding that unconscious emphasis on the word. Perhaps she wasn't even equating the two of them—the knight who rode with Paladine's blessing, the cleric who had given up the favor of his goddess by choosing to stay in this world—but the pain burned. He said nothing, however.

She might think he was jealous of the knight, but Michael wasn't, not really. Nikol was not in love with Lord Soth. She saw in him what she had been raised to see—the epitome of honor, godliness, nobility. The Oath and the Measure placed the knights above the faults and foibles of other, lesser men.

Michael left the castle for a few hours, until his hurt subsided. Catching fish, wading up to his shins in the stream, helped him rationalize, understand. Her faith was touching, childlike. Who was he to destroy it?

"Perhaps, if more had believed as she does, we would not be facing this dreadful fate," he said to the strange wind and the cloudless, lead-colored sky.

The night before the Cataclysm, Michael woke from dreams of fire and blood to find himself prostrate upon the floor, shivering and sweating. The gods' anger crackled in the air, rumbled in the empty sky. A timid knock at his door roused him.

"Are you all right, Brother?" called Nikol.

Michael flung open the door, startled her. She stared at him, backed up a step. He knew he must look wild, disheveled—thin from lack of food, bleary-eyed from sleepless nights. He caught hold of her.

"We must go somewhere, somewhere safe."

"It's a storm, that's all," said Nikol, uneasy, nervous. "Michael, you're hurting me."

He did not loosen his hold. "It is coming. The Day of Wrath."

"Lord Soth—" she began.

"He couldn't stop it, Nikol!" Michael had to shout to be heard over the low rumble of thunder that shook the manor walls. "I don't know why or how or what happened, but he failed! Men do fail, you know! Even Knights of Solamnia. They're human, damn it, like the rest of us."

"I have faith in him!" Nikol cried angrily.

"He is a man. We must have faith in the gods." Saying this, reminding himself of it, Michael was calm. "This house, these walls are strong. Blessed, the knight said. Yes, here, inside these walls, we will be safe.

"No! It cannot be! He *will* stop it."

She broke free of his grasp, ran inside the small family

chapel. Michael followed her, to try to reason with her. Looking around, he realized at once that this room—built in the castle's interior, without windows—was the safest place. Nikol was kneeling before the altar.

"Paladine! Be with Lord Soth! Accept his sacrifice, as you once accepted Huma's!"

The strange wind, hot and dry, blew harder and harder, shrieked about the castle walls with inhuman voices. Lightning slashed, split trees. Thunder shook the ground, like the footsteps of an angry giant.

All that morning the storm raged, growing more and more intense. The sun vanished. Day became darker than night. Violent winds blew, lifted huge trees from the ground, hurled them about like newly planted saplings. Those trees that held fast against the wind fell victim to the savage lightning. Michael, daring to leave the chapel, ventured back into his room, stared out the window.

Fires lit the darkness, trees consumed by flames. Grass fires scorched the land. Nikol, shivering, came to stand by his side. "The gods have forsaken us," she whispered.

"No," said Michael, taking her in his arms. "It is we who have forsaken them."

They returned to the chapel. The wind blew harder. The voices in it were horrible, conjuring up visions of dragons, screaming over their kill. It buffeted the castle walls, trying to beat them down. The earth began to shudder, as if the very ground was appalled at the horrors it was witnessing. The first quakes hit. The castle rocked and shivered. The two crouched and shivered before the altar, unable to move, unable to speak or even pray. Beyond the chapel, they could hear crashes, shattering cracks.

Michael knew they were doomed. The walls must collapse, the ceiling cave in. He held fast to Nikol's hands and began to describe, in a feverish voice, the beautiful bridge of starlight he'd seen before, the wondrous worlds where they soon would find peace and freedom from this terror.

Then it was over.

The tremors ceased. The storm abated, clouds blown away as if by a mournful sigh. All was quiet. They were not dead.

"We're safe, beloved!" Michael cried, not thinking of what he was saying. He clasped Nikol in his arms.

She was stiff, rigid in his grasp. Then, suddenly, she threw her arms around him, held him fast. They sank to the floor, before the altar of Paladine. Huddled in each other's gasp, they were grateful for the comfort of being together.

"'The land will be sundered, seas will rise, and mountains topple. Countless numbers will die. Countless more, who will live in the dark and terrible days to follow, will come to wish they had died.' That's what he said, the black-robed wizard. Why? Why did this happen, Michael?" Nikol cried brokenly. "Certainly, some deserved the gods' wrath—that horrible, fat cleric who came here before Nicholas died—but this terror has surely destroyed the innocent as well as the guilty. How can the gods, if they are good, do this?"

"I don't know," Michael said helplessly. "I wish I had the answer, but I don't."

"At least I'm not alone," Nikol continued softly. "You're here. I'm glad you're here, Michael. It's selfish of me, I know, but if you had left with the goddess, I think I would be dead by now."

He didn't answer. He couldn't. The words wouldn't come past the ache of love and longing.

"Hold me closer," she said, burrowing into his arms.

He did as she commanded, pressed her head against his breast, bent, and kissed the shining hair. To his amazement, Nikol returned his kiss. Her lips met his hungrily.

"Nikol," he said, when he could breathe. "I've no right to ask this. You're the daughter of a knight. Your family is noble. My father was a shopkeeper in Xak Tsaroth, my mother a nomad, who roamed the plains. I have nothing to give. . . ."

"I will marry you, Michael," she said.

"Nikol, think about what I said—"

"Michael," she whispered, laying her hand upon his lips. "You think about it. Does any of that matter now?"

Perhaps Paladine heard their vows of marriage, spoken silently in their hearts. Perhaps the god turned aside his wrath one moment to bless their union, for the manor walls continued to stand strong and sheltering above them.

When the morning came, a heavy sadness, mingled with their joy, oppressed them both. Nikol stood before the altar of Paladine, which now had a crack in it, traced the crack with her finger. "We will find out why, won't we, Michael," she said firmly. "We will find out why this happened. We will search until we discover the answer. Then you and I will make it right."

In a world of the faithless, you are the only one who is faithful. And, because of that, you will be reviled, ridiculed, persecuted. But I see one who loves you, who will risk all to defend you.

The words of the black-robed wizard, Raistlin.

"Yes," Michael answered, as he would have answered yes to anything she asked of him at that moment. "We will search for the answer."

Part III

A cold and bitter wind closed in on them soon after the Cataclysm. Their small supply of food dwindled rapidly. The stream in which Michael fished vanished during the quakes, swallowed by the ground. A killing frost shriveled any plants that had survived the fires.

Then, one day, a small band of humans, up from the south, had offered to trade game for shelter. The manor, they said, looking at it in awe, was one of the few buildings in these parts still standing. Michael agreed, was forced to eat animal flesh to stay alive. He hoped, all things considered, the goddess would forgive him.

But, once they were rested and had buried their dead, the refugees left, looking for new hunting grounds. Michael had figured, only this morning, that they had dried meat and berries to last them another few days. South, at least, there apparently was game to be had in the forests, the plains. Besides, Michael had a sudden urgent longing for his home.

"Xak Tsaroth," said Michael.

"What about it?" Nikol asked him.

"The Temple of Mishakal is there. And so are the holy disks. Why didn't I think of these sooner?" He began to pace the room excitedly.

"What disks? What are you talking about?"

"The Disks of Mishakal. All the wisdom of the gods are written on these disks. Don't you see, beloved? It's on those disks that we will find the answers!"

"If there *are* answers," Nikol said, frowning. "We buried a child yesterday. A little child! What had that babe to do with Kingpriests or clerics? Why should the gods punish the innocent?"

"If we find the disks, we'll find the answers," he said.

"In Xak Tsaroth!" Nikol scoffed. "Don't you remember what those refugees told us about Xak Tsaroth?"

"I remember." Michael turned, started to walk away. Having been born and reared in Xak Tsaroth, he had listened in disbelief to the tales of its destruction, told by the refugees. He had to see for himself.

Nikol ran after him, laid a remorseful hand on his arm. "I'm sorry, dearest, truly I am. I wasn't thinking. I forgot that was your home once. We'll travel there. We'll leave tomorrow. We have nothing to keep us here. We would have had to leave soon anyway."

As they were leaving, Nikol pulled shut the castle's heavy oaken door, made to lock it. Then, abruptly, she changed her mind. "No," she said, shoving it wide open. "This home is blessed, as the knight said. Let it shelter those who come. I have the feeling I will never see it again anyway."

"Don't speak words of ill omen," Michael waned her.

"It's not an ill omen," Nikol said quietly, looking up at him with a sad smile. "Our path lies far from here, I think."

She placed her hand upon the cold stone wall in final farewell, then the two gathered their meager belongings and started down the road, heading south.

****

If they had known how long the journey would take them, or how hard and dangerous it would be, they would have never left the castle's walls. They had been forewarned of terrible destruction farther south, but they were unprepared for the tremendous changes that had occurred, not the least of which was a sea where no sea had been before.

Reaching Caergoth, they were amazed to discover that the ground had sunk. Seawater, rushing in from the Sirrion Sea, now hid the scars of sundered lands. The two were forced to a halt and work to pay their passage on a crude raft, run by a group of villainous-looking Ergothians, who had been separated by the sea from their homeland to the west.

The Ergothians ambushed them outside of Caergoth, demanded they hand over food and valuables. Nikol, disguised as a knight, refused. A fight ensued that left no one seriously injured, but gained Nikol the men's respect. They eyed Michael's blue robes with sneering suspicion, but accepted Nikol's explanation that "her brother" had made a vow to their dying mother to remain faithful to his goddess.

As it turned out, the Ergothians were basically honest folk, made savage in their ways by the hardships they had been forced to endure. Nikol, maintaining her disguise as a knight, aided them in wiping out a band of goblins that had been raiding their hovels. Michael showed them plants and herbs they could use to supplement what had been a steady diet of fish. In return, the Ergothians ferried them across what they were calling "Newsea" and promised that they would have a return voyage, should they care to come back.

Which they soon would, they promised, once they saw what had become of Xak Tsaroth.

On the opposite shore, Michael and Nikol soon lost their way, wandered in the mountains for weeks. No map was trustworthy. The land had altered and shifted beyond recognition. Roads that once led somewhere now would up nowhere—or worse. Survival itself was a struggle. Game was scarce. Farmland was either scorched by drought or flooded by newly created rivers. Famine and disease drove people to flee wrecked homes and villages and seek a better life that, rumor had it, was always over the next mountain. Even good men and women became desperate as they listened to their children cry from hunger. Rumor had it that several elven cities in nearby Qualinost had been attacked by humans.

This must have been true, for when Michael and Nikol accidentally came too near the borders of that land, a flight of elven arrows warned them to turn aside.

Nikol wore her sword openly; the bleak and chill sun shone on the blade. Her armor and breastplate and her knightly air of confidence daunted many. Most robbers were nothing more than ruffians, who wanted food in their bellies, not a sharp blade. But, on occasion, she and Michael met with those who were well armed and were not afraid of a "beardless knight."

Nikol and Michael fought when they were cornered, ran when they were outnumbered. The cleric had taken to carrying a stout staff, which he learned to swing with clumsy effect, if not skill. He fought for Nikol's sake, more than his own. Plunged into despair over the chaos he saw in the world, he would, if he had been alone, gone the way of so many others before him.

Nikol credited him with keeping her alive during the dark days before the Cataclysm. Now it was she who returned the favor, Her love alone bore him along. Michael even ceased to ask Mishakal's forgiveness when he bashed a head. Eventually, after many months of weary travel, they reached their destination.

****

"The Great City of Xak Tsaroth, whose beauty surrounds you . . ." Michael whispered the inscription on the fallen obelisk, traced it with his hand on the broken stone. His voice died before he could finish reading. He lowered his head, ashamed to be seen weeping.

Nikol patted his shoulder. Her hand was roughened, its skin tough and calloused, cracked and bleeding from the cold, scarred from battle. But its touch was gentle.

"I don't know why I'm crying," Michael said harshly, wiping his hands over his cheeks before his tears froze on his skin. "We've seen so many horrible sights—brutal death, terrible suffering. This"—he gestured at the fallen obelisk—"this is nothing but a hunk of stone. Yet, I remember . . ."

His head sank into hands, hurting sobs wrenched him. He thought he'd prepared himself. He'd thought he was strong enough to return, but the devastation was too much, too appalling.

From this point, long ago, one could have seen the city of Xak Tsaroth, heard its life in the throbbing, pulsing cries of its vendors and hawkers, the shrill laughter of its children, the rush and bustle of its streets. The silence was the most horrible part of his homecoming. The silence and the emptiness. They told him Xak Tsaroth was gone, sunk into the ground on which it had been built. He had not believed them. He had hoped. Bitterly, he cursed his hope.

Nikol pressed his arm in silent sympathy, then drew away. His grief was private; she did not feel that even she had a right to share in it. Hand on her sword hilt, she kept watch, staring out over the ruins that surrounded the obelisk, peering intently into the shadows beyond.

Gradually, Michael's sobs lessened. Nikol heard him draw a shivering breath.

"Do you want to keep going?" she asked, purposefully cool and calm.

"Yes. We've come this far." He sighed. "It's one thing to see strange cities lying in ruins, another to see one's home."

Nikol climbed on the obelisk, used it as a bridge to cross the swamp water. Michael, after a moment's hesitation, followed after her. His feet trod over the inscription: *The gods reward us in the grace of our home.* Grace. The land was barren, almost a desert, its trees charred stumps, its flowering plants and bushes nothing but soft ash. There was no sign of any living being, not even animal tracks.

Michael looked out over the ruins of the city's outskirts. "I can't believe it," he said softly to himself. "Why did I come? What did I expect to find here?"

"Your family," said Nikol quietly.

He looked at her in silence a moment, then slowly nodded. "Yes, you're right. How well you know me."

"Perhaps you will find them," she said, forcing a smile. "People might live around here still."

Nikol tried to sound cheerful, for Michael's sake. She did not believe herself, however, and she knew she hadn't fooled Michael. The quiet was oppressive, perhaps because it was not true quiet. A thin undercurrent of sound disturbed the surface. She could tell herself it was the wind, sighing through the broken branches of dead trees, but its sorrow pierced her heart.

Michael shook his head. "No, if they survived, which I doubt, they must have fled into the plains. My mother's people came from there. She would have gone back to find them."

Nikol paused, uncertain of her way. "You know, I could almost think that Xak Tsaroth *is* haunted, that its dead do lament."

Michael shook his head. "If any of the dead walk these broken streets, it is those who are unable or unwilling to pass beyond, to find the mercy of the gods."

What mercy? Nikol almost asked bitterly, but she bit her tongue, kept silent. Their relationship over these past hard months had deepened. Love was no longer the splendid, perfect bridal garment. The fabric was worn now, but it fit better, was far more comfortable. Neither could imagine a night spent outside the refuge of the other's arms. But there were several rents and tears in the shining fabric.

The terrible things they'd seen had left their mark upon them both. When these cuts were mended, they would serve to make the marriage stronger, but now the arguments were growing bitter, had inflicted wounds that were still tender and sore to the touch.

"It's midafternoon," she said abruptly. "We don't have much time if we're going to make use of the daylight to aid our search. Which way do we go?"

He heard the chill in her voice, knew what she was thinking as well as if she'd said it.

"Straight ahead. We will come to a large well and, beyond that, the Temple of Mishakal."

"If it's still standing. . . ."

"It must be," said Michael firmly. "There we will find the answers to your questions and to mine."

The remnants of what once had been a broad street took them to an open, paved courtyard. To the east stood four tall, free-standing columns that supported nothing; the building lay in ruins around them. A circular stone wall, rising four feet above the ground, had once been a well. Nikol stopped, peered down, and shrugged. She could see nothing but darkness. Michael ran his hand over the low wall."

"We used to come out of temple classes and sit on the wall and talk of our plans—how we would go forth and, with the help of the gods, change the world for the better."

"Obviously, the gods weren't listening." Nikol gazed around. "Is that the temple?" She pointed.

Now it was Michael who bit his lips on the words that would have precipitated another quarrel.

"Yes," he said instead. "That is the temple."

"I see *it* escaped the destruction unscathed," Nikol stated, her tone bitter.

Michael walked toward the building that was so familiar—its beautiful white stone shining pure and cold—and, at the same time, so alien. Perhaps that was because he missed the sight of the other buildings, now lying in rubble; missed the crowds of people strolling about the courtyard, meeting at the well to exchange the latest news. He ascended the stairs, approached the large, ornate double doors that led into the temple. Made of gold, the doors gleamed coldly in the winter sun. Michael pushed on them.

They did not open.

He pushed again, harder. The doors remained shut fast. Stepping backward, he stared at them in perplexity.

"What's wrong?" Nikol called from her place, guarding the foot of the stairs.

"The doors won't open," Michael answered.

"They're barred, then. Keep a look out, will you?" Nikol climbed the stairs, studied the doors. "But they should be easy to pry apart—"

"They're not barred. They couldn't be. They had no locks on them. The temple was always open. . . ."

"This is ridiculous. There *must* be a way inside."

Nikol shoved at the doors, leaned her shoulder against them. The temple doors did not move.

Nikol stared at them, frustrated, angry. "We have to get inside! Is there another way?"

"This was the only entrance."

"I *will* enter, then!" She drew her sword, was about to thrust it between the doors.

Michael laid his hand upon her arm. "No, Nikol. I forbid it."

"You *forbid* it!" Nikol rounded on him in fury. "I'm the daughter of a Knight of Solamnia! You dare to give me orders, you who are nothing but a—"

"Cleric," finished Michael. "And now not even that." He touched the holy medallion around his neck, the symbol of the goddess. He looked at the temple sadly. "She will not open her doors to me."

"Now is not the time," came a voice.

Nikol drew her sword. "Who's there?" she demanded.

"Put your weapon away, Knight's Daughter," said the voice meekly. "I mean you no harm."

A middle-aged woman clad in threadbare clothing sat at the foot of the stairs. She sat very still; the dark shadow of a broken column had hidden her from view. Perhaps that was why neither Michael nor Nikol had noticed her until now. Nikol sheathed her sword but kept her hand on the hilt. The Cataclysm had not destroyed magic-users, or so rumor had it. This seemingly harmless woman might be a wizardess in disguise.

They both descended the stairs, walking slowly, warily. Nearing her, Nikol saw the woman's face more clearly. The sorrow etched on the aged and wrinkled skin was heart-breaking. Nikol's hand slipped from her sword's hilt. Tears came to her eyes, though she had not cried in all the long months of weary journeying.

"Who are you, Mistress?" Michael asked gently, kneeling beside the woman, who had not moved from where she sat. "What is your name?"

"I have no name," said the woman quietly. "I am a mother, that is all."

Her clothes were thin. She had no cloak and was shivering in the chill twilight. Michael took his own cloak from his shoulders, wrapped it around the woman.

"You cannot stay here, Mistress," he said. "Night is coming."

"Oh, but I must stay here." She did not seem to notice the cloak. "Otherwise, how will my children know where to find me?"

Nikol knelt. Her voice, which had been so strident when she was arguing with Michael, was now soft and low and filled with compassion. "Where are your children? We'll take you to them."

"There," said the woman, and she nodded toward the destroyed city.

Nikol caught her breath, looked at Michael. "She's gone mad!" she mouthed.

"How long have you been waiting here, Mistress?" he asked.

"Since that day," she answered, and they had no need to ask which day she meant. "I have never left them. They left me, you know. They were supposed to meet me here, but they didn't come. I'll keep waiting. Someday, they will return."

Nikol brushed her hand across her eyes. Michael gazed at the woman. He was at a loss to know what to do. He couldn't leave this poor, mad creature here. She would surely die. But it was obvious that she would not go without a struggle, and the shock of that might well kill her. Perhaps, if he could draw her thoughts away from her tragedy . . .

"Mistress, I am a cleric of Mishakal. I have returned to the temple in search of the disks that were kept here. You said that now is not the time to enter. When will the golden doors open?"

"When the evil comes out of the well. When the blue crystal staff shines. When dark wings spread over the land. Then my children will come. Then the doors will open." The woman spoke in a dreamy voice.

"When will that be?"

"Long . . . long." The woman blinked dazedly. The mists of madness parted, and she seemed to return to reality. "You seek the disks? They are not in there."

"Where, then?" Michael asked eagerly.

"Some say . . . Palanthas," the woman murmured. "Astinus. The great library. Go to Palanthas. There you will find the answer you seek."

"Palanthas!" Michael sat back on his heels, appalled. The thought of more months of traveling, of venturing back out into the savage land, came close to driving him to the pathetic state of this pitiable woman.

But Nikol's eyes shone. "Palanthas! The High Clerist's Tower, strong bastion of the Solamnic Knights, Yes, *that* is where we will find answers. Come, Michael," she said, rising briskly to her feet. "We can get in an hour's journeying before sunset."

Michael stood reluctantly. "Are you sure you won't come with us, Mistress?"

"This is my place," she said to him, fingering the cloak. "How will they know where to find me otherwise? Thank you for the wrap, though. I will be warm now, as I wait."

He started to go, felt a strong tugging at his heart. Turning, he stared at her. Suddenly, she seemed very familiar. Perhaps he'd known her—a friend, a neighbor.

"How can I leave you?"

She smiled a strange, sad smile. "Go with my blessing, child. Someday, you, too, will return. And when you do, I will be waiting."

Part IV

The great seaport city of Palanthas, built by dwarves, fabled as far back as the Age of Might, was, according to swift-flying rumor, one of the few cities to come through the Cataclysm almost unscathed. Michael and Nikol, to their astonishment and disquiet, found themselves two drops in a steadily slowing stream of refugees, flowing toward what was purportedly a rich, safe harbor.

Located in west Solamnia, on the Bay of Branchala, the Cityhome, as it was known among its inhabitants, was governed by a noble lord under the auspices of the Knight of Solamnia, whose stronghold—the Tower of the High Clerist—guarded the mountain pass that kept goods and wealth flowing from Palanthas to the lands beyond.

But, though the city's walls and pavement, its tall towers and graceful minarets, may have survived the Cataclysm without damage, the disaster opened cracks within its population. These cracks had always been there, but the rifts had been covered by wealth, reverence for the gods, respect for (and fear of) the knights.

Now, almost a year after the Cataclysm, wealth had ceased to enter Palanthas. Few ships sailed the sea. Beggars, not gold, came pouring through the gates. The city's economy collapsed beneath the weight. Here, as in other places throughout Ansalon, the people looked for someone other than themselves to blame.

Michael and Nikol, along with numerous other fellow travelers, arrived at the city of Palanthas in midmorning. They'd heard rumors in abundance, some good, but many more dark—tales of beating, looting, murder. Mostly, they'd discounted them, but rumor had not prepared them for the sight that met their eyes.

"May the gods have mercy," said Michael, staring in pity and horror.

Throngs of people—ragged, wretched—crouched on the road outside the walls. At the sight of the new arrivals, they surged forward, begging for anything that might, for a moment, relieve their misery and suffering.

Michael, sick at heart, would have given them all he owned, but Nikol, her face pale, her lips pressed tight, steered him with a firm hand through the grasping, wailing mob that surrounded the city gates.

The gates stood open wide, people pouring in, shoving their way out. The guards kept traffic moving, but did little else. One of them, however, eyed Nikol, and the weapon she wore, with interest.

"Hey you, Mercenary. The Revered Son's looking for swords," said the guard. "You can earn yourself a meal, a place to sleep." He jerked a thumb. "Head for the Old City."

"Revered Son?" Michael repeated, in disbelief.

"Thank you," said Nikol, catching hold of her husband and dragging him away. Outside the walls, they could hear the disappointed cries of the beggars.

Inside the walls, things were not much better. People lay sleeping in doorways or on the bare, cold pavement. Evil-looking men drifted near, saw Nikol's sword and Michael's stout staff, and drifted away. Two slatternly women caught hold of them and tried to drag them into a tumble-down hovel. The city stank of filth and disease.

They were loathe to stop and ask anyone for directions. Nikol's father had visited Palanthas often, however, and had described the layout of the city, which was like a gigantic wheel. The great and ancient library stood in the city's center, known as Old City, along with the palace, the homes of the knights, and other important structures. They made their way through the wall that separated the Old City from the New. Here the streets were not as crowded, almost empty. The air was cleaner, easier to breathe.

Michael and Nikol hurried forward, certain that the library must be a haven of peace in this wretched city. They had barely passed through the Old City wall when they discovered why the streets had been deserted. All the people—and there must have been hundreds—were gathered here.

"Where's the library?" Michael asked, peering over the heads of the crowd.

"There," said Nikol, pointing to the building the mob surrounded.

"What's going on here?" Michael asked a woman standing near him.

"Hush!" she said, glaring at him. "The Revered Son is speaking."

"Over here!" Nikol drew Michael into a grove of trees that bordered one of the broad avenues of Old City. From this vantage point, both could see and hear the speaker, who stood upon the very steps of the Great Library of Palanthas.

"Do you know what is behind those walls, good citizens? I'll tell you! Lies!" A man pointed an accusing finger at the large, elegant, columned building behind him. "Lies about the Kingpriest!"

The crowd gathered around him muttered angrily.

"Yes, I've seen them, read them with my own eyes!" The man tapped those eyes, remarkable only for the fact that they were squinted and sly-looking. "The great Astinus"—the voice was poisoned with sarcasm—"writes that the Kingpriest called down the wrath of the gods by making demands of them! And who had a better right? What man has lived who was as good as that man? I'll tell you the real reason the gods hurled the fiery mountain upon Istar!"

He paused, waited until the crowd hushed.

"Jealousy!" he breathed in a stage whisper that carried clearly through the chill air. "They were jealous! Jealous of a man more godly than the gods themselves! They were jealous and afraid that he might challenge them. And so he might have! And he would have won!"

The crowd roared its approval, with an undercurrent of anger frightening to hear.

"But, though he is gone," continued the man, clasping his hands in pious grief, "some of us have vowed to carry on, to keep his memory alive. Yes," he cried, raising his fist to heaven. "We defy you, gods! We are not afraid! Drop a fiery mountain on us if you dare!"

Michael stirred restlessly, opened his mouth.

"Are you mad?" Nikol whispered. "You'll get us killed!" Taking hold of his medallion, she tucked it down the front of his blue robes, hiding it from sight.

Michael sighed, kept silent.

No one else in the crowd saw them. All eyes were on the speaker.

"Lord Palanthas sides with us," the man cried. "He would agree to pass our laws, for he knows they are right and just, but he is prevented from doing so by that old man in there!" Again he pointed at the columned building behind him.

"Then *we'll* pass the laws and enforce them ourselves!" shouted a voice from the crowd, who, by the quickness of his response, obviously had been waiting for a cue. "Read us your laws, Revered Son. Let us hear them."

"Yes, read us the laws!" The crowd picked up the shout, turned it into a chant.

"I will, good citizens," said the squint-eyed speaker. He drew forth a scroll from the bosom of robes that were rich and snowy white—a marked contrast to the worn and shabby clothing of those who hung upon his every word.

"First: no elf, dwarf, kender, gnome, or anyone with so much as a drop of blood of any of these races is to be allowed in the city. Any now residing here will be expelled. Any caught here in the future will be put to death.

The people looked at each other, muttered their approval.

"Second: any wizard or wizardess, witch or warlock, apprentice mage, sorcerer or sorceress"—the man ran out of breath, paused to catch it—"caught within these city walls will be put to death."

This met with nods and shrugs and even some incredulous laughter, as though such an occurrence was almost beyond the realm of possibility. Palanthas had divested itself of such evil along ago, though at a heavy cost.

"Third: all Knights of Solamnia—"

Boos and hisses and angry shouts interrupted the speaker. He smiled in satisfaction and raised his voice to be heard above the uproar.

"All Knight of Solamnia or any member of a knight's family found henceforth within the city limits shall be expelled!"

A loud cheer.

"All lands and goods and properties of said Knights of Solamnia shall be confiscated and turned over to the people!"

An even louder cheer.

Now it was Nikol who flushed in anger and seemed about to speak.

"Are *you* mad?" Michael whispered, wrapping her cloak more closely about the telltale breastplate, twitching the folds over the sword in its antique silver sheath, decorated with kingfisher and crown.

The two drew back to stand in the shadows of a large, spreading oak.

"Fourth: the library will be razed to the ground! All the books and scrolls and the lies that they contain will be burned!"

The speaker snapped his own scroll shut. Leaning toward the crowd, he made a sweeping gesture with his arm, as if he would scoop them up and send them in a surging tide toward destruction. The mob shouted its agreement and made a tentative movement toward the steps of the ancient library.

No one came out from the library. No defender appeared in the doorway. The building itself, the weight of years, its age and veneration and dignity, spoke a silent, eloquent defense and daunted the crowd.

Those in the front ranks seemed unwilling to proceed, fell back to let those behind come forth if they wanted. Those behind, finding themselves about to become those in front, had second thoughts, with the result that the mob began to mill about aimlessly at the foot of the library stairs. Some shouted threats; others threw rotten eggs and vegetables at the venerable structure. No one wanted to go any nearer.

The speaker gazed at them with a grim face, realized that the time was not propitious. He stepped down from the platform and was immediately surrounded by people, who cried out for his blessing or reached out to touch him reverently or held up their children for him to kiss.

"In the name of the Kingpriest," he said humbly, moving from one to another. "In the name of the Kingpriest."

"What is this mockery?" Michael gasped, appalled, no longer able to keep quiet. "I can't believe this! Haven't they learned? This is worse, far worse—"

"Hush!" Nikol hissed and dragged him even farther back into the shadows.

The speaker moved through the crowd, handling the people skillfully, giving them what they wanted, yet subtly ridding himself of them. A small retinue, led by the man who had asked the speaker to read the laws, formed a circle around the Revered Son and managed to extricate him from the press. He and his henchmen emerged near where Michael and Nikol stood, hidden by the trees.

Some of the mob continued to surge sluggishly about the library steps, but most grew bored and wandered off to the taverns or whatever other amusements could cheer their dreary existence.

"You had them eating out of your hand, Revered Son. Why didn't you urge them on?"

"Because now is not the time," the Revered Son answered complacently. "Let them go to their friends and neighbors and tell what they have heard this day. We'll have a hundred times more people than this at our next rally and a hundred times a hundred more after that. In the meantime, we'll whip up their fear and their hatred.

"Remember that half-elf baker we talked to yesterday, the stubborn one, who refused to leave the city? See to it that his loaves make a few people sick. Use this." The Revered Son handed over a small glass vial. "Let me know who's taken ill. I'll be around to 'heal' them."

One of the henchmen, taking the vial, looked at it dubiously. The Revered Son regarded him with some impatience. "The effects wear off naturally after a while, but these ignorant peasants don't know that. They'll think I've performed a miracle."

The man pocketed the vial. "What about the library?"

"We'll hold another rally in front of it day after tomorrow, after we've had time to stir up trouble. If you could get me one of those books, the one with the lies about the Kingpriest—"

The man nodded, shrugged. "Nothing to it. That fool old man, Astinus, lets anyone read 'em."

"Excellent. I'll read it aloud to the crowd. That should seal the library's fate and the old man's. He's been the main one opposing my takeover of the city's government. Once he's out of the way, I'll have no trouble with the namby-pamby Lord Palanthas.

"Now, tonight," continued the Revered Son, "I want you and others in the taverns, spreading stories about that knight, the one that was god-cursed—"

"Soth."

"Yes, Lord Soth."

Nikol sucked in her breath softly. Michael caught hold of her hand, squeezed it, counseling silence.

"I'm not certain we should rely on that story to drive the mob to attack the knights, Revered Son. There's more than one tale about him going around."

"What's the other?" the speaker asked sharply.

"That he was forewarned about the Cataclysm. He was riding to Istar, planning to try to *stop* the Kingpriest—"

"Nonsense!" The Revered Son snorted. "Here's the story you tell them. Soth was furious because the Kingpriest was about to make public the knight's dalliances with that elven trollop of his. Make that clear. Oh, and throw in that bit abut him murdering his first wife. That always goes over—"

"Shush, someone's wanting a blessing."

A young woman, carrying a baby, was hovering timidly on the outskirts of the group. The Revered Son glanced about, saw the woman, and smiled at her benignly.

"Come closer. What may I do for you, Daughter?"

"Pardon me for disturbing you, Revered Son," the woman said, with a blush, "but I heard you speak at the temple yesterday, and I'm confused."

"I'll do my best to help you understand, Daughter," said the Revered Son humbly. "What do you find confusing?"

"I have always prayed to Paladine, but you say we're not to pray to him or any of the other gods. We're to pray to the Kingpriest?"

"Yes, Daughter. When the wicked Queen of Evil attacked the world, the other gods fled in terror. The Kingpriest alone had the courage to stand and fight her, just as did Huma, long ago. The Kingpriest fights her today, on the heavenly plane. He needs your prayers, Daughter, to aid him in his struggles."

"And that's why we must drive out the kender and the elves—"

"And all of those whose disbelief come to the aid of the Powers of Darkness."

"I understand now. Thank you, Revered Son." The young woman curtseyed.

The Revered Son laid his hand upon her head, and upon

her child's. "In the name of the Kingpriest," he said solemnly.

The young woman left. The Revered Son watched after her, a pleased smile upon his lips. He cast a glance at his cohorts, who grinned and nodded. Their heads bent together in continued plotting, the Revered Son and his minions walked off in the opposite direction.

Neither Nikol nor Michael could speak for long moments. The shock of what they'd heard and seen took their breath, made them dizzy and sick, as if they'd been physically assaulted.

"Oh Michael," murmured Nikol, "this can't be happening! I don't believe it. Lord Soth was so valiant, so brave. No knight would do such terrible things—"

"Lies!" said Michael. His face was pale. He literally shook with anger and outrage. "That false cleric has twisted the truth—"

"But what is the truth, Michael?" Nikol cried. "We don't know!"

"Hush, we're attracting attention," he cautioned, noting that several men were casting suspicious glances in their direction. "The truth about that friend of ours," Michael continued loudly. "We'll find out, I'm certain, now that we're here in this fair city. A city obviously blessed."

Several men, burly and unwashed and smelling strongly of dwarf spirits, lurched over to stare at them.

"Strangers, are you?" one said, scowling.

"From Whitsund, Sire," said Michael, bowing.

"At least you're human. Refugees? Thinkin' of movin' in?" He glowered at them. "'Cause if you are, you got another think comin'. We got beggars enough as it is." Those with him muttered their assent. "Why don't you two just head on back to wherever it is you came from?"

Nikol shifted restlessly; her arm jingled, her sword clanked. The man turned, looked at her with drunken interest.

"That steel I hear?" The man took a step nearer Nikol. Reaching out a filthy hand, he caught hold of her by the chin, wrenched her face to the light. "You look as if you've noble blood in you, boy. Don't he, fellas? Not some noble's son, by any chance? With a fat purse?"

"Let go of me," said Nikol through clenched teeth. "Or you're a dead man."

"Please," said Michael, trying to come between them, "we don't want any trouble—"

But he only made matters worse. His staff caught on Nikol's cloak, dragged the fabric aside. The shining breastplate she wore glittered in the sun.

"A knight hisself!" The man howled in glee. "Look, fellas. Look what I've caught! I'm gonna have a little fun." He drew a long dagger from his belt. "Let's see if your blood does run yellow—"

Nikol thrust her sword into the man, yanked it out before he or his drunken companions knew what had happened. The man stared at her in blank astonishment, then groaned and toppled to the ground. A pool of blood spread beneath him. The sight sobered up his friends, who growled in anger. Some drew knives; one wielded a blackthorn cudgel. Michael whirled his staff. Nikol set her back to his, her sword, red with blood, swinging in a slow arc.

The men made a half-hearted show of attacking. Michael's staff lashed out, caught one on the side of one man's head, sent him into the dust. Nikol gave another a slash on the cheek that he would carry to his grave. The men, eyeing the knight and the cleric, decided they'd had enough. They broke and ran.

"Cowards!" jeered Nikol, cleaning her sword with the tail of the dead man's shirt. "Thieves and knaves."

"Yes, but they'll be back," said Michael grimly. "And they'll bring help. We can't stay in the city. We'll have to leave." He cast a longing, disappointed glance at the great library.

"We'll return," said Nikol confidently. "I have an idea. Hurry up. One of the thugs is talking to that so-called Revered Son."

Sure enough, the Revered Son was turning, staring hard in their direction. The man was pointing at them excitedly.

The two ran, blended in with the rest of the flotsam and dregs of humanity that had washed ashore in Palanthas. Reaching the gates, they were walking out just as one of the Revered Son's henchmen came pounding up, breathless, to deliver a message to guard.

Michael and Nikol ducked behind a wagon that had become mired in the crowd.

"Knight of Solamnia!" the man shouted. "A huge fellow with a sword six feet long! He's got a friend, some fellow wearing the blue robes of the false goddess."

"Yeah, sure, we'll watch for them," said the guard, and the henchmen dashed off, to spread the alarm at other gates. "Get that wagon moving! What's the matter with you?"

Nikol drew her cloak close around her, pressed her sword against her thigh. Michael made certain his holy medallion was well hidden. The guard didn't even bother to spare them a glance. Once outside the gate, they fended off the beggars, traveled some distance up the road, finally stopping in a grove of stunted trees.

"What's your plan?" Michael asked.

"We'll travel to the High Clerist's Tower," Nikol replied. "The knights must be told about what is going on in Palanthas, how this false cleric is plotting to take control. They'll put a stop to it, then we can go into the library and find the Disks of Mishakal. We'll use them to prove to people that this Revered Son is a crook and a charlatan."

Michael looked doubtful. "But surely the knights must know—"

"No, they don't. They can't or they would have stopped him before now," Nikol argued. Serene, confident, she looked up into the mountains that loomed over Palanthas, to the road that led to the knights' stronghold. "And we'll find out the truth about Lord Soth, too," she added softly, her cheeks flushing. "I don't believe what they said, not a word of it. I want to know the truth."

Michael sighed, shook his head.

"What?" Nikol demanded sharply. "What's the matter?"

"I was thinking that perhaps there are some truths we are better off not knowing," he replied.

Part V

A chill wind, which blew from the plane of dark and evil magic, tore aside the cloak of the knight who stood upon that plane, allowed the icy blast to penetrate to the center of his empty being. He drew the cloak closer around him—a human gesture made from force of habit, for this ephemeral fabric, spun of memory, would never be sufficient to protect him from death's eternal cold. The knight had not been dead long, and he clung to the small and comforting habits of blessed life—once taken for granted, now, with their loss, bitterly regretted.

Other than drawing his cloak closer around the body that no longer was there, he did not move. He had urgent business. He was spying on the city of Palanthas. And though he was quite near it, none of the living saw him or were aware of his presence. The shadows of his dark magic shrouded him, hid him from view. The sight of him would have terrorized these weak vessels of warm flesh, rendered them useless to him. He needed the living, needed them alive, and, knowing his own cursed power, he wasn't certain how to approach them.

He watched them, hated them, envied them.

Palanthas. Once he's owned that city. Once he'd been a power there. He could be a power still, a power for death and destruction. But that wasn't what he wanted, not now, not yet. A city saved from the terror of the Cataclysm. There had to be a reason, something blessed within it, something he could use.

The Revered Son? The knight had assumed so, at first. A dark joy had filled what once had been his heart when he'd heard that a Revered Son had arrived from the east, claiming to be a survivor of the shattered Istar, come to take over the spiritual well-being of the populace. Was it possible? Had he discovered a true cleric left in the land? But, after long days and nights (for what was time to him?) spent listening to the Revered Son, the knight came to the conclusion he'd been deceived.

In life, he'd known men and women like this charlatan, made use of them for his own ends. He recognized that man's tricks and deceits. He toyed with the idea of destroying this Revered Son, found it amusing, for the knight hated the living with a hatred born of jealousy. And he would be doing these fool Palanthians a favor, ridding them of one who would end up tyrant, despot.

But what would he gain out of it, except the fleeting pleasure of watching warm flesh grow as cold as his own?

"Nothing," he said to himself. "If they are stupid enough to fall for that man's lies, let them. It serves them right."

Yet something within Palanthas called to him, and so he stayed, watching, waiting with the patience of one who has eternity, the impatience of one who longs for rest.

He was there, invisible to living eyes, when two people—a beardless youth armed with a sword, and a man in shabby blue robes—emerged from the city gates with haste enough to draw the knight's attention, piqued his interest by taking themselves away from the sight of the guards.

The knight gazed at the man in blue with interest that increased when he saw, with the clear sight of those who walk another plane of existence, the symbol of Mishakal hidden beneath the man's robes. And the beardless youth; there seemed something familiar about him. The dark knight drew closer.

"We'll travel to the High Clerist's Tower," the youth was saying to his friend. "The knights must be told about what is going on in Palanthas, how this false cleric is plotting to take control. They'll soon put a stop to it, then we can go into the library and find the Disks of Mishakal. We'll use them to prove to people that this Revered Son is a crook and a charlatan."

High Clerist's Tower! The knight gave a bitter, silent laugh.

The youth's friend appeared to share the listener's doubts. "But surely the knights must know—"

"No, they don't," the youth returned. 'They can't or they would have stopped him before now. And we'll find out the truth about Lord Soth, too. I don't believe what they said, not a word of it. I want to know the truth."

The knight heard his name, heard it spoken in admiration. A thrill passed through him, a thrill that was achingly human and alive. Soth was so astounded, so lost in wonder and puzzlement, trying to think of where he'd known this young man, that he didn't hear whatever reply the friend made in response.

The two started on their way up the winding road to the High Clerist's Tower. Summoning his steed, a creature of flame and evil magic as dark as his own, Lord Soth accompanied them—an unseen companion.

****

The Tower of the High Clerist had been built by the founder of the knights, Vinas Solamnus. Located high in the Vingaard Mountains, it guarded Westgate Pass, the only pass through the mountains.

The road to the High Clerist's Tower was long and steep, but, because it was so well traveled, the knights and the citizens of Palanthas had always worked together to keep it in good repair. The road had become legendary, in fact. A quick route to anything was termed "as smooth as the road to Palanthas."

But that had changed, as had so much else, since the Cataclysm.

Expecting a swift and easy journey, Michael and Nikol were dismayed and disheartened to discover the once smooth road now in ruins; at points, almost impassable.

Huge boulders blocked the way in some places. Wide chasms, where the rock had split apart, prevented passage in others. Mountain wall on one side of them, sheer drop on the other, Michael and Nikol were forced to climb over these barriers or—heart in mouth—make a perilous leap from one side of a cut to another.

After only a few miles journeying, both were exhausted. They reached a relatively level place, a clearing of fir trees that once might have been a resting area for travelers. A mountain stream ran clear and cold, bounding down the cliff's side to disappear into the woodlands far beneath them. A circle of blackened rocks indicated that people had built campfires on this spot.

The two stopped, by unspoken consent, to rest. Although the way had been hard, both were far wearier than they should have been. A pall had come over them shortly after starting out and lay heavily on them, drained them of energy. They had the feeling they were being watched, followed. Nikol kept her hand on her sword; Michael stopped continually, looked behind. They saw nothing, heard nothing, but the feeling did not leave them.

"At least," said Nikol, "we have a clear view of the road from here." She stared long and hard down the mountain, down the way they'd come. Nothing stirred along the broken path.

"It's our imagination," said Michael. "We're jumpy, after what happened in Palanthas, that's all."

They sat down on the ground that was smooth with a covering of dead pine needles and ate sparingly of their meager supplies.

The sky was gray, laden with heavy clouds that hung so low, wisps seemed to cling to the tall firs. Both were oppressed, spirits subdued by a feeling of dread and awe. When they finally spoke, they did so in low voices, reluctant to shatter the stillness.

"It seems strange," said Michael, "that the knights do not clean up this road. The Cataclysm was almost a year ago, time enough to build bridges, remove these boulders, fill in the cracks. Do you know," he continued, talking for the sake of talking, not realizing what he was saying, "it looks to me as if they've left the road in disrepair on purpose. I think they're afraid of being attacked—"

"Nonsense!" said Nikol, bristling. "What do the knights have to fear? That drunken scum in Palanthas? They're nothing more than paid henchmen for that false cleric. The citizens of Palanthas respect the knights, and well they should. The knights have defended Palanthas for generations. You'll see. When the knights come riding down in force, those cowards will take one look and beg for mercy."

"Then why haven't they ridden forth before now?"

"They don't know the danger," she snapped. "No one's brought them word."

Rubbing her shoulders beneath her heavy cloak, Nikol abruptly changed the subject. "How hard the wind blows up here, and how bitter it is. The cold goes through flesh and bone, strikes at the heart."

"So it does," said Michael, growing more and more uneasy. "A strange chill, not of winter. I've never known the like."

"I suppose it's just the high altitude." Nikol tried to shrug it off. Rising to her feet, she paced the clearing, peering nervously into the woods. "Nothing out there."

Coming back, she nudged Michael gently with the toe of her boot. "You didn't hear a word I said. You're smiling. Tell me. I'd be glad of something to smile about," she added with a shiver.

"What?" Michael jumped, glanced up, startled. "Oh, it's nothing, really. Funny what memories come to you for no good reason. For a moment, I was a child, back in Xak Tsaroth. An uncle of mine, one of the nomads, came into town one day. I don't suppose you ever saw the Plainsmen. They dress all in leather and bright-colored feathers and beads. I loved it when they came to visit our family, bringing their trade goods. This uncle told the most wonderful stories. I'll never forget them, tales of the dark gods, who were never supposed to be mentioned then, in the time of the Kingpriest. Stories of ghosts and ghouls, the undead who roam the land in torment. I was terrified for days after."

"What happened?" asked Nikol, sitting beside him, crowding near for warmth and comfort. "Why do you sigh?"

"I told my teacher one of the stories. He was a young man, a cleric sent from Istar. He was furious. He called the Plainsman a wicked liar, a dangerous blasphemer, a corrupting influence on the impressionable youth. He told me my uncle's tales were ridiculous fabrications or, worse, downright heresy. There were no such things as ghosts and ghouls. All such evil had been eradicated by the almighty good of the Kingpriest. I can still feel the knock on the head the priest gave me—in the name of Mishakal, of course."

"What made you think of all this?"

"Those ghost stories." Michael tried to laugh, but it ended in a nervous cough. "When one of the undead comes near, my uncle says you feel a terrible chill that seems to come from the grave. It freezes your heart—"

"Stop it, Michael!" Nikol bounded to her feet. "You'll end up scaring us both silly. There's snow in the air. We should go on, whether we're rested or not. That way, we'll reach the tower before nightfall. Hand me the waterskin. I'll fill it, then we can be on our way."

Silently, Michael handed over the waterskin. Nikol walked over, filled the skin at the bubbling brook. Michael pulled the symbol of Mishakal out from beneath his robes, held it in his hand, stared at it. He could have sworn in glowed faintly, a shimmer of blue that lit the gray gloom surrounding them, deepening around them, deepening to black. . . .

And in the black, eyes of flame.

The eyes were in front of Nikol, staring at her from across the stream. She had risen to her feet, the waterskin in her hand, water dripping from it.

"This is how I know you," came a deep and terrible voice.

Michael tried to call to her, but his own voice was a strangled scream. He tried to move, to run to her side, but his legs were useless, as if they'd been cut off at the knees. Nikol did not retreat, did not flee. She stood unmoving, staring with set, pale face at the apparition emerging from the shadows.

He was—or had once been—a Knight of Solamnia. He was mounted on a steed that, like himself, seemed to spring from a terrible dream. A strange and eerie light, perhaps that cast by the black moon, Nuitari, shone on armor that bore the symbol of the rose, but the armor did not gleam. It was charred, scorched, as if the man had passed through a ravaging fire. He wore a helm, its visor lowered. No face was visible within, however. Only a terrible darkness lighted by the hideous flame of those burning eyes.

He came to a halt near Nikol, reached down a gloved hand, as if for the waterskin. In that motion, Michael knew him.

"You gave me water," said the knight, and his voice seemed to come from below the ground, from the grave. "You eased my burning thirst. I wish you could do so again."

The knight's voice was sad, burdened with a sorrow that brought tears to Michael's eyes, though they froze there.

The knight's words jolted Nikol, drove her to action. She drew her sword from its sheath.

"I do not know what dark and evil place you sprang from, but you desecrate the armor of a knight—"

Michael shook free of his fear, ran forward, caught hold of her arm. "Put your weapon away. He means us no harm." Pray Mishakal that was true! "Look at him, Nikol," Michael added, barely able to draw breath enough to speak. "Don't you recognize him?"

"Lord Soth!" Nikol whispered. She lowered her sword. "What dread fate is this? What have you become?"

Soth regarded her long moments without speaking. The chill that flowed from him came near to freezing their blood, the terror freezing their minds. And yet Michael guessed that the knight's evil powers were being held in check, even as he held the reins of his restive steed.

"I hear pity in your voice," said the knight. "Your pity and compassion touch some part of me—the part that will not die, the part that burns and throbs in endless pain! For I am one of the undead—doomed to bitter agony, eternal torment, no rest, no sleep. . . ."

His fist clenched in anger. The horse shied, screamed suddenly. Its hooves clattered on the frozen ground.

Nikol fell back a step, raised her sword.

"The rumors we heard about you, then, are true," she said, trying to control her shaking voice. "You failed us, the knights, the gods. You are cursed—"

"Unjustly!" Soth's voice hissed. "Cursed unjustly! I was tricked! Deceived! My wife was warned of the calamity. I rose forth, prepared to give my life to save the world, but the gods had no intention of being merciful. They wanted humankind punished. The gods prevented my coming to Istar and, in an attempt to cleanse their hands of the blood of innocents, they laid this curse on me! And now they have abandoned the world they destroyed."

Michael, frightened and sick at heart, clasped his hand around the symbol of Mishakal. The death knight was swift to notice.

"You do not believe me, Cleric?"

The flame eyes seared Michael's skin; the dreadful cold chilled his heart. "No, my lord," said Michael, wondering where he found the courage. "No, I do not believe you. The gods would not be so unjust."

"Oh, wouldn't they?" Nikol retorted bitterly. "I've kept silent, Michael, for I did not want to hurt you or add to your burden, but what if you're wrong? What if you've been deceived? What if the gods *have* abandoned us, left us alone at the mercy of scoundrels like those in Palanthas?"

Michael looked at her sadly. "You saw Nicholas. You saw him blessed, at peace. You heard the promise of the goddess, that someday we would find such peace. How can you doubt?"

"But where is the goddess now, Michael?" Nikol demanded. "Where is she when you pray to her? She does not answer."

Michael looked again at the medallion in the palm of his hand. It was dark and cold to the touch, colder than the chill of the death knight. But Michael had seen it glow blue—or had he? Was it wishful thinking? Was his faith nothing but wishful thinking?

Nikol's hand closed over his. "There, you see, Michael? You don't believe. . . ."

"The Disks of Mishakal," he said desperately. "If we could only find those, I could prove to you—" Prove to myself, he said silently, and in that moment admitted for the first time that he, too, was beginning to lose his faith.

"Disks of Mishakal? What are these" Lord Soth asked.

Michael was reluctant to answer.

"They are holy tablets of the gods," the cleric said finally. "I . . . hoped to find the answers on them."

"Where are these disks?"

"Why do you want to know?" Michael asked, growing daring.

The shadows deepened around him. He felt Soth's anger, the anger of pride and arrogance at being questioned, his will thwarted. The knight controlled his anger, however, though Michael senses it took great effort.

"These holy disks could be my salvation," Soth stated.

"But how? If you don't believe—"

"Let the gods prove themselves to me!" said the knight proudly. "Let them do so by lifting this curse and granting me freedom from my eternal torment!"

This is all wrong, Michael thought, confused and unhappy. Yet, in his words, I hear an echo of my own.

"The disks are in the great library," said Nikol, seeing that Michael would not reply. "We would have gone to look for them, but the library is in peril from the mobs. We travel to the High Clerist's Tower to warn the knights, that they may ride to Palanthas, quell this uprising, and restore peace and justice."

To their horror and astonishment, Lord Soth began to laugh—terrible laughter that seemed to come from places of unfathomable darkness. "You have traveled far and seen many dreadful sights," said the knight, "but you have yet to see the worst. I wish you luck!"

Turning the head of his wraithlike steed, he vanished into the shadows.

"My lord! What do you mean?" cried Nikol.

"He's gone," said Michael.

The darkness lifted from his heart; the icy chill of death retreated; the warmth of life flowed through his body.

"Let's leave this place swiftly," he said.

"Yes, I agree," Nikol murmured.

She went to lift the waterskin, hesitated, loathe to touch it, fearful, perhaps, of the death's knight return. Then, resolute, face pale, lips set, she picked it up. "He has been cruelly wronged," she said, flashing Michael a glance, daring him to disagree.

He said nothing. The silence became a wall between them, separated them the rest of the way up the mountain.

Part VI

The Tower of the High Clerist was an imposing structure, its central tower rising some one thousand feet into the air. Tall battlements, connected by a curtain wall, surrounded it. Michael had never seen any building this strong, this impregnable. He could now well believe the claim made by Nikol that the "tower had never fallen to an enemy while knights defended it with honor."

Both stopped, stared at it, overcome with awe.

"I have never been here," said Nikol. The lingering horror of the meeting with the undead knight had faded; her lingering anger at Michael was all but forgotten. She gazed on the legendary stronghold with shining eyes. "My father described it to Nicholas and me often. I think I could walk it blindfolded. There is the High Lookout, there the Nest of the Kingfisher—the knight's symbol. We planned to come here, Nicholas and I. He said a man was never truly a knight until he had knelt to pray in the chapel of the High Clerist's Tower—"

She lowered her head, blinked back her tears.

"You will kneel there for him," said Michael.

"Why?" she demanded, regarding him coldy. "Who will be there to listen?"

She walked up the broad, wide road that led to one of several entrances into the fortress. Michael followed after, troubled, uneasy. The tower was strangely quiet. No guards walked the battlements, as he might have expected. No lights shone from the windows, though the sun had long since sunk behind the mountains, bringing premature night to the tower and its environs.

Nikol, too, appeared to find this silence, this lack of activity odd, for she slowed her walk. Tilting back her head to try to see through the gloom, she started to hail the tower. Her call was cut off.

Cloaked and hooded figures surged out of the night. Skilled hands laid hold of Michael, swiftly relieved him of his staff, pinned his arms behind his back. He struggled in his captors' grasp, not so much to free himself, since he knew that was impossible, but to try to keep sight of Nikol. She had disappeared behind a wall of bodies. He heard the ring of steel against steel.

"You are a prisoner of the Knights of Solamnia. Yield yourself," said a harsh voice, speaking in the crude trade tongue.

"You lie!" Nikol cried, answering in Solamnic. "Since when do true knights move in the shadows and ambush people in the darkness?"

"We move in the dark because these are days of darkness." Another man approached, emerging from the gate leading into the High Clerist's Tower. More men followed after him.

Torchlight flared, half blinding Michael. Its light shone on polished armor, steel helms, and, beneath the helms, the long, flowing moustaches that were the knights' hallmark. One man, the one who'd answered Nikol, wore on his shoulder a ribbon. Once bright, it was now somewhat frayed and discolored. Michael had lived among knights long enough to recognize by this insignia a lord knight, one who commands in time of war.

"What have we here?"

"Spies, I believe, my lord," answered one of Michael's captors.

"Bring the torches closer. Let me take a look."

Michael's guard escorted him to the front. The knights were efficient, but not rough, according him a measure of respect even as they let him know who was in charge.

Nikol looked somewhat daunted at the sight of the lord knight, but she flushed angrily at the charge.

"We are not spies!" she said through clenched teeth. Remaining on guard, she used the flat of her blade to strike out at any who came near her.

The knights outnumbered her, could have taken her, but that would have meant unnecessary bloodshed. They glanced at the lord knight for orders.

He walked over to her, held the light to shine upon her. "Why, it is but a beardless youth, yet one who wields a sword with a man's skill, it seems," he added, looking at a companion, who was wiping blood from a cut cheek. Frowning, he studied the sword in Nikol's hand. The lord knight's face hardened. "How did you come by such a weapon and this armor that belongs to a Knight of the Crown? Stolen from the body of a gallant knight, no doubt. If you thought to sell it to us for your own gain, you have made a mistake that will prove costly. You will end up paying—with your life!"

"I did not steal it! I carry it by—" Nikol paused. She had started to say she carried it by right, but the thought occurred to her that she did not have the right to bear the arms of a true knight. Flushing, she amended her words. "My father is Sir David of Whitsund, now deceased. My twin brother, Nicholas, who is also dead, was a Knight of the Crown. This sword is his, as is the armor. I took them from his body—"

"And she put them on and cut her hair and bravely defended the castle and those of us within it," struck in Michael.

"And who are you?" The lord knight glowered at Michael.

"Perhaps that false cleric from Palanthas, my lord," said a knight. "See, he wears the holy symbol of Mishakal."

The lord knight barely spared Michael a glance, turned to stare at Nikol.

"*She*?" the lord knight repeated. He stepped forward, scrutinized Nikol's features, then fell back, his gaze traveling swiftly over her body. "By Paladine, the false cleric speaks the truth. This is a *woman*!"

"Michael is not a false cleric," Nikol began angrily.

"We will deal with him later," said the lord knight. "You have yourself to explain first."

Biting her lip, her face stained crimson, Nikol looked irresolute. Michael guessed at the struggle within her breast. She had lived the Oath and the Measure, fought evil, defended the innocent. She had come to think of herself as a knight. Yet, by the Measure, she knew she was in the wrong. Kneeling on one knee before the lord knight, she presented her sword hilt-first, over her arm, as was correct for a knight, when yielding to one superior in rank or to a victor in a tournament.

"I have broken the law. Forgive me, my lord."

Nikol was pale and grave, but she held her head proudly. She did not kneel from shame, but out of respect.

The lord knight's face remained stern and cold. Reaching out, he took hold of the sword she offered him and tried to remove it from her grasp. She let it go reluctantly. Not since her brother's death had anyone other than herself handled his blade.

"You did indeed break the Measure, Daughter, which prohibits the hand of a woman from wielding the blade of a true knight. We will take into consideration the fact that you came to us of your own free will, to surrender yourself—"

"Surrender? No, I have not, my lord!" Nikol stated. Rising to her feet, she shifted her gaze, which had been fixed wistfully on the sword, to the lord knight's granite face. "I have come to warn you. That false cleric, of whom you speak, is rousing citizens to violence against the great library! Tomorrow they threaten to burn it, and all the knowledge it holds, to the ground."

Nikol looked from one to the other, expecting shock, action, expressions of outrage. No one moved, no one said a word. The knights didn't even seem surprised. Their faces grew more grim and rigid, and dark lines deepened.

"Am I correct in understanding that you did not come here to ask forgiveness for your crime, Daughter?" the lord knight said.

Nikol stared at him.

"You . . . What . . . *My* crime? Didn't you hear what I just said, my lord? The great library is in danger! Not only that, but the city of Palanthas itself could fall into the hands of this evil man and his henchmen!"

"What happens in Palanthas is none of our concern, Daughter," said the lord knight.

"None of your concern? How can you say that?"

"Many of these men came from Palanthas, as did I myself. The people drove us out. They attacked our homes, threatened our families, My own lady died at the hands of the mob."

"Yet," said Michael quietly, "by the Measure, Sir Knight, you are bound in Paladine's name to protect the innocent—"

"Innocent!" The lord knight's eyes flashed. "If the city of Palanthas burns to the ground, it will be no more than the rabble deserve! Paladine, in his righteous wrath, has turned his face from them. Let the Dark Queen take them and be damned!"

"The wrath of the gods has fallen upon all of us," said Michael. "How can any of us say we didn't deserve it?"

"Blasphemy!" thundered the lord knight, and he struck Michael across the face.

He staggered beneath the blow. Putting his hand to his cut lip, he saw his fingers stained with blood.

The lord knight turned to Nikol. "The blasphemer will not be allowed within our walls. You, Daughter, since you are the child of a knight, may stay here in the fortress, safe from harm. You will remove your armor, turn it over to us, then you will spend night and day on your knees in the chapel, begging forgiveness of the father and the brother whose memories you disgrace."

Nikol went livid, as if she'd been run through by her own sword, then hot blood flooded her cheeks.

"I'm not the one who disgraced the knighthood. You! You're the disgrace!" Her gaze flashed around at the knights. "You hide away from the world, whining to Paladine about the injustice of it all. He doesn't answer you, does he? You've lost your powers and you're scared!"

Moving swiftly, she reached out, grabbed hold of her sword, wrested it from the lord knight before he knew what was happening. Lifting her weapon, she fell back, on guard.

"Seize her!" the lord knight ordered.

The knights drew their swords, began to close in.

"Hold," came a deep voice.

A blast of bitterly cold wind blew out the torches, chilled flesh and blood. Swords fell from numb hands, clattered to the ground with a hollow sound that was like a death knell. The knights' faces went stark white beneath their helms. Their eyes widened in horror at the sight of the terrible apparition riding down upon them.

"The Knight of the Black Rose!" cried one, in panic.

"Paladine forfend!" shouted the lord knight, raiding his hand in a warding gesture.

Lord Soth laughed, a sound like the grinding of rocks in a mountain slide. He reined in his nightmare steed, regarded the knights cowering before him with scorn.

"This woman is far more worthy than any of you to wield the sword and wear the armor of a knight. She stood up to me. She faced me, unafraid. What will you do, noble knights all? Will you fight me?"

The knights hesitated, cast terrified, questioning glances at their leader. The lord's face was yellow, like old bone.

"They are all in league with the Queen of Darkness!" he shouted. "Retreat, for the sake of your souls!"

The knights picked up their swords. Massing around their leader, they fell back until they had reached the massive wooden doors, which opened wide to let them in. Once inside, the doors slammed and the portcullis rang down.

The High Clerist's Tower stood dark and silent, as if it were empty.

Part VII

Nikol and Michael spent the night in a cave they found in the mountains. Huddled together for warmth, they slept only fitfully. Again they had the feeling they were being watched. Both were up with the dawn, made haste to return to Palanthas, though what they would do when they arrived was open to question.

"If we can only find the holy disks, then all will be put right," Michael said more than once.

"We can warn Astinus about the library's danger," said Nikol. "And we can take the Disks of Mishakal to safety."

"Take them to Lord Soth, don't you mean?" Michael asked her quietly.

"He saved us at the tower. We are in his debt. If I can end his torment, I will. *He* is a true knight," she added, casting a sad and wistful look back up into the mountains. "I know it in my heart."

Michael said nothing. Soth had saved them, but for their sake or his own? Had he been cursed unjustly or had his dread fate been forged by his own evil passions? Michael could only repeat what had become a litany: the blessed disks would make everything clear, everything right again.

Neither wayfarer was overly concerned at the thought of reentering the city. Having seen the confusion at the main gate, they doubted if the guards would even remember they were supposed to be looking for a beardless knight and blue-robed cleric. They timed their arrival for midday, when the traffic should be at its peak.

But, when they reached Palanthas, they found the road before the city empty, its gates standing wide open.

Alarmed at the sudden and inexplicable change, they ducked into the same grove of stunted trees, waited, and watched.

"Something's definitely wrong," said Nikol, eyeing the city walls. "I haven't seen one guard go past on his rounds. Come on," She buckled on her sword, wrapped her cloak around her. "We're going inside."

No beggars accosted them. No guard hailed them. No one challenged them or demanded to know their business within the city. The walls were deserted, the streets empty. The only living being they saw was a mongrel dog, trotting past with a head hen in its mouth, having taken advantage of the situation to raid an unguarded chicken coop.

They hurried through the merchandising district of New City, the streets of which should have been filled with people at this time of day. Stalls were closed. Shop windows were barred and shuttered.

"It looks like a city preparing for a holiday," said Michael

"Or a war," Nikol said grimly. She walked with her hand on the hilt of her sword. "Look. Look at that."

One of the shops was not closed. It had been destroyed, its windows smashed. The shop's goods—gaily colored silks from the elven lands of Qualinesti—lay strewn about the streets. Ugly epitaphs had been scrawled across the walls, written in blood. Lying in front of the shop was the body of an elven woman. Her throat had been cut. A dead child lay beside her.

"May the gods forgive them," murmured Michael.

"I trust your disks can explain this," Nikol said bitterly.

They continued on, passing other sites of senseless destruction, other wanton acts of violence. Palanthas itself may have escaped the ravages of the Cataclysm, but the souls of its people had been cracked and shattered.

It was at the Old City wall that they first heard the sound of the mob, the sound of a thousand people gone mad, a thousand people finding anonymity in their numbers, driven to commit crimes one alone would have been ashamed to consider. The noise was frightful, inhuman. It prickled the hair on Michael's neck, sent a shiver down his spine.

Smoke boiled up from beyond the walls of Old City. Under its cover, Michael and Nikol slipped through the gates without attracting anyone's attention. Reaching the other side, they came to a halt, stared in disbelief. Nothing, not the sight of the destruction, not the tumult that raged around them, prepared them for what they saw.

Several large and beautiful houses had been set ablaze and were burning furiously. Large crowds dances drunkenly in front of the fires, cheering and waving bottles and other, more gruesome, trophies. But the largest concentration of the mob was farther on, gathered around the great library.

Here the crowd was more or less hushed, heads craning to see and hear. A voice rose, exhorting them to further acts of terror. Nikol climbed a drainpipe that ran up the side of a house, and stood on the roof to gain a better view.

"The Revered Son is on the library stairs," she reported on her return. "His men are with him. They're armed with clubs and axes and carrying torches. He's—" Her words were drowned out by a roar that set the windows rattling.

"We must get inside the library!" Michael was forced to shout to be heard over the clamor. He was starting to feel panicked. The idea that the holy disks might fall victim to this unholy chaos appalled him.

"I have an idea!" Nikol shouted in return, then motioned him to follow her. They slipped past on the fringes of the crowd, ducked down an alleyway, ran its length. Reaching the end, they stopped, peered out cautiously. They stood directly opposite one of the library's semidetached wings. The mob, intent upon hearing the speaker, blocked the front, but not the sides, of the building.

"We can climb in through the windows," said Nikol.

They headed for the ornamental grove of trees, the same grove that had provided them shelter the last time they were here. Keeping to the shadows, they trampled on dead, unkempt flower beds and shoved through the hedges, once clipped, now left to grow wild. A narrow strip of open lawn stood between them and the library. Breaking free of their cover, they ran across the well-kept grass, came to a window on the ground level. They flattened themselves against the building, trying to keep out of sight of the mob.

"The window's probably guarded," said Michael.

Nikol risked peeping over the ledge. "I don't see anyone, not even the Book Readers," she added, using a common slang term that referred to the Order of Aesthetics, followers of the god Gilean who devoted their lives to the gathering and preserving of knowledge.

Nevertheless, she drew her sword from its sheath. "Quickly!" whispered Nikol.

A blow from Michael's staff broke the window, knocking down fragments of glass. Nikol clambered through, kept her sword raised. She stared about intently. Seeing no one, she reached back to help Michael.

He climbed inside, came to a halt. He had heard all his life about the great library, but he'd never seen it, and this was beyond anything he could have imagined. A vast room held row after row of bookshelves, each shelf filled with neatly arranged, lovingly dusted, leather-bound volumes. His heart yearned, suddenly, for the wisdom stored within these walls, ached to think that all this irreplaceable knowledge was in such dire danger.

"Michael!" Nikol called a warning.

A robed monk, wielding a sword, had crept out from the shadows of one of the bookcases, stood blocking the Aesthetic. "Don't . . . don't m-m-move."

The monk was thinner than the heavy, antique, two-handed broadsword he was trying his best to hold. His face was chalk-colored, sweat ran down his bald head, and he shook so that his teeth clicked together. But, though obviously frightened out of his wits, he was grimly standing his ground. Nikol had been about to laugh. She remembered the brutal mob, their hands already stained with blood, and her laughter changed to a sigh.

"Here," she said, stepping forward, accosting the terrified monk, who stared at her, wide-eyed. "You're holding that sword all wrong." Wrenching the poor man's hands loose from the weapon, she repositioned them. "This hand here, and this hand here. There. Now you have a chance of hurting someone besides yourself."

"Th-thank you," murmured the monk, gazing at the weapon and Nikol in perplexity. Suddenly, he brought the sword, point-first, to her throat. "Now . . . I s-s-suggest you . . . leave."

"For the love of Paladine! We're on *your* side," said Nikol in exasperation, shoving the wavering blade away from her. Outside they could hear the mob raise its voice in response to the Revered Son's harangues.

"We want to help you," Michael said, coming forward. "We don't have much time. We're looking for the disks—"

"What is going on in here, Malachai?" questioned a stern voice. "I heard glass breaking."

A robed man who seemed old, but whose face was unlined, smooth, and devoid of expression, entered the library room. Calm and unruffled, he walked down the aisle between the bookcases.

"They . . . broke in, M-master," the monk gasped.

The man's stern gaze shifted to the couple. "You are responsible for this?" he said, indicating the broken window.

"Well, yes, Master," answered Michael, astonished to feel his skin burning in shame. "Only because we couldn't get in the front."

"We don't mean any harm," said Nikol. "You must believe us. We'd like to help, in fact, Master—"

"Astinus," said the man coolly. "I am Astinus. Did I hear you say you were searching for the Disks of Mishakal?" His gaze went to Michael's breast.

The cleric had been careful to hide the medallion beneath his robes, but this man's ageless eyes seemed able to penetrate the cloth.

"The *true* clerics have all departed Krynn," observed Astinus, frowning.

"I was given the chance," said Michael defensively. "I chose to stay. I could not leave—"

"Yes, yes. It is all recorded. You've come for the disks. This—"

A howl rose from the mob outside. Shouts of anger and rage surged up against the library walls like the pounding of a monstrous sea. The monk, hearing that terrible sound, seemed likely to faint. He was sucking in breath in great gulps. His eyes were white-rimmed and huge.

"Sit down, Malachai. Put your head between your knees," advised Astinus. "And for the gods' sake drop that sword before you slice off your toe. When you feel better, fetch a broom and sweep up this glass. Someone could get cut. Now, if you two will come with me—"

Nikol stared at the man. "You daft old fool! Listen to that! They're out for blood! *Your* blood! You should be preparing for your defense! Look, we can barricade these windows. We'll overturn these bookcases, then shove them up against—"

"Overturn the bookcases!" Astinus thundered, his placid calm finally disturbed. "Are you mad, young woman? These hold thousands of volumes, catalogued according to date and place. Do you realize how long it would take us to put every volume back in its proper position? No to mention the damage you might do to some of the older texts. The binding is fragile. And the method of making paper was not as advanced—"

"They're about to burn you to the ground, old man!" Nikol shouted back. "You're not going to have anything *left* to catalogue!"

Astinus pointedly ignored Nikol, shifted his gaze to Michael. "You, Cleric of Mishakal, are, I take it, not here to overturn bookcases?"

"No, Master," said Michael hurriedly.

"Very well. You may come with me." Astinus turned, started to leave.

"Pardon, Master," Michael said meekly, "if my wife could accompany us . . ."

"Will she behave herself?" Astinus demanded, regarding Nikol dubiously.

"She will," said Michael. "Put your sword away, dear."

"You're all mad!" muttered Nikol, staring from one to the other.

Michael lifted his eyebrows. "Humor the old man," he said silently.

Nikol sighed, slid her sword in its sheath. The monk, Malachai, was sitting on the floor, his hand still clasped over the hilt of the sword.

Astinus led them out of the room, into the main portion of the library. He walked at a leisurely, unhurried pace, pointing out this section and that as they passed. Outside they could hear the mob gathering its courage. Smoke, drifting in through the broken window, hung ominously in the still air.

Michael moved as if in a dream. Nothing seemed real. Inside the library, all was as quiet, calm, and unperturbed as Astinus himself. Occasionally, they caught sight of some monk running down a hallway, a scared look on his face, some precious volume clutched in his arms. At the sight of the master, however, the monk would skid to a halt. Eyes lowered before Astinus's frown, the monk would proceed at a decorous walk.

They passed from what Astinus said were the public reading rooms, through a small hallway, up two flights of stairs, into the private section of the library. Here, at high desks, perched on tall stools, some of the Aesthetics sat at their work, pens scratching, a ghastly counterpoint to the roaring outside. But a few had left their work, were clustered in a frightened knot at one of the windows, staring down at the mob below.

"What is the meaning of this?" Astinus barked.

Caught, the monks cast swift, apologetic glances at the master and hastened back to their seats. Pens scratched diligently. Work resumed.

Astinus walked among them, eyes darting this way and that. Pausing beside one pale-faced older man, the master of the library stared down at the manuscript, pointed.

"That is a blot, Johann."

"Yes, Master. I'm sorry, Master."

"What is the meaning of that blot, Johann?"

"I—I'm afraid, Master. Afraid we're all going to die!"

"If we do, I trust it will be neatly. Start the page over."

"Yes, Master."

The Aesthetic removed the offending sheet, slid a clean one in its place. He bent to his task, but, Michael, noticed, the monk's fear had eased. He was actually smiling. If Astinus could be concerned over blots at a time like this, surely there was no danger—that's what he was telling himself.

Michael would have liked to believe that as well, but more and more he was becoming convinced that the master of the library was either drunk or insane or perhaps both.

They left the main library, entered what Astinus termed the living area. He guided them through long hallways, past the small, comfortless cells where the monks resided.

"My study," said Astinus, ushering them into a small, book-lined room that contained a desk, a char, a rug, a lamp, and nothing else. "I rarely permit visitors, but today I will make an exception, since you seem unduly disturbed by the noise in the streets. You"—he indicated Michael—"may sit in the chair. You"—he glowered at Nikol—"stand by the door and touch nothing. Do you understand? Touch nothing! I will be back shortly."

"Where are you going?" Nikol demanded.

He stared at her, face frozen.

"Master," she added in a more respectful tone.

"You asked for the Disks of Mishakal," said Astinus, and left.

"At last!" Michael said, sitting in the chair, glad to rest. "Soon we'll have the disks and the answers—"

"If we live long enough to read them," Nikol stated angrily. She left her place by the door, began pacing the small room, waving her hands. "That old man is a fool! He'll let himself and these poor, wretched monks be butchered, his precious library torn down around his ears. When we get the disks, Michael, we'll take them and leave. And if that old man tries to stop us, I'll—"

"Nikol," said Michael, awed. "Look . . . look at this."

"What?" She stopped her pacing, startled by the odd tone of his voice. "What is it?"

"A book," said Michael, "left open, here, on the desk."

"Michael, this is no time to be reading!"

"Nikol," he said softly, "it's about Lord Soth."

"What does it say?" she cried, leaning over to him. "Tell me!"

Michael read the text silently to himself.

"Well?" Nikol demanded, impatient.

He looked up at her. "He's a murderer, Nikol, and worse. It's all here. How he fell in love with a young elven maid, a virgin priestess. He carried her off to Dargaard Keep, then murdered his first wife, to have her out of the way."

"Lies!" Nikol cried, white-lipped. "I don't believe it! No

true knight would break his vows like that! No true knight would do such a monstrous thing!"

"Yet, one did, " came a deep voice.

Lord Soth stood in the room.

Part VIII

Michael, trembling, rose to his feet. Nikol turned to face the knight. Her hand went to her sword, but fell, nerveless, at her side. The accursed knight's chill pervaded the small room. His flame-eyes were fixed, not on the two who stood before him, but upon the book.

"That tells my story?" Soth asked, gesturing with his gloved hand to the book on the table.

"Yes," Michael answered faintly. Nikol fell back, to stand by his side.

"Turn the book toward me, that I may read it," Soth ordered.

Hands shaking, Michael did as he ordered, shifting the heavy, enormous volume around for the death knight to view. An awful darkness filled the room, doused the lamp-light, grew deeper and darker as time passed. The only light was the burning of the flame-eyes, which did not read, so much as devour, each page. Michael and Nikol drew near each other, clasped each other tightly by the hand.

"You did these terrible deeds?" Nikol asked, her voice as small and unhappy as a child's, whose dream has been shattered. "You murdered . . ."

The blazing eyes lifted; their gaze pierced her heart.

"For love. I did it for love."

"Not love," Michael said, the warmth of Nikol's touch giving him strength. "Lust, dark desire, but not love. She—the elven maid—she hated you for it, when she found out, didn't she?"

"She loved me!" Soth's fist clenched in anger. He glanced down at the page. His hand slowly relaxed. "She hated what I had done. She prayed for me. And her prayer was answered. I was to be given the power of stopping the Cataclysm. I was on my way to do so, when I stopped at your castle, Lady."

The deep voice was sad, filled with regret, a bitter sorrow that wrung the heart. The darkness deepened until they could see nothing except the flaming eyes, the reflection of their fire in the charred and blackened armor. The noise of the mob faded away, became nothing more than the keening of the wind.

"And I turned aside, as it says here." Soth gestured at the flame-lighted page. "But it was Paladine who tempted me to do so. Elven priestesses, enamored of the Kingpriest, told me that the woman I loved was unfaithful. The child she had borne was not mine. Wounded pride, soul-searing jealousy, overwhelmed me, drove me to abandon my quest. I rode back, accused my love, falsely accused her. . . . The Cataclysm struck. My castle fell. She died in the fire . . . and so did I.

"But not to stay dead!" Soth's mailed fist clenched again. His anger flared. "I awoke to endless torment, eternal pain! Free me, Cleric. You can. You must. You are a true cleric."

He stretched out his ghostly hand to the medallion. "The goddess has blessed you."

"Yet she does not bless you," said Michael, the words falling from fear-numbed lips. "You lied to us, my lord. The gods did not curse you unjustly, as you would have had us believe. All the evil passions that led you to disgrace and downfall are still alive within you."

"You dare speak so to me? You dare defy me? Wretched mortal! I could slay you with a word!" Soth's finger hovered near Michael's heart. One touch of that death-chilled hand, and the heart would burst.

"You could," Michael answered, "but you won't. You won't kill me for speaking the truth. I hear your regret, my lord. I hear your sorrow. Better feelings within you war with the dark passions. If you were wholly given over to evil, my lord, you would not care. You would not suffer."

"Bitter comfort you offer me, Cleric," Soth sneered.

"It could be your redemption," Michael said softly.

Soth stood long moments in silence. Slowly, his hand lowered. It went to the book, lying on the table. The fingers followed the words, as though the death knight were reading them again. Michael clasped the medallion in one hand, Nikol's hand in the other. Neither spoke. Not that it would have mattered. The death knight seemed unaware of their presence. When he spoke, it was not to them.

"No!" he cried suddenly, lifting his head, his voice to the heavens. "You tempted me, then treated me unjustly when I fell! I will *not* ask your forgiveness. It is you who should ask mine!"

Flames sprang up, engulfing the page, the book, seemed likely to set fire to the room. Michael fell back with a cry, shielding Nikol with his body, his hand raised to ward off the searing heat.

"*What* is the meaning of this?"

Astinus's voice fell over them like cool water, doused the flames in an instant. Michael lowered his hand, blinked, staring through an afterimage of fiery red that momentarily blinded him.

Lord Soth was gone; in his place stood the library's master.

"I cannot let you two out of my sight a moment, it seems," stated Astinus coldly.

"But, Master. Didn't you see him?" Michael gasped, pointed. "Lord—"

Nikol dug her nails into his arm. "Tell this old fool nothing!" she whispered urgently. "Forgive us, Master," she said aloud. "Have you brought the Disks of Mishakal?"

"No," said Astinus. "They are not here. They have never been here. They will never be here."

"But . . ." Michael glared at the man. "You said you went to get them . . ."

"I said you wanted them. I did not say I would get them," Astinus replied with calm. "I went to open the doors."

"The great doors! The doors to the library!" Nikol gasped. "You . . . opened them! You're mad! Now there's nothing to stop the mob from entering!"

"At least," said Astinus, "they will not harm the woodwork."

The rising clamor of the mob was much louder than before. They were chanting, "Burn the books, burn the books, burn the books!"

Michael looked at the book on the table. It was whole, unharmed. The fire had not touched it. He stared at Astinus and thought he saw the tiniest hint of a smile flicker on his stern lips.

"You two can escape out the back," said the master.

"We should," said Nikol, regarding him with scorn. Shoving past Michael, she drew her sword, started for the door. "We should leave you to the mob, old man, but there are others here besides you, and, by the Oath and the Measure, I'm bound to protect the innocent, the defenseless."

"You are not bound. You are not a knight, young woman," said Astinus testily.

Nikol, however, had already gone. They could hear her booted footsteps racing down the hall. And they could hear, as well, the rising tumult of thousands. Michael took hold of his staff, set out after Nikol. As he passed Astinus, who continued to regard him with that faint smile, Michael paused.

"'This woman is far more worthy than any of you to wield the sword and wear the armor of a knight,' he quoted, pointing back at the book that stood upon the desk. "Soth said that. You can read it here."

He bowed to Astinus and left to join Nikol in death.

****

The mob had been astonished to see the master open the great doors that led into the Library of Palanthas. For a moment, the sight of Astinus, standing framed in the doorway, even curbed the loquacity of the Revered Son, who certainly had never expected such a thing. His jaw went slack. He stared foolishly at the master, who not only opened the doors, but also bowed silently to the people before leaving.

Then Nikol appeared. Alone, she advanced to stand before the great doors.

"Astinus asked me to tell you," she called, spreading her hands in a gesture of welcome, "that the library is always open to the public. The wisdom of ages is yours. If you enter, do so with respect. Lay down your weapons."

The cruelest, most murderous villain in the crowd could not help but applaud such courage. And most of the people were not murderers or villains, but ordinary citizens, tired of fighting poverty and disease and misfortune, seeking to place the blame for their problems on someone else. They looked ashamed of what they'd done, what they'd been about to do. More than a few began to slink away.

The Revered Son realized he was losing them.

"Yes, it's open to the public!" he shouted. "Go inside! Read about the gods who brought this misery upon you! Read about the elves, the favored of the gods, who are living well while your starve! Read about the knights!" He pointed at Nikol. "Even now, they feed off your misery!"

The people stopped, exchanged glances, and looked uncertain. The Revered Son sent a swift glance at the leader of his henchmen, who nodded. A stone hurtled from the crowd, struck Nikol on her shoulder. Hitting her breastplate, the stone knocked her back a step but did no harm.

"Cowards!" Nikol cried, drawing her sword. "Come and fight me face-to-face."

But that is not the way of a mob. A second stone followed the first. This one hit its mark, struck her on the forehead. Nikol reeled, dazed from the blow, and fell upon one knee. Blood streamed down her face. At the sight, the crowd howled in glee, excited. The henchmen, shouting, urged them on. Nikol staggered to her feet, faced them alone, glittering steel in her hand.

****

Michael saw her fall. He started toward the door, to her. A hand clapped over his shoulder.

The touch chilled him to the very marrow of his bones, drove him to his knees. Looking up into fiery eyes, Michael stifled a gasp of pain, knowing that the touch, if the knight had wanted, could have killed him.

"The book will remain here forever—for all to read?" Lord Soth asked.

"Yes, my lord," Michael answered.

Soth nodded slowly. It had not been a question, so much as a reaffirmation. "I cannot be saved, but perhaps my story can save someone else."

The flame-eyes seemed to burn clear for a moment in what might have been a smile. "Ironic, isn't it, Cleric? Two false knights defending the truth." He let go his hold, turned, and walked out the library doors.

****

The mob surged forward. Men came at Nikol with clubs raised. She struck out at the leader, had the pleasure of seeing him fall back with a cry, clapping his hand over a broken, bleeding arm. For a moment, the rest held back, daunted, fearful of the gleaming steel. Then someone threw another rock. It struck Nikol on her hand, knocked the sword from her grasp.

The mob gave an exultant shout, rushed at her. She tried to reach her weapon, beating those nearest her back with fists, kicking and gouging, knowing all the time she must fall.

She heard Michael shout her name, turned her head, tried to find him, then she was hit from behind. Pain exploded in her brain. She stumbled to her knees, weak, unable to rise.

A shadow fell over her. Someone was standing at her back. Someone was helping her to her feet. Someone had retrieved her sword, was handing it to her. Wiping away blood, she peered through mists of pain and failing consciousness.

A Knight of Solamnia stood beside her. His armor shone silver in the sunlight. His crest fluttered bravely in the wind. His sword gleamed, argent flame, in his strong hand. With respect and reverence, he lifted his sword to her in the knight's salute, then he turned and faced the mob.

Nikol put her back against his, did the same. At least now she would not die alone, without making one last, glorious stand for the honor of the knights. True knights . . .

Nikol blinked, stared in dazed astonishment, unable to comprehend what was happening. She and the knight were outnumbered a thousand to one, yet the mob was not yet attacking. Faces that had been contorted in bloodlust were now twisted in horror. Curses and threats shrilled to terrified shrieks. Men who had been racing up the library stairs were tumbling over themselves and each other in a panicked race back down.

The Revered Son was among the first to flee, running for his life, driven by such stark terror that it seemed likely he would stop running only when he reached the Newsea.

Nikol's sword was suddenly too heavy for her to hold. It slid from her grasp. She was tired, so tired. She sank to the stone steps, wanting only to sleep. Strong arms took hold of her, gathered her close.

"Nikol!" a voice cried. "Beloved!"

She opened her eyes, saw only Michael's face, illuminated by a soft blue light.

"Is the library . . . safe?" she asked.

Michael nodded, unable to speak for his grief and fear for her.

Nikol smiled. "Cowards," she murmured. "They dared not stand and fight a true knight."

"No," said Michael, through his tears, "they dared not."

Blue light surrounded her, soothed her. She slept.

Part IX

"Are you certain you are well enough to travel, my lady?" The young Aesthetic, Malachai, gazed at Nikol anxiously. "You were grievously hurt."

"Yes, I'm fine," said Nikol, with a hint or irritation.

"My dear . . ." Michael reprimanded gently.

Nikol glanced at him, glanced at the young monk, who was looking downcast. She sighed. She detested being "fussed over."

"I'm sorry I snapped at you. You've all been very kind to me. I thank you for everything you've done," said Nikol.

"We would have done more, much more, but you seemed to be in good hands," Malachai said, with a smile for Michael. "I'll never forget that terrible day," he added, with a shudder. "Looking down from the window, seeing you standing beside that evil knight, so brave, so courageous—"

"What evil knight?" Nikol asked.

The Aesthetic flushed crimson, clapped his hand over his mouth. Casting a guilty look at Michael, Malachai made a brief, bobbing bow and scuttled from the tiny room.

"What was he talking about?" Nikol demanded. "There was no evil knight there. He was a Knight of the Rose. I saw him clearly."

"Astinus wants to see us, before we go," Michael said, turning from her. "Everything's packed. The Aesthetics have really been very kind. They've given us food, warm clothing, blankets—"

"Michael," Nikol came to stand in front of him, forcing him to face her. "What did that Book Reader mean?"

Michael took hold of her, held her tightly, thinking of how he'd almost lost her. "Lord Soth was the one who fought at your side, Beloved."

She stared at him. "No! That's not possible. I saw a knight, a true knight!"

"I think you saw the part of him that still struggles toward the light. Unfortunately, I think it is a part of him that few will ever see again." Michael added, with a sigh, "Now, come. We must bid farewell to Astinus."

****

The Aesthetics led them to the master's study. The ageless man with his expressionless face was hard at work, writing in a thick book. He did not glance up at their entry, but continued working. They stood for long moments in silence, then Nikol, growing bored and restless, walked over to look out the window.

Astinus lifted his head. "Young woman, you are standing in my light!"

Nikol jumped, flushed. "I beg your pardon—"

"Why are you here?" he asked.

"You sent for us, Master," Michael reminded him.

"Humpf." Carefully Astinus replaced his pen back in the inkwell. Folding his hands, he regarded the two impatiently.

"Well, go ahead. Ask your question. I'll have no peace until you do."

Michael stared. "How did you know I meant to ask—"

"Is that your question?"

'No, Master, it isn't, but—"

"Then out with it! Entire volumes of history are passing while you stand there yammering, wasting my time."

"Very well, Master. My question is this: Why were we directed here to search for the Disks of Mishakal when they are not here?"

"I beg your pardon," said Astinus. "I thought you came here searching for the answer."

"I came here searching for the disks that hold the answer," said Michael patiently. "I didn't find them."

"But did you find the answer?"

"I—" Michael stopped, taken aback. "Perhaps. . . . Well, yes, in a way."

"And that is?"

"Those people out there are searching for the answer.

Lord Soth was searching for his answer. The knights in the tower are searching for theirs. They were all looking, like we were, in the wrong place. The answer is here . . . in our hearts."

Astinus nodded, lifted his pen, delicately shook off a drop of ink. "And you discovered that without overturning my bookshelves. Gilean be praised."

"There is one more thing," said Nikol. She laid a bundle that clanked and rattled down on the floor in front of Astinus's desk. "Would one of your people see that this is returned to the knights in the High Clerist's Tower?"

"Your armor," said Astinus, still holding the pen poised above the inkwell. "Or should I say, your brother's armor. What's the matter? Ashamed of being thought a knight?"

"I am not!" Nikol retorted. "I would wear this armor with more pride than ever, but in the lands where we're planning to travel, the people don't use metal armor. They've never seen anything like it, in fact, and may be frightened."

"You are going to join up with the Plainsmen," Astinus said. He put his pen to paper, began to write. "Some of the few who still believe in the true gods. But, eventually, even their faith will weaken and diminish and die. Still, your mother will be glad to see you, Cleric."

Nikol stared. "His mother! How did you know—We never told anyone—"

Astinus made an impatient gesture. "If that is all the business you have with me, Malachai will see you out."

Michael and Nikol exchanged glances. "He's not even going to say thank you," Nikol whispered.

"For what?" Astinus growled.

Nikol only smiled, shook her head. Malachai waited for them at the door. The two turned to leave.

"Cleric," said Astinus, without pausing in his work.

"Yes, Master?"

"Keep searching."

"Yes, Master," said Michael, taking hold of Nikol's hand. "We will."

Afterword

Michael, cleric of Mishakal, and Nikol, daughter of a knight, left the city of Palanthas, never to return. They traveled south into the plains of Abanasinia. Here they joined a tribe of the nomadic Plainsmen.

A child of a child of a child of a child of Michael and Nikol would come to be called Wanderer—a man whose ancestors, so it was said, never lost faith in the true gods.

And Wanderer would have a grandson named Riverwind.

They Were Not Yet Famous

A flashback by Michael Williams

I first met Margaret and Tracy when my hair was dark and they were not yet famous.

I have known Tracy a little longer and Margaret a little better. But twenty years at least for each of them, and twenty years of the best of knowing. If invited to roast either of them, I'd be hard pressed for insults.

Then again, Tracy *has* had the same haircut for two decades. Looks basically the same, while Margaret looks better and better.

They both have portraits in their attics that are rotting away, you know. That's the price they pay for perpetual youth.

But back in the '80s, when the DRAGONLANCE setting was first taking shape, we were all perpetually young, with the excitement of this sprawling, magnificent project in front of us, and a group of our own Companions, ready and willing to bring a world to life.

Don't get me wrong: I think that credit has been apportioned fairly. Some of us contributed to the initial vision, but at the start it was Tracy's world, pure and simple.

I remember sitting on the third floor of some rickety building in Lake Geneva, the old designer/editor ward, so architecturally unsound that you could roll a marble into a room and watch it spiral on the floor in diminishing circles like some science experiment gone incredibly wrong.

Tracy had maps of Krynn even then—1982, unless I've been chronologically impaired by Jack Daniels. I remember seeing them in some kind of folder on his desk, and remember that my first reaction was, "Damn! It must have taken him a long time to do *those!* Bet he's glad to be finished with *that* project, whatever it is!"

Tracy was pure entertainment from the get-go. Had me laughing through the work day with his "Johnny Nylon / Trademark Cop" musical. I had never touched a computer until my first day at TSR, and when my screen went blank on my second day at work, he informed me soberly that I had "blown out all the computers east of the Mississippi." Had he said, "all the computers in Wisconsin"—narrowed his sights a little—I would probably still believe him.

Margaret was another story. We met each other more on . . . well, literary grounds. We liked a lot of the same writers, and as I recall, our first conversations were mainly about books. We intimidated each other, I found out later. She intimidated me because she was pretty, smart, and slated as the editor in charge of the DRAGONLANCE books. That was, of course, before she took on the even more daunting task of *writing* the blessed things!

I intimidated her because I wore red suspenders a lot. Don't ask me why I wore them (other than to keep my pants up), or why they intimidated her. They have never worked in my favor in other circumstances, but apparently they got her attention. It wasn't long into our acquaintance until I showed her some of my poetry. She told me that she dreaded reading it, but it ended up that she really liked it.

I'm glad she did. It was my ticket into this wonderful project. And you can blame Margaret Weis for the poetry and fiction I've inflicted on readers for a number of years now. I don't think it's an overstatement to say that I owe her my writing career.

Those first DRAGONLANCE meetings were pretty heady and contentious. Some of the names you've come to recognize in association with the series were there already—the amiable Doug Niles, Larry Elmore (who remains on my Top 10 list of people), Carl Smith, Jeff Grubb, Gali Sanchez. Others contributed as well, but those are the ones I remember. And spearheading the whole project was Tracy Hickman.

At this stage in our lives, I think I can finally confess to him that he was brilliant. If you have to serve someone else's creative vision, it is best done with someone who is first of all genuinely creative and visionary, but it also helps if that person is generous and kind. Tracy was all of that stuff. I continue to thank him and always will.

But that brilliance needed Margaret to breathe life into flesh, to give the vision form, to help create and shape the story that ultimately created and shaped the world. As our friendship progressed, I came to respect Margaret more and more deeply. She is a *daily* person—all of her talents focus amazingly in what needs to be done next. That's a great gift for a novelist, who, instead of indulging in a poet's sporadic flashes of passion and insight, carries on a sustained love affair with the world. She writes daily, she works out daily, and (I think) most importantly she attends daily to those around her.

I believe I've written this elsewhere, but it doesn't hurt to say it again: for all the talents I could praise in Margaret and Tracy, both have an extraordinary gift for friendship. It is the thing about them that I regard most highly and that their readers should know.

Known to some as the Bard of DRAGONLANCE, Michael Williams has written poetry for DRAGONLANCE games and books since its inception. He has also written or co-written eleven novels, five set in the world of Krynn and another five of his own devise. He is presently working on his twelfth book, a magical realist novel set in the 1960s Midwest.

The Story That Tasslehoff Promised He Would Never, Ever, Ever Tell

Margaret Weis and Tracy Hickman

Originally published in *Tales Vol. VI: The War of the Lance*

Chapter One

So I guess you're wondering why I'm telling you this, since I promised not to. I'm sure Tanis wouldn't mind, seeing that it's you. I mean, you've heard the other stories, all about the War of the Lance and the Heroes of the Lance (of which I, Tasslehoff Burrfoot, am one) and how ten years ago we defeated the Dark Queen and her dragons. This is just one more story, one that never was told. As to why it was never told, you'll find that out when I get around to the part about promising Fizban.

It all began about a month ago. I was traveling up the Vingaard River, heading for Dargaard Keep. You've heard the stories about Dargaard Keep, how it's cursed and Lord Soth is supposed to haunt it. I hadn't seen Lord Soth in a while—he's a death knight and while we're not exactly friends, he is what you might call a close personal acquaintance. I was thinking about him one night and how he very nearly killed me once. (I don't harbor a grudge; death knights have to do these things, you see.) And it occurred to me that he might be bored, what with having nothing to do for the past ten years, ever since we defeated the Dark Queen, except haunt people.

Anyway, I thought I'd go find Lord Soth and fill him in on Recent Events and maybe he'd glare at me with his fiery eyes, and make me go all wonderfully cold and shivery inside.

I was on my way to Dargaard Keep when I stopped over in a little town that I can show you on my map, though I can't remember the name. They have a very nice jail there. I know, because I was spending the night in it, having become involved in an argument with a butcher over a string of sausages that had followed me out of his shop.

I tried to point out to the butcher that they must be magical sausages, because I couldn't think of any other way they would have ended up trailing after me like that. I thought he'd be pleased, you know, to realize he had the power to make magical sausages. And if I did eat two of them, it was just to find out if they did anything magical in the stomach. (They did, but I don't think that counts as magic. I'll have to ask Dalamar.) To make a long story short, he was not pleased to hear he had magical sausages and I was taken away to jail.

Things have a way of working out, though, as my grandmother Burrfoot used to say. There were a whole lot of other kender in the jail. (Quite a remarkable coincidence, don't you think?) We had a very agreeable time together, and I caught up on all the news of Kendermore.

And I found out that someone had been looking for me!

He was a friend of a friend of a friend and he had an important message for me. Just think! An Important Message. Kender all over Ansalon had been told to give it to me if they ran into me. This was the Important Message.

"Meet me at the Silver Dragon Mountain during this anniversary. Signed, FB."

I must say that I thought the message a bit confused, and I still think it probably lost something over having been passed around by so many people. But my friends assured me that was exactly how they'd heard it or close enough as not to make any difference. I knew right off who FB was, of course, and you must too. (Tanis did. I could tell that from the groan he gave when I mentioned it.) And I knew where the Silver Dragon Mountain was. I'd been there before, with Flint and Laurana and Gilthanas and Theros Ironfeld and Silvara before we knew she was a silver dragon herself. You remember that story, don't you? Astinus wrote it all down and called it Dragons of Winter Night.

I was puzzling over this message and wondering what anniversary he was talking about, when the kender who gave it to me said that there was another part to it.

"Repeat the name Fizban backwards three times and clap your hands."

That sounded like magic to me and I am extremely fond of magic. But, knowing Fizban as I did, I thought it wise to take precautions. I told the other kender in the cell with me that this spell might be Quite Interesting and that maybe I should wait until we were all out of jail in the morning.

But the other kender said that, while it would be shame to blow up this nice jail, if I did blow it up, they didn't want to miss it. They all gathered around and I began.

"Nabzif, Nabzif, Nabzif!" I said quickly, kind of holding my breath, and I clapped my hands.

Poof!

Once I cleared away the smoke, I discovered I was holding a scroll. I unrolled it quickly, thinking it might be another spell, you see. But it wasn't. The other kender were considerably disappointed and rather miffed that I hadn't blown up either the jail or myself. They went back to comparing jails in other parts of Solamnia. I read what I was holding in my hands.

It turned out to be an invitation. At least I think that's what it was. It was hard to tell, what with all the burn holes and smudges and smears of what smelled like grape jelly.

The writing was very pretty and elaborate. I can't copy it, but this is what it said (I'm including smudges and blots):

A Celebration of the Tenth Anniversary of the
(Blot) *of the Dragonl*(smudge)
to be held at the
Silver Dragon Mountain
Yuletime.
Hero of the Lance
Your Presence is Most Earnestly Requested.
We Honor the Knight of Solamnia
Who First Did Battle with the (bob, blot),
Sir (smear and tarbean tea-stain)*ower*

It was signed *Lord Gunthar Uth Wistan.*

Well, of course, this explained everything (not counting the blots). The knights were holding a celebration in honor of something, probably the War of the Lance. And, since I'm one of the Heroes, I was invited! This was incredibly exciting. I put off my visit to Lord Soth (I hope he understands, if he reads this), let myself out of jail with a key I found in my pocket, and headed immediately for the Silver Dragon Mountain.

It used to be you couldn't find Silver Dragon Mountain, but after the War, the knights turned it into a Monument and fixed the roads so that they could get to it easier. They left the Ruined Keep ruined. I traveled past it and wandered through the Wood of Peace awhile, then I stopped to admire the hot springs that boil just like Tika's tea kettle and I crossed the bridge where I saw the statues that looked like my friends, only they were just statues now. Probably because of the Monument. And then I came to Foghaven Vale.

Foghaven Vale has a lot to do with the rest of my story, so I'll tell you about it, in case you've forgotten from the last time I was there.[1] The Hot Springs mixing with the water of the Cool Lake makes fog so thick that it's hard to see your

1. *Dragons of Winter Night*, DRAGONLANCE Chronicles, Volume 2. Available in the Library at Palanthas, which is a very nice city to visit, especially since they've cleaned up after the dragons. The library is one block south and two east of the jail. You can't miss it.

topknot in front of your nose. No one used to know where this Vale was, a long time ago, except Silvara and the other silver dragons, who guarded Huma's Tomb, the final resting place of a truly great knight from long, long ago. His tomb is there, only he isn't.

At the north end of Foghaven Vale stands Silver Dragon Mountain. You can get into the mountain through a secret tunnel inside Huma's Tomb. I know, because I accidentally fell into it and got sucked up the statue dragon's windpipe. That's where I found Fizban after he was dead, only he wasn't.

And it was in this mountain that Theros Ironfeld forged the dragonlances. And that's why it's a Monument.

Every year at Yuletime the knights come to the Silver Dragon Mountain and Huma's Tomb and they sing songs of Huma and of Sturm Brightblade—a very good friend of mine! They "tell tales of glory by day, and spend the night on their knees in prayer before Huma's stone bier." Those quotes are from Tanis.

I knew about this, but I'd never been invited to come before, probably because I'm not a knight. (Though I would really like to be, someday. I know a story about a half-kender who was almost a knight. Have you heard it? Oh, all right.) I guess I was invited this year because this year was special, being the tenth anniversary of Something that I couldn't read for the blot. But I didn't care what it was, as long as there was to be a big party in honor of it.

I was traipsing through the fog of Foghaven Vale, wondering where I was (I had wandered off the path), when I heard voices. Naturally, I stopped to listen and while stopping to listen I may have sneaked behind a tree. (This is not snooping. It is called "caution" and caution is conducive to a long life. Something Tanis is very big on. I'll explain later.)

This is what I heard the voice say.

" 'The tenth anniversary is to be a reverent, solemn, holy time of rededication for all good and righteous people of Krynn.' " It was Tanis! I was sure it was his voice, only he was talking in a Lord Gunthar-kind of tone. Then Tanis said in his own voice. "Crap. It's all a lot of crap."

"What?—" said another voice, and I knew that voice was Caramon's, and he sounded the same dear old confused Caramon as always. I couldn't believe my luck,

"Tanis, my dear," came a woman's voice and it was Laurana! I knew that because she's the only one who ever calls Tanis *my dear*. "Don't talk so loudly."

"But what?—" That was Caramon again.

"No one can hear me," said Tanis, interrupting. He sounded really irritated and in a Bad Mood. "This damn fog muffles everything. The truth is that the knights are having political problems at home. That draconian raid of Throtl touched off a riot in Palanthas. People think the knights should go into the mountains and wipe out the draconians and the goblins and anything else that doesn't wipe them out first. It's all the fault of this new group of boneheads who say we should go back to the golden days of the Kingpriest!"

"But doesn't Lady Crysania—" Caramon tried again.

"Oh, she reminds people of the truth," Tanis told him. "And I think most understand. But the fanatics are gaining converts, especially when the refugees come forward and tell their tales of Throtl in flames and goblins killing babies. What no one seems to realize is that the knights couldn't possibly raise an army large enough to go into the Khalkists, even if they did ally with the dwarves. The rest of Solamnia would be left defenseless, which is probably just exactly what these goblin raids are trying to accomplish. But these fools won't listen to reason."

"Then why are we—"

"—here? That's why," Tanis answered. "The knights are turning this into a public spectacle in order to remind everyone how truly great and wonderful we are. Are you sure we're going in the right direction?"

I could see them now from where I was hiding. (Caution, not snooping.) Tanis and Caramon and Laurana were riding on horses, and an escort of knights was riding behind—a long way behind. Tanis had reigned in his horse and was looking around like he thought he was lost, and Caramon was looking, too.

"I think—" Caramon began.

"Yes, dear," said Laurana patiently. "This is the trail. I came this way before, remember?"

"Ten years ago," Tanis reminded her, turning to look at her with a smile.

"Yes, ten years," she said. "But I'm not likely to ever forget it. I was with Silvara and Gilthanas . . . and Flint. Dear old Flint." She sighed and brushed her hand across her cheek.

I felt a snuffle coming on, so I kept behind the tree until I could choke it back down. I heard Tanis clear his throat. He shifted uncomfortably in his saddle and moved closer to Caramon. Their horses were nose to nose and almost nose to nose with me.

"I was afraid this would happen," Tanis said quietly. "I tried to talk her out of coming, but she insisted. Damn knights. Polishing up their armor and their memories of glory from ten years ago, hoping that people will remember the battle of the High Clerist's Tower and forget the Sacking of Throtl."

Caramon blinked. "Was Throtl really?—"

"Don't exaggerate, Tanis," said Laurana briskly, riding up to join them. "And don't worry about me. It's good to be reminded of those who have gone before us, who wait for us at the end of our long journey. My memories of my dear friends aren't bitter. They don't make me unhappy, only sad. It is our loss, not theirs." Her eyes went to Caramon as she spoke.

The big man smiled, nodded his head in silent understanding. He was thinking of Raistlin. I know because I was thinking of Raistlin, too, and some fog got into my eyes and made them go all watery. I thought about what Carmon had put on the little stone marker he set up in Solace in Raistlin's honor.

Our granted peace for his sacrifice. One who sleeps, at rest, in eternal night.

Tanis scratched his beard. (His beard has little streaks of gray in it now. It looks quite distinguished.) He looked frustrated.

"You'll see what I mean when we get there. The knights have gone to all this trouble and expense, and I don't think it's going to help matters. People don't live in the past. They live in the present. That's what counts now. The knights need to do something to bolster our faith in them now, not remind us of what they were ten years ago. Some are beginning to say it was all wizard's work back then anyway. Gods and magic." He shook his head. "I wish we could forget the past and get on with the future."

"But we should remember the past, honor it," said Caramon, actually managing to finish a complete sentence. He wouldn't have managed that—Tanis was so worked up—only Tanis had been forced to stop talking by a sneeze. "If people are divided now, then it seems that we should remind them of a time they came together."

"If it would do that, it might be of some worth," Tanis muttered, sniffing. He was searching through his pockets, probably for a handkerchief. He's quite careless about losing things. I know because I was holding onto his pack at the time.

Here's how it happened that I had his pack. I had stepped out from behind the tree, ready to surprise him. I caught hold of the pack, which had been tied (not very well) onto the back of the saddle. Suddenly the pack bounced loose and came off in my hand. I would have said something to him then, but he was talking again and it wouldn't have been polite to interrupt. So I took the pack and stepped back behind the tree and looked inside it to see if it was really his and not someone else's by mistake.

"But the knights won't do anything except wallow in the past," Tanis was saying. "Mark my words. Have you heard that latest song they've made up about Sturm? Some minstrel sang it for us the other night, before we left. I laughed out loud."

"You deeply offended him," said Laurana. "He wouldn't even stay the night. And there was no need to follow him out to the gate, yelling at him."

"I told him to sing the truth next time. Sturm Brightblade wasn't a paragon of virtue and courage. He was a man and he had the same fears and faults as the rest of us. Sing about that!"

Tanis sneezed again. "Blast this damp! The cold eats into the bone. And we'll be spending the night on our knees in a mouldy old tomb. Where the blazes did I put my handker—"

Well, of course it was in his pack,

"Is this it, Tanis? You dropped it," I said, coming out of the fog.

Once they were over being amazed, they were all very happy to see me. Laurana hugged me (she is so beautiful!) and they asked me where I was going and I told them and then they didn't look so happy.

"You were supposed to invite him to come," said Laurana.

(She either said that or "You *weren't* supposed to invite him to come." I wasn't certain. She was talking so softly I had to strain my ears to hear.)

"I didn't," said Tanis, and he glared at Caramon.

"Not me!" said the big man emphatically.

"Oh, don't worry," I said, not wanting them to feel bad that they'd each forgotten to invite me. "I have my own invitation. It found me, so to speak." And I held it up.

They all stared at it and looked so amazed and astonished that I thought I better not say who had sent it to me. Like I said, Tanis always groans whenever I mention Fizban.

Tanis said something in a low voice to Caramon that sounded like, "It will only make things worse if we try to get rid of him . . . follow us . . . this way, keep an eye on him."

I wondered who it was they were talking about.

"Who are you talking about?" I asked. "Who'd follow you? Keep an eye on who?"

"I'll give you three guesses," Tanis growled, holding out

his hand to me and pulling me up to ride behind him.

Well, I spent the rest of the trip to the Silver Dragon Mountain guessing, but Tanis said I never got it right.

Chapter Two

"I asked you not to bring the kender," said Lord Gunthar.

He thought he was talking a low voice, but I heard him. I looked around, wondering where this other kender was that they were talking about.

I knew it couldn't be me, because I'm one of the Heroes of the Lance.

We were standing in the Upper Gallery that is inside the Silver Dragon Mountain. It is a large room with dragonlances all around one end and it is meant for formal celebrations like this one. We were all of us dressed in our very best clothes because, as Tanis said, this was a reverent and solemn occasion. (I was wearing my new purple leggings with the red fringe that Tika sewed for me and my buckskin shirt with the yellow and orange and green bead work that was a gift from Goldmoon.)

There were lots of knights in their shining armor and Caramon (Tika was home with the babies) and Laurana were there and some people I didn't know. Lady Crysania was expected any minute. It was very exciting, and I wasn't the least bored, or I wouldn't have been if I could have walked around, talking to people. But Tanis said I was to stay close to him or to Caramon or Laurana.

I thought it was sweet that they wanted me close by them that much, and so I did what Tanis said, though I pointed out that it would be more polite if I were to mingle with the other guests.

Tanis said that on no account was I to mingle.

"I didn't bring him," Tanis was telling Lord Gunthar. "Somehow or other he got hold of an invitation. Besides, he has a right to be here. He's just as much as hero as any of us. Maybe more."

Again I wondered who Tanis was talking about. This person sounded like an interesting fellow to me. Tanis was going to say more except he sneezed. He must have caught a really nasty cold out here in Foghaven Vale. (I've often wondered why we say "you've caught a cold." I mean, no one I ever knew went out after a cold. And I never heard of anyone going cold-chasing. It seems to me that it would make more sense to say the cold's caught you.)

"Bless you," Lord Gunthar said, then he sighed. "I suppose there's no help for it. You'll keep an eye on him, won't you?"

Tanis promised he would. I gave him his handkerchief. Odd, the way he kept losing it. Lord Gunthar turned to me.

"Burrfoot, my old friend," he said, putting his hands behind his back. A lot of people have a habit of doing that when we're introduced. "So glad to see you again. I hope the roads you travel have been sunny and straight." (That is a polite form of greeting to a kender and I thought it very fine of the knight to use it. Not many people are that considerate.)

"Thank you, Sir Gunthar," I said, holding out my hand.

He sighed and shook hands. I noticed he was wearing a very nice set of silver bracers and a most elegant dagger.

"I hope your lady wife is well?" I asked, not to be outdone in politeness. This was, after all, a Formal Occasion.

"Yes, thank you," said Gunthar. "She . . . um . . . appreciated the Yule gift."

"Did she?" I was excited. "I'm really glad she liked it. I always think of the time Fizban and I spent Yule at your castle, right after . . . er . . . after . . ."

Well, I almost told the story I wasn't supposed to tell, right there! Which would have been terrible! I caught myself in time.

"I—I mean right before the Council of Whitestone. When I broke the dragon orb. And Theros smashed the rock with the dragonlance. Has she used it yet?"

"The lance?" Gunthar seemed somewhat confused.

"No, no, the Yule present," I corrected him.

"Well . . . that is . . ." Gunthar looked embarrassed. "The wizard Dalamar advised us that we shouldn't . . ."

"Ah, so it *was* magical." I nodded. "I had a feeling it might be. I wanted to try it myself, but I've only had a couple of experiences with magic rings and while they've certainly been interesting experiences, I didn't feel like being turned into a mouse or being magicked into the castle of an evil wizard just at that particular time. It wasn't convenient, if you know what I mean."

"Yes," said Lord Gunthar, tugging on his moustaches. "I understand."

"Plus, I think we should share experiences like that. It's selfish to keep them all to ourselves. Not that I'd want your lady wife to be magicked into the castle of an evil wizard. Unless she really felt inclined for the trip, that is. It does make a nice change of pace. For example, did I ever tell you about the time I was—"

"Excuse me," said Lord Gunthar. "I must go welcome our other guests."

He bowed, checked to see that he was still wearing his bracers, and left.

"A very polite man," I said.

"Give me the dagger," Tanis said, sighing.

'What dagger? I'm not carrying a dagger."

Then I noticed I *was* carrying a dagger. An elegant dagger decorated with roses on the hilt. Imagine my surprise!

"Is this yours?" I asked wistfully, because it was such a truly elegant dagger.

"No, it belongs to Lord Gunthar. Hand it over."

"I guess he must have dropped it," I said, and gave it to Tanis. After all, I have my own dagger, which I call Rabbitslayer, but that's another story.

Tanis turned to Caramon, saying something about tying someone's hands and head up in a sack. That sounded extremely interesting, but I didn't hear who it was they were talking about because I suddenly saw someone I wasn't expecting to see.

Someone I didn't want to see.

Someone I wasn't supposed to see.

I felt very strange for a moment, kind of like you feel right after you've been clunked in the head and right before you see all the stars and bright lights, then everything goes dark.

I looked at him very closely. And then I realized it couldn't have been him because he was too young. I mean, I hadn't seen this knight for ten years and I guess he must have aged during that time. So I was feeling a little better, when I saw the other knight. He was standing a little ways behind the first man I'd seen. Then I realized that the young man must be his son. I still hoped I might be wrong. It had been ten years, after all.

I tugged on Tanis's sleeve.

"Is that Owen Glendower over there" I asked, pointing.

Tanis looked. "No, that's Owen's son, Gwynfor. Owen Glendower is the one standing in back, over by the lances." Then he looked at me and frowned. "How do you know Owen Glendower? I didn't meet him until after the war was over."

"I don't know him," I said, feeling sicker than ever.

"But you just said his name and asked me if that was him."

Tanis is thick-headed, sometimes.

"Whose name?" I asked, truly miserable.

"Owen Glendower's!"

I didn't think Tanis should shout on a Formal Occasion and I told him so.

"Never heard of him," I added. And then, to make matters worse, in walked Theros Ironfeld!

Do you know who Theros Ironfeld is? I'm sure you do, but I think I should mention it, in case you've forgotten. Theros is the blacksmith with the silver arm who forged the dragonlances from the magical pool of dragonmetal that some people think is under the Silver Dragon Mountain.

"Theros too!" I was having trouble breathing.

"Yes, of course," Tanis said. "It is the tenth anniversary of the Forging of the Lance. Didn't you know that? It says so right on your invitation. We're meeting here to honor Sir Owen Glendower, the first knight who ever used the dragonlance against a dragon."

It didn't say that on *my* invitation! I fished it out of my pouch and looked at it again. My invitation said we were honoring *Sir* (Splot)*ower.*

Well, let me tell you it was a wonder I didn't fall down on the spot in a state of nervous prostration. (I'm not certain what that is, but it describes the way I felt.)

"I'm not feeling very good, Tanis," I said, putting one hand to my forehead and the other to my stomach, for they both were acting very queer. "I think I'll go lie down."

I meant to leave, truly. I was going to get as far from the Silver Dragon Mountain as possible. Only I didn't tell Tanis that, because he and Laurana and Caramon had all been so glad to see me and were so nice about wanting me around. I didn't want to hurt their feelings.

But Tanis took hold of my arm and said, "No, you're staying with me, at least until after the ceremony."

That was awfully good of him, if inconvenient and uncomfortable for me. I decided maybe I could get through the ceremony, especially if Owen Glendower didn't talk to me, and I suspected that he wouldn't want to talk to me anymore than I wanted to talk to him. Tanis said all I would have to do was go up with him when my name was called out by Lord Gunthar as one of the Heroes of the Lance. I wasn't to say anything, just bow and look honored.

Then the knights would sing and go off to pray at Huma's Tomb and, since I wasn't permitted to go there (which I don't know why since I was there several times before, as you'll hear), I could leave and maybe we'd go have dinner.

I didn't feel at all hungry, but I told Tanis that would

be fine with me. And I hid behind Caramon (six kender could hide behind him), so that Owen wouldn't see me, and I hoped it would all be over soon. I was so nervous I'd forgotten to ask Lord Gunthar about Fizban, who hadn't come anyhow.

The ceremony started. Lord Gunthar and all the dignitaries lined up in front of the dragonlances that stand all around the front end Upper Gallery. I heard the beginning of Lord Gunthar's speech. This was it:

"We knights come to rededicate ourselves to continue the fight against the evil that exists still in the world.

"For the Queen of Darkness wages unceasing eternal war against the powers of good. Though her dragons have retreated to hidden places, they continue to ravage the land. Her armies of goblins and draconians and ogres and other wicked creatures rise up from dark places to slaughter and burn and plunder."

This was interesting and I began to breathe easier, but right then he started going on about the magic of the dragonlances that had been blessed by Paladine himself and how the magic dragonlances had been responsible for defeating the Dark Queen's dragons. The more Lord Gunthar talked like this, the worse the queer feeling in my stomach grew.

Then I was hot and cold, both at the same time, which might sound entertaining to you, but I can assure you it isn't. Take my word. It's very uncomfortable. Then the room began to bulge in and out.

Lord Gunthar introduced Theros Ironfeld and talked about how he forged the magical lance. Then Lord Gunthar brought forth Sir Owen Glendower.

"The first knight ever to use the dragonlance in battle."

And someone gave a kind of strangled choke and tumbled down on the floor in what Tanis said was a fit, but which I think was a state of nervous prostration. At first I thought it was me, but I realized it wasn't, because I was on my feet.

It was Sir Owen Glendower.

That put an end to the ceremony real quick.

I could have left then, because Tanis let loose of me and ran over to Owen. Everyone was running over to Owen—to see him having his fit, I suppose. I'm sure it must have been exciting, to judge by the sounds he was making—gurgling and thrashing about on the floor—and I would have liked to have seen it myself, except I wasn't certain that I wouldn't be having a fit of my own any minute.

"Stand back!" cried Caramon. "Give him air."

Poor Caramon. As if he thought we'd suck up all the air in that big chamber and not leave any for Owen to have his fit with. But everyone did what Caramon said (they generally do, I've noticed, especially when he flexes his arm muscles) and they all backed up, except for Owen's son, who was kneeling beside his father and looking terribly worried and anxious.

Lady Crysania . . . (Did I mention she was there now?) Anyway, Lady Crysania (she was there) knelt down and put her hands on the knight's head and she prayed to Paladine and Owen Glendower quit flopping around. But I couldn't see that he'd improved much. He was lying still as death and his breathing sounded real funny—when he remembered to breathe at all.

"He needs rest and quiet," said Lady Crysania. "No, it would be better not to move him. We must keep him warm. Make a pallet for him here."

They all piled up cloaks and furs and Theros and Caramon lifted the knight very, very gently and laid him on the pallet. Laurana covered him up with her own fur cape. Gwynfor sat down beside his father and held his hand.

Tanis said something in a low voice to Lord Gunthar. Lord Gunthar nodded his head and announced that his might be a convenient time for the knights to all go down to the tomb and pray and rededicate themselves to fighting evil. The knights thought so, too, and off they went. That cleared a lot of people out of the room.

Lord Gunthar next said that he thought all the other guests should go to dinner, and Caramon saw to it that the other guests did, whether they wanted to or not. That cleared out about everyone else. I couldn't go to the Tomb and I wasn't hungry and my legs felt wobbly, so I stayed.

"Will my father be all right?" Gwynfor was asking Lady Crysania. Theros Ironfeld was standing over Owen, looking down at the knight with grimmest expression I'd ever seen Theros wear.

"Yes, my lord," Crysania said, turning in the direction of Gwynfor's voice. (Lady Crysania is blind. That is another interesting story, only kind of sad, so I won't tell it here.) "He is in Paladine's hands."

"Perhaps we should leave," suggested Tanis.

But Lady Crysania shook her head. "No. I would like you all to stay. There is something very wrong here."

I could have told her *that!*

"I've done what I could to heal him, but Sir Glendower's affliction isn't in his body. It's in his mind. Paladine has given me to know that there is a secret locked inside the knight, a secret he's been carrying by himself for a long, long time. Unless we can discover the secret and free him of it, I'm afraid he will not recover."

"If Paladine's given you to know the knight has a secret, why doesn't Paladine just tell you what the damn secret is?" Tanis asked, and he sounded a bit testy. He gets put out at the gods sometimes.

Laurana cleared her throat and gave him one of Those Looks that married people give each other sometimes. One reason I've never been married myself.

"Paladine has done so," said Lady Crysania with a smile.

And you may believe this or not, but she turned her head and looked straight at me, even though she couldn't see me and she couldn't have had any idea I was in the room for I was being as quiet as the time I accidentally turned myself into a mouse.

"Tasslehoff!" Tanis said, and he didn't sound at all pleased. "Do you know anything about this?"

"Me?" I asked, looking around. I didn't think it likely he

could have been talking to any other Tasslehoff, but I could always hope.

He meant me, however.

"Yeeessss," I said, drawing out the word a long time, as long as possible, and not looking at him. I don't like it when he looks so stern. "But I promised not to tell."

Tanis sighed. "All right, Tas. You promised not to tell. Now I'm certain you must have told this story a dozen times since then so I won't hurt it you tell it—"

"No, Tanis." I interrupted him, which was not very polite, but he truly had it all wrong. I looked up at him and I was extremely solemn and serious. "I haven't told. Not ever. Not anyone. I promised, you see."

He stared at me real hard. Then his eyes crinkled. He looked worried. Kneeling down, he put his hand on my shoulder. "You haven't told anyone?"

"No, Tanis," I said, and for some reason a tear slid out of my eye. "I never have. I promised him I wouldn't."

"Promised who?"

"Fizban," I said.

Tanis groaned. (I told you, he always groans when I mention FB.)

"I, too, know," said a voice unexpectedly.

And at this we all turned to look at Theros. And he was as grim and dour and stern as I've ever seen Theros, who is usually quite nice, even if he does pick me up by the topknot sometimes, which isn't at all dignified.

"Sir Owen Glendower and I have discussed it between ourselves, often, each looking for his own truth. I have found mine. And I thought he had found his. Perhaps I was wrong. It is not for me to tell his tale, however. If he had wanted it told, he would have done so before now."

"But surely," Tanis said, growing more irritated than ever, "if the man's life is at stake . . ."

"I can tell you nothing," Theros said. "I wasn't there." He turned and talked out of the Upper Gallery.

Which left me. You see, I *was* there.

"C'mon, Tas," said Caramon in that wheedling way of his that makes me feel like I'd like to hit him sometimes. "You can tell me."

"I promised not to tell anyone," I said. They were all standing around me now, and I had never in my life felt more miserable, except maybe when I was in the Abyss. "I promised Fizban I wouldn't."

Tanis started to get red in the face and he would have yelled at me for sure but two things—a sneeze and Laurana digging her elbow into his ribs—put a stop to it. I didn't even remember to give him his handkerchief, I was so unhappy.

Lady Crysania came over to me and put out her hand and touched me. Her touch was soft and gentle. I wanted to run into her arms and cry like a big baby. I didn't because that wouldn't have been dignified for a kender my age and a hero, to boot, but I wanted to, most desperately.

"Tas," she said to me, "how did you happen to come here?"

I thought it was a strange question, since I was invited, so I told her about the sausages and the jail and the message and the invitation from Fizban.

Tanis groaned and sneezed again.

"Don't you see, Tasslehoff?" asked Lady Crysania. "It was Fizban who sent you here. You know who Fizban really is, don't you?"

"I know who he *thinks* he is," I said, because Raistlin told me once that he wasn't really certain himself if the wacky old wizard was telling the truth or not. "Fizban thinks he's the god Paladine."

"Whether he is or he isn't"—Lady Crysania smiled again—"he sent you here for a reason, you may be sure. I think he wants you to tell us the story."

"Do you?" I asked hopefully. "I'd like to, because it's been weighing on my mind."

I handed Tanis his handkerchief and gave the matter some thought. "But you don't know that for sure, Lady Crysania," I said, starting to feel miserable again. "I'm always *not* doing the right thing. I wouldn't want to not do the right thing now."

I thought some more. "But I wouldn't want Sir Owen to die either."

I had an idea. "I know! I'll tell you all the secret, then you can tell me whether or not I should tell anyone. And if you say I shouldn't, then I won't."

"But Tas, if you tell us—" Caramon began.

At which point Laurana gave him a nudge on one side and Tanis gave him a nudge on the other, so that Caramon coughed and was all sort of nudged out, I guess, because he didn't say anymore.

"I think that is very wise," said Lady Crysania, and she said she wanted to keep near Owen Glendower, so we all followed her. There weren't any chairs. We sat down on the floor in a circle, with Lady Crysania keeping beside Owen and everyone else around her and me opposite.

And it was there, sitting on the floor next to Owen Glendower, stretched out in his armor on the fur cloaks, that I told the story I had sworn by my topknot I would never, ever, ever tell.

I took hold of my topknot and held it fast, because I thought this might be the last time I'd ever see it.

Chapter Three

Well, I'm certain you must remember the part in the old story where most of us went to the Silver Dragon Mountain. There was me and Flint and Laurana and her brother Gilthanas and Theros Ironfeld and Silvara, the silver dragon, except we didn't know she was a silver dragon then.

Silvara took us to the Silver Dragon Mountain on purpose to find the dragonlances and to tell us how to forge them. But once we got there, she began to have second thoughts about telling us, because of the oath the good dragons had taken.

It's all very complicated and doesn't have anything much

to do with my story, but it sets the scene for you, so to speak. While we were inside Huma's Tomb, Silvara cast a spell on everyone, except she missed me, because I was hiding under a shield. I went to get help for my friends, who were under her sleep spell, and I got sucked up inside the Silver Dragon Mountain. And it was there that I found Fizban, who was dead. Only he wasn't.

I brought him down, and he had a talk with Silvara. It was after that talk that she decided to tell everyone who she was really. And she led Theros Ironfeld to the pool of dragonmetal that would be used to forge the lances. Only that comes later. Where I'm starting now is the part right after Fizban had the talk with Silvara. He'd decided that he had to leave.

"Good-bye, good-bye," Fizban told us. We were all inside Huma's Tomb, in the Silver Dragon Mountain. "Nice seeing you again. I'm a bit miffed about the chicken feathers"—(I could explain that part but it would take too long. Astinus has it written down in his Chronicles.[2])—"but no hard feelings."

Then Fizban glared at me.

"Are you coming?" he demanded. "I haven't got all night."

The chance to travel with a wizard! Especially a dead wizard! I couldn't pass it up. (Though I guess he wasn't really dead but none of us were sure of that at the time, especially Fizban.)

"Coming? With you!" I cried.

I was all excited and would have left right then and there, but it occurred to me that if I left, who would look out for everyone else in the group? (If I had known then that Silvara was really a silver dragon, I wouldn't have felt so bad, I didn't.) I had no idea what sort of trouble my friends would get into without me. Especially Flint, my best friend, the dwarf.

2. *Dragons of Autumn Twilight,* DRAGONLANCE Chronicles, Volume 1.

Flint was truly a wonderful person and had many good qualities, but—since I have to be honest—I thought he lacked a bit in the common-sense line. He was constantly getting into trouble and it was me who was always having to drag him out.

But Fizban promised me that Flint and the rest of my friends would be fine without me and that we'd see them again in Famine Time, which was coming up soon. So I grabbed my pack and my pouches and off Fizban and I went together on an adventure.

And adventure that I never told anyone about until now.

THE STORY I NEVER TOLD

"Where are we going?" I asked Fizban, after we'd left Huma's Tomb far, far behind us.

The wizard was moving in a tremendous hurry, huffing and puffing and stomping down the trail, his arms flying, his hat pulled low over his forehead, his staff thumping the ground.

"I don't know," he said fiercely, and walked faster than ever.

This struck me as a bit odd. I mean, I've set off on journeys to places that I didn't know precisely where I was going but I never rushed to get there. I took my time. Enjoyed the scenery. Which is maybe why we were traveling so fast, because at that point there wasn't much scenery to enjoy. We hadn't gone very far when—smack—we walked right into Foghaven Vale.

I suppose you're wondering about that *smack* sound. Maybe you think *squish* might be more appropriate for talking about walking into fog. Or perhaps *whoosh*. But I thought "smack" at the time because that's what it felt like. Smack into a gray-white wall of fog. It was thick. Extremely thick. I know because I held my hand up to my face and walked right into it myself. I wondered if the fog had thickened up on purpose in our honor.

"Drat!" said Fizban, waving his arms. "Get out of my way! Can't see a confounded thing. What's the meaning of this? No respect for the aged! Absolutely none at all."

He stood there waving his arms and shouting at the fog. I watched for a while as best I could for not being able to see him all that well. But it seemed to me that the more he shouted the thicker the fog got—sort of an "I'll Show You, Old Man!" type of reaction. And my topknot was soaking wet and dripping water down the back of my shirt, and my shoes were slowly filling up with oozing muck all of which was very entertaining for a while, but soon lost a lot of its charm.

"Fizban," I said, going up to tug on his sleeve.

I guess I startled him, coming up on him suddenly out of the fog like that.

At any rate, he apologized very handsomely for hitting me on the nose with his staff and helped pick me up out of the muck and patted my head until it quite ringing. And we thought at first my nose was broken, then decided it wasn't and when the bleeding stopped, we started on our way again.

We walked and we walked. Finally, Fizban said he thought the fog had let up considerably. The result, he said, of a marvelous spell he'd cast on it. I didn't think it was polite to contradict him and besides I could almost sort of see the grass under my feet if I bent down and looked for it, so I figured he must be right. But we slowed our pace quite a bit, especially after Fizban walked *blam* into the tree.

It was either right before or right after he set the tree on fire that we came to Huma's Tomb.

It was daylight now. (We'd spent the night getting here.) The fog lifted just enough for us to see where we were, which I thought was quite sneaky of the fog. Almost like it was laughing at us.

I must tell you I was somewhat disappointed to see Huma's Tomb again. Not that it isn't a wonderful place. It is. Huma's Tomb, for those who haven't made the pilgrimage there, is really a temple. It is rectangular in shape and made out of black rock that Flint called obsidian. The outside is carved all over with knights fighting dragons and it is a very solemn and reverent place.

Inside is Huma's bier where they laid his body to rest. And his shield and sword are still there, but his body isn't. The Tomb is sad because it makes you think about your life and how you wish you'd done things better. But it's a good kind of sad because you realize that there's still the rest of your life for you to change and make better.

That was how I felt when I *first* saw Huma's Tomb, but now maybe all the fog was making it look different. All I felt now was the kind of sad that doesn't make you feel good inside.

"Ah, ha!" Fizban shouted. "I know where I am."

"Huma's Tomb," I said.

"No!" He was thunderstruck. "Didn't we just leave here?"

"Yes. We must have been walking in circles. Maybe I'll go say good-bye to Flint, while I'm here," I said, and started to climb the stairs.

"No, no," Fizban said quickly, grabbing hold of me. "They're not here. All gone inside the Silver Dragon Mountain. Silvara's taken them to the magical pool of dragonmetal, used to forge the magic dragonlances. Come along. We have other fish to fry."

Well, I had to admit that the temple did look dark and deserted now. And fried fish sounded good. So we set out.

We hadn't taken two steps before the fog came back, only this time it was mixed with smoke from the smoldering tree and I couldn't see the grass beneath my feet. I couldn't see my feet.

We walked and walked and walked and stopped and rested and ate dinner. We began to walk again and Fizban told me what a marvelous tracker he was, much better than Riverwind, and how he (Fizban) never ever got lost and how he always kept the wind on his right cheek so moss wouldn't grow on his north side. And then we came to Huma's Tomb. The second time.

"Ah! Ha!" cried Fizban, charging out of the fog, and stubbed his toe on the stairs leading up to the temple.

When he saw where we were (for the second time), he shouted. "You again!" He scowled and shook his fist at the temple. And he kicked the stairs with the same toe he used to bump into them.

Fizban hopped around on one foot and yelled at the stairs, which was fun to watch for a while, but must have got pretty boring later on because the next thing I knew I was asleep.

What I mean to say is that the next thing I knew I was awake, but I must have fallen asleep in order to have woken up, mustn't I? I think I slept for a considerable length of time because I was all stiff and sore from lying on the slick, black stairs, and I was wet and cold and hungry.

"Fizban?" I said.

He wasn't there.

I felt sort of creepy, maybe because the Tomb was sort of creepy. My stomach twisted up, because I was afraid something might have happened to Fizban and, to be honest, this fog was starting to make my skin shiver, as Flint would say. Then I heard him snore. (Fizban.) He was sleeping on the grass with his injured foot propped up on a step and his hat over it (his foot).

I was very glad to see him and guess I startled him, waking him up suddenly with a yell like that. He apologized for letting off the fireball, and we were able to have a hot breakfast, due to the fact that another tree was burning. He said that my eyebrows would grow back any day.

After breakfast, off we went again—Fizban with his foot wrapped up in a dish towel I'd found in my pouch. We walked around in the fog for I forget how long except I remember eating again and sleeping again and then we came to Huma's Tomb.

For the third time.

I don't mean to offend any knights when I say this, but I was beginning to be a little bored at the sight of it.

"This does it," Fizban muttered, and he started to rollup his sleeves. "Follow us, will you!"

"I don't think it's following us," I pointed out, and I'm afraid I spoke pretty sharp. "I think we're following it!"

"No!" Fizban looked amazed. Then confused. "Do you think so?"

"Yes," I snapped, wondering if my eyebrows would truly grow back and wishing I could see what I looked like without them. In fact, I was wishing I could see anything besides Huma's Tomb and fog and burning trees.

"Then you don't think I should let loose with a real rip-snorter of a spell and blow it sky high?" he asked, in a kind of wistful tone.

"I don't think the knights would like that," I pointed out testily. "And you know how they can be."

(No offense. I don't mean all knights. Just some knights.)

"Besides," I continued, "Huma might come back and be really put out to find that someone blew up his Tomb while he was gone. And I can't say I'd blame him."

"No, I suppose not," said Fizban, unhappily. "Maybe I could just blow up the stairs?"

"How will Huma get up to the door if the stairs are gone?"

"I see your point." Fizban heaved a sigh.

"You know, Fizban," I said sternly (I decided I had to be stern), "this has been a lot of fun. Really. It's not everyday I get my nose almost broken and both my eyebrows singed off and watch you set fire to two trees and see Huma's Tomb in the fog three times (four to me) but I think we've done just about everything exciting there is to do around here. It's time to move on. *Wherever it is we're going.*" I said the last words in an extra firm tone, hoping he'd take the hint.

Fizban muttered around awhile and did a few magic tricks that were kind of interesting, like shooting off some white and purple stars. He asked me how I liked that one and would I like to see some more?

I said no.

Then he got real flustered and took off his hat and took off the dish towel from around his hurt foot and put his hat back on, only he put it on his foot and put the disk towel over his head.

Suddenly he said, "I've got it! A spell—"

"Wait! Not yet!" I cried, jumping up and covering my face with my hands.

"A spell that will take us right where we want to go!" he shouted triumphantly. "Here, grab hold of my sleeve. Hang on tight, there's a good lad. Keep your hand out of my pouch. Wizard-stuff in there. And some rather fine liverwurst. Ready? Here we go!"

Well, I thought. Finally! At last!

I grabbed hold of Fizban's sleeve and he spoke some words that sounded like spiders crawling around inside my head. Everything went blurry and I heard a sound like wind blowing in my ears.

And when I opened my eyes, there we were.

Inside Huma's Tomb.

Chapter Four

"Fizban!" I said and this time I was stern *and* firm. "Did you mean to do that?"

"Yes," he said, twisting the dish towel in his hands and sneaking peeks around the room. "Got us right where I wanted. Uh, do you happen to know where that might be? Just testing you," he added quickly.

I'm afraid I shouted. "We're in Huma's Tomb!"

"Oh, dear," he said.

Well, by this time I'd had enough. "I hate to hurt your feelings, Fizban, but I don't think you're much of a wizard and—"

I didn't finish that because Fizban's eyebrows (*he* still had eyebrows) came together and got real bristly and stuck out over his nose and he looked suddenly very fierce and angry. I was afraid he was angry at me, but as it turned out, he wasn't.

"Enchantment!" he cried.

"What?" I didn't know what we were talking about.

"Enchantment!" he said again. "We're under an enchantment! We're cursed!"

"How marvelous—I m-mean, how awful," I stammered, seeing his fierce look grow even fiercer. "Who . . . who would put us under an enchantment?" I asked in very polite tones.

"Who else? The Dark Queen." He glared at me and stomped around the tomb. "She knows I'm after the dragon orb and she's trying to thwart me. I'll fix her. I'll . . . (mumble, mumble, mumble)."

I put the mumbles in because I really couldn't make out what Fizban said he was going to do to the Dark Queen if he ever got his hands on her. Or if I did at the time I can't remember now.

"Well," I said briskly, hopping up. "Now that we know we're cursed and under an enchantment, let's leave and get on with our journey."

Fizban bristled at me. 'That's just it, you see. We can't leave."

"Can't leave?!" My heart sank down to the hole in my sock. "You mean . . . we're . . ."

"Trapped," said Fizban gloomily. "Doomed forever to wander in the fog and always come back here, where we started. Huma's Tomb."

"Forever!"

My heart oozed right out of the hole in my sock and ended up in my shoe. A snuffle rose up in my throat and choked me. "I'm very glad you're not dead anymore, Fizban, and I'm truly quite fond of you, but I don't want to be trapped in a cursed enchantment in a tomb with you forever! Why, what would Flint do without me? And Tanis? I'm his advisor, you know. You have to get us out of here!"

I'm afraid I went a bit wild, just because I was so tired of being in this Tomb and of the fog and everything, I grabbed hold of Fizban's robes and the snuffle turned into a whimper, then into a wail, and I lost control of myself for a fairly good stretch of time.

Fizban patted my topknot and let me cry into his robes, then he slapped me on the back and said to brace myself and keep a stiff upper torso. He was going to offer me his handkerchief to wipe my nose only he couldn't find it. Fortunately, I found it and so I used it and felt some better. Funny, the way getting those snuffles and wails out of your insides makes you feel better.

And I was so much better that I had an idea.

"Fizban," I said, after giving the matter thought, "if the Dark Queen has put us under an enchantment, it must mean she's watching us—right?"

"You betcha!" he said, and he looked around quit fierce again.

It occurred to me then that maybe I shouldn't talk so loud because if she was watching us she might be listening to us, too. So I crept over to Fizban and, once I found his ear under all that hair, I whispered into it, "If she's watching the front door, why don't we sneak out the back?"

He looked sort of stunned, then he blinked and said, "By George! I have an idea. If the Dark Queen's watching the front door, why don't we sneak out the back?!"

"That was my idea," I pointed out.

"Don't be a ninny!" he said, miffed. "Are you a great and powerful wizard?"

"No," I was forced to admit.

"Then it was my idea," he said. "Hang on."

He grabbed hold of my topknot and I grabbed hold of his robes and he spoke some more of those spider-leg words. The Tomb got blurry and wind rushed around me and I was dizzy and turned every which way. All in all quite a delightful sensation. And then everything settled down and I heard Fizban say "oops" in a kind of way that I didn't like much, having said it myself a time or two on occasion and knowing what it meant.

I opened my eyes kind of cautiously, thinking that if I saw Huma's Tomb again I'd be upset. But I didn't. See Huma's Tomb, that is. I opened my eyes wide and my mouth opened at the same time to ask where we were, when suddenly a hand clapped over my mouth.

"Shush!" said Fizban.

His whiskers tickled my cheek, and, before I knew what was happening, he'd lifted me clean off my feet and was dragging me backward into a really dark part of wherever it was we were.

"Mish, muckgup, whursh, blimp," I said. What I meant to say was, "But, Fizban, that's Flint!" only it sounded like the other since he had his hand over my mouth.

"Quiet! We're not supposed to be here!" he hissed back at me, and he looked incredibly angry and not at all pleased with either me or himself and probably the Dark Queen, too. So I kept quiet.

Though, of course what I really wanted to do was to shout, "Hey, Flint! It's me, Tas!" 'cause I knew the dwarf'd be really glad to see me.

He always is, though he pretends he isn't, because that's the way dwarves are. And Theros Ironfeld was with Flint, too, and I knew Theros would be glad to see me because just a while back up in Huma's Tomb he's saved me from falling into a hole and ending up on the other side of the world.

With Fizban's hand clapped tight over my mouth and his whiskers tickling me I didn't have much else to do except look. So I looked. We were in what appeared to be a blacksmith's shop, only it was the largest and finest blacksmith's shop I'd ever seen in my entire life. And I guessed then that this blacksmith's shop must be making Theros happy because he is the finest blacksmith I'd ever known in my life. He and this shop just seemed to go together.

There was an anvil bigger than me and a forge with a bellows and a lake of cool water that you put the hot metal in to hear it hiss and see steam rise up and when the metal comes out it's not hot anymore.

But the most wonderful thing was a huge pool or what looked like molten silver that gave off a most beautiful light. It reminded me of Silvara's hair in the light of Solinari, the silver moon. That silver light was the only light in the forge and it seemed to coat everything with silver, even Flint's beard. Theros's black skin shone like he's been standing out in the moonlight. And his silver arm gleamed and glistened and it was so lovely and wonderful that I felt a snuffle come up on me again.

"Shhhh!" Fizban whispered.

I couldn't have talked now anyhow, what with the snuffle, and he knew that, I guess, because he let loose of me. We stood quietly in the shadows and watched. All the time Fizban was muttering that we shouldn't be here.

While Fizban muttered to himself trying to remember his spell, I suppose I fought the snuffle and listened to Flint and Theros talk. For awhile I was too busy with the snuffle to pay much attention to what they were saying, but then it occurred to me that neither of them looked very happy, which was odd, considering that they were down here with this wonderful pool of silver. I listened to find out why.

"This is what I'm to use to forge the dragonlances?" asked Theros, and he stared into the pool with a very grim expression.

"Yes, lad," said Flint, and he sighed.

"Dragonmetal. Magical silver."

Theros bent down and picked up something from a pile of somethings lying on the floor. It was a lance, and it gleamed in the light of the silver pool, and it certainly seemed very fine to me. He held it in his hand and it was well-balanced and the light glinted off its sharp spearlike point. Suddenly, Theros's big arm muscle bunched up and he threw the lance, hard as he could, straight in to the rock wall.

The lance broke.

"You didn't see that!" Fizban gasped and clapped his hand over my eyes, but, of course, it was too late, which he must have realized, cause he let me look again after I started squirming.

"There's your magical dragonlances!" Theros snarled, glaring at the pieces of the shattered lance.

He squatted down at the edge of the pool, his big arms hanging between his knees and his head bowed low. He looked defeated, finished, beaten. I had never seen Theros look that way, not even when the draconians had cut off his arm and he was near dying.

"Steel," he said. "Fair quality. Certainly not the best. Look how it shattered. Plain ordinary steel." Standing up, he walked over and picked up the pieces of the broken lance. "I'll have to tell the others, of course."

Flint looked at him and wiped his hand over his face and beard, the way he does when he's thinking pretty hard and pretty deep. Going over to Theros, the dwarf laid a hand on the big man's arm.

"No, you won't, lad," he said. "You'll go on making more of these. You'll use your silver arm and say they're made of dragonmetal. And you won't say a word about the steel."

Theros started at him, startled. Then he frowned. "I can't lie to them."

"You won't be," Flint said, and he had That Look on his face.

I knew That Look. It was like a mountain had plunked down right in the middle of the path you want to walk on. (I heard that actually happened, during the Cataclysm.) You can say what you like to it, but the mountain won't move. And when the mountain won't move it has That Look on its face.

I said to Theros, under my breath, *You might as well give up right now, because you'll never budge him.*

Flint was going on. "We'll take these lances to the knights and we'll say, 'Here, lads, Paladine has sent these to you. He hasn't forgotten you. He's fighting here with you, right now.' And the faith will fill their hearts and that faith will flow into their arms and into their bright eyes and when they throw those lances it will be the strength of that faith and the power of their arms and the vision of their bright eyes that will guide these lances into the evil dragons' dark hearts. And who's to say that this isn't magic, perhaps the greatest magic of all?"

"But it isn't true," argued Theros, glowering.

"And how do you know what is true and what is not?" Flint demanded, glowering right back, though he only came up to Theros's waist. "Here you stand, alive and well with the silver arm, when you should—if you want truth—be lying dead and moldering in the ground with worms eating you.

"And here we are, inside the Silver Dragon Mountain, brought here by that beautiful creature who gave up everything, even love itself, for the sake of us all, and broke her oath and doomed herself, when if you want the truth she could have magicked us all away and never said a word.

"Now I'll tell you what we're going to do, Theros Ironfeld," Flint went on, the stubborn look on his face getting stubborner. He rolled up his sleeves and hitched up his pants. "We're going to get to work, you and I. And we're going to make these dragonlances. And we're going to let the truth each man and woman carries in his or her own heart be the magic that guides it."

Well, at this point Fizban got the snuffles. He was dabbing his eyes with the end of his beard. I guess I wasn't much better. We both stood there and snuffled together and shared a handkerchief that I happened to have with me and by the time we were over the snuffles Flint and Theros had gone away.

"What do we do now?" I asked. "Do we go help Flint and Theros?"

"A lot of help you'd be," Fizban snapped. "Probably fall into the dragonmetal well. No," he said, after chewing on the end of his beard, which must have been quite salty from his tears, "I think I know how to break the enchantment."

"You do?" I was truly glad.

'We've got to grab a couple of those lances." He pointed to the pile of lances lying by the pool.

"But those don't work," I reminded him. "Theros said they don't."

"What do you use these for?" Fizban demanded, grabbing hold of my ears and giving them a tug that brought water to my eyes. "Doorknobs? Weren't you listening?"

Well, of course I had been. I'd heard every word and if some of it wasn't exactly clear that wasn't my fault and I don't know why he had to go and pull my ears nearly off my head, especially after he'd already almost broken my nose and burned off my eyebrows.

"If you ask Theros nicely I'm sure he's lend you a couple of lances," I said, rubbing my ears and trying not to be mad. After all, Fizban had gotten me caught in an enchantment and, while it was a dull and boring enchantment, it was an enchantment nonetheless and I felt I owed him something. "Especially since they don't work."

"No, no!" Fizban muttered, and his eyes sparkled in quite a cunning and sneaky manner. "We won't bother Theros. He's over firing up the forge. You and I'll just sneak in and borrow a lance or two. He'll never notice."

Now, if there's one thing I'm good at, it's borrowing. You won't find a better borrower than me, except maybe Uncle Trapspringer, but that's another story.

Fizban and I sneaked out of the shadows where we'd been hiding and crept quiet as mice over to where the lances lay by the shining pool of silver. Once I got close to the lances, I had to admit they were beautiful things, whether they worked or not. I wanted one very badly and I was glad Fizban had decided he wanted one, too. I was a bit uncertain, at first, as to how we were going to make off with them, for they were long and big and heavy, and I couldn't very well stuff one in my pouch.

"I'll carry the butt-end," said Fizban, "and you carry the spear-end. Balance it on our shoulders, like this."

I saw that would work, though I couldn't quite balance my end on my shoulders, since Fizban's shoulders are higher than mine. But I held my end up in the air and Fizban managed the butt-end. We lifted up two of the lances and ran off with them.

And while we were running, Fizban said some more of those spider-foot words and the next thing I knew I was running straight into . . .

You guess it. Huma's Tomb.

Chapter Five

"Oh, now really!" I began, quite put out.

But I didn't get the rest of my sentence finished, which was probably just as well, since it would have most likely made Fizban angry and he might have sent my topknot to join my eyebrows.

The reason I didn't get the rest of my sentence finished was that we weren't alone in Huma's Tomb anymore. A knight was there. A knight in full battle armor and he was kneeling beside the bier in the silver moonlight, with tears rolling down his cheeks.

"Thank you, Paladine!" he was saying, over and over again in a tone that made me feel I'd like to go off somewhere and be very, very quiet for a long time.

But the lances were growing extremely heavy, and I'm afraid I dropped my end, which caused Fizban to overbalance and nearly tumble over backward, and he dropped his butt-end. Which meant we both dropped the middles. The lances fell to the stone floor with quite a remarkable-sounding clatter.

The knight nearly leapt out of his armor. Jumping to his feet, he drew his sword and whipped right around and glared at us.

He had taken off his helmet to pray. He was older, about thirty, I guess. His hair was dark red and he wore it in two long braids. His eyes were green as the vallenwood leaves in Solace, where I live when I'm not out adventuring or residing in jails. Only his eyes didn't look green as leaves just at the moment. They looked hard and cold as the ice in Ice Wall.

I don't know what the knight expected maybe a dragon or at least a draconian, or possibly a goblin or two. What he obviously didn't expect was Fizban and me.

The knight's face, when he saw us, slipped from fierce into muddle and puzzled, but it hardened again right off.

"A wizard," he said in the same tone of voice he might have said "ogre dung." "And a kender." (I won't tell you what *that* sounded like!) "What are you two doing here? How dare you defile this sacred place?"

He was getting himself all worked up and waving his sword around in a way that was quite careless and might have hurt somebody namely me, because I was suddenly closest, Fizban having reached out and pulled me in front of him.

"Now wait just a minute, Sir Knight," said Fizban, quite bravely, I thought, especially since he was using me for a shield, and my small body wouldn't have done much to stop that knight's sharp sword, "we're not defiling anything. We came in here to pay our respects, same as you, only Huma was out. Not in, you see," the wizard added, gesturing vaguely to the empty bier. "So we . . . er . . . decided to wait a bit, give him a a chance to come back."

The knight stared at us for quite a long time. He would have stroke his moustaches, I thought, like Sturm did when he was thinking hard, except that this knight didn't have any moustaches yet. Only the beginnings of some, like he was just starting to grow them out. He lowered the sword a little, little bit.

"You are a white-robed wizard?" he asked.

Fizban held out his sleeve. "White as snow." Actually it wasn't, having been dragged through the mud and spotted with blood from my nose and slobber from both of us and ashes from the burning tree and some soot we'd picked up in the dragonlance forge.

Fizban's robes didn't impress the knight. He raised his sword again and his face was extremely grim. "I don't trust wizards of any color robe. And I don't like kender."

Well, I was just about to express my opinion of knights, which I thought might help him—(Tanis says we should come to know our own faults, to be better persons)—but Fizban grabbed hold of my topknot and lifted me up like you pick up a rabbit by the ears and shuffled me off to one side.

"How did you find this sacred place, Sir Knight?" Fizban asked, and I saw his eyes go cunning and shrew like they do sometimes when they're not vague and confused.

"I was led here by the light of the fire of two burning trees and a celestial shower of white and purple stars . . ." The knight's voice faded to an awed breath.

Fizban smirked at me. "And you said I wasn't much of a wizard!"

The knight appeared dazed. He lowered his sword again. "You did that? You led me here purposefully?"

"Well, of course," said Fizban. "Knew you were coming all along."

I was about to explain to the knight about my singed eyebrows and even offer to show him where they'd been, in case he was interested, but Fizban accidentally trod on my foot at that moment.

You wouldn't think one old man, especially one who looks as frail and skinny as Fizban, could be so heavy, but he was. And I couldn't make him understand that he was standing on my foot—he kept shushing me and telling me to have respect for my elders and that kender should be seen and not heard and maybe not even seen—and by this time I managed to pull my foot out from under his, he and the knight were talking about something else.

"Tell me exactly what happened," Fizban was saying. "Very important, from a wizard's standpoint."

"You might tell us your name, too," I suggested.

"I am Owen of the House of Glendower," said the knight but that was all he would tell us. He was still holding his sword and still staring at Fizban as if trying to decide whether to clap him heartily on the shoulder or clout him a good one on the headbone.

"I'm Tasslehoff Burrfoot," I said, holding out my hand politely," and I have a house myself, in Solace, only it doesn't have a name. And maybe I don't even have a house anymore now," I added, remembering what I'd seen of Solace the last time I was there and growing kind of sad at the thought.

The knight raised his eyebrows (*he* had eyebrows) and was staring at me now.

"But that's all right," I said, thinking Owen Glendower might be feeling sorry for me because my house had most likely been burned down by dragons. "Tika said I could come live with her, if I ever see Tika again," I added, and that made me sadder still, because I hadn't seen Tika in a long time either.

"You came all the way from Solace?" asked Owen Glendower, and he sounded no end astonished.

"Some of us came a lot farther than that," Fizban said solemnly, only the knight didn't hear him, which was probably just as well.

"Yes, we came from Solace," I explained. "A large group of us, only some of us aren't with us anymore. There was Tanis and Raistlin and Caramon and Tika, only we lost them in Tarsis, and that left Sturm and Elistan and Derek Crownguard and they went to—"

"Derek Crownguard!" Owen gasped. "You traveled with Derek Crownguard?"

"I'm not finished," I said, eyeing him sternly. "And it isn't polite to interrupt. Tanis says so. Inside there's Laurana and Flint and Theros—"

"But it's Sir Derek I'm searching for," said the knight, completely ignoring me. (I'm not certain but I believe that ignoring people is against their knightly code, though Sturm often ignored me, now that I come to think of it. But Tanis says that if ignoring kender isn't in the Measure it should be.)

"I'm a courier from Lord Gunthar and I've been sent to find Sir Derek—"

"You've just missed him," I said, and tried to look sad about it, though I wasn't, not in the least. "He went off with the dragon orb."

"The what?" Owen stared at me.

"Dragon *herb*," said Fizban, giving me a tug on the top-knot that made tears come to my eyes. "Similar to wolfbane. Only different."

Well, I had no idea what he was talking about, but it wasn't important anyway and I could see Owen was getting a bit impatient. So I went on.

"I don't know why you were looking for him. Derek Crowngard is *not* a nice person," I informed him.

"Describe him to me," said Owen.

"Don't you know him?" I asked, amazed. "How can you find him if you don't know him?"

"Just describe him, kender," growled the knight.

"Tasslehoff Burrfoot," I reminded him. Obviously he'd forgotten. "Well, Derek's mad at most everyone all the time and he's not at all polite and I don't think he has much common sense either, if you want my opinion."

Well, as it turned out, Owen didn't want my opinion; what he wanted was a description of what Derek looked like, not what he acted like, so I gave him that, too. My description seemed to please him, only it was hard to tell, because he was so confused.

"Yes, that's Derek Crownguard," he said. "You've described him perfectly. You must be telling the truth."

He thought another moment, then looked at Huma's bier, to see if it might help, and it looked very peaceful and beautiful in the moonlight. (If you are wondering why there was moonlight when there should have been fog, keep listening and I'll explain later on when the moonlight has its proper turn.)

"I was sent to find Derek Crownguard," Owen said, talking slowly, as if he might decide to stop any moment and take back everything he'd just said. "I have . . . dispatches for him. But I lost his trail, and I prayed to Paladine to help me find it again. That night, in a dream, I was told to seek Huma's resting place. I didn't know where it was no one knows. But I was told that if I studied Solinari, on a cloudless night, I would see a map on the moon's surface. The next night, I did so. I saw what appeared to be a map of my homeland, Southern Ergoth. I have walked these mountains and valleys thirty years, yet I never knew this place existed. I followed Solinari's guidance, but then fog overtook me. I could no longer see the moon.

"The path led into a valley inside the mountains and vanished. I could not find my way out and have wandered about for days, perhaps. I'm not sure how long: time has lost all meaning to me. Then I saw a fire, burning in the distance. I followed it, thinking that I should at least find someone to guide me back to the trail. Then it went out and I was lost again. Then another fire and then clouds of purple stars and then I discovered this holy place, Huma's Tomb. And you."

Looking at us, he shook his head and I could tell we weren't exactly what he'd been praying to Paladine to find.

"But if my Lord Crownguard left with the dragon orb, what are you two doing here?" he asked, after he'd stared at us longer than was really polite. "Why did you stay behind?"

"We're under an enchantment," I said. "Isn't it exciting? Well, to be honest, not all that exciting. Actually it's been pretty boring, not to mention cold and icky and damp. The Dark Queen has put us under a spell, you see. And we can't get out of here because every time we leave we keep coming back. And we have to get out of here because we're on a Very Important Mission to . . . to . . ."

I stopped because I wasn't quite sure what our Important Mission was.

"Lord Gunthar. Important mission to Lord Gunthar,"

said Fizban. "Must see him right away. Most urgent."

"You're under black enchantment?" Owen pulled back from us both, raised his sword, and laid his hand on Huma's bier.

"Well, now. As to the enchantment part." Fizban scratched his head. "It could be that I exagger—"

"Oh yes!" I averred. (I'm fond of that word, averred.) "The Dark Queen is most dreadfully afraid of Fizban, here. He's a great and powerful wizard."

Fizban blushed and took off his hat and twirled it around in his hands. "I do my best," he said modestly.

"Why did you send for me?" Owen asked, and he still seemed suspicious.

Fizban appeared somewhat at a loss. "Well, I . . . you see . . . that is . . ."

"I know! I know!" I cried, standing on my tiptoes and raising my hands in the air. Of course, anyone who's ever been a child knows the reason, but maybe knights were never children or maybe he didn't have a mother to tell him stories like my mother told me. "Only a true knight can break our enchantment!"

Fizban breathed a deep sigh. Taking off his hat, he mopped his forehead with his sleeve. "Yes, that's it. True knight. Rescue damsels in distress."

"We're not damsels," I said, thinking I should be truthful about all this, "but we are in considerable distress, so I should think that would count. Don't you?"

Owen stood beside Huma's bier, eyeing us, and he still seemed confused and suspicious probably because we weren't damsels. I mean, I could see how that would be disappointing, but it wasn't our fault.

"And there's these dragonlances, I said, waving my hand at them, where we'd dropped them, on the floor at the back of the temple. "Only they don't—"

"Dragonlances!" Owen breathed, and suddenly, it was like Solinari had dropped right down out of the sky and burst on top of the knight. His armor was bright, bright silver and he was so handsome and strong-looking that I could only stare at him in wonder. "You have found the dragonlances!"

He thrust his sword in its sheath and hurried over to where I'd pointed. At the sight of the two lances, lying on the floor in the moonlight, Owen cried out loudly in words I didn't understand and fell down on his knees.

Then he said, in words I could understand, "Praise be to Paladine. These are dragonlances, true ones, such as Huma used to fight the Dark Queen. I saw the images, carved on the outside of the Temple."

He rose to his feet and came to stand before us. "Now I know that you speak the truth. You plan to take these lances to Lord Gunthar, don't you, Sir Wizard? And the Dark Queen has laid an enchantment on you to prevent it."

Fizban swelled up with pride at being called Sir Wizard and I saw him look at me to make certain I noticed, which I did. I was very happy for him because generally he gets called other things that aren't so polite.

"Why, uh, yes," he said, puffing and preening and smoothing his beard. "Yes, that's the ticket. Take the lances to Lord Gunthar. We should set out right away."

"But the lances don't—" I began.

"—shine," said Fizban. "Lances don't shine."

Well, before I could mention that the lances not only didn't shine but didn't work either, Fizban had upended one of my pouches, causing my most precious and valuable possessions in the whole world to spill out all over the floor. By the time I had everything picked up and resorted and examined and wondered where I'd come by a few things that I didn't recognize, Fizban and Owen were ready to leave.

Owen Glendower was holding the lances in his hand—did I mention that he was very strong? I mean, it took Fizban and me both to carry them, and here this knight was holding two of them without any trouble at all.

I asked Fizban about this but he said it was reverence and thankfulness that gave the knight unusual strength.

"Reverence and thankfulness. But we'll see about that as we go along," muttered Fizban, and I thought he looked cunning again.

Owen Glendower said good-bye to Huma and was very unhappy over leaving the Tomb.

"Don't worry," I told him. "If you haven't broken the enchantment, we'll be back."

"Oh, he's broken it, all right," said Fizban, and we all trooped out the door and into the moonlight.

And then I realized that it *was* moonlight. (I told you I'd tell you all this when it came its proper turn in the story, and this is it.) The fog was gone and we could see the Guardians and the Bridge of Passage and behind us the Silver Dragon Mountain. And Owen was so fascinated that we almost couldn't drag him off. But Fizban reminded him that the dragonlances were the "salvation of the people" and this got the knight moving.

He'd had a horse, but somehow or other he'd lost it. He said that when we reached civilized lands we'd find other horses to ride and that would get us to Lord Gunthar's faster.

I considered telling him that Fizban could get us all to Lord Gunthar's much, much faster, if he wanted to cast one of his spells on us. Then I thought that with Fizban's spells, all things considered (especially my eyebrows), we might end up in the middle of the Hot Springs. And maybe Fizban thought the same thing because he didn't mention his spells either. So we set off, with Owen Glendower carrying the dragonlances and me carrying my pouches and Fizban carrying a tune, sort of.

And, praise be to any and all of the gods, we did *not* go back to Huma's Tomb!

Chapter Six

Let me point out right here and now that it wasn't my fault we ended up in the Wasted Lands. I had a map and I told Fizban and Sir Owen we were heading the wrong direction. (It was a perfectly good map; if Tarsis By the Sea chose to get itself landlocked, I don't see how anyone can blame me for it!)

It was night. We were wandering around in the mountains when we came to a pass. I told Fizban that we should go left. That would lead us out of the mountains and take us to Sancrist. But Fizban scoffed and said my map was outdated (outdated!) and Owen Glendower vowed he'd shave his moustaches before he ever took advice from a kender. (Which seemed a fairly safe vow to me, considering that he didn't have all that much yet to shave.) This after he'd admitted that he'd gotten himself all turned around in Foghaven Vale and wasn't real sure where he was now!

He said that we should wait until morning and that when the sun came up we'd know what direction to take, but Fizban said he had a feeling in his bones that the sun wouldn't come up in the morning, and, by gosh, he was right. The sun didn't come up or if it did we missed it what with the snow and all.

So we turned right when we should have turned left and came to the Wasted Lands and the adventure, but this isn't the adventure's proper place in the story yet, so it'll have to wait its turn.

I could tell you about the days we spent traveling through the mountains in the snow but, to be honest, that part wasn't very exciting . . . if you don't count Fizban accidentally melting our snow shelter down around us one night while he was trying to read his spell book by the light of a magical candle that turned out to be more magic than candle. (I got to keep the wick.)

One nice thing about that time was traveling with Owen Glendower. I was getting to like the knight a lot. He said he didn't even mind being around me much (which may not sound very gracious to you but is a lot more than I expected).

"Probably," he said, "because I don't have many valuables to lose."

I didn't quite understand that last part, especially since he kept losing what he said was his most treasured possession: a very beautiful little painting of his wife and son that he carried in a small leather pouch over his left breast underneath his armor.

He discovered it missing one night when we were relaxing in our snow shelter (the one Fizban melted) and we all hunted for the painting most diligently. It was right when Owen said he was going to turn me upside down and maybe inside out if I didn't get it back to him that Fizban happened to find the painting inside my shirt pocket.

"See there," I said, handing it back to Owen, "I kept it from getting wet."

He wasn't the least appreciative. For a minute I thought he was going to throw me out off the side of the mountain and for a minute he thought he was going to, too. But after a while he calmed down, especially when I told him that the lady inside the painting was one of the prettiest ladies I'd ever seen, next to Tika and Laurana and a certain kender maid I know whose name is engraved forever on my heart. (If I could remember it, I'd tell you, but I guess that it isn't important right now.)

Owen sighed and said he was sorry he shouted at me and he wasn't really going to slit my pockets or maybe my gut, whichever came first. It was only that he missed his wife and son so much and was so very worried about them because he was here in the snow with us and the dragonlances, and his wife and son were back in their house alone without him.

Well, I understood that, even if I didn't have a wife or a son or a house anymore. We made an agreement then and there. If I found the painting I was to give it right back to him immediately.

And it was amazing to me that he lost the painting as often as he did, considering how much it meant to him. But I didn't mention this to him, because I didn't want to hurt his feelings. As I said, I was beginning to like Owen Glendower.

"Life hasn't been easy for my lady wife," he told us one other night while we were thawing out after having spent the day trekking about lost in the snow. "From what you've told me about your friend Brightblade, you know how the knights have been persecuted and reviled. My family was driven from our ancestral home years ago, but it was a point of honor among us that someday we would return to claim it. Our holdings have passed from one bad owner to the next. The people in the village have suffered under their tyrannies and though they were the ones who drove us out, they have more than paid for that now.

"I worked as a mercenary, to keep body and soul alive, and to earn the money to buy back lawfully what had been stolen from us. For I would be honorable, though the thieves that took it were not.

"At last, I was able to save the necessary sum. I am ashamed to say that I was forced to keep my identity as a knight secret, lest the owners refuse to sell to me."

He touched his moustaches as he said this. They were coming out fairly well, now, and were dark red as his hair.

"As it was, the thieves made a good bargain, for the manor was crumbling around their ears. We have repaired it ourselves, for I could not afford to hire the work done. The villagers helped. They were glad to see a knight return, especially in these dangerous times.

"My wife and son toiled beside me, both doing far more than their share. My wife's hands are rough and cracked from breaking stone and mixing mortar, but to me their touch is as soft as if she wrapped them in kid gloves every night of her life. Now she stands guard while I am gone, she and my boy. I did not like to leave them, with evil abroad in the land, but my duty lay with the knights, as she herself reminded me. I pray Paladine watches over them and keeps them safe."

"He does," said Fizban, only he said it very, very softly, so softly that I almost didn't hear him. And I might not have if I hadn't felt a snuffle coming on and so was searching in his pouch for a handkerchief.

Owen could tell the most interesting stories about when he was a mercenary and he said I was as good a listener as his son, though I asked too many questions.

We went on like this and were really having a good time and so I guess I have to admit that I didn't really mind that we took the wrong way. We'd been wandering around lost for about four days when it quit snowing and the sun came back.

Owen looked at the sun and frowned and said it was on the wrong side of the mountains.

I tried to be helpful and cheer him up. "If Tarsis By the Sea could move itself away from the sea, maybe these mountains hopped around, too."

But Owen didn't think much of my suggestion. He only looked very worried and grim. We were in the Wasted Lands, he said, and the bay we could see below us (Did I mention it? There was a bay below us.) was called Morgash Bay, which meant Bay of Darkness and that, all in all, we were in a Bad Place and should leave immediately, before it Got Worse.

"This is all your fault!" Fizban yelled at me and stamped his foot on the snow. "You and that stupid map."

"No it isn't my fault!" I retorted. (Another good word—retorted.) "And it isn't a stupid map."

"Yes it is!" Fizban shouted and he snatched his hat off his head and threw it on the snow and began to stomp up and down on top of it. "Stupid! Stupid! Stupid!"

Right then, things Got Worse.

Fizban fell into a hole.

Now, a normal person would fall into a normal hole, maybe twist an ankle or tumble down on his nose. But no, not Fizban. Fizban fell into a Hole. Not only that but he took us into the Hole along with him, which I considered thoughtful of him, but which Owen didn't like at all.

One minute Fizban was hopping up and down in the snow calling me a doorknob of a kender (That wasn't original, by the way. Flint yells that at me all the time.) and the next the snow gave way beneath his feet. He reached out to save himself and grabbed hold of me and I felt the snow start to give way beneath my feet and I reached out to save myself and grabbed hold of Owen and the snow started to give way beneath his feet and before we knew it we were all falling and falling and falling.

It was the most remarkable fall, and quite exciting, what with the snow flying around us and cascading down on top of us. There was one extremely interesting moment when I thought we were all going to be skewered on the dragonlances that Owen had been carrying and hadn't had time to let go of before I grabbed him. But we weren't.

We hit bottom and the lances hit bottom and the snow that came down with us hit bottom. We lay there a little bit, catching our breath. (I left mine up top somewhere.) Then Owen picked himself up out of a snowbank and glared at Fizban.

"Are you all right?" he demanded gruffly.

"Nothing's broken, if that's what you mean," Fizban said in a sort of quavery-type of voice. "But I seem to have lost my hat."

Owen said something about consigning Fizban's hat to perdition and then he pulled me out of a snowbank and stood me up on my feet and picked me up when I fell back down (my breath not having made it this far yet) and he asked me if I was all right.

I said yes and wasn't that thrilling and did Fizban think there was a possibility we could do that again. Owen said the really thrilling part was just about to begin because how in the name of the Abyss were we going to get out of here?

Well, about that time I took a good look at where we

were and we were in what appeared to be a cave all made out of snow and ice and stuff. And the hole that we'd fallen through was a long, long, long way up above us.

"And so are our packs and the rope and the food," said Owen, staring up at the hole we'd made and frowning.

"But we don't need to worry," I said cheerfully. "Fizban's a very great and powerful wizard and he'll just fly us all back up there in a jiffy. Won't you, Fizban?"

"Not without my hat," he said stiffly. "I can't work magic without my hat."

Owen muttered something that I won't repeat here as it isn't very complimentary to Fizban and I'm sure Owen is ashamed now he said something like that. And he frowned and glowered, but it soon became obvious that we couldn't get out of that hole without magic of some sort.

I tried climbing up the sides of the cave walls, but I kept sliding back down and was having a lot of fun, though not getting much accomplished, when Owen made me stop after a whole great load of snow broke loose and fell on top of us. He said this whole mountain might collapse.

There was nothing left to do but look for Fizban's hat.

Owen had dug the dragonlances out of the snow and he said the hat might be near where they were. We looked, but it wasn't. And we dug all around where Fizban had fallen and the hat wasn't there either.

Fizban was getting very unhappy and starting to blubber.

"I've had that hat since it was a pup," he whimpered, sniffing and wiping his eyes on the end of his beard. "Best hat in the whole world. Prefer a fedora, but they're not in for wizards. Still—"

I was about to ask who Fedora was and what did she have to do with his hat when Owen said "Shush!" in the kind of voice that makes your blood go all tingly and your stomach do funny things.

We shushed and stared at him.

"I heard something!" he said, only he said it without any voice, just his mouth moved.

I listened and then I heard something, too.

"Did you hear something?" asked a voice, only it wasn't any of our voices doing the asking. It came from behind a wall of snow, that made up one end of the cave.

I'd heard that kind of voice before slithery and hissing and ugly. I knew right off what it was, and I could tell from the expression on Owen's face angry and loathing—that he knew too.

"Draconian!" Owen whispered.

'It was only a snowfall," answered another voice, and it boomed, deep and cold, so cold that it sent tiny bits of ice prickling through my skin and into my blood and I shivered from toe to topknot. "Avalanches are common in these mountains."

"I thought I heard voices," insisted the draconian. "On the other side of that wall. Maybe it's the rest of my outfit."

"Nonsense. I commanded them to wait up in the mountains until I come. They don't dare disobey. They better not disobey, or I'll freeze them where they stand. You're nervous, that's all. And I don't like dracos who are nervous. You make me nervous. And when I get nervous I kill things."

There came a great slithering and scraping sound and the whole mountain shook. Snow came down on top of us again, but none of us moved or spoke. We just stared at each other. Each of us could match up that sound with a picture in our minds and while my picture was certainly very interesting, it wasn't conducive to long life. (Tanis told me once I should try to look at things from the perspective of whether they were or were not conducive to long life. If they weren't, I shouldn't hang around, no matter how interesting I thought it might be. And this wasn't.)

"A dragon!" whispered Owen Glendower, and he looked kind of awed.

"Not conducive to long life," I advised him, in case he didn't know.

I guess he did, because he glared at me like he would like to put his hand over my mouth but couldn't get close enough, so I put my own hand over my own mouth to save him the trouble.

"Probably a white dragon," murmured Fizban, whose eyes were about ready to roll out of his head. "Oh, my hat! My hat!" He wrung his hands.

Perhaps I should stop here and explain where we were in relation to the dragon. I'm not certain, but I think we were probably in a small cave that was right next to an extremely large cave where the dragon lived. A wall of snow separated us and I began to think that it wasn't a very thick wall of snow. I mean, when one is trapped in a cave with a white dragon, one would like a wall of snow to be about a zillion miles thick, and I had the unfortunate feeling that this one wasn't.

So there we were, in a snow cave, slowly freezing to death (did I mention that?) and we couldn't move, not a muscle, for fear the dragon would hear us. Fizban couldn't work his magic because he didn't have his hat. Owen didn't look like he knew what to do, and I guess I couldn't blame him because he'd probably never come across a dragon before now. So we didn't do anything except stand there and breathe and we didn't even do much of that. Just when we had to.

"Go on with your report," said the dragon.

"Yes, O Master." The draconian sounded a lot more respectful, probably not wanting to make the dragon nervous. I scouted the village, like you said. It's fat—lots of food laid in for the winter. One of those (the draconian said a bad word here) Solamnic Knights has a manor near it, but he'd off on some sort of errand."

"Has he left behind men-at-arms to guard his manor?"

The draconian made a rude noise. "This knight's poor as dirt, Master. He can't afford to keep men-at-arms. The manor's empty, except for his wife and kid."

Owen's face lost some of its color at this. I felt sorry for him because I knew he must be thinking of his own wife and child.

"The villagers?"

"Peasants!" The draconian spit. "They'll fall down and wet themselves when our raiding parties attack. It'll be easy pickings.

"Excellent. We will store the food here, to be used when the main force arrives to take the High Clerist's Tower. Are there more villages beyond this?"

"Yes. O Master. I will show you on the map. Glendower is here. And then beyond that there are—"

But I didn't hear anymore because I was afraid suddenly that Owen Glendower was going to fall over. His face had gone whiter than the snow and he shook so that his armor rattled.

"My family!" he groaned, and I saw his knees start to buckle.

I can move awfully quietly when I have to and I figured that this was one time I had to. I crept over to him, put my arm around him, and propped him up until he quit shaking.

He was grateful, I think, because he held onto me very tightly, uncomfortably tightly (did I mention he was really strong) and my breath almost left me again before he relaxed and let loose.

By now some blood had come back into his cheeks and he didn't look sick anymore. He looked grim and determined and resolved, and I knew then and there what he was planning to do. It was not conducive to a long life.

The dragon and draconian had gone into a rather heated discussion over which village they should burn and pillage and loot next after Glendower.

I took advantage of the noise they were making to whisper to Owen, "Have you ever seen a dragon?"

He shook his head. He was tightening the buckles on his armor and pulling at straps and things and, having seen Sturm do this before a battle, I knew what it meant.

"They're huge," I said, feeling a snuffle coming on, "and extremely big. And enormous. And they have terrible sharp teeth and they're magical. More magical than Fizban. More magical than Raistlin, even, only you don't know him, so I guess that doesn't mean much. And the white dragons can kill you just by breathing on you. I know because I met one in Ice Wall. They can turn you into ice harder than this mountain, and kill you dead."

I said all this, but it didn't seem to make any impression on Owen Glendower. He just kept buckling and tightening and his face got more and more cold and determined until I began to think that it might not make much difference if the white dragon breathed a cone of frost on the knight because he looked already frozen to me.

"Oh, Fizban!" I'm afraid I may have whimpered a bit here, but I truly didn't want to see Owen turned into a part of this mountain. "Make him stop!"

But Fizban was no help. The wizard got that crafty, cunning look on his face that makes me feel squirmy, and he said, real soft, "He can do it. He has the dragonlances!"

Owen lit up. He stood tall and straight and his eyes shone bright green, fueled from inside by a beautiful, awful, radiant light.

"Yes, " he said in a reverent voice, like he was praying. "Paladine sent the lances to my hand and then sent me here, to save my family. This is Paladine's work."

Well, I felt like telling him, No, it wasn't Paladine. It was just an old, skinny and occasionally fuddled wizard who got us into this by falling into a hole. But I didn't. I had more important things on my mind.

Like the dragonlances.

I looked at them lying in the snow, and I could hear Theros's voice in my head. And I looked at Owen, standing so tall and handsome, and I thought about the painting of his wife and child and how sad they'd be if he was dead. Then I thought that if he was dead they'd be dead, too. And I heard Theros's voice again in my head.

Owen reached down and picked up one of the dragonlances and before I could stop it, a yell burst out of me.

"No! Owen! You can't use the dragonlances!" I cried, grabbing hold of his arm and hanging on. "They don't work!"

Chapter Seven

Well, at that moment, a whole lot of things happened at once. I'll try to keep them straight for you, but it was all pretty confusing and I may put some things not in quite the right order.

Owen Glendower stared at me and said, "What?"

Fizban glared at me and snapped, "You fool kender! Keep your mouth shut!"

The draconian probably would have stared at me if it could have seen me through the wall of snow and it said, "I heard that!"

The dragon shifted its big body around (we could hear it scraping against the walls) and said, "So did I! And I smell warm blood! Spies! You, draco! Go warn the others! I'll deal with these!"

Wham!

That was the dragon's head, butting the ice wall that separated us. (Apparently, the wall was much thicker and stronger than I'd first supposed. For which we were all grateful.) The mountain shook and more snow fell down on top of us. The hole at the top grew larger not that this was much help at the moment, since we couldn't get up there.

Owen Glendower was holding the dragonlance and staring at me. "What do you mean the lances don't work!"

I looked helplessly at Fizban, who scowled at me so fiercely that I was afraid his eyebrows would slide right off his face and down his nose.

Wham!

That was the dragon's head again.

"I have to tell him, Fizban!" I wailed. And I spoke as quickly as I could because I could see that I wasn't going to have time to go into a lot of detail. "We overheard Theros Ironfeld say to Flint that the lances aren't special or magical or anything they're plain ordinary steel and when Theros threw one against the wall it broke I saw it!"

I stopped to suck in a big breath, having used up the one

I'd taken to get all that out.

And then I used the next breath to shout, "Fizban! There's your hat!"

The dragon's head-whamming had knocked over a snow bank and there lay Fizban's hat, looking sort of dirty and crumpled and nibbled on and not at all magical. I made a dive for it, brought it up and waved it at him.

"Here it is! Now we can escape! C'mon, Owen!" And I tugged on the knight's arm.

Wham! Wham! That was the dragon's head twice.

Owen looked from the shaking wall (We could hear the dragon shrieking "Spies!" on the other side.) to me, to the lance, to Fizban.

"What do you know about this, Wizard?" he asked, and he was pale and breathing kind of funny.

"Maybe the lance is ordinary. Maybe it is blessed. Maybe it is flawed. Maybe you are the one with the flaw!" Fizban jabbed a finger at Owen.

The knight flushed deeply, and put his hand to his shaven moustaches.

Wham! A crack shivered up the wall and part of a huge dragon snout that was white as bleached bone shoved through the crack. But the dragon couldn't get its whole mouth through and so it left off and started butting the ice again. (That ice was much, much stronger that I'd first thought. Very odd.)

Owen stood holding the dragonlance and staring at it, hard, as if he was trying to find cracks in it. Well, I could have told him there wouldn't be any, because Theros was a master blacksmith, even if he was working with ordinary steel, but there wasn't time. I shoved Fizban's hat into the wizard's hand.

"Quick!" I cried. "Let's go! C'mon, Owen! Please!"

"Well, Sir Knight" said Fizban, taking his hat. "Are you coming with us?"

Owen dropped the dragonlance. He drew his sword. "You go," he said, "Take the kender. I will stay."

"You, ninny!" Fizban snorted. "You can't fight a dragon with a sword!"

"Run, Wizard!" Owen snarled. "Leave while you still can!" He looked at me and his eyes shimmered. "You have the painting," he said softly. "Take it to them. Tell them—"

Well, I never found out what I was supposed to tell them because at that moment the dragon's head punched right smack through the ice wall.

The cave we were trapped in was smallish compared to the dragon, and the wyrm could only get its head inside. Its chin scraped along the floor and its snaky eyes glared at us horribly. It was so huge and awful and wonderful that I'm afraid I forgot all about it not being conducive to long life and mine would have ended then and there except Fizban grabbed hold of me by the collar and dragged me against the far wall.

Owen staggered backward, sword in hand, leaving the dragonlances in the snow. I could tell that the knight was fairly well floored at the immensity and sheer terribleness of the dragon. It must have been obvious to him right then that what Fizban said was right. You can't fight a dragon with a sword.

"Work some magic, Wizard!" Owen shouted. "Distract it!"

"Distract it! Right!" Fizban muttered and, with a great deal of courage, I thought, the old wizard leaned out from around me (I was in front of him again) and waved his hat in the dragon's general direction.

"Shoo!" he said.

I don't know if you're aware of this or not, but dragons don't shoo. In fact, being shooed seems to have an irritating effect on them. This one's eyes blazed until the snow started melting around my shoes. It began to suck in a deep, deep, deep breath and I knew that when it let that breath out we'd all be permanently frozen statues down here beneath the mountain forever and ever.

The wind whistled and snow whirled around us from the dragon's sucking up all the air. And then, suddenly, the dragon went "Ulp!" and got an extremely startled and amazed look in its eyes.

It had sucked up Fizban's hat.

Fizban had been waving his hat at the dragon, you see, and when the dragon started sucking up air it sucked the hat right out of Fizban's hand. The hat whipped through the air and in between the dragon's fangs and the "Ulp!" was the hat getting stuck in the dragon's throat.

"My hat!" wailed Fizban, and he swelled up until I thought he was going to burst.

The dragon was tossing its head around, choking and wheezing and coughing and trying to dislodge the hat. Owen dashed forward, not bothering to take the time to give the knight's salute to an enemy, which I thought was sensible of him, and stuck his sword (or tried to stick it) in the dragon's throat.

The sword's blade shivered and then shattered. The dragon thrashed out at Owen, but it couldn't do much except try to thump him on the head since it was still trying to breathe around the hat. Owen stumbled away and slipped and fell in the snow. His hand landed on the dragonlance.

It was the only weapon we had except for my hoopak, and I would have offered him the hoopak at the time only I forgot I had it. This was all so thrilling.

"Save my hat!" Fizban was shrieking and hopping up and down. "Save my hat!"

Phuey!

The dragon spit out the hat. It flew across the cave and hit Fizban in the face and flattened him but good. Owen leapt to his feet. He was shaking all over, his armor rattled, but he lifted the dragonlance and threw with all his might.

The dragonlance struck the dragon's scaly hide and broke into about a million pieces.

The dragon was sucking in its breath again. Owen slumped. He looked all defeated and hurting. He knew he was going to die, but I could tell that didn't matter to him. It was the thought that his wife and little boy and maybe all those villagers too were going to die that was like a spear in his heart.

And then it seemed to me that I heard a voice. It was Flint's voice, and it sounded so close that I looked all around, more than half-expecting to see him come dashing at me, all red in the face and bellowing.

"You doorknob of a kender! Didn't you hear anything *I* said? Tell him what I told Theros!"

I tried to remember it and then I did remember it and I began to babble, "When you throw the lance, it will be the strength of your faith and the power of your arm and the vision of your eye that will guide the lances into the evil dragon's heart. That's what Flint said, Owen, except I changed it a little. Maybe I was wrong!" I shouted. "Try the other lance!"

I don't know whether he heard me or not. The dragon was making a lot of noise and snow was falling and swirling around us. Either Owen did hear me and took my advice (and Flint's) or else he could see as plain as the hat on Fizban's face that the lance was our last and only hope. He picked it up and this time he didn't throw it. This time he ran with it, straight at the dragon, and with all his strength and might and muscle he drove the lance right into the dragon's heart.

Blood spurted out, staining the white snow red. The dragon gave a horrible yell and flung its head from side to side, screaming in pain and fury. Owen hung onto the lance, stabbing it deeper and deeper into the dragon. The lance didn't break, but held straight and true.

Blood was all over the place and all over Owen and the dragon's shrieks were deafening. Then it made a terrible kind of gurgling sound. The head sank down onto the blood snow, shuddered, and lay still.

None of us moved—Fizban because he was unconscious and Owen because he's been battered about quite a bit by the dragon's thrashing, and me because I just didn't feel quite like moving at the time. The dragon didn't move, either, and it was then I realized it was dead.

Owen crouched on his hands and knees, breathing heavily and wiping blood out of his face and eyes. Fizban was stirring and groaning and mumbling something about his hat, so I knew he was all right. I hurried over to help Owen.

"Are you hurt?" I cried anxiously.

"No," he managed and, leaning on me, he staggered to his feet. He took a stumbling step backward, like he didn't mean to, and then caught himself, and stood gasping and staring at the dragon.

Fizban woke up and peered around dazedly. When he saw the dragon's nose lying about a foot from him, he let out a cry, jumped to his feet in panic, and tried to climb backward through a solid wall.

"Fizban," I told him. "The dragon's dead."

Fizban stared at it hard, eyes narrowed. Then, when it didn't move and its eyes didn't blink, he walked over and kicked it in the snout.

"So there!" he said.

Owen could walk some better now, without using me for a crutch. Going over to the dragon, he took hold of the dragonlance and jerked it out of the dragon's hide. That took some doing. The lance had bit deep and he'd buried it almost to the hilt. He wiped the lance in the snow, and we could all see that the tip was sharp and finely honed as ever, not a notch or crack anywhere. Owen looked from the good dragonlance to the broken dragonlance, lying in pieces underneath the dragon's chin.

"One broke and one did what no ordinary lance could do. What is the truth?" Owen looked all puzzled and confused.

"That you killed the dragon," said Fizban.

Owen looked back at the lances and shook his head. "But I don't understand . . ."

"And whoever said you would. Or were entitled to!" Fizban snorted. He picked up his hat and sighed. The hat didn't even look like a hat anymore. It was all scrunched and mushed and slimy.

"Dragon slobber," he said sadly. "And who'll pay for the dry cleaning?" He glared round at us.

I would have offered to pay for it, whatever it was, except I never seem to have much money. Besides, neither Owen nor I were paying attention to Fizban right then. Owen was polishing up the good dragonlance and when he was done with that, he gathered up the pieces of the flawed dragonlance and studied them real carefully. Then he shook his head again and did something that didn't make much sense to me. He very reverently and gently put the pieces of the broken dragonlance all in a heap together, and then wrapped them up in a bundle and tied it with a bit of leather that I found for him in one of my pouches.

I gathered together all my stuff, that had gotten sort of spread out during the running and jumping and hat-waving and dragon-fighting. By that time Owen was ready to go and I was ready to go and Fizban was ready to go and it was then I realized we were all still stuck down in the cave.

"Oh, bother," muttered Fizban, and walking over to the back part of the cave, he kicked at it a couple times with his foot, and the wall tumbled right down.

We were staring out into bright sunshine and blue sky and when we quit blinking we saw that what we'd thought was a wall wasn't. It had only been a snow bank, and I guess we could have walked out anytime at all if only we'd known it was there.

Well, Owen gave Fizban a really odd look.

Fizban didn't see it. He stuck his maltreated hat in a pocket of his robes, picked up his staff, which had been lying in the snow waiting for him, I guess, and walked out into the sun. Owen and I followed; Owen carrying the dragonlances and me carrying my most precious possessions.

"Now," said Fizban, "the kender and I have to travel to Lord Gunthar's, and you, Owen Glendower, have to return to your village and prepare to face the draconian raiding party. No, no, don't mind us. I'm a great and powerful wizard, you know. I'll just magic us to Lord Gunthar's. You haven't got much time. The draconian ran off to alert its troops. They'll move swiftly now. If you go back into the dragon's lair, you'll find that the cave extends all the way through to the other side of the mountain. Cut your distance in half and it will be safe traveling, now that the dragon's dead.

"No, no, we'll be fine on our own. I know where Lord Gunthar's house is. Known all along. We make a left at the pass instead of a right," he said.

I was about to say that's what I'd said all along, only Owen was obviously real anxious to get on his way.

He said good-bye and shook hands with me very formally and politely. And I gave him back the painting and told him rather sternly that if he thought so much of it he should take better care of it. And he smiled and promised he would. And then he shook hands with Fizban, all the time looking at him in that odd way.

"May your moustaches grow long," said Fizban, clapping Owen on both shoulders. "And don't worry about my hat. Though, of course, it will never be the same." He heaved a sad sigh.

Owen stood back and gave us both the knight's salute. I would have given it back, only a snuffle took hold of me right then, and I was looking for a handkerchief. When I found it (in Fizban's pouch) Owen was gone. The snuffle got bigger and it probably would have turned into a sob if Fizban hadn't taken hold of me and given me a restorative shake. Then he raised a finger in the air.

"Tasslehoff Burrfoot," he said, and he looked very solemn and wizardly and so I paid strict attention, which I must admit sometimes I don't when he's talking, "you must promise me that you will never, ever, ever, tell anyone else about the dragonlances."

"What about them?" I asked, interested.

His eyebrows nearly flew up off his head and into the sky, which is probably where my eyebrows were at the moment.

"You mean . . . um . . . about them not working?" I suggested.

"They work!" he roared.

"Yes, of course," I said hurriedly. I knew why he was yelling. He was upset about his hat. "What about Theros? What if he says something? He's a very honest person."

"That is Theros's decision," said Fizban. "He'll take the lances to the Council of Whitestone and we'll see what he does when he gets there."

Well, of course, when Theros got to the Council of Whitestone, which in case you've forgotten was a big meeting of the Knights of Solamnia and the elves and some other people that I can't remember. And they were all ready to kill each other, when they should have been ready to kill the evil dragons, and I was only trying to prove a point when I broke the dragon orb (That's *orb* not *herb!*) and I guess they would have all been ready to kill me, except Theros came with the dragonlances and he threw a lance at the Whitestone and shattered it—the stone, not the lance—so I guess he had decided the lances worked, after all.

Fizban took his slobbered-on hat out of his pocket and perched it gingerly on his head. He began to hum and wave his hands in the air so I knew a spell was coming on. I covered my face and took hold of his sleeve.

"And what about Owen?" I asked. "What if he tells the other knights about the lances?"

"Don't interrupt me. Very difficult, this spell," he muttered.

I kept quiet or at least I meant to keep quiet, but the words came out before I could stop them, in the same sort of way a hiccup comes out, whether you want it to or not.

"Owen Glendower's a knight," I said, "and you know how knights are about telling the truth all the time. He's bound by whatever it is that knights are bound by to tell the other knights about the lances, isn't he?"

"If he does, he does. It's his decision," said Fizban. And he was suddenly holding a flapping black bat in his hand. "Wing of bat!" he shouted at nobody that I could see. "Not the whole damn . . ." Muttering, he let the bat loose, glared at me, and sighed. "Now I'll have to start over."

"It doesn't seem to me very fair," I commented, watching the bat fly into the cave. "If it's Theros's decision to tell or not to tell and Owen's decision then it should be my decision, too. I mean whether or not to say anything about the lances. Working," I added.

Fizban stopped his spell casting and stared at me. Then his eyebrows smoothed out. "By gosh. I believe you've caught on at last. You are absolutely right, Tasslehoff Burrfoot. The decision will be yours. What do you say?"

Well, I thought and I thought and I thought.

"Maybe the lances aren't magical," I said, after thinking so hard that my hair hurt. "Maybe the magic's inside us. But, if that's true, then some people might not have found the magic inside themselves yet, so if they use the lances and think that the magic is outside themselves and inside the lances, then the magic that isn't inside the lances will really be inside them. And after a while they'll come to understand—just like Owen did, though he doesn't—and they'll look for the magic inside and not for the magic outside."

Fizban had the sort of expression that you get on your face when you're sitting in a rope swing and someone winds the rope up real right, then lets it loose and you spin round and round and throw up, if you're lucky.

"I think I better sit down," he said, and he sat down in the snow.

I sat down in the snow and we talked some more and eventually he knew what I was trying to say. Which was that I would never, ever, ever say anything to anybody about the dragonlances not working. And, just to make certain that the words didn't accidentally slip out, like a hiccup, I swore the most solemn and reverent oath a kender can take.

And I want to say right here and now, for Astinus and history, that I kept my oath.

I just wouldn't be me without a topknot.

Chapter Eight

I finished my story. They were all sitting in the Upper Gallery, next to poor Owen Glendower, listening to me. And they were about the best audience I'd ever had.

Tanis and Lady Crysania and Laurana and Caramon and Owen's son and Lord Gunthar all sat staring at me like they'd been frozen into statues by the white dragon's frost breath. But I'm afraid the only thing I was thinking about then was my topknot shriveling up and falling off. I was hoping it didn't, but that's a risk I figured I had to take. I just couldn't let Owen Glendower die of a fit when telling this story might help him, though I didn't see how it could.

"You mean to say," said Lord Gunthar, his moustaches starting to quiver, "that we fought that entire war and risked our very lives on dragonlances that were supposed to be magical and they were just ordinary lances?"

'You said it," I told him, hanging onto my topknot and thinking how fond I was of it. "I didn't."

"Theros of the Silver Arm knew they were ordinary," Lord Gunthar went on, and I could see him getting himself all worked up over it. "He knew the metal was plain steel. Theros should have told someone."

"Theros Ironfeld knew, and Theros Ironfeld split the Whitestone with the dragonlance, Lady Crysania said coolly. "The lance didn't break when he threw it."

"That's true," said Lord Gunthar, struck by the fact. He thought this over, then he looked angry again. "But, as the kender reminded us, Owen Glendower knew. And by the Measure he should have told the Knight's Council."

"What did I know?" asked a voice, and we all jumped up to our feet.

Owen Glendower was standing up in the middle of the pile of cloaks and, though he looked almost as bad as he had when he was fighting the dragon, he had at least come out of his fit.

"You know the truth, Sir!" said Lord Gunthar, scowling.

"I came to know the truth for myself. But how could I know it for any other? That was what I told myself and what I believed until . . . until . . ." He glanced at his son.

"Until I became a knight," said Gwynfor.

"Yes, my son." Owen sighed, and stroked his moustaches that were extremely long now, though they weren't red so much as mostly gray. "I saw you with the lance in your hand and I saw again the lance—the first lance I threw—shatter and fall to pieces in front of my foe. How could I let you go to battle the evil in this world, knowing as I did that the weapon on which your life depended was plain, ordinary? And how could I tell you? How could I destroy your faith?"

"The faith you feared to destroy in your son was not in the dragonlance, but in yourself, wasn't it, Sir Knight?" Lady Crysania asked, her sightless eyes turning to see him.

"Yes, Revered Daughter," answered Owen. "I know that now, listening to the kender's story. Which," he added, his mouth twisting, "wasn't precisely the way it all happened."

Tanis eyed me sternly.

"It was so, too!" I said, but I said it under my breath. My topknot didn't appear to be going anywhere for the time being and I intended to keep it that way.

"It was my faith that faltered the first time," Owen said. "The second, my heart and my aim held true."

"And so will mine, father," said Gwynfor Glendower. "So will mine. You have taught me well."

Gwynfor threw his arms around his father. Owen hugged his son close, which must have been hard to do with all the armor they were wearing, but they managed. Lord Gunthar thought at first he was going to keep being mad, but the more he thought about it, the more I guess he decided he wouldn't. He went over to Owen and they shook hands and then they put their arms around each other.

Laurana went to get Theros, who'd walked out of the room, you remember. He was awfully gruff and grim when he first came back, as if he thought everyone was going to yell at him or something. But he relaxed quite a bit when he saw that

Owen was walking around and smiling, and that we were all smiling, even Lord Gunthar—as much as he ever smiles, which is mostly just a twitch around the moustaches.

They decided to go on with the ceremony of the Forging of the Lance, but it wasn't going to be a "public spectacle" as Tanis put it, when he thought Lord Gunthar wasn't listening. It was going to be a time for the knights to rededicate themselves to honor and courage and nobility and self-sacrifice. And now it would have more meaning than ever.

"Are you going to tell them the truth about the lances?" Laurana asked.

"What truth?" asked Lord Gunthar and for a moment he looked as craft and cunning as Fizban. Then he smiled. "No, I'm not. But I am going to urge Owen Glendower to tell his story to them."

And with that he and Owen and Gwynfor left (Owen said good-bye to me very politely) and went down to Huma's Tomb, where all the other knights were getting ready to fast and pray and rededicate themselves.

"His story!" I said to Tanis, and I must admit I was a bit indignant. "Why, it's my story and Fizban's story just as much as it is Owen's story."

"You're absolutely right, Tas," said Tanis seriously. One thing I do like about Tanis is that he always takes me seriously. "It is your story. You have my permission to go down into Huma's Tomb and tell your side of it. I'm certain that Lord Gunthar would understand."

"I'm certain he better," I said loftily.

I was about to go down to Huma's Tomb, because I was afraid Owen would leave out a lot of the very best parts, only about then Caramon came up to us.

"I don't understand," he said, his big face all screwed up into thought-wrinkles. "Did the lances work? Or didn't they?"

I looked at Tanis. Tanis looked at me. Then Tanis put his arm around Caramon's shoulders.

"Caramon," he said. "I think we better have a little talk.

We used the lances, and we won the war because of them. And so you see . . ."

The two of them walked off. And I hope Caramon understands the truth about the lances now, though I think it's more likely that he just caught Tanis's cold.

I was on my own, and I started once again to go down to Huma's Tomb when the thought occurred to me.

Huma's Tomb. Again.

Now, please don't misunderstand, all you knights who read this. Huma's Tomb is a most wonderful and solemn and sorrowful and feel-sad-until-you-feel-good kind of place.

But I'd seen about all of it I wanted to see in a lifetime.

Right then I heard Tanis sneeze, and I figure he'd need his handkerchief, which he'd left behind in my pocket, so I decided I'd go take it to him instead.

And I figure that about now Owen Glendower must be looking for that little painting of his that he keeps losing. I plan to give it right back to him . . . when he leaves Huma's Tomb.

A Dead Dragon in the Road

(And Other Difficulties to Be Overcome In Getting that First Book Out)

A flashback by Jean Blashfield Black

It wasn't easy, folks. Here are only a few of the difficulties:

1. Persuading the corporate powers-that-be that TSR, a game company, could and should be publishing full novels, not just gamebooks. Fortunately, two steps had already been overcome. First, Tracy Hickman and his cohorts in the game department had convinced said powers that it was possible—nay, even desirable—to create a series of AD&D© game modules that told a continuing story with specific characters. And second, Rose Estes had put TSR in the book business by creating the first Endless Quest© books.

What! You want to compete with the big guys!? Sure, why not! Just picture the number of meetings it took to get the approval for that crazy idea.

2. Finding an author. By some wonderful quirk of fate, I had recently hired Margaret Weis as an editor in the book department. I knew I had made a good decision in getting her to move to Lake Geneva, Wisconsin, from Missouri, but I didn't know how good. Together we developed a plan to offer a story outline to specific known authors, knowing full well that most of them wouldn't be interested. After all, who had ever heard of TSR as a book publisher? But we got a response, and sample chapters from several good writers . . . but it didn't work. They just didn't come to grips with the already existing characters and plotlines. But we already had a novel in the publishing budget for the coming season—autumn (what else?)—1984. We had to do *something.* Without my knowing, Margaret and Tracy spent a weekend writing several sample chapters. Hemming and hawing, they shuffled into my office with it on Monday morning. "Just read it," they said. My first thought was, "Oh dear, how am I going to tell them that it didn't work, that their trying to write the novel was a bad idea?" I fretted over that during a day filled with meetings. Finally, that evening, children tucked in bed, husband out at a meeting, I sat down with their manuscript. 'Nuff said. They had achieved exactly what we wanted.

3. However, by that time it was March, and the manuscript was supposed to be ready by June. They each had to put in their own regular full day of work—Tracy writing games and Margaret editing gamebooks—and then go home at night and write something very different. All while learning to work together—two strong personalities, one a published book writer, the other a game designer with quite firm opinions about the DRAGONLANCE world. Fortunately, they're both workaholics. They did it, folks. By June I had a 1,500-page manuscript for *Dragons of Autumn Twilight.*

4. Stopping Tracy from destroying all the photocopy machines in the building in his zeal to make an infinite numbers of copies of all 1,500 pages. However, it paid off. Turned out that a power-in-his-own-right from Penguin in England obtained a copy. Having nothing better to do on a plane trip back home, he read the rough manuscript.

5. Squeezing all those 1,500 pages in the original manuscript into the format approved by the powers-that-be. This was literally the first time I experienced the total joy of word processing. After Margaret did her editing, I did mine, and somehow we still had a manuscript that didn't have to be retyped! It was glorious. Even more wonderful was actually fitting it into real pages. I cut and snipped here, did a major chopping there, each time checking to see if it now fit into the agreed-upon number of pages.

6. Persuading the legal powers-that-be to allow us to use the word "dragonlance" without a capital and trademark symbol every time it appeared in the book. The Forestmaster might have had to say, "I recognize your blade as ancient and most valuable! . . . but even the great Huma laid the DRAGONLANCE© at my feet." Shudder.

7. Getting the finished books on the shelves of bookstores. Seems like a simple task, but TSR's major distributor to the book trade had seen "Margaret Weis and Tracy Hickman" as authors, said, "Well, who ever heard of them?" and failed to order books. But gamers were finding the book in game stores—finding it, loving it, and telling others about it. They went into bookstores to buy copies, but none were to be had. The stores hadn't even heard of it.

Margaret got mad. I suggested she call a bookstore she knew in Kansas City and find out what was going on. They said no, they didn't have the book, but they'd had several requests for it. Margaret then bravely called the buyer at B. Dalton (before Barnes & Noble bought it). She didn't identify herself but found that the buyer had just had requests for it. Did she know where it could be obtained? You bet, she did! So the sales logjam was broken.

In the meantime, the Penguin editor (see above) liked it so much that Penguin bought the British rights to the book. They had no qualms about unknown authors in bookstores, and the book was selling in the British stores almost as soon as the original American edition.

8. Knowing that success would eventually drive Margaret and Tracy to leave TSR and venture out on their own as successful published fantasy novelists. But what a world had been opened up for fantasy fans everywhere!

Jean Blashfield Black, the founding editor of the TSR Book Department, is currently writing and designing and producing a series of six books on the geologic history of North America. She has published more than a hundred similar books for young people.

Master Tall and Master Small

Margaret Weis and Don Perrin
Originally published in *The Dragons of Chaos*

They called themselves Master Tall and Master Small.

We knew those weren't their real names, of course. We may be mostly farmers in Goodland, but we hadn't just fallen off the hay cart. We knew those names had to be made up. We had no idea what their real names were, however, or why they chose to hide them. That was their business. We're pretty easygoing in Goodland. So long as the strangers didn't cause any trouble, we didn't trouble them.

Master Tall was the taller of the two and he was extremely tall, probably the tallest man that any of us had ever seen and there's been many of us that have traveled out of our lush vale on either business or pleasure, though we never stay long. I'm Lord Mayor of Goodland and so I admit that I may be prejudiced, but of all the places I've been, I've never found one to equal to my valley homeland.

Master Tall was so tall that he had to stoop not only his head, but his shoulders and half of his back to get in through the tavern door and Goodland's tavern was not some ramshackle dive. The only tavern I've seen to match it was one in Solace whose name escapes me.

We assumed that Master Tall had some elf-blood in him. We have nothing against elves in Goodland. We have nothing against anybody in our sunny valley, so long as they're good-humored, good-natured, and don't mind taking a glass of ale and smoking a fine bit of pipe-weed. If they happen to be chess players on top of that . . . but I'm getting ahead of myself.

We call our valley Bread Bowl Valley. It's a large valley, with three towns: one at the north, called Fairfield; one at the south, called Sunnyvale; and our own, Goodland, at the west. In the east is Mount Benefice, named because of the crystal clear water which cascades down from that high peak and waters our valley. Due to the water and the fact that we have more days of sunshine in our valley than almost any other place on Ansalon, our farms are truly blessed by the good gods. We grow food enough not only to feed all the people in our valley, but to ship to lands around us.

This summer, we had heard terrible tales of a severe drought hitting other parts of Ansalon. I myself had traveled down to Northern Ergoth and back and what I saw dismayed me. Crops withering under a blistering sun, creek beds gone dry, grass fires everywhere. On my return, I gazed up at Mount Benefice and offered thanks to Paladine that we remained blessed. The water continued to flow from our mountain top. Our crops were doing excellently well this year.

They would be needed. We began to make plans to distribute our harvest to all those lands near us who would have no food at all this winter.

But it was not harvest time yet. The two strangers came to us in late summer. They entered the tavern in Goodland, bought ale, requested pipes, and very politely drank to the health of the innkeeper. She returned the favor. Next the strangers turned to me. I was wearing my gold chain of office, of course, and so they knew who I was.

"Lord Mayor," they said, "we drink to your fine town and its people."

I raised my glass, more than happy to return the favor. "To your health, friends," I said.

I meant that, too. Outside of the strangeness of their names, which we took for a joke, the two were well dressed and well-spoken, though they were certainly odd looking.

One man was, as I said, inordinately tall, with sharp features that came to a point around his nose, which is what made me think of elves. He was mostly human, however, somewhere around middle age, with silver-gray hair, dark eyes, and a sad, almost wistful, smile. His hands were fine boned, the fingers long and thin.

Master Small was human, too, but I guessed that he had dwarf-blood in him. He was the shortest human I'd ever seen. I've known kender who might top him. He had a chest like an ale barrel, though, and arms that looked as if they could punch through solid rock if he took it into his head to do so. He jingled when he walked, which meant that he was wearing chain mail under his clothing. That wasn't as peculiar as it sounds, since we'd heard rumors of war way, way off to the northwest, somewhere around the Khalkists. Seems like they were forever fighting wars in that part of the country.

Being not only the lord mayor, but the owner of one of the largest grain mills in the valley, I felt it behooved me to make the strangers welcome, and so I made a little speech, welcoming the two to the valley, and then ended by asking if they were on business or pleasure.

"Business *and* pleasure, my Lord Mayor." Master Small rose to his feet and bobbed from the waist. He climbed up on a chair so that all of us in the tavern could see him and continued, "You good people of Goodland are no doubt wondering why we have come to pay your bountiful valley a visit. We've heard that your children are beautiful, your ale superb, and"—he paused with the timing of a thespian—"that you consider yourselves to be the finest chess players in all of Ansalon."

"What do you mean 'consider'?" called out Farmer Reeves, and we all laughed heartily.

As I started to say earlier, if we have one passion in Bread Bowl Vale, (not counting farming), it is playing chess. There was a chessboard on every table in the tavern, a chessboard in every home in the valley, and even a giant chessboard in the town square, which was used for the annual inter-valley match. We had children's chess clubs, the League of Women Chess Players, the League of Men Chess Players, the League of Men and Women Chess Players, the Chess Association, the Chess Guild, and many more. Our chess players traveled throughout Ansalon, wherever there was a tournament, in order to compete. We had to build a hall to house our trophies. We not only knew we were the best, we had carried the proof of that home with us from tourneys all over the land.

Master Small bowed to us to acknowledge this fact, then continued, "For that reason, Master Tall and I have come to Goodland to admire your children, drink your ale, and to challenge each and every one of you to a chess game with Master Tall, who considers himself to be the finest chess player on all of Krynn."

"We'd be delighted to play Master Tall," I said, pulling up a chessboard. "As the lord mayor, I'll go first."

Master Small raised his hand, which, I noted, was callused and sun-browned and seemed more suited to holding a sword than a chess piece. "Ah, a game in a tavern—while enjoyable and friendly—is not quite what we had in mind. Master Tall and I have to eat." Master Small said this in apology, as if this were a weakness. Master Tall nodded sadly. "Chess is a way for us to earn our living. If you will come to where we have pitched our tents, out in the Midsummer Fair grounds, we'll show you what we have in mind. I think you'll find it worth your while."

I said that I'd be out the next day to take a look. The next day, several of us tramped out to the Midsummer Fair grounds, where the strangers had pitched their tents.

The tents were of rich material, made up of panels of red, white, and gold silk sewn together. There were three tents—two small and one large. The two small ones were where Master Tall and Master Small slept. (I couldn't help but wonder if Master Tall slept with his feet sticking out the front, because it didn't seem possible that this tent would hold him.) The big tent was open on all four sides and inside the big tent was a table and two chairs.

The table was round, about three feet in diameter, with four legs. Inlaid in the center of the tabletop was a checkered playing board, the squares made up of light and dark wood.

There sat Master Tall in a chair on one side of the table. The chair in front of him was empty, waiting for an opponent. On the table was a chess set and a small brass dish.

I only saw the small brass dish later. At first, I couldn't see anything but the chess set.

It was simply the grandest, most wonderful, most valuable, most beautiful chess set any of us had ever set eyes upon.

The chess sets we played with were mostly carved of wood, though some of us had brought back sets made of stone from Thorbardin or steel made in Palanthas. We had kings and queens, and knights and castles. This chess set was different. This chess set was made up of dragons and it *wasn't* carved of wood or stone or steel. If there was a precious metal or a rare gem on Ansalon, it was in this chess set.

The golden dragon Paladine ruled the side of light. The chess piece stood at least eight inches high and was carved out of solid gold, crafted with such skill that I could pick out every single one of the dragon's thousand scales. The piece shone like flame in the summer sun. Next to it, where the queen would have customarily stood, was a female dragon. It was carved of solid silver and was so delicate and beautiful that it brought tears to the eyes just to gaze at it.

Across from these was the side of darkness, represented by a five-headed dragon of many colors. This dragon was encrusted with gems. It sparkled with a myriad of colors that dazzled the eye. Next to the five-headed dragon on the board was a black dragon carved from a rare black opal.

The rest of the pieces were equally valuable and equally gorgeous. The rooks were dragon-guarded keeps, with dragons twined about them, made of precious metals on one side and diamond on the other. The knights were dragons mounted with riders, the pawns were smaller brass dragons on the side of good, draconian warriors on the side of darkness. Every piece was made of precious metal—gold, silver, and platinum, or precious gems—diamond, emerald, sapphire, and ruby.

I have heard it said that certain objects are "worth a king's ransom." The Kingpriest of Istar himself may have been worth the price of this chess set, though I doubt it.

I stood and stared at the chess set and was not ashamed to wipe the tears of admiration from my eyes. More than one person around me was doing the same.

Master Small waited until we had all seen our fill of the wondrous dragon chess set, then he announced, "Here are the conditions. You will pay one steel coin for the privilege of playing chess with Master Tall. If you beat him, you leave here with this magnificent chess set."

I couldn't believe my ears. I shifted my stare from the gold and jewels to Master Small and Master Tall.

"Are you gentlemen serious?" I demanded.

"We are serious, Lord Mayor," said Master Small.

I dug my hand into my coin purse, as did everyone else standing around the tent. Steel coins rattled in the brass dish. We put lots into Master Small's hat, to see who the first player would be—Bommon. I groaned in good-natured disappointment. Bommon was one of our champion players. A wing of the trophy hall belonged to Bommon alone.

"Well, friends, we might as well go home," I said to the rest. "Bommon here will win the chess set."

But none went home. Everyone stayed to watch.

Bommon took the side of darkness and, for a moment, it

was all he could do to force his attention to play—he was so fascinated by touching and admiring and exclaiming over all the details of the wonderful chess pieces. But, eventually, he settled down and the game began.

For nearly three-quarters of an hour, Bommon and Master Tall exchanged moves. The rest of us watched, with the exception of Master Small, who apparently had no interest in the game. He gathered up the steel coins and carried them into his tent, then replaced the brass dish on the table. Then he puttered about, polishing up a very handsome sword, which hung in a shabby leather harness outside his tent, and arranging several very fine chessboards and pieces on display for sale, though none as fine as those his partner used.

In the end, Master Tall moved his silver dragon forward one space, smiled, and leaned back in his chair as if to signify the game was at an end. It occurred to me then that I'd never heard him speak a word, not since the two came to town.

Bommon studied the situation, then shook his head.

"Aaagh! You are right. Check and checkmate. You have me, Master Tall," Bommon conceded. He sighed deeply and smiled. "That was, however, the best match I've ever played. I'll remember that combination of moves. I was particularly impressed by your move of your knight to my denied flank. It proved to be brilliant!"

Master Tall bowed slightly in his chair and waved his hand toward the brass dish, as if to invite Bommon to deposit another coin.

Bommon shook his head regretfully.

"I cannot today, I fear! I must get back to my work. I thank you for the game, though. Perhaps tomorrow?"

"Tomorrow, anytime," said Master Small, bustling forward and rattling the brass dish.

Bommon cast one final, longing look at the beautiful chess set, rose and departed.

The rest of us exchanged glances. We'd met our match.

That much was obvious. Rubbing my hands in satisfaction, I sat down to play.

It took Master Tall only fifteen minutes to finish me off. One by one, the rest of us fell to Master Tall's unparalleled skill. But none of us considered our steel wasted. We left that day, but only to go home to practice our moves and prepare for the morrow.

Word of the challenge, the valuable chess set, and Master Tall's skill spread quickly throughout the valley. When I arrived the next day, I had to stand in line behind fifteen people: men, women, and children, eager to try their skill. By the end of the week, there were so many people clamoring to play that Master Small was forced to hand out numbered tickets and schedule appointed times.

Large crowds gathered around the main tent, watching in a breathless silence that was broken only by the ring of steel coins in the brass dish. More tents had sprung up, the business-minded of Goodland not failing to take full advantage of this opportunity. The Widow Peck was doing a brisk business selling fresh fruit to those who grew hungry while waiting. Alderman Johannson was offering to impart guaranteed winning strategies to anyone who would pay him three steel. The crowd was in a good humor.

"Today's my big day, eh, Master Tall?" called out Goodwife Bacon.

Otto Smithy behind her shouted, "You'll only need to play as far as me, Master Tall! After that, you won't have your fine chess set anymore."

The first match for the day began. It was clear by the sixth move that Master Tall had won. His opponent, a short man from the Tailor's Guild, stood up and shook Master Tall's hand.

"I fear I am not at my best today. You are truly the best chess player I've ever come across, with one exception."

Master Tall looked startled, lifted his head.

Master Small strode up, his interest piqued at last. "And who would that one exception be, good sir?"

"The man we call Blackshanks, Master. We don't know much about him. He hasn't been here long, or at least if he has we haven't seen him before this summer. He lives somewhere up in the mountain, and he comes down to the valley every now and then for a game of chess. He's a loner, sort of a rough fellow and not very friendly. But he's a fierce lover of chess, and as good as Master Tall here or better, if you'll excuse my saying so."

Master Tall did appear extremely put out by the remark. He frowned down at the chessboard and pushed the pieces back and forth with his long index finger.

Master Small smoothed things over with a smile and a clap on the back. "Well, then, perhaps this Blackshanks'll come by and give us a match, eh, Tailor? Then we'll see."

Perhaps he would. I myself had played a game with the mysterious Blackshanks and, though he was far from being a genial opponent, he was certainly an excellent player. He had demolished me in three moves, using a gambit I'd never seen before nor have I seen it since. From that moment on, we in Goodland began to talk of what a great game that would be, and we started looking out for Blackshanks, hoping he'd make one of his rare visits to our town.

"Next player," called Master Small.

A tall woman in well-worn boots and fighting breeches took her seat. Master Tall stood, bowed slightly, and reseated himself. By twenty moves, Master Tall had proven himself again. Without a word, the woman rose and stalked out of the tent.

The day continued on with match after match. Master Tall never took a break, not even to eat. Master Small busied himself around the area, occasionally darting into his own tent to restock his supply of chess sets. Sales were brisk, with many a potential challenger purchasing a set for playing while waiting—practicing against the other players.

By the end of that day, Master Tall had defeated seventeen opponents. The line outside the tent had not diminished. Master Small went out to address the fifty players waiting.

"We will continue the matches until sundown. Those who have not yet played are welcome to return in the morning. If you cannot play tomorrow, then please be good enough to return your tickets and let someone else take your place. For a full refund, of course."

The wonderful chess set glowed and sparkled in the late evening sunshine that filtered through the tent. Everyone who sat down to play with those marvelous pieces longed to see them shine in his or her own dwelling place. Master Tall's phenomenal skill amazed and delighted all who watched and all who played against him.

No one turned in a single ticket.

The next day was a repeat of the one before. People arrived at the tent long before the two men were even awake, sitting quietly on the grass outside the big tent, practicing their moves.

Master Tall set to work immediately. By noon-sun, he had defeated eleven players, and his pace seemed to be accelerating. His eleventh player, Toby Wheeler, one of our more inquisitive ten-year-olds, asked, "Why is it that the human kings and queens are dragons on your set, Master Tall?"

Master Tall cast a sad-eyed glance in the direction of Master Small, who hurried over to reply.

"A wise question, son. Master Tall and I believe that the forces of good and evil are far more influenced by dragons than by any human. The power, intelligence, and wisdom of dragons make them more appropriate for the primary pieces on the board, wouldn't you agree?"

Toby shrugged, not much interested in the philosophy, far more interested in winning. He made his move. Master Tall neatly countered, and within four more moves had the game decided in his favor.

"I don't suppose I could take home just a pawn?" Toby said, fingering a jewel-encrusted draconian with longing.

Master Tall shook his head. Toby set down the pawn and ran off to rejoin his playmates.

Two more days passed, with Master Tall defeating all

who came before him. He had just passed his one hundredth victory mark early on the fifth day, when the line of people waiting to play and those standing around watching began to buzz and whisper and point. I had been over visiting the Widow Peck and, turning, looked to see what all the fuss was about. A man dressed in black, with black leather pants and long black boots, came strolling up the hill.

"Blackshanks!" The excited whisper went about.

Such was the nickname we'd given him, since he never volunteered to give us a name of his own.

Blackshanks quietly took his place at the end of the line. Master Small hurried over and offered the brass dish. Blackshanks dropped one steel coin into it. A ripple of anticipation passed through the crowd. Several small boys dashed into town to spread the news, and soon most of the population of Goodland had left their crops and their washing, their blacksmiths and their innkeeping to watch what we knew would be the chess match of the century.

Master Tall was obviously looking forward to this game as much as the rest of us. He kept glancing down the line at Blackshanks, and finished off the next players rapidly, with what seemed absentminded skill. Even Master Small appeared to be excited at the prospect of a match. He ended the sale of his chessboards and, settling down to polish his sword, rubbed it with such fervor that it gleamed.

Blackshanks waited and watched and spoke to no one. He was not a likable fellow. In fact, most of us always felt rather uneasy when he was around and were generally extremely glad when he left. He had cold black eyes, cold pale skin, and cold, clammy hands. I myself had hinted that there were other valleys just as nice as ours in other parts of the world where I was sure he would be more comfortable, but he always maintained that he liked Goodland best.

Which was quite flattering, so how could I argue?

Still, I had to admit that I was glad Blackshanks hadn't left quite yet. Not before he played chess with Master Tall.

At last, it was Blackshanks's turn. He strode up to the

table, stood and looked at the wonderful chessboard. A faint tinge of color rose into his cold pallid cheeks. He gazed at the chess set with a longing that, truly, I don't believe any of us had felt—and most of us wanted that chess set pretty badly. Blackshanks didn't just want it. He coveted it, lusted after it. He reached out a hand to touch the five-headed dragon made up of different colored precious jewels. His hand shook with his longing and I heard him breathe a soft sigh.

"Is it true," he said in a sepulchral voice that set the teeth on edge and made goose bumps chase themselves up my back, "that you will give this fine chess set to anyone who beats you?"

"True enough, sir," said Master Small.

Blackshanks silently took his seat. Master Tall sat forward. Master Small actually ceased polishing his sword and, elbowing his way through the crowd, stood beside his partner to watch, something he'd never done before. He had an anxious expression on his face. Master Tall looked grim.

Undoubtedly, they feared they might lose their valuable chess set.

Blackshanks made the opening move, a bold jaunt forward with a knight. Master Tall nodded, then looked over at Master Small, something he'd never done before. Master Small nodded back. Master Tall looked to the board, thought for a long, long time, then made a counter move with a rook.

Blackshanks grunted and settled down to serious play.

The game continued for thirty moves with neither side gaining an advantage. The crowd gathered around the board was as silent as if they had all been watching from their graves.

The game reached fifty moves, and the advantage was beginning to sway to the challenger. Master Tall appeared nervous. His hand trembled as he touched his golden dragon king. Master Small was sweating and looking even more anxious than before. Master Tall nodded once again to his partner, then made a move with his gold dragon.

Blackshanks laughed slowly, and moved his own five-headed dragon into a winning position. "Check and checkmate, Master Tall."

A collective sigh swept through the crowd. We had just witnessed a chess match that we would be talking about for the rest of our lives, but it wasn't that. It seemed a terrible shame to us that the cold and unlikable Blackshanks should now be the owner of the exquisite chess set.

Master Tall sat back in his chair, pale and broken. Master Small appeared to be in shock. His mouth opened and shut, but he had been robbed of speech.

"It looks as if I've bested you, Master Tall," said Blackshanks, leering. "I'd be obliged if you'd hand over the prize now."

We all waited, hope against hope, for Master Tall to make some brilliant move that would yet win the day. He stared at the board, shook his head, then, slowly, he rose to his feet. He bowed to his opponent.

"It is true that you have beaten me, sir." He motioned for the crushed and quivering Master Small to come forward. "Bring the box, Master Small. We must pack up the chess set."

"Pack it well," ordered Blackshanks in a nasty tone. "I've a long way to go and I don't want it harmed."

Master Small stifled a sob, walked with feet dragging into his tent. Master Tall sank back down in his seat, as if his legs had gone weak and could not bear his weight. He touched each piece lovingly, saying good-bye. I had to turn away. I could not bear to see the pain on his face.

Long moments went by. Master Small did not reappear and Blackshanks began to grow impatient.

"Not thinking of trying to back out on our deal, are you, Master Tall?" Blackshanks said, his face paling in anger. "Keep your box. I don't need it."

Reaching out his hand, he picked up the golden dragon and was about to thrust it into his pocket when Master Small emerged from his tent.

Those standing near him gasped and drew back, while people in the back of the crowd strained to see what was causing all the commotion.

Master Small wasn't carrying a box. The only object he carried was his sword. He was dressed in full plate mail that shone silver in the sunlight and over the armor he wore the tabard of a Knight of the Rose.

He marched up to Blackshanks, who was regarding him with suspicion and disdain.

"What's this?" Blackshanks demanded, with a harsh laugh. "Dressed up for the Night of the Eye, are you?"

Master Small slid his sword from his scabbard and held it in front of him in a knightly salute.

"I am Sir Michael Stoutbody, Knight of the Order of the Rose. The Holy Writ of Paladine requires me, as a Knight of Solamnia, to counter evil wherever I find it. It is my duty, therefore, Blackshanks or whatever it is you call yourself, to best you in combat. Prepare yourself, sir."

Blackshanks stared, then he began to laugh. Sir Michael came to Blackshanks's waist. "You little runt!" Blackshanks snorted. "Better put that sword down before you hurt some-one."

I looked at Master Tall, hoping he might intervene to save his partner from further embarrassment. He merely watched, a half-smile playing about his mouth.

As lord mayor, I would have to take things into my own hands.

I made my way forward. "Here, now, Master Small," I said. "Blackshanks won fair and square. It was a great game. It's a shame to lose your valuable chess set, but you were the ones who offered it, you know."

Sir Michael bowed to me. "Lord Mayor, if you will take my advice, you will warn your people to leave this area and return to their homes."

"But, really, my dear sir—" I stopped.

Blackshanks was glaring at the knight with such hatred that it made me wish I was well on the other side of Mount

Benefice with a good horse and a clear road. I began to back off, away from the tent.

"Ladies and gentlemen," I called out, "I think it would be a good idea if you did as advised. Especially those of you with small children."

A feeling of dread, of danger, spread over us like the creeping of a dark, dank fog through our sunny vale. Children began to whimper in fear and I must admit that I felt as if a whimper or two might be in order. As Lord Mayor of Goodland, it was my duty to remain on the scene, as did some of the aldermen. The rest of our townspeople ran down the hillside in a panic that seemed to grow and spread like wildfire.

All the time, Blackshanks had not moved. He stood, holding the golden dragon in his hand, his gaze shifting from Master Small to Master Tall and back again.

"You have been challenged, sir," said Sir Michael in cool tones. He drew his sword from his scabbard. "Fight or perish where you stand, Evil One."

Blackshanks suddenly hurled the golden dragon piece straight at Sir Michael. The knight lifted his arm; the piece struck him on the shoulder and bounced off.

"Evil I am, little knight," Blackshanks snarled, "but not as you might suspect. I have a surprise for you, Sir Michael."

Blackshanks placed his hand on a ring he wore and suddenly the man's appearance began to change. He started to grow. He'd been about my height, maybe a bit more, but within a minute he was taller than the center pole holding up the tent. His clothes seemed to melt from his body, and in their place glistened black scales! Wings sprouted from his back. His jaw thrust forward, his nose stretched out to meet it, and became a snout over a mouth filled with hideous fangs. His eyes were red as the rubies in the chess set. Claws curled from his fingers. A black tail lashed savagely.

"This is my true form!" he announced, enjoying our terror.

Quivering in the air around Blackshanks was the transparent image of a black dragon. He had not completed his shapeshifting yet, but that is what he would be when the transformation was finished.

The dragon was enormous. It loomed over us with snapping maw and deadly acid breath and a wingspan that banished the sun, shrouded us in darkness.

At the sight, some of the people who had remained with me shrieked and began to flee down the hillside. I would have liked to run away, but I was paralyzed from the shock of it all.

A black dragon!

We'd been harboring a black dragon in our peaceful valley!

"You are doomed!" Blackshanks hissed. "How can a runt like you battle a powerful creature like me?"

In another moment, he would be taller than the tallest oak trees, his acid breath would come raining down on us. In another moment . . .

"You should have fought me in your man-form," advised Sir Michael. "I gave you that chance."

He jumped to attack the half-man, half-beast. Had the sword encountered flesh, it would have finished Blackshanks. The knight's sword hit scales, however, and the blow glanced harmlessly off.

Blackshanks kicked out with his dragon-haunch leg, struck Sir Michael in the chest, and sent the knight reeling backward. Sir Michael crashed into the table holding the chess set. The table smashed. Sir Michael tumbled down and lay dazed amid the wreckage. The wondrous pieces fell over him, like rose petals scattered over a grave.

Master Tall knelt beside his friend, looking anxious, and checked to make certain he was all right.

"I'm not hurt!" Sir Michael gasped, already struggling to get back on his feet. "You must . . . stop him! Don't . . . let him grow. . . ."

Sensible words. The dragon was growing larger by the

second. His wings were starting to unfurl, his neck snaked out in a sinuous curve. More and more scales covered his body, rapidly closing up all areas that might be vulnerable to attack.

Master Tall sprang to his feet. Holding up his right hand, he spoke a single word. The word sounded among us like the call of a silver trumpet bringing an army of knights to our rescue. I did not understand the word, but it brought faint hope to my heart and, for a moment, lifted my fear.

Whatever it meant, that word seemed to be one of arcane power. It struck Blackshanks as if it had been a spear. He gasped, quivered in rage and gnashed his teeth.

The shapeshifting spell came suddenly to an end. Now Blackshanks was caught in between two forms: half man, half dragon.

The beast howled and gibbered and lashed at Master Tall with a lethal claw, but Master Tall kept carefully out of range. Slowly, Master Tall, chanting more strange words, began to circle around Blackshanks, who was endeavoring to follow the man's movements with his snaky head.

As he circled, Master Tall made twining motions with his hands, as though he were braiding a chain, a chain that he alone could see.

The man-dragon was caught in mid-transformation, like a chick half in and half out of its shell. Enraged, Blackshanks lunged with snapping jaws at Master Tall. The man-dragon couldn't move with the speed of a black dragon, however, and the deadly fangs closed over air. Master Tall began racing around and around the infuriated dragon, winding fast the great invisible chain he was weaving.

"Hurry, lord knight!" Master Tall shouted. "I can't hold this spell for long!"

Sir Michael was on his feet, his sword in his hand. Puffing beneath his heavy armor, he dashed forward at the furious, spitting and clawing man-dragon.

Sir Michael thrust his sword. The man-dragon parried the strike with a swipe of its claw, or at least Blackshanks would have parried it, had the blow actually been struck. As it was, Sir Michael's attack had been a feint. He held his blade until the dragon's lethal claws had swiped past, then Sir Michael lunged forward, stabbing with all his strength, aiming for a part of the chest that had not yet been fully covered over with black scales.

The blade passed through the chest of the half man, half dragon and emerged, covered with blood, out the back of the beast. Blackshanks roared in pain and tried to free himself from the sword. Sir Michael held on gamely, though he was lifted clean off his feet by the efforts of the pain-maddened beast.

The dying dragon whipped back and forth. Blood and its acid breath rained down on Sir Michael, burning the knight's flesh wherever it touched. At length, Sir Michael was forced to let loose. He fell heavily, groaning in pain.

The black dragon plucked the sword from his chest, but it was too late. The wound was mortal. Blackshanks began to slump toward the ground. He gazed with fury at the two who had defeated him, particularly the tall, skinny chess player.

"Who?" he managed to gasp. "Tell me! Who are you who has slain me? No ordinary human, as you pretend!"

Master Tall stepped forward. "This is for my family and my clan. In the name of Vloorshad the Swift, and of Huma the bravest of them all, it is my honor to end the line of Basalt Blackdragon, his stain upon Krynn finally at an end. You are his final progeny, and with you dies great evil in Ansalon."

Blackshanks looked up with his dying gaze. He saw, as all of us saw then, rippling around Master Tall, the transparent outline of a silver-scaled body, the graceful shape of a large silver-scaled dragon's head. Silver wings lifted over Blackshanks. He snarled, turned his face away, and died.

The image of the silver dragon faded, leaving only Master Tall, chess player, behind.

Master Tall helped Sir Michael to his feet. The rest of us

stood staring at the two of them in wordless and somewhat wary amazement.

Sir Michael smiled reassuringly. "Don't be afraid, my friends. This is Sheen Vloorshad, youngest of the silver dragon clan of Vloorshad. We are sorry to have deceived you and the fine citizens of Goodland, my Lord Mayor," the knight added, turning to me, "but we had to lure Basalt from his lair in order to slay him, and this was the one way which we were certain would work."

Master Tall gazed down at the twitching black carcass. "It is well known—Basalt Blackdragon could never resist a game of chess."

****

And so ends the story of the greatest chess game for the highest stakes ever to be played in our valley.

We carried Sir Michael into town, where the two were celebrated as heroes. Our cleric attended to his injuries and he was well enough to have dinner as my guest, along with Master Tall.

"How were you so certain that Blackshanks was a black dragon?" I asked.

"Because he was the only one who defeated me," said Master Tall, with a smile. "No offense, Lord Mayor, to you or your fine townspeople. You are skilled chess players, no doubt of it. But you're only human, after all."

I must admit that rankled a bit. "I'll play you right here and now," I said, reaching for the chessboard.

Master Tall rose to his feet, smiling and shaking his head. "I'm sorry, Lord Mayor, but if I never in my next thousand years play another game of chess, it will be too soon."

Sir Michael also rose. "Farewell, Lord Mayor. We must return to make our report and take up the fight against Lord Ariakan. If you people of Bread Bowl Valley will take my suggestion, you will put aside the chessboards and start preparing to face a real enemy."

"We will do it. I can't begin to thank you two enough," I

said, giving them each a parting handshake. "May Paladine guide your footsteps."

Sir Michael and the silver dragon left the tavern, amid shouts and cheers from the populace.

I was just about to call a meeting of the town aldermen, when a young boy came dashing up to me. He held, in his hand, a large wooden box.

"What's this?" I asked.

"Them two strangers said I was to give it to you, my Lord Mayor," said the boy.

On top of the box was a note:

We leave this with you, Lord Mayor. We think it would make a fitting addition to your trophy hall. May it bring you and your people good fortune.

I opened the lid to the box.

There, glittering and sparkling in the torch light, was the magnificent chess set.

It was missing only one piece: that of the black dragon.

DEMONS OF THE MIND

Margaret Weis and Don Perrin

Originally published in *Tales of the Fifth Age: Relics and Omens*

Crockery crashed to the floor, plates smashing, mugs cracking, sounding like the last note from the last trump of doom. The noise—coming on a warm, gently quiet, sunny afternoon in midsummer—startled Caramon, who jumped violently and struck his head on an overhanging shelf. Rising ponderously to his feet, he glared over the counter, wincing and rubbing his head.

Tika dashed past, giving Caramon The Look on her way. Caramon always thought of her look as The Look, spelled with capital letters. He had been on the receiving end of The Look very often in his married life. The Look said, plain as speech, "Not a word to me, Caramon! Not a single word!"

Caramon had fought goblins, hobgoblins, draconians, dragons, and the odd assorted thief, rogue, and evil cleric. But he knew better than to challenge The Look.

Caramon loved his wife dearly. If anyone on Krynn had asked him to name the most beautiful and wonderful, the wisest and bravest woman he'd ever known, he would have said Tika Waylan Majere instantly, without a qualm or a second thought.

Gray streaked her red hair now, her face showed the marks of laughter, the tracks of tears. She had fought at his side during a war to bring the gods back to Krynn, she had stood by his side during the war that presumably saw the gods leave Krynn. Caramon and Tika had buried two dearly loved sons during the last war, been present at the funerals of two dearly loved friends. Their love kept them strong, comforted them in their sorrow.

Most important, Caramon credited Tika with saving his life during the terrible time when he had come close to falling a victim to the brain-rotting effects of the potent liquor known as dwarf spirits. She had sent him on a quest to find himself, to find his own strength, his own worth as a person. A world without Tika was a world in which Caramon would not want to live. But when she gave him The Look, he wished a portion of that world might open up and swallow him.

Biting his tongue, he ducked back behind the bar, continued to mop up spilled ale.

"There, Jassar," Tika said, her voice coming to him from the kitchen. "There, girl, don't take on so. It's only a few broken plates and a mug or two."

Caramon groaned. He knew how Tika counted. "A few" meant fifteen or twenty, in all likelihood. Caramon had never known a barmaid to be so clumsy.

He bided his time, said nothing until that night when the inn's doors had closed on the last customer and he and Tika were making ready for bed. Caramon sat on the bed, pulling off his boots. Tika sat before her mirror, which hung on the wall before her. She brushed her hair one hundred strokes as she did every night. Caramon felt safe in bringing up the subject, for her back was to him.

"I know you're fond of her, my dear," Caramon said, "but that Jassar's got to go."

Caramon had not taken the mirror into account. He discovered, too late, that The Look worked equally well by reflection. Bouncing off the mirror, The Look struck him squarely between the eyes.

"She hasn't been with us that long. She needs a bit of training. The trays are awkward and hard to balance. She was upset about something that happened at home," said Tika, brushing her hair with unusual force so that it actually crackled.

Caramon breathed a sigh. When Tika started handing out excuses, he knew he was safe. The Look had been reflexive, apparently. He had to tread cautiously, however.

"Jassar's been with us for three months now, my dear," Caramon said mildly, careful to make it an observation, not an argument. "She was okay when she started—not great, but okay. But she hasn't gotten any better. In fact, she's gotten worse! The customers are complaining. She mixes up orders, when she remembers to bring the orders at all. She's jumpy as a kender in a prison cell. That's the fifth tray of plates she's dropped this week. I've had to replace them at least once a week, and now the potter grins from ear to ear when he sees me coming. He's planning to build a new house on our business alone! We're losing customers and we're losing money. I'm sorry, Tika, Jassar's a nice girl and all, but we can't afford to keep her."

He prepared to duck, should The Look come his way. But Tika only sighed, set down her brush—after only seventy-nine strokes—and turned to face him. Her face was drawn, softened.

"This is the fourth job she's had in a year. Without her work, she and her husband will starve."

"What's the matter with her husband?" Caramon asked. "Why doesn't he pull his share? Come to think of it, I don't believe I've ever seen him around."

"You would if you went to the Trough," Tika said, her voice low.

"Ah, that's the way of it, is it?" Caramon looked grave. He had spent considerable time at the Trough himself once, back in the dwarf-spirit days.

"He's a cripple. He lost his arm in the war," Tika added by way of explanation.

"Our sons lost more than that," Caramon returned quietly. "They gave their lives. This man's the lucky one"

"He doesn't seem to think so. Anyway, that's why Jassar's mind isn't on her work. She's worried about him. I know how she feels, Caramon. I understand. I know what it was like when you were drinking. At least you didn't . . ." She stopped.

"Didn't what?" Caramon frowned. "He doesn't beat her, does he?"

"He always says he's sorry afterward," Tika said. "Now, Caramon, it's none of our business—"

"Yes, it is!" Caramon stood up, his fist clenched. "I'll give him a taste of his own medicine and see how he likes it! There's no bigger coward than a man who beats a woman."

"Caramon, don't! Please!" Tika crossed over to him, put her hands pleadingly on his chest. "You'll only make things worse for her."

"Well, now," said Caramon, smoothing down his wife's rampant hair, "I won't be rough with him, though I'd like to. But I can at least talk to him. I know what it's like to have your head in a bottle."

"Then Jassar can stay?" Tika asked, nestling against her husband's broad chest.

"She can stay," said Caramon, sighing. "And the potter can have his new house."

****

The next day, Caramon took off his apron, folded it neatly over the bar, and left the inn. As he walked along the boardwalks—the town of Solace was built in the tops of the giant vallenwood trees, its buildings connected by swinging bridges and boardwalks—people called out greetings, came to shake his hand, engage him in conversation. Children ran to be lifted onto his broad shoulders, cats rubbed around his ankles, dogs jumped up to lick his hands.

A modest man, Caramon was always astonished at the attention, received it with true pleasure. When he looked into Tika's mirror, he saw a middle-aged, stout (not fat, stout) man, with maybe a chin or two more than was absolutely necessary. He honestly could not understand what people saw in him. What he couldn't see, but which others did, was a face whose customary cheerfulness was tempered by a gravity that opened hearts to him, for he seemed to say, "Whatever your sorrow, I have known it, and yet I can still find joy in every sunrise." Caramon Majere was now one of the best liked, most admired men in Solace.

But that hadn't always been the case. Caramon remembered when he'd been the most detested man—a sodden, blubbering drunk. People had avoided him then, children had fled in terror, dogs sniffed him and trotted off in disgust. He hadn't liked himself then, and so he wasn't surprised that no one else liked him either. He pondered on his own past as he followed his wife's directions to Jassar Lathhauser's dwelling, located in the old, run-down, and mostly abandoned part of Solace.

Few people came here anymore. No respectable citizens, only transients, rogues, squatters, and derelicts. The houses perched sullenly and precariously in the trees, ready to tumble down at the slightest provocation. Caramon had proposed more than once that these unsafe houses be torn down and new homes built in their place. He made a mental note to bring it up again at the next town meeting.

He found the house, which he was relieved to see was actually somewhat sturdier than the others around it, and knocked on the door.

No answer.

Jassar's husband was inside. The smell of dwarf spirits was rank. He was probably sleeping off last night's toot. Caramon banged loudly on the door, then recollected that this would have little effect. He recalled the dwarves who had spent the night hammering in his head after a drinking bash. The man wouldn't be able to hear the knock on the door for the thuds between his ears.

The door wasn't locked, didn't even have a lock on it. Caramon shoved it open. The smell of dwarf spirits and vomit hit him full in the gut. He wrinkled his nose, glanced about the one-room shack. The man lay facedown on the bed, still in his clothes. The sun coming in the window seemed repulsed by the sight, for it glanced off the foot of the bed, didn't come near the head.

Caramon turned on his heel, walked out the door, and headed for the nearest town pump. He filled a bucket with water, ice-cold from the deep well, and brought it back to the house. He flung the water on the slumbering drunk.

The man sat bolt upright, sputtering and gasping with the shock. "You bitch! What do think you're doing?"

Bleary-eyed, he couldn't see who was there. Assuming it was his wife, he swung out with his left fist. He had no right fist. His sleeve hung bare from the shoulder down. "You know better than to wake me. . . ."

"I'm not your wife," said Caramon sternly, his booming voice rattling the cracked windowpanes. "You can take a swing at me and welcome, Gemel Lathhauser. But it's only fair to warn you that I hit back."

The man looked up, startled. Then he scowled. "What's the idea . . . bargin' in here? . . . Get lost. . . ."

"My name's Caramon Majere. Your wife works for me at the inn. I've come to talk to you about her."

"Did she say I hit her? If she did, she's a liar. It's none of your damn business anyway." Gemel lurched to his feet. He was unshaven, unwashed, his clothes much the worse for wear. Yet he must have been a good-looking man once. His body was still strong and well muscled, though he had the pot belly of a drinker. The jawline that was now weak and puffy must have once been firm, decisive. And when he had referred to his wife as a liar, he'd actually had the grace to look ashamed of himself. He obviously didn't like what he'd become any more than she did.

"Your wife loves you," Caramon began.

"She doesn't love me!" Gemel snarled, anger burning away the fog left by the spirits. "She pities me because of this"—he grabbed hold of his empty sleeve, gave it a shake—"and won't leave me alone. I'd be better off without her, but she keeps hanging around."

"You figure if you hit her enough you'll drive her away," Caramon said. "Look, Gemel, I've been where you are. I know what you're going through—"

"No, you don't!" Gemel shouted, with a vehemence that shocked Caramon. "You've got two good arms, blast you! How in the name of the gods who forsook us can you know what I'm feeling! Get out, you bastard!"

Gemel grabbed hold of Caramon's shirt with some wild thought of shoving the big man out the door.

Caramon brushed off the man's trembling hand with ease. "Now, look here," he said, trying to be patient.

"No. You look!" Gemel kicked Caramon in the stomach.

Caramon doubled over, groaning, fell back a step.

"Get out!" Gemel said again, grinding his teeth. "Mind your own damn business."

Caramon sucked in a breath. "You just made this my business," he said and, head down, he charged straight at Gemel.

The two crashed to the floor, shaking the house and causing it to creak ominously. The men punched and jabbed. Though Gemel lacked an arm, he was younger than Caramon and someone somewhere had trained the man for combat.

Caramon was rapidly becoming winded. He drew back his great fist, thinking to end it with a single punch, when he saw tears streaming down the face of his opponent.

Caramon lowered his fist. "What's the matter?"

"C'mon, hit me, damn it! Hit me!" Gemel collapsed into a heap. He began to sob uncontrollably, violent sobs that tore at him.

Stunned and embarrassed to see a grown man weeping like a child, Caramon didn't know what to do. Reaching out, he patted the man tentatively on the shoulder.

"It's my arm!" Gemel cried, his voice choked. "It aches. It aches constantly, and I can't stop the pain."

"Did I land on it too hard? I'm really sorry," Caramon said, overcome with guilt.

"Not my left arm," Gemel said. He sat upright, wiped his face. "It's my right arm. My sword arm. My hand's clenched around the hilt so tightly, I can't let loose. I can't make the aching stop."

Caramon stared blankly at Gemel. "But you don't have a right arm."

"I can damn well see that," Gemel snapped, glowering. "It still hurts, though. I can feel it! Day and night. I can't let loose of the sword! I can't sleep. I can't work! I'm going to go crazy! I'd chop my arm off if it weren't already gone."

Privately Caramon thought Gemel might already be crazy. He decided it would be best to humor him.

"So you drink to . . . um . . . ease the pain?"

"Hah!" Gemel smiled bitterly. "You'd think that would help, wouldn't you? But it doesn't. I can still feel my arm ache no matter how drunk I get. But at least I can sleep."

"That's not sleep. It's a drunken stupor," said Caramon. "How did you lose your arm?"

"Why should you care?" Gemel returned, sullen. "It happened."

Caramon regarded him thoughtfully for a few moments. "Here, let's get you cleaned up. When was the last time you had a good meal? One you didn't wash down with dwarf spirits."

"I don't know," Gemel said wearily. He stood up and almost fell over. Staggering to a rickety chair, he sat down, covered his eyes with his good hand. "What does it matter to you, anyway? I'm sorry I kicked you, but if I want to drink myself to death, what right have you got to stop me?"

"It's a matter of crockery," said Caramon. "And the potter building a new house."

"Huh?" Gemel stared up at him.

"Never mind," Caramon said. "I'll give the problem some thought. Now, let's get a good breakfast inside you. There's nothing much goes wrong with a man that ham and eggs can't cure. And while you're eating, you can tell me all about the battle. I was a soldier myself once, you know," he added modestly.

****

"You're right, Caramon," said Tika the next morning. "That Gemel's gone raving mad. How can an arm that isn't there hurt? How can a hand that doesn't exist hold a sword? I'm going to tell Jassar to leave him right this minute. She can live here with us until . . ." Tika paused, stared at her husband. "What are you doing?"

"Just packing up a few things," Caramon said, stuffing a shirt and a change of stockings into a leather bag. "I'm going to take a little trip. He doesn't know it yet, but Gemel's coming with me. We'll ride the horses. They could use the exercise."

"They could? He is? You are?" Tika stared at her husband in astonishment. Perhaps one reason their marriage had been so enduring was that he could still surprise her. "All right, Caramon," she said briskly, hands on her hips. "What have you got planned?"

Caramon paused in the act of rummaging for his walking boots. "I know what Gemel means about the arm that isn't there hurting him. I felt that way when Raist left to take the black robes. Like part of me had been cut away, and yet that part still ached. You sent me away on a quest to find myself. I think it's time Gemel made the same journey.

"In the meanwhile"—Caramon slowly unfolded a piece of paper he'd had stuffed in his pocket—"take this to John Carpenter. Have him make me a box to these dimensions: three feet in length, two feet wide and one foot high. Cut three holes in the end, two of them six inches in circumference. No lid. The box is open on the top, and I want a wooden divider running down the center.

"Tell him to make the box of used wood from some of the dilapidated shacks, so that it looks really old. Oh, and tell him to carve a Sign of the Eye on it—you know, the symbols the wizards used to use. He should have it ready for me when I get back, say in about three weeks."

Tika walked over, placed her hand on Caramon's broad forehead. "You're not running a fever." She eyed him suspiciously. "*You* haven't been at the Trough, have you?"

"I'm fine and I'm sober," he said, smiling at her. Leaning down, he kissed her. "I'll be back in three weeks. Take good care of Jassar."

"You're not going to tell me, are you?"

Caramon shook his head, looked grave. "You are my wife, Tika, and I love you better than I love life itself but you can't keep a secret to save your soul."

Tika's cheeks flushed, but Caramon was so earnest and so serious that her anger changed to laughter. She admitted, grudgingly, that he might be right.

"The gods go with you, Caramon," she said, kissing him tenderly.

"There aren't any gods, remember?" he said.

"Who says? Fizban? You'd take the word of an old fool who can't remember his name half the time? Be off with you, Caramon Majere. I haven't got all day to stand around and talk nonsense."

Gemel had at first refused to go. He had been adamant in his refusal. Caramon had not argued with him. The big man had simply planted himself in Gemel's house, immovable as Prayer's Eye Peak, stating that he intended to sit there for a month if necessary. In vain, Gemel had argued and threatened and cursed. Caramon had said only two words: "Get dressed." He had refused to even tell Gemel where they were going.

Now they'd been on the road for a week, and Gemel still didn't quite know why he'd come, except it seemed the only way to get this big, galumphing oaf of an innkeeper out of his life. Yeah, so Majere had been a Hero of the Lance. Gemel had heard the bard's stories, the minstrel's songs. He knew all about Caramon Majere—how he'd fought dragons and even the Dark Queen herself. How his brother had been the greatest wizard who had ever lived.

Maybe. Maybe not. Minstrels and bards were singing songs about the Chaos War, too. About the glory and the honor. They never sang about the fear that turns a man into a whimpering child. They never sang about the blood, the death, the pain.

Gemel rode along morosely, gritting his teeth against the aching of his arm, refusing to talk except to hint now and then that they might stop at a tavern and break the journey's monotony. Caramon always refused. They ate what food he'd brought, and when that was gone, they ate what they could catch. The hot sun and activity baked the dwarf spirits out of Gemel. Food began to taste good to him again. Caramon was an excellent cook on the road; his rabbit stew was the best Gemel had ever eaten. By nightfall, Gemel was so tired he fell asleep immediately. But he always woke in the night, woke with a cry, clutching the arm that wasn't there.

On the eighth day, they rode into northern Abanasinia, not far from the coastline, and Gemel realized where they were headed. He came to a stop, glared at Caramon.

"What the hell do you think you're doing? Is this some sort of sick joke?"

"The battle was close by here, wasn't it?" Caramon said, looking around. "The graves were marked with a sword, so you said."

"My sword," said Gemel thickly. Tears wet his eyelashes. He blinked them away, tugged on the reins so violently that the horse whinnied in protest. "I'm leaving."

Caramon reached out, caught hold of the horse's bridle.

"The sword," said Caramon urgently. "The sword that you hold in your right hand. You've got to find that sword."

"You're the one who's crazy," Gemel returned. "What the devil does my sword have to do with anything?"

"You know that my brother was a great wizard," Caramon said.

"Yeah, so what?"

"I learned a good deal from him." Caramon's tone was solemn. He spoke in a hushed whisper. "There's magic at work here, Gemel. I know it. I can feel it. You've been cursed by a Chaos demon. I can lift the curse, Gemel. But I need your sword to do it."

A curse! Gemel considered it. Of course. That would explain everything. But could a Chaos demon really be removed by a fat, middle-aged innkeeper? He regarded Caramon doubtfully.

"Magic doesn't work anymore. I've heard wizards complain that their spellcasting abilities are gone. So even if your brother was some great archmage, what does that matter now?"

"Raistlin traveled to the Abyss," said Caramon. "He was master of the Tower of High Sorcery in Palanthas. He knew a great many magical spells. Now, no one else knows this"—Caramon lowered his voice conspiratorially—"but he taught me some of his spells. I think one of them will help you."

"How? Make me a new arm, a silver arm, perhaps, like that blacksmith the bards are always yammering about?" Gemel sneered.

"No," Caramon said quietly. "But I think the magic will take away your pain."

Gemel gazed at Caramon long and suspiciously, searching the big man's open, genial, and sympathetic face for the least hint of laughter, of guile, of pity.

Caramon returned his gaze steadily.

"C'mon. I'll show where I put the damn sword," Gemel said grudgingly at last.

They found the mass grave where the knights had been hastily buried. The hilt of Gemel's sword—a plain iron sword, not a fancy sword like the Solamnic knights wielded—rose from a barren plain. Though the site was far removed from any village or town, it was swept clean and neat, almost as if some loving hand took care of the grave site by brushing away dead leaves and sticks. In the center of the small burial mound, near where Gemel had thrust his sword, a wild rose bush grew and flourished.

Dismounting from his horse, Gemel walked slowly to the graves. He gazed in wonder at the rose bush, tears stinging his eyes. He laid his hand upon the sword's hilt. . . .

****

Rain dripped from his sodden hair into Gemel's eyes, momentarily blinding him. He blinked the water away, trying desperately to see and not having much luck. A tree branch scraped across his face. He shoved it aside and pressed forward. Sir Trechard, the battle commander, was somewhere up ahead.

Gemel felt for the message case for the hundredth time, checked to make certain it was securely strapped to his thigh. He had an urgent message from the captain to deliver to the commander, and Gemel didn't have time to waste stumbling about in the rain and the darkness. Since he couldn't see all that well, he used his other senses to try to make out what was happening. He could hear the jingling of chain mail, the cries of men in battle. And there was that strange smell, the peculiar smell that had stung his nostrils for the last fifty paces or so.

He could identify the scent of pine and the smell of wet, decaying vegetation. But there was another odor, one he could not place. Vague childhood memories returned—a scorched tree in his village, a tree blasted apart by lightning. The smell brought back the memory of the dazzling, flaring light, the deafening boom of the thunderclap. Gemel peered ahead through the torrential rain, trying desperately to see something, anything.

Strange, this rain. After months of drought, the worst drought Krynn had seen, this rain should be welcome. But it wasn't. It had an oily feel and an iron taste to it, almost as if the skies rained blood.

"How do those idiots in command expect me to deliver a message if I can't see a damned thing?" he muttered to himself, using the soldier's customary method of routing fear, which was to complain about his superiors. Though he couldn't see a thing, his hearing told him that he was drawing close to the battle.

The fir trees came to an end finally. Gemel looked out onto a windswept plain, and he breathed a relieved sigh. He'd been told to find this very plain. Sir Trechard and his forces were supposed to be around here somewhere. The knight commanded the left wing of the small army that was fighting for its life in the forests far north of Qualinesti, fighting the terrible demons of Chaos.

Gemel could hear the sounds of battle, but he still couldn't see a thing. He waited in the shelter of the forest, hoping to be able to determine what was going on before he walked into the midst of it.

Lightning flashed, illuminated the scene. Gemel saw, but though he saw, he didn't believe. He didn't want to believe.

A group of knights and a small band of spearmen were drawn up on the barren plain. Approaching them were several gigantic monsters the likes of which had never before been seen on Krynn. Perhaps the monsters had emerged from the sea, perhaps they sprang up from the riven ground or were formed of the black clouds that hung low and menacing from the sky. Whatever they were, they came from Chaos—shapeless masses of oozing darkness. Huge tentacles dangled from their bodies. If they had eyes or ears or mouths, these could not be seen, but they knew where to find their prey, for they advanced steadily on the knights.

The knights held their ground.

"Throw!" cried a voice that Gemel recognized as that of Sir Trechard.

A deadly volley of spears hurtled through the rain toward the tentacled monsters. Gemel's heart was cheered, for the spears were well thrown, their aim was true. They must destroy the Chaos spawn.

The monsters made no attempt to duck or avoid the spears. Instead, the hulking creatures began to spin around and around, whirling fast and then faster, spinning now so rapidly that their tentacles blurred with the motion, and Gemel was dizzy from the sight. The spears struck the whipping tentacles, which sliced up the wooden hafts as easily as a knife slices through butter. The broken spears plummeted harmlessly and ineffectually to the ground.

The whirling monsters began to surge forward toward the knights. The wind generated by their spinning hit Gemel a blast that nearly knocked him down; the smell of ozone and sulfur was pungent, gagging.

The spearmen wavered, then, panic-stricken, they turned and fled. The knights in their bright armor remained to hold the line.

"Hold steady, Knights of Solamnia," called Sir Trechard to his remaining men, his voice calm. "We've faced worse than this. Paladine is with us."

Gemel's first thought was to follow the example of the spearmen and run. Then he recalled his message, its urgency. He was not a knight, nor ever hoped to be a knight, but he had taken an oath of fealty and loyalty to his commander. Gemel would not let his comrades down. He would not let himself down by breaking that oath.

Gemel forced himself to move forward, clutching his sword in a deathlike grasp. The hilt was slippery from the strange rain. Gemel gripped the sword tightly, so tightly that his right arm ached with the strain.

The monsters were closing with the knights.

Sir Trechard dashed forward, struck at one of the monsters, thrusting his blade straight into the dark and whirling center. The sword, blessed by Paladine, glowed blue, and the whipping tentacles had no effect on it. The sword struck the heart of the monster. Lightning crackled and the monster blew apart, spattering the knights and Gemel with foul-smelling gore. Nothing daunted, the other monsters whirled on toward their prey.

"They can be killed, men!" Sir Trechard shouted. "Stand fast."

Emboldened by the sight, Gemel reached for the message case. He prepared to make his final dash, when he felt wind on the back of his neck, heard a horrible whip, whip sound coming from behind him. The smell of ozone was intense.

He turned fearfully to see one of the whirling monsters bearing down on him.

Gemel swung his sword wildly at the monster, but his blow was deflected by a spinning tentacle. Another whiplike tendril smacked Gemel in the thigh. The force of the blow flung him backward, tumbling head over heels. He landed heavily on the rain-soaked ground.

Terrified that the monster would come after him, Gemel scrambled to his feet, his sword ready. The whirling monster was intent upon attacking the knights, the greater threat. It paid no more attention to Gemel.

He stood still a moment, weak and shaking, glad for the respite. He couldn't stay here long, however. He had to complete his mission. Taking a step forward, he sucked in a breath as pain flared through his injured leg.

He tried to examine the extent of his injuries but could see nothing for the strange darkness. Every fiber of his clothing was soaked, either with blood or rain. He couldn't tell which.

Sir Trechard was only a few feet away. Gemel lurched toward the commander, every step bringing a gasp of pain to his lips. The knight attacked one of the monsters with his sword, only to have his blow deflected as Gemel's had been.

"Sir Trechard!" Gemel yelled.

Sir Trechard looked over his right shoulder, attempting to find the shouting voice.

Gemel yelled again. "Sir! I have a message from Rac Vandish for you. He requests—Look out, sir!"

The Chaos monster surged forward. Sir Trechard stabbed at it desperately, but the whipping tentacles tore the sword from his grasp, sent it flying. And then it was as if the knight were being struck from all sides by a thousand whips. The tentacles sliced through the knight's metal armor as if it were sheerest silk, laying bare the flesh beneath, stripping away that flesh. The blows flailed the flesh from his bones, his face dissolved in a welter of blood and bone. And still, horribly, Sir Trechard lived, though now his very innards were exposed.

With a bubbling scream of agony, he fell to the ground.

Gemel choked on his own bile. He gripped his sword even harder, the hilt cutting painfully into his hand. Using all his strength, he brought his sword down upon the monster. The blade entered the maelstrom and hit something substantial and, he hoped, vital. Lightning flickered from inside the monster, its whirling motion slowed, but the monster was not yet dead. Gemel's sword was lodged inside it. He tried to let go of the hilt but discovered, to his horror, that he could not.

A bone snapped in his upper arm. Then the monster pulled Gemel's arm from out of his shoulder socket. The arm, still holding the sword, tore loose, spraying him with his own blood.

Gemel sank into a spinning torment of whirling, lightning-tinged darkness.

He woke to find himself inside a tent. Looking through an opening in the top, he saw clouds still covering the sky. The air was hot and smelled of blood and lightning and death. Memory returned, and with it the pain in his right arm. Yet he remembered clearly having seen the arm torn away. Perhaps it hadn't happened! He'd been dreaming. He could feel his arm. His arm hurt. He had not lost his arm after all.

Lying on a blanket on the ground, he looked over to where his right arm should have been.

There was nothing there, nothing except some blood-soaked bandages wrapped around his mangled shoulder. He began to weep.

A soldier entered the tent.

"You're awake. Excellent. How do you feel?"

"How the hell do you think I feel?" Gemel snarled savagely. "My arm is gone!"

"Still, you can count yourself lucky," the soldier answered. "You were the only one we found alive on that plain. It's a good thing we had one of our druid healers with us, or you'd be dead, too. He cauterized your wound, stopped the bleeding, and gave you a potion to ease the pain."

"How long have I been unconscious?" Gemel asked.

"Maybe a day and a half. We're still burying the dead."

"What about—" Gemel swallowed his sudden fear—"what about the Chaos monsters?"

"Destroyed. You and the knights did a good job. The reserves pushed forward and killed the monsters that were left. Hey, what are you doing?"

"Standing up." Gemel grunted. "I've got two good legs at least. Show me where you found me."

"I don't think—"

"Show me!" Gemel yelled.

"It's pretty horrible," the soldier said.

"I know," Gemel said grimly. "I was there."

The soldier eyed him dubiously, then, seeing Gemel standing upright if a little unsteadily, the soldier shrugged and nodded.

"Here's where we found you." The soldier pointed to a spot on the rain-swept plain.

The ground, the straggling grass, the weeds, were all covered with blood, as if the sky had rained blood, not water. Nearby, a group of soldiers, pale-faced and sweating, were digging an enormous pit in which to bury the dead.

To bury what was left of the dead, that is.

There were no recognizable bodies, only parts of bodies—a foot here, a leg there, a trunk somewhere else. Metal armor, cut to ribbons, chain mail scattered about in bits and pieces. The scene was horrible, gruesome. Every so often, one of the soldiers would turn from his task and go off quietly by himself to retch and heave.

Gemel began to shake. The bile surged up in his throat, but he forced it back down. His arm, the arm that wasn't there, ached and burned.

A pile of weapons stood near the bodies, gathered together to be laid to rest with the knights. Among them was his own sword. His was easy to recognize. The knights had carried valuable swords with engraved remarques and roses on the hilts. His was just a sword.

The soldiers placed the body parts in the ditch. Gemel just stood there watching. One-armed, weak, and light-headed, he could do nothing to help. He could give nothing now but his respect and his remorse. If it hadn't been for his distracting the knight, Sir Trechard might not be dead.

The soldiers completed their work quickly, eager to have the horrible job finished, eager to hide the bloody remains beneath mounds of dirt. They held no ceremony, made no speeches about the knights' courage and loyalty. There wasn't time. The war still raged. The soldiers shoveled dirt into the ditch until it was filled.

Gemel retrieved his sword, held it clasped tightly in his left hand. His grip was painful, it hurt him and he let go. His sword fell from his left hand. But his right hand only clasped the blade harder, tighter.

The soldiers finished the grave. There was no stone, no way to mark the place where Solamnic knights had died fighting for a noble cause. Gemel leaned over and picked up his sword again. Carrying his blade awkwardly in his left hand, he walked over to the foot of the grave site.

He jammed the sword, point first, into the soft ground.

Gemel turned and started to walk back. He collapsed before he had taken a step.

****

"I was the only survivor of that battle," Gemel said. Holding the sword, he jabbed the rusted point again and again into the soft ground. "People say I'm the lucky one."

He snorted, glanced over at the grave site. "Their pain is over. They can sleep."

"Yeah, I know," said Caramon quietly. "They told me the same thing after the end of the Chaos War. After a dark knight brought me the torn and bloodied bodies of my sons. After I had to tell their mother that two of her children were dead. After I had to plant the vallenwood on their graves, when I should have been picking flowers for their weddings. It took me a long time before I finally admitted to myself that people were right. Before I quit feeling guilty because I was alive and my sons weren't."

Gemel looked down at the ground, said nothing.

"What were those monsters you fought?" Caramon wisely changed the subject.

"Some sort of Chaos monster. The very gods themselves fled from them, or so they say."

"You didn't flee," Caramon said. "You held your ground. You and the knights."

"Yeah. We held our ground." Gemel was bitter. "And what did they get for it? That bit of ground right there where they're lying. Well, Majere, I have the damned sword. Now what? You going to rub bat guano on it or something?"

"We have to take it back to Solace," said Caramon. "The magic spell my brother taught me will only work back there."

"And Jassar thinks *I'm* crazy," Gemel muttered. He paused a moment longer at the grave site, then turned away. He and Caramon had taken only a few steps when Gemel stopped. "Wait a minute. If I take my sword, there won't be a marker anymore."

"Yes, there is." Caramon pointed to the rose bush, whose red and white blossoms filled the air with fragrance. "That is their marker. Look at it, Gemel. Have you ever seen a rose like it? And where did it come from? Nothing but grass and weeds for miles. Yet here roses bloom, here roses flourish."

"That's true," Gemel said. He gazed out over the barren, sandy plain covered with tall brown grass and scraggly weeds. And there in the center of the small mound stood the rose bush with its green leaves and white blossoms, each with a drop of red at its heart. "That's true."

"And people say the gods have left us," Caramon said, smiling and shaking his head. "Now let's go back home."

****

"Caramon!" Tika was scandalized. "What are you doing? That's my best linen bed sheet!"

Caramon looked up, flushed a guilty red. "I'm sorry. I thought it was an old one. I . . . um . . . I need some wizard robes. . . ."

Tika glared at him. "Caramon Majere, this has gone far enough. You couldn't work a magic spell if your life depended on it, and you know it!"

"It's not *my* life we're talking about," Caramon said, holding the sheet up to his chin and attempting to measure it on himself.

"Gemel's, you mean? You're giving that poor man false hopes, Caramon, and I think it's cruel! And now—Oh, for mercy's sake, give that to me!"

Snatching the bed sheet from her husband, Tika spread it out on the bed, eyed it thoughtfully. "Now, if I cut it this way, we'll have room for the sleeves. . . ."

"Thank you, my dear," Caramon said, kissing her cheek.

"I hope you know what you're doing," Tika said darkly.

"I hope I do, too," Caramon muttered, but not until he was sure Tika couldn't hear him.

****

The next morning, the Inn of the Last Home was not open for business, much to the dismay and shock of the citizens of Solace. Rumors abounded. The younger members of Solace's population risked their necks climbing the great vallenwoods to try to peep into the windows. Since the windows were stained glass, this proved a failure. The inn had remained open through war and plagues. What dread incident had caused it to close this day, no one knew. But everyone in town waited out front to find out.

Only four people were inside the inn—Caramon, dressed in white robes and looking very magnificent; Tika, looking grim and nervous; Jassar, wan and despairing; and Gemel, dubious, doubtful, and hung-over.

"Finding that cursed sword only made him worse, not better," Jassar said tearfully to Tika. "He holds it and stares at it and then flings it to the floor, then picks it up again and hurls it down again. And all the time he complains of the pain!"

"There, there," said Tika, holding Jassar in her arms and soothing her tenderly. "It will be all right. Caramon's a good man. A little daft, maybe, but a good man. That must count for something."

On a table in the middle of the inn sat the magical box. Three feet long, two feet wide, and one foot high, the box looked very impressive and mysterious with its cabalistic symbols carved into the wooden sides. The top of the box was open, revealing two compartments running the length of the box, compartments that were separated by a wooden divider. Two round openings were in the front of the box, one for either compartment. A slit had been cut in the center. Laid over the top of the box was a thin, diaphanous cloth, thin as cobweb, which Tika recognized as one of her very best elf-woven scarves.

"Bring me your sword, Gemel Lathhauser," said Caramon in a suitably impressive-sounding voice.

Gemel came forward, surly and embarrassed. Standing in front of the box, he looked up, his expression so desperate, yet so hopeful, that Caramon was forced to avert his head a moment, rub his eyes, and clear his throat before he could continue.

"Place the sword into the slot here in the front of the box," Caramon ordered.

Gemel's hand shook. He missed the slot the first few times, but then managed to slide the blade into the slit in the front of the box between the two compartments. The blade disappeared.

"Very good." Caramon drew in a deep breath, let it out in a gust. He was prepared. "Now, whatever you do, do not touch the cloth covering the top of the box. It has been enchanted with powerful spells taught to me by my brother, the great archmage, Raistlin Majere. You must follow my directions exactly. If you deviate from them even in the slightest, the spell will fail. Do you understand?"

"He sounds very powerful," whispered Jassar, awed.

Tika only shook her head and rolled her eyes.

Gemel stood straight and stiff-backed. "I understand," he said gruffly.

"Take your place in front of the box."

Gemel breathed deeply. Steeling himself, he walked forward.

"Now close your eyes," Caramon continued. "I will cast the spell upon the box and cloth, and then, when I count three, you will place both your arms, real and phantom, inside the box, up to your elbows."

"Then what?" Gemel was suspicious.

"And then the magic happens. Close your eyes," Caramon ordered testily.

Gemel sighed, shook his head, and closed his eyes.

Caramon began to chant mystical words, words with a spidery feel to them. His voice rose to a crescendo, and he clapped his hands loudly and suddenly, startling all of them, including himself.

Gemel jumped at the sound, but he did not open his eyes.

"The spell is cast. Place your arms in the box," Caramon instructed.

Gemel hesitated, then, stepping forward, he put his left arm into the hole on the left side of the box, made as if to put the missing right arm into the hole on the right.

He gasped in astonishment. "I don't believe it! It's incredible! I can feel both my arms in the box!"

"Good," said Caramon, smiling in satisfaction. "Now you may open your eyes."

Gemel opened his eyes, looked into the box, and sucked in an awestruck breath. Jassar and Tika crept forward to see.

"My god!" Jassar whimpered.

Inside the box were Gemel's two arms, left and right, and two hands. Both Gemel's hands were clasped tightly into fists.

"We must be silent," said Caramon, "and let the magic work."

They were all quiet, all awed and amazed. Outside, the breeze freshened, the limbs of the vallenwood swayed, the inn rocked gently, as it was sometimes wont to do. A kettle, balanced precariously on the hearth, fell to the floor with a sharp bang. Tika gasped and clasped her hands over her mouth.

"That is the sign! The magic has worked! Through the power of my brother," Caramon said, "I have given form to your arm within the box." He repeated the magic words, then cried out in stentorian tones. "Chaos demon, I charge you, release your grasp on this man's flesh!"

He looked at Gemel. "Now open both of your fists and relax your arms."

Slowly Gemel released the tightly clenched muscles in his hands. His fingers uncurled, unclasped. His hands relaxed. Both hands relaxed. Gemel stared down at his hands through the cloth.

"Quickly!" Caramon cried. "Pull your arms out of the box! The demon has freed you. I have it under enchantment, but I can't hold it for long!"

Gemel jerked his arm from the box. He stood staring at the place where his right arm had been, dumbfounded.

"I don't believe it! I don't feel my arm anymore! The pain is gone!"

Gemel's knees gave way. With a shuddering sob, he sank down into a chair. Jassar, weeping joyfully, put her arms around him. He reached out with his left arm, took hold of her, held her tightly.

Tika stared at Caramon with wide-eyed wonder. “Caramon?”

“Yes, my dear?” Caramon said, turning to regard her with calm serenity.

“Nothing.” Tika looked dazed. She peered trepidly into the box. “Is . . . is the demon really trapped inside there?”

“Right here,” Caramon said. He plucked the scarf from the top of the box and tossed it into to the inn’s gigantic fireplace. There was a flash of blue flame and the scarf disappeared. Though it had been her very best scarf, Tika never said a word.

“The demon is gone. It can never harm you again.” Caramon stated. Removing the sword from the box, he handed it to Gemel. “Keep this to remind you of the brave men who died . . . and those who live.”

Gemel reached out, clasped hold of Caramon’s hand. “You have saved my sanity and my life. How can ever I repay you?”

“Stay out of the Trough, for one thing,” Caramon said sternly. “You owe that to yourself. As for repaying me, there’s odd jobs you can do around here.”

Gemel smiled ruefully. “Jobs for a man with only one arm?”

“Build up the strength in that arm,” Caramon answered, “and there will be work for you aplenty anywhere.”

****

Rumor flashed around Solace that Caramon Majere had performed a magic spell, had caused a one-armed man to grow a new arm. Panic ensued. Some people flocked to the inn, hoping for a miracle of their own, while others took fright and insisted that they would never again set foot inside the accursed place.

Throughout the day, Caramon maintained steadily to one and all that he hadn’t done anything out of the ordinary, and since everyone knew that Caramon Majere was incapable of telling a lie and since he went about his business the same as usual and did not pluck any Chaos demons out of the spiced potatoes, people began to think the rumor was just that—a rumor. By dinnertime, everyone in Solace was laughing heartily at the thought of Caramon the wizard.

All except Tika. She had seen the two arms inside the box, she had seen Gemel freed from his pain. She treated her husband with newfound respect all that day—treatment that he thoroughly enjoyed, for where is the married couple, no matter how happy, who don't now and then take each other for granted?

That night, alone in their bedroom, Tika sat down wearily.

"What a day!" She sighed. "I'm glad it's over."

"So am I," said Caramon. He carried with him the magical box, which he placed on Tika's nightstand.

Tika cast the box an uncomfortable glance. "Don't you think you should keep that locked up somewhere safe?"

"Oh, I think it's safe enough," Caramon replied complacently.

Tika, looking doubtful, picked up her hairbrush.

"Where's my mirror?" she demanded suddenly, staring at the blank space on the wall. "It's gone! Caramon, some thief has stolen my mirror!"

"I didn't steal it, my dear," said Caramon slyly.

He reached into the box and pulled out the mirror, which he solemnly handed back to his wife. "As the kender said, 'I only borrowed it.' "

Tika gazed at the mirror, she gazed at the box. Then she threw the hairbrush at him.

Arguments, Anger, and Tears

A flashback by Larry Elmore

Dragonlance. Now there is a word that has had a great impact in my life. Harold Johnson came to me one day way, way back in 1983 or '84 and told me that Tracy Hickman, one of our new game designers, had an idea for a story that could spin off at least twelve game modules and perhaps three novels. The only catch is that we had to sell this idea to the board of directors at TSR. He and Tracy had decided that if I did some quick paintings or drawings to illustrate some of the characters, perhaps giving a visual feel for the project, it might help in selling this idea to the "suits." I think the main person we had to sell it to was Gary Gygax. Harold also told me that I had to do this artwork on my own time and not on TSR's time. I told him that I might want to do it, but first I wanted to know if this story was any good or not. I didn't want to waste time on an idea that sucked!

Harold and Tracy made a date to come over to my house and tell me the story of Dragonlance. They came over around seven it the evening and started telling me this big epic adventure and finally finished the story around eleven-thirty. Man, what a story! I liked it and told them that I would do whatever I could to help make this product a reality. With the help of a few more TSR employees we convinced the powers that be to let us develop this project. The project was planned to help us (TSR) produce a few extra products for the next three years. Three years?!

We were lucky back then because everyone was under one roof. The artists worked close to the game designers and editors, so that made it very easy for Margaret and Tracy to help us develop the "look" of the world and its characters. We were all young and not very experienced, but thanks to Tracy and Margaret, this project developed a life of its own and seemed to pull the best out of us. Tracy and Margaret were like a torch. They had a burning desire to get this project done right, and when that torch touched you, you were caught up in that same flame and then you wanted to do your best. There were arguments, anger, and tears—all for the sake of making this project the best we could possibly create at that time in our lives.

Many people have asked me about the creation of the dragons in the DRAGONLANCE setting. Some people really liked them. Well, I didn't design them all. I was sort of the art director of the DRAGONLANCE setting, and the one thing that I didn't want to do was paint the same kind of dragons that were in that old Monster Manual. Up until then, when we painted dragons they were supposed to resemble or look exactly like the ones in the manual, and I had begun to hate them. I thought this was a perfect time to come up with some new designs that look like *real* dragons . . , like they truly existed!

Well, I had a fight on my hands with the suits. Even before they gave us an official go-ahead we had already started doing paintings for the first DRAGONLANCE Calendar, so some of the first dragons that I painted look a little like the ones in the manual. I was sort of splitting the difference between the way I wanted them to look and the way they had always looked. Eventually we just started doing them the way we wanted, and to heck with the "official Monster Manual" dragons.

I told all the artists that were working on the project that when they painted a DRAGONLANCE dragon for the first time (for instance, a black dragon) it was up to them to look at the Monster Manual and if they wanted to use some of the components of that particular dragon, okay, but at the same time make it "your" dragon. And I wanted us to try to make the dragons consistent. For example if Clyde Caldwell was the first to paint a black DRAGONLANCE dragon, then we should always try to make our black dragons look somewhat like his.

The same rule applied to the characters. If I painted Tanis first, then the rest of the artists should make Tanis look like the way I painted him. If Keith Parkinson painted Sturm first, then we would always try to paint Sturm the way Keith had imagined him.

This plan seemed to work okay, but there were some characters and monsters that evolved a little. The best examples are the draconians and Goldmoon. I never had time to really design the draconians. I think some of my earliest sketches of them were published, but I didn't particularly like them. They needed more thought, more sketches, and development. Keith and I talked about that, and he solved the draconian problem when he did the painting titled "Whadda Mean We're Lost?" Those dudes were perfect. Goldmoon meanwhile went through a few wardrobe changes. Sometimes she was painted too sexy, so we had to tone down her outfits. The first time or two she was visualized, the books weren't even written yet. We knew who the character was, but we didn't have a true "feel" for the character until we read the first novel.

When I look back, it is a miracle that the DRAGONLANCE project, both story and art, came out as good as it did. So many people worked on it (all at the same time); so many different personalities, egos, and talents were involved in its creation. But everyone put their differences aside and gave it their best shot . . . and we still do.

Part of the original team of artists and designers of the DRAGONLANCE setting, well-known artist Larry Elmore recently finished covers for the next DRAGONLANCE Game Book and the Elves Game Book for Sovereign Stone. He is starting on the cover art for the next EverQuest computer game box.

The Raid on the Academy of Sorcery

Margaret Weis

Originally published in *Tales of the Fifth Age: Rebels and Tyrants*

He would not give up. He would try the spell again.

"Though I have no idea why," Ulin muttered beneath his breath, "for it won't work."

In truth, the "why" was his father. Ulin had watched Palin Majere cast the same spell over and over until the words to the spell thickened on his tongue. Sometimes the magic worked, but more often, these days, the spell did not.

When that happened, Ulin watched his father grow old.

Palin had never before now seemed old to his son, not until this last year, when the wild magic his father had, in essence, "discovered" began to slip through his fingers like quicksilver. At first Palin had blamed his ineptitude on the infirmities of age, although that seemed implausible. His father, Caramon Majere, was still hale and hearty into his eighties. Palin had lost nothing else to age. Although he was of slender build, like his uncle Raistlin Majere, Palin was not cursed with ill-health, as had been his uncle. Palin was active and in good physical condition. His mind was keen. He enjoyed being out-of-doors, enjoyed walking and riding. He still liked a game of goblin ball and often outplayed the young scholars who did nothing all day but keep indoors with their noses pressed between the covers of a book.

Ulin realized now that his father had never truly thought the dwindling of the magic had anything to do with a dwindling of his mental or physical capacity. Palin had wished it to be so. Wished it desperately. He would have made that sacrifice gladly rather than come to understand the truth.

The spell Ulin was attempting to cast was a simple one—he was trying to put a wizard lock on a door. He drew in a deep and cleansing breath, endeavored to clear his mind of all nagging worries and cares—a difficult task, these days—and closed his eyes, concentrating on the magic that he could feel in the stone floor beneath his feet, feel in the cool stone walls at his side, feel in the wood of the door itself. That was the frustrating part. He could feel the magic. He knew it was there as he knew that blood ran red and warm in his veins. He could feel the magic flowing into him, but when he attempted to make the magic work for him, it was as if some other mouth than his was gulping it all down before he could get a draught. When he tried to cast the spell, he was left with nothing inside. He was drained, empty, the magic dissipated.

Ulin sighed, brushed irritably at some annoying insect that he could feel crawling on his skin. Gnats, he thought. Or fruit flies. He would have to remember to see if the servants had left open the cellar door again. As for this particular door, he glared balefully at the inoffensive object as if it were personally responsible for thwarting him and even gave it a swift kick in his frustration.

Sighing and muttering imprecations, he took out an ordinary iron padlock from the pocket of his robes, affixed it to the door, and locked it with an iron key.

"A sad pass we've come to, isn't it, Ulin?" said a voice behind him.

"What do you mean, Lucy?" he asked with forced cheerfulness.

"You tried to cast a wizard-lock and it failed," she said.

Ulin smiled ruefully and shrugged. "You know me. Ham-fisted. Butter-fingers. I should be a cook. I wouldn't be a bad cook, you know. The alchemy, that's much like cooking. One reason I enjoy it. A pinch of this. A cup of that."

"It's not just you, Ulin," she said. "It's—"

Ulin laid a hand to his lips, glanced around swiftly to see if anyone else was in earshot.

"We're alone," she said, exasperated. "Look, Ulin, it's no use going on this way. Pretending everything's right when it's not. You and I both know the truth. Some of our pupils know the truth. That's why they're leaving. The masters know the truth. That's why your father disbanded the Conclave. The magic is failing. It's not just failing you. It's not just failing your father. It's failing all of us!"

Ulin didn't answer. Turning away from those green eyes that had the disconcerting habit of seeing inside his head, he gave the padlock a vicious tug. The lock held. Satisfied, he dropped the heavy key into a pocket.

"Time was when we didn't need locks on the doors here at the Academy. But these days, with the madness for god-crafted artifacts and their value so high, my father felt it was unwise to leave the mage-ware room free for all to enter. I suppose he's right, though I do detest these iron padlocks. They tell everyone who passes by, 'Hey! We have something valuable in here! And we figure you'll steal it!' Wizard-locks at least have the advantage of being subtle and invisible."

He glanced back at his companion hopefully. "I don't suppose that you, Lucy—"

She shook her head. "My spells have been working about half the time. And if I put a wizard-lock on, odds are I might not be able to take it off. I'd rather not try. The fact is, Ulin . . ." She hesitated, as if unwilling to impart bad news.

They had been friends for years, ever since his arrival to take up his post as Assistant Master at the Academy. He understood her silences now as well as he understood her spoken words. The bond was that close between them.

"No, not you, too, Lucy," he said quietly, taking hold of her hand. "You can't leave. What we would do without you?"

Those were the words he said with his mouth. The words he said in his heart were: What will I do without you?

Plump Lucy she was called or Plain Lucy, to distinguish her from another Lucy who had been a student at the Academy. Although that other Lucy had left, the appellation had stuck, much to Ulin's indignation. Lucy wasn't beautiful, by any means, not like Ulin's mother Usha Majere, not like Mistress Jenna, not like Ulin's late wife Karynn. But Lucy's smile, which brought a dimple into each freckled cheek, could warm Ulin like spiced wine. Her rolling laughter could tease him to laughter, even in his darkest moods. Her green eyes sparkled in his dreams.

The green eyes were not sparkling now. They were shadowed, distressed. Lucy was his closest friend, his dearest friend. He had not thought he could ever love anyone again after his young wife had died untimely, stricken by a plague for which the healers had no cure, a plague most believed had been inflicted on them by the monstrous green dragon Beryl. Ulin had been away from home searching for magical artifacts. He had arrived back just in time to hold his dying wife in his arms. His heart had died then, too, or at least he wished it so. But he was young himself, only in his late twenties, and his heart had a perverse way of continuing to beat. Now it seemed to have found a perverse way of allowing him to love again, to find pleasure in life again. He had begun to think that Lucy might become more than a friend to him and he had thought, on occasion, that perhaps she was thinking the same way.

"Ulin, I don't want to leave," she said, holding his hand fast. "But, let's face it. I'm not earning my keep. I have only two pupils. Another left last week. I tried to talk him into staying but his parents said that they weren't paying good money for no results. They're making him a carpenter's apprentice and I can't say that I blame them. At least he'll be taught a skill that will gain him a living. As for the other pupils, they can join the class with Master Dowlin. He's lost several of his, as well."

"Stay here and do research, then," Ulin said. He gestured back to the room behind him, to the locked door. "Alchemy is a fascinating study, Lucy." His golden eyes gleamed like the precious metal they resembled as he thought of it. "It's much more satisfying than magic. I'm relying on myself, my own creativity and intelligence, to create something—not on some force that comes from the gods or from the air or the ground or wherever. Magic maybe works with you and maybe it doesn't. Magic is completely unreliable. I control my experiments, Lucy! I do." He thumped himself on the chest. "And, if my measurements are correct and accurate, the chemicals *always* react in the *very* same way *every single time*. No guess work involved. No wondering if this time the magic will work for me, or if this time it will fail. I must show you, I've just come up with the most amazing concoction—"

He paused, then said contritely, "I'm sorry. I know you're not interested. And you don't have to work with my smelly old chemicals. There's a lot of work to be done cataloging artifacts and old spellbooks and scrolls—"

"Cataloging them to sell them," said Lucy gently, folding her other hand over Ulin's. She smiled as he shook his head stubbornly. "I saw Mistress Jenna here last week. I know what your father is doing."

"They're old friends," Ulin said.

"That may be, but she's also the largest dealer in magical artifacts in all of Ansalon and although I don't know this for a fact, my guess is that she left with several choice ones tucked away safely in her robes. Your father's selling off his own collection to keep the Academy going, isn't he, Ulin?"

He wanted very much to say no, but he knew he could not lie to the dimples and the freckles and the green eyes.

"I've seen the change in him," Lucy continued. "Everyone has. We're all worried about him. He's thin and gaunt. He avoids all of us. He won't speak to anyone. He spends all his time locked in his study."

"He's studying new spells," Ulin said, and the excuse sounded lame, even to him.

Lucy just shook her head. "I'm proud, Ulin. I've made my own way in life since I was little. I've supported myself and my family. None of us ever took a copper we didn't earn and I won't start now." She squeezed his hand. "Cheer up, dear friend. The moment the magic returns, I'll be back. You won't be able to keep me away, not with a hundred wizard-locked doors!"

Her laughter made Ulin smile, but the smile didn't last long. He was tempted to ask her to stay because of him, because he loved her, but this wasn't the right time for those words. A declaration of love now would be mistaken for charity. He'd had countless opportunities before this. For one reason or another, he'd never taken them. And now, when he desperately wanted to tell her, the time had passed.

"Where will you go?" he asked. "What will you do?"

"I'm a good teacher. If I can't teach children to read the language of magic, then maybe I can teach them to read Solamnic or Common. Your grandmother Tika's come up with the idea of a school for the refugee children. Better than having them run wild in the streets, she says. She's offered me the job. The pay isn't much, but I'll have room and board at the Inn—" She halted, chuckling. "Ulin, you look just like a landed fish."

"You're not leaving!" he said, gaping and staring. "You're not leaving Solace!" He caught her in his arms and hugged her close.

He held her for a long time, reveling in the warmth of her body, the smell of her chestnut hair. She clasped him just as firmly, nestled her head into his chest. In that moment, everything was settled between the two of them, though neither of them spoke of it aloud.

"I was looking for your father," she said, emerging reluctantly from his embrace. She glanced toward the door across the hallway, where Palin had his study. "I wanted to tell him myself. That is, if he'll even see me—"

"He's not here," Ulin replied. "No, that's the truth this time." Palin had made it a practice lately to tell his son to say that he was away, when in fact he was locked up in his study, searching for some reason that the magic was failing. "He's meeting with the commander of the Solamnic garrison here. They sent for him. There've been reports of troop movements in the east. Dark Knights massing on the Qualinesti border. They think the dragon may be gathering her forces to attack Haven."

Lucy's forehead crinkled in a frown. "But what about the pact of the dragons? Beryl—the old green bitch—should know that if she attacks Haven, her cousin Malys will have something to say about it."

"Pact!" Ulin snorted. "As if any of us really thought the treacherous beasts would honor a pact. The key word is 'honor' and we know that none of them can probably even spell it!"

"What does your father think?"

Ulin sighed, shook his head. "I have no idea. He's not talking to anyone these days, Lucy. Not even my mother. But then, she's gone so much of the time. Her portraits are in such demand . . ." Recalling vividly the last violent clash between his parents at home, he let that subject lapse.

"I'd like to see this new concoction of yours," Lucy said, hoping to cheer him.

"Would you?" Ulin brightened.

He always considered himself homely. He was rail-thin and gangly with his grandfather's big bones but no meat to cover them. The mirror showed him only his inadequacies. It never showed him what other people saw in him, for only the mirror of the soul can do that. His face was transformed in his eagerness.

"You'll find this really interesting," he said, walking with rapid strides down the hall, tugging her along after him. "I guarantee it."

At the end of the corridor stood a laboratory that had been established for the use of students and masters. Only a few years ago, the laboratory had been crowded with mages practicing their spellcasting, studying the nature of ancient artifacts, creating their own magical devices. The laboratory was almost completely empty now. Ulin and his father were the only two who used it and Palin was here rarely. The twenty or so masters and students still in residence at the Academy were busy researching ancient texts, hoping to find clues as to why the wild magic had suddenly ceased to work for them or, if it did work, why it was unpredictable and unreliable.

Ulin entered the laboratory, hustling Lucy along with him.

She coughed and wrinkled her nose. "It smells dreadful. What have you done? Invented gully dwarves?"

"That's the brimstone. Or maybe the saltpeter." Ulin led her to a large stone table covered with numerous black splotches, as if someone had been mashing blackberries. The room reeked with a peculiar acrid odor that made Lucy sneeze violently. Several large crocks holding various substances were lined up on the table.

Lcuy glanced at the black splotches. "If you're searching for gold, you've missed the mark."

"Bah! Gold!" said Ulin. He sat down at the table. "What I've created is much more interesting than gold."

"What *have* you created?" Lucy looked around. "I don't see anything?"

Ulin grinned shamefacedly. "Well, maybe 'creation' isn't the right word. Watch this."

"I have here a small sampling of saltpeter. Did you know," he added, mixing the strange concoction together, "that my great uncle Raistlin used saltpeter to fool his enemies into thinking he was working magic when he was really too exhausted to cast a spell? Watch this."

He struck a spark from flint. The spark landed on the white, crystalline substance and it flashed brightly, so brightly that Lucy blinked. The flash vanished almost immediately.

"Impressive," she said dryly. "He must have scared a lot of goblins in his time."

"He did, so my grandfather told me." Ulin dipped a scoop into one of the crocks, drew out six measures of a black powdery substance. "Charcoal," he said. "Add to that one measure of brimstone." He dumped in a bright yellow powder and continued to talk while he mixed his concoction assiduously. "Well, that started me to thinking. What if I could make the flash do something. Something more than just flash. Like lightning. Lightning gave me the idea of using brimstone. I began trying various substances—

Ulin halted in his mixing to look up at her. "I was never a very good mage, Lucy. I was born into a world the gods had forsaken. A world where godly magic was lost. True, my father found the wild magic, and that helped sustain him and the other mages. Somehow, I never took to it. Or it never took to me. Father says I lack discipline and perseverance. I used to think he was right, but now I'm not so sure. I seem to have all the discipline and perseverance I need when I'm pursuing my alchemic studies. I spend hours here and never notice the time pass at all. But trying to cast magic leaves me frustrated and with a pain in my belly. And that was in the days when the magic was working! I'm much happier here in the laboratory than I am in the mage-ware room."

"I think your mother was scared by a gnome when you were in her womb," Lucy said, teasing.

"Maybe so." Ulin laughed. "I'll have to ask her." Having mixed together the substances, he packed the resultant powder into a small salt cellar. "Now watch this. You better stand back."

Lucy retreated backward, holding her nose. She had been involved in some of Ulin's experiments before and knew that, if nothing else, they tended to be odiferous. Flint and tinderbox in hand, he held his arms outstretched over the salt cellar. He struck a spark over the salt cellar and jumped back.

Again a flash, but this was accompanied by a loud bang. The salt cellar blew apart, bits of it flying all over the laboratory. The force of the blast shook the stone table and the floor on which they were standing.

The noise was alarming, deafening. Lucy hastily covered her ears, but by that time, the boom was over, like thunder after a lightning strike. She blinked, staring at what was left of the salt cellar, which wasn't much. Ulin's face was blackened with powdery residue. He had a bloody gash on his forehead from where he'd been struck by a portion of the salt cellar. He never noticed. He gazed at his achievement with pride.

"I'd say that would definitely put the scare in more than a few goblins, wouldn't you, Lucy? I call it 'thunder powder'. Come closer. It's safe now."

"What did you say? I can't hear you." Still keeping her hands near her ears, just in case the thunder powder was not yet finished thundering, Lucy advanced cautiously, staring warily at the black splotch on the table, as if fearing it might go off again. "That was very nice, Ulin. Very . . . entertaining."

"Yes, I know," he said gleefully. "It can blow up great huge piles of stones. One day last week I took it out into the woods and I did just that. Then I blew a boulder out of the ground. After that, I blew up a tree stump. You could hear the explosion for miles." He smiled impishly, looking very much like a mischievous small boy. "When I came back into town, people were out looking at the sky for storm clouds. That's what gave me the idea for the name."

He began to pour out more powder. "If you had enough of this stuff, you could knock down a stone wall. Like one of these walls here." He waved a hand vaguely.

"I think your father might notice one of his walls missing," Lucy said.

"Don't worry," Ulin said, looking at her with the same impish grin. "It's just a theory. One I won't be testing. Would you like to see it again?"

"Uh, no," she said, adding hastily, at his look of disappointment. "It was quite impressive, Ulin, but my ears are still ringing! Maybe some time we'll . . . uh, blow up stumps together. We'll take a picnic lunch . . ." She couldn't help it. She began to giggle.

"Laugh at me, will you?" he said, pretending to be hurt. "I don't mind. You unbelievers may scoff now, but when the time comes, when you absolutely have to have a stump removed, you won't be laughing then, will you, Mistress Lucy?"

She pursed her lips, eyed him critically. "You look a fright. You've got black stuff all over your face and hands. And you've got a cut on your forehead. Come along and wash up like a good boy and make yourself useful. Help me pack my things and carry them over the Inn."

"Yes, ma'am," he said, playfully meek. Sliding off his tall stool, he finished the destruction of his person by wiping his powder-stained hands on his robes.

Lucy herded him out of the room, looking very much like a short, plump sheepdog harrying a tall, thin sheep. Once they were outside the laboratory, though, he halted.

"You should have seen how high that stump flew up into the air!"

"You," said Lucy, giving him a shove in the direction of the washroom, "are incorrigible!"

****

Lucy's possessions were few. Ulin carried the iron-banded box that held the few magical artifacts she'd managed to acquire over the years. Lucy carried a wicker basket filled with her clothes. Leaving the Academy, heading for the Inn of the Last Home, that was run by Ulin's grandfather and grandmother, Caramon and Tika Majere, the two crunched companionably through the dried, dead leaves of autumn, admiring the beauty of the flaming reds and yellows of the leaves that still clung to the branches. The two enjoyed each other's company, as always, but Ulin was glad when the Inn came in sight. The handles of the box were digging into his palms. Lucy was huffing and puffing with the weight of the basket and they had just mutually agreed to set down their loads and rest a spell, when the town bell began to clang, sounding the alarm that would call all citizens of Solace to the central square.

The bell was rung by the sheriff and then only in dire emergency. The clanging could mean anything from a child lost in the woods to a barn catching fire to the approach of a flight of dragons. The smith in his leather apron came running, leaving his apprentices to mind the forge fire. Women came clattering down the stairs that led to the tree-top houses, wiping away flour from the day's baking, carrying babes in arms who were too little to be left at home alone. Old folk, who had been basking blissfully in the sun, perked up on hearing the bell and reached for their canes. Dogs began to bark wildly and small boys, like squirrels, slithered and slid down out of the trees.

"We'll drop off this stuff and go see what's happening," Lucy said and Ulin agreed.

Picking up their burdens hastily, they hurried toward the Inn. Halfway there, they saw Palin Majere. He was walking with rapid steps against the flow of the crowd, heading for the Academy. His head was down, his hands folded in the sleeves of his robes.

"Father!" Ulin called.

Palin either didn't hear his son over the commotion or he was deliberately ignoring him. He kept walking.

"Father!" Ulin called more loudly and made a move to intercept his father.

Only then, when Palin had practically walked into his son, did he lift his head. His face was grim. His eyes shadowed.

"I don't have time to talk now, son," he said brusquely, starting to pass by. "I am in a hurry."

"What is it, Father?" Ulin demanded, detaining him. "What's going on?"

"Beryl is preparing to attack Solace," Palin said. He walked off, then, as if struck by a thought, he halted and turned back.

Ulin stood gaping at him. "But . . . that's ridiculous, Father. Is she insane?"

"I don't know whatever gave you the impression the dragon was sane to begin with," Palin retorted. "Ridiculous or not, the knights have received reports that a force they have been watching, led by Dark Knights, is not marching to Haven, as was thought. They have turned toward Solace, coming up from the south. The knights are planning to march as swiftly as possible to meet their advance long before they can reach our city. We're calling out the town militia. I was on my way back to the Academy to collect some of the artifacts that have to do with battle-magic."

"I'll come with you," Ulin offered.

"And I will, too," Lucy added stoutly.

Palin was shaking his head. "No, I need you both to remain in the Academy. The pupils should not be abandoned, nor the masters. I want you to go back to the Academy, son. Make sure everyone remains calm."

"You don't think the Academy will be attacked, do you, father?" Ulin asked.

Palin shrugged his shoulders. "Lord Warren is confident that the knights will halt the enemy's advance. Our scouts report that the force is a small one. The Dark Knights are getting cocky, he thinks, to attack with so few men. I'm more worried that a few of Solace's own ne'er-do-wells might decide to take advantage of the turmoil to do a little thieving. And now I *must* be going. May luck be with you and with us all this day."

He left them abruptly, without waiting to hear their answer, taking it for granted they would do as he bid them.

"Well, that's that," said Ulin, grunting as he hefted the box. They started once more for the Inn. From the square, they could hear the loud and authoritative voice of Lord Warren formally calling the Solace militia to arms. "No glory in battle for us. Only stanching Master Thomas's nosebleed that he always gets when he's over stimulated."

"But your father's right, you know," said Lucy, lugging the clothes basket. "The pupils can't be left alone. Goodness knows what the little dears would do. Half of them in hysterics and the others ready to rush out to fight. And the masters no better, some of them. To tell you the truth, I don't really think I'd be much good in a fight." She glanced down cheerfully at her plump body.

"Whether we are or whether we're not, it looks like we're not going to get the chance to find out," Ulin said and he sounded glum.

****

Wary of the dragon lurking so near their borders, the knights and the Solace town militia had long been preparing for just such an eventuality. The muster of troops was swift, for they had practiced monthly, and within six hours after the first reports came in, the knights were riding southward, followed by a regiment of doughty, arms-bearing citizens. A small force had been left behind under the command of Caramon Majere, who ordered everyone to fill whatever containers they could find with water in case the dragons launched a fiery assault against their city.

Riding at the head of his column of knights, Lord Warren turned on his horse to motion to an aide. "Where is Master Majere?"

"Riding by himself at the back of the column, sir," the aide reported. "At least that's where I last saw him."

Lord Warren nodded. "Tell Master Majere I want to speak with him."

The aide raised an eyebrow, looked shocked.

Lord Warren said gruffly, "Very well, damn it, ask Master Majere politely if it would be convenient for him to speak with me. Civilians," he muttered after the aide had departed.

Palin rode forward along the long line of men-at-arms

and knights to confer with the knight commander, Lord Warren. The two were not exactly friends, but they held a mutual respect for each other. Lord Warren was completely opposed to the use of magic in battlefield situations, believing firmly that the men required to guard a spell-casting mage could be of better use elsewhere on the field. But he was forced to concede that on occasion, magic had its place, particularly pyrotechnics, and so he asked the mage to ride along. Lord Warren trusted immeasurably in Palin's good sense and his courage, if he did not trust completely in his magic.

"Master Majere," Lord Warren said. "Thank you for taking the time to speak with me."

Palin bowed from the saddle, wordless. He wore a hooded traveling cloak, kept the hood pulled low over his face. Removing the hood, he found, merely encouraged people to talk to him.

Lord Warren cleared his throat. He found speaking to the shadowed face extremely disconcerting. "I know you mages have your secrets and all that, but I need to know . . . in order to plan the attack, mind you, I need to know . . ."

"What magic spells I intend to use?" Palin finished, as a way of bringing the conversation to a swift conclusion. "Certainly, my lord." Palin reached into a pouch, produced a rosewood box, banded with silver. He opened the box to show twenty silver balls nestled in red velvet. Each ball was decorated with runes engraved upon the sides.

Lord Warren eyed the silver balls warily. "What do they do?"

"Toss one of these on the ground in the midst of enemy cavalry, and it will burst apart, sending out a swarm of magical insects. Their bite is like that of the horsefly, only a hundred times more painful. They will drive even the best-trained war-horse mad within seconds, send him plunging out of control, thus completely disrupting a cavalry unit, rendering them not only useless in the field, but making them a danger to their own troops."

"Amazing," said Lord Warren, impressed. He could well gauge the value of such a weapon. "How does it distinguish friend from foe?"

"It does not, my lord," Palin replied, not bothering to hide his scorn.

Lord Warren frowned. "Then what good is it, if it drives the mounts of my own knights crazy?"

Palin endeavored to curb his impatience with those who were magic-ignorant. "My lord, you need only attach one of these silver balls to an arrow and have your best archer send it flying deep into the enemies' ranks. Your knights will remain unaffected so long as they keep out of the spell's radius for fifteen minutes. After that, the spell will dissipate, the insects disappear."

"I see." Lord Warren was pleased. "I'll have our best archer assigned to you, Majere. But you won't fire until you have my signal?"

"Of course not, my lord," Palin said coldly. "I have had some experience in battle myself, my lord."

"That's good," said Lord Warren, relieved. "That's very good."

Palin started to ride away, then paused. "My lord, don't you find this all rather odd? I know something of military matters from both my own past experience and that of my father. This seems a very small force to send out against a city as well-prepared for attack as Solace."

"Bah! These Dark Knights have a new leader now. A man named Targonne. He's an accountant, an office-flunky. Not a general. He knows little of military matters, so our spies tell us. His own officers have no respect for him, though they're all terrified of him. He gained his post through assassination, you know. This is probably some hare-brained scheme of his thinking to catch us napping." Lord Warren grunted. "He'll find that we're awake. Wide awake."

Palin remained unconvinced. Turning his horse's head, he rode back to the rear, well behind the knights, behind even the footsoldiers. Palin was troubled, but unable to explain his anxiety. As he had said, the actions of the Dark Knights made no sense to him and he could not, as could Lord Warren, so easily pass off their actions as being those of an obtuse commander. Whatever else the Dark Knights may be, they were not stupid and they did not allow stupid people to remain in positions of command.

Palin could not explain it, but he had the strangest feeling that he was riding away from battle, not toward it.

****

"So you see, there is nothing to worry about," Ulin told the assembly of students and masters. "The knights have everything well in hand. According to my grandfather, they face only a small enemy force and will likely rout it without any problem. My father has asked that we continue with our daily routine—" He paused, checked a sigh. "Yes, Mistress Abigail?"

The small red-haired, sharp-eyed, sharp-tongued little girl was the bane of the masters' existence. She was one of those extremely intelligent children who are brighter than most of the adults around them and who make no secret that they hold the adult-world in contempt. When the other students had departed the school, saying they had nothing left to learn since the magic was failing, Palin had hoped that the one good which might come out of this evil was the departure of Mistress Abigail. Sadly, she stayed on. Word was that she terrified her parents and that they were quite content to let others deal with her.

"What if the knights don't hold them?" she asked petulantly. "What if we're attacked?"

"That's a very unlikely possibility," said Ulin, striving to remain patient. Lucy had just stanched Master Thomas's nosebleed and now Ulin could see the boy's eyes starting to widen in terror. "Very unlikely," he said emphatically. "We are in a secure fortress. The walls of this building are made of stone and very thick. The gate is guarded by a very powerful magic spell. Nothing can possibly harm us."

"A dragon could," said the little girl.

"Dragon!" Master Thomas's chin quivered. His hand flew to his nose.

"Tilt your head back," Ulin snapped. "We are not going to be attacked by dragons. Return to the classroom, all of you."

"Blue dragons with lightning breath," hissed Mistress Abigail, leaning near Master Thomas and contorting her face grotesquely. "They'll breath fire on you and your flesh will snap and crackle and turn black. And after they cook you they eat you! They start by biting off your head—"

"Oohhhh," Master Thomas moaned. Blood dribbled down his nose and into his mouth.

Ulin, with a grim face, marched Mistress Abigail to the library, figuring that an afternoon of dusting books would settle her much too vivid imagination.

The day passed in relative quiet at the Academy of Sorcery. Master's Thomas nosebleed finally stopped. Mistress Abigail was sent to bed early as a reminder that it wasn't nice to frighten little boys.

Or big boys either, for that matter.

"I think you should stay here tonight," Ulin said to Lucy. "Not go back to the Inn. Not tonight."

"Is that a proposition?" she asked, her dimple flashing.

"No." Ulin flushed. "I didn't mean it like that. It's just—Well, I don't want you in Solace in case anything should happen. Not that I think it will, mind you, but ..."

"I'll stay," she said. "I was planning on it in any case. Master Thomas was in such a state I had to cast a sleep spell over him. A sleep spell, mind you!" she reiterated proudly. "The first spell I've cast in days. And I cast a wizard-lock spell on the mage-ware room. I think it's the state of crisis. Brings out the best in me. It won't stop a dragon, but—"

"Dragons!" Ulin grimaced. "You've been listening to Mistress Abigail. You know, I think I'd rather face a dragon than ever spend five hours alone with that little imp again. She asked, by my count, seven hundred and eighty-five questions, of which seven hundred and eighty-four could not possibly be answered by the great Astinus himself. And the seven hundredth and eighty-fifth was 'How do babies get inside a mommy's tummy?'" He sighed deeply, then cheered up. "I don't feel much like sleeping. What about a game of fox and hounds after you cast the spell? Will you be fox or hounds?"

"Hounds," said Lucy promptly, heading off for the mage-ware room. "Two coppers a point?"

"It's a deal." Ulin went to find a deck of cards.

****

"That's it!" Lucy said wearily, tossing in her hand. "I give up. You win."

"You owe me"—Ulin peered down at the slash marks he'd made on a chalk board—"eight steel and ten coppers."

"You cheat," Lucy accused. "I know there were six huntsmen in that last hand, when there's only supposed to be four in the deck. I would have called you on it, but I was too tired."

"I do not cheat," Ulin returned indignantly. "If you'd just learn to count the cards when they fall—"

The town bell rang out, wildly, frantically. At almost the same moment, someone was heard bellowing from down below.

"Ulin!" a voice shouted. "Open the gate!"

"Grandfather!" Ulin said, jumping to his feet.

"You don't suppose—" Lucy couldn't finish the thought. It was too terrible to speak. "Ulin, we have all these children!"

He was up and gone, dashing down the stairs, taking them recklessly two or three at a time in his haste to reach the door. Lucy caught up the skirts of her robes and followed as fast as she dared.

Ulin threw open the main door. He ran across the courtyard that was rimed with frost, spent several moments wrestling with the enormous wooden bar that held the gates closed. At this moment, he was thankful that he didn't have to contend with removing a wizard lock. He pulled open the gates.

The Academy was located several miles outside of Solace. Built on a hilltop, the tall towers and high walls made of it a small fortress. The night air was chill and crisp. The full moon shone brightly and the grass beyond sparkled with frost. Caramon Majere was big and brawny still, though he was in his eighties. His hair was iron gray, but his eyes were clear and keen, his body unstooped and unbowed. He loomed large against the starlit darkness. Behind his grandfather stood two big draught horses, hitched to a large hay cart. Caramon had driven here in a hurry, apparently, for the horses were puffing and blowing, sending up clouds of breath that smoked in the chill air.

"Grandfather! What—"

"We were duped, Ulin," Caramon said bluntly. "The knights have gone off on a wild kender chase. I sent some of the lads out on patrol to the west, just in case some Beryl's forces might decide to try circle around and attack from that direction. The lads have come hot-footing it back with word that a small force of draconians is headed this way."

"They're going to attack Solace!" Ulin gasped.

"Not Solace, grandson," said Caramon, placing his hand on Ulin's shoulder. "The Academy of Sorcery."

"No! That can't be! How do you know, Grandfather?"

"I had lads posted in the lookout towers high up in the vallenwoods," Caramon answered. "A force of about seventy-five draconians passed right underneath them. They could hear them talking. The draconians were all excited about the loot they were going take from the Academy and how Beryl is going to reward them for every magical artifact they bring to her. And double that reward for any mage they capture alive."

"The knights," said Ulin thickly, his brain stumbling around like a drunkard. "The army—"

"I've sent word," Caramon said. "Mistress."

He doffed his cap and nodded his head to Lucy, who had come to join Ulin and now stood calm and mute at his side, offering her silent support.

"But they can't possibly return in time," Caramon continued, replacing his cap. "If they force-marched all night, as they planned, they will have covered some thirty miles by now. The men and horses will be exhausted. They couldn't possibly turn around and march back to Solace without rest. The quickest they could come would be tomorrow night. And that's many long hours away."

"Still, we could hold out until then," Ulin said hopefully, fumbling his way through the fog of fear and dismay to see clearly at last. "The Academy walls are stone, thick enough to withstand even a draconian assault, especially from a small force. We have a store of artifacts, some of them meant for battle-magic, to say nothing of our spell-casting—What is it, Grandfather?" Ulin asked sharply, noting Caramon's grave expression. "You're not telling me something."

"The draconians spoke of dragons, Grandson. We don't know . . . the lads didn't see any, but . . ."

"Dragons! Then perhaps we will be safe and Solace is their target!"

"Ulin," Lucy chided him. "What are you saying?"

Realizing what he had been wishing, if not exactly saying, Ulin felt his face flush. "I'm sorry, Grandfather. Of course, I don't want Solace to be attacked. It's just . . ." He looked behind him, at the stone walls standing tall against the stars, gleaming a soft pearl gray in the moonlight. "My father loves this place, Grandfather. He will be devastated."

"Buildings can be rebuilt," said Caramon briskly. "The Inn's been burned down and built back twice in my lifetime and better each time. But lives once lost cannot be recovered."

"You're right, of course," Ulin agreed. He was calm now and in control. "We have the children to consider, as well as the masters." He looked out to the courtyard. "That's why you brought the cart."

"I'll take them to the Inn," said Caramon. "Make haste! We don't have much time!"

Lucy was already racing back across the courtyard. Ulin followed her, thankful that they didn't have their full complement of students. He woke the masters and explained the situation. Fortunately, they kept their heads. They woke the children, soothed their first startled fears and, wrapping them in blankets, hustled them out of the Academy and out the gate to the waiting cart. All they were told was that they were going to Solace to stay in the Inn of the Last Home for a little while. All the children knew Caramon, who was a favorite. The sight of his jovial face, calm and reassuring, set them at ease, and the idea of a ride in a hay cart at this time of night, when they should be in bed, more than allayed any terrors.

Mistress Abigail guessed the truth right away, of course, but kept her mouth shut and was actually seen to be daubing Master's Thomas bleeding nose with a handkerchief in a motherly fashion and admonishing him, once they were settled in the cart, to tilt his head back. When all were packed in, Caramon looked down from his place on the seat of the hay cart to Ulin, who was standing in the gate, with Lucy staunchly at his side.

"Ulin—" Caramon began.

Ulin shook his head. "I'm staying here, Grandfather. I can't let all our artifacts come into Beryl's possession. I have to make some provision for them. But Mistress Lucy will go with you."

"Mistress Lucy will not, thank you, Master Ulin," Lucy returned placidly. "You better be on your way, sir," she said to Caramon. "Don't worry! We can manage."

Perched on the driver's seat, the whip in his hand, Caramon seemed about to argue. Realizing that time was running short and realizing, too, that what Ulin said was right, that they could not allow such powerful artifacts as Palin had collected to fall into Beryl's claws, Caramon urged them not to take any unnecessary chances and then snapped the whip over the horse's ears. The big animals lunged forward, pulling their heavy load with ease. The cart's wheels went spinning up the road, heading into the thick woods.

The night was eerily quiet once they were gone. Ulin peered intently into the trees, but he saw no movement. Draconian raiders would be silent and circumspect. He had no doubt but that they'd never see them until they were upon them. As for the dragons, the first they would know of them would be the terrible debilitating dragonfear, which robbed a man of his wits, his courage and, most horribly, even his will to live. Whatever he did, he must do now, before the fear rendered him helpless as a child, lost and forsaken.

"What *are* we going to do, Ulin," Lucy asked, as if she'd heard his thoughts. "They could be on us at any moment." She helped him swing shut the heavy gate. "They could be out there right now, for all we know."

"Yes," he said. He slid the huge bar into the gate. He paused to consider it. "When the Academy was first built, my father and the other mages cast a powerful spell on this gate, a spell that is supposed to activate if anyone attempts a forced entry."

"Do you think it still works?" Lucy asked.

Ulin shrugged. "Who knows? I guess we're about to find out." He glanced at her sharply as they hurried back across the courtyard. "Are you all right?"

"No," she returned cheerfully. "To be honest, I'm so scared I could run away down that road this moment and probably beat the horses back to Solace. But I'm not leaving you behind. Especially since you have a plan. You do have plan, don't you?"

He smiled ruefully, took hold of her hand and squeezed it tight. "Yes, I have a plan. But it's dangerous and I'm not sure you should be here, Lucy. It might fail."

"Can you use my help?"

"Yes," he admitted.

"Then let's get to it. What are you going to do? We can't hide the artifacts. The draconians will almost certainly find them and if they don't, the dragons will. Reds have a nose for magic, or so I've heard."

"I'm not going to hide them," Ulin said. "I'm going to bury them."

****

The captain of the draconian raiding party was a large aurak named Izztmel. He was already a favorite of Beryl's and this night's raid would go a long way toward increasing his influence with the dragon. The raid was Izztmel's idea, based on a "conversation" he'd had with a young human magic-user, a friend of Palin Majere's.

A month ago, Izztmel had come across the unfortunate young mage, capturing him as he was attempting to return to the Academy from a journey to the Tower of High Sorcery at Waywreth, a Tower Beryl longed to acquire but which the wizards managed to continue to successfully conceal from her.

The young mage had not provided any useful information regarding the Tower, but he had revealed, before he died, the fact that Palin Majere, fearing Beryl might stumble across the Tower, had a great many valuable magical artifacts secretly stored in the Academy.

When Izztmel suggested to the dragon that they raid the Academy, Beryl embraced the idea. She had never breathed a word to anyone, but she had felt a decrease of her magical powers in the past few months. In her heart, she feared that her cousin Malys was responsible, but Beryl also had to consider that the culprit might be these troublesome human mages at the Academy. Beryl gave orders for the Dark Knights to feint an attack coming from the south, drawing out the garrison of Solamnics and the Solace town militia, leaving the Academy isolated and undefended.

Izztmel had pointed out that this would leave the rich city of Solace undefended, as well, but Beryl had refused to even consider attacking Solace. Her cousin Malys would almost certainly view this as a breaking of the pact and

Beryl was not strong enough yet to win a battle against the immense and powerful red. But Malys would not mind a little midnight raid against an Academy whose mages had on more than one occasion thwarted the great red's ambition to rule all of Ansalon.

Solace's time would come, but it was not now.

Izztmel and his small force of raiders marched from Beryl's lair, heading toward Solace, keeping under cover. In the meantime, the Dark Knights marched from another direction, making their movements as open and blatant as possible.

A few hours past midnight, the main body of the draconian raiding party joined up with their advance scouts, who had been hiding in the woods ever since sundown, keeping watch. Izztmel noted with disappointment that lights shown in some of the windows of the immense stone structure. He'd been hoping to catch them all asleep.

"Your report?" Izztmel asked one of the scouts.

"Sir." The scout saluted. "They were tipped off. Your force was seen by some humans hiding in the trees."

Izztmel muttered curses. "I thought I smelled human flesh in the forest. I couldn't spare the time to check it out. Have they all fled then? Taken their goods with them?"

"They loaded some of their young into a wagon," said the scout. "Your orders were not to do anything that might alert them and so we let the wagon leave. That was about an hour ago. But there are still at least two mages inside. We heard them talking. They said they were going to stay to protect the artifacts. We haven't seen them come out."

"Come now," said Izztmel, rubbing his clawed hands. "This is not so bad. Two prisoners and all the artifacts. And no one defending the place. We have only to wait for the reds—"

"Sir," one of his draconians called, "you can see the red dragons just coming over the horizon."

Izztmel, looking to the west, saw the shadows of dragon wings blotting out the starlight.

"Launch the attack," he ordered.

The word passed quietly down the line from one draconian to another. They drew their curved bladed swords and ran over the frost-rimed ground toward the main gate. They ran in silence, no cheering or yelling. Reaching the gate, they halted.

"Bring up the battering ram," Izztmel ordered.

Draconians carrying an enormous iron-shod ram ran at full speed toward the gate. The ram struck the gate and instantly disintegrated as if it had been made of ice, not wood. The draconians who had been holding onto it flew backward, struck by some unseen force.

"Some sort of spell on it, sir," reported one of the draconians.

"You don't say." Izztmel sneered. "Stand back, the lot of you."

Approaching the gate, he stood before it. He held out his clawed hands, brought his spell to mind. He could feel the power of the spell on the gate working against him. He could feel, too, those little annoying stinging gnats or whatever insects seemed to flock around him when he was spell-casting. His spell wavered and for a moment he thought he'd lost it, and then suddenly the spell on the gate snapped. Izztmel's magic flowed inside him, warm and exhilarating. The magic flared from his hands, forming a wall of fire that struck the gate and set it ablaze.

Now yelling wildly, the Draconians battered down the flaming gate and dashed through.

****

At the sound of the shattering boom of the battering ram, Lucy flinched, spilling some of the charcoal she was scooping into a barrel.

"Careful," Ulin said coolly. "We don't have all that much of this stuff that we can throw it around."

"I'm not throwing it around," Lucy snapped. "I'm shaking like a leaf. You did hear that, didn't you? They're out there!" She lifted her head fearfully. "And something else is out there, too! Something awful!"

"Dragons," he said grimly. "That's the first taste of the dragonfear. Fight against it, Lucy. The dragons aren't close yet. And hopefully it will take them some time for the draconians to break the gate down." He carefully scooped up the small amount Lucy had spilled and poured it into the barrel. "Now we put the lid on these two."

"Why a lid?" Lucy asked nervously.

"Because I've discovered in my experiments that the thunder powder is more effective when it's contained than when loose."

Ulin hefted the barrel filled with the black powder and, carrying it carefully, hauled it down the hallway to the room where the artifacts were stored. Lucy brought the other barrel. They had only managed, in the short time they had, to produce an amount of the thundering black powder sufficient to fill three barrels, two large and one small. Ulin placed each of the large barrels at the foot of two large, load-bearing columns that stood near the door to the mage-ware room.

"Now, if I'm right," he said, eyeing the barrels and the columns and glancing up at the massive stone ceiling above, "when these two go off, the force of the blast will knock down the columns and that will cause the roof to collapse on top of the artifacts. Not even the dragon will be able to get to them then."

The dragons were drawing ever nearer. He could feel his stomach start to clench. He took in a deep breath to calm himself.

"*If* you're right," Lucy said. She looked skeptical. "Ulin, you blew up a *salt cellar!*"

Ulin shrugged. "Whether I am or not, there's not much to be done about it now."

Upending the third small barrel, he poured lightning powder on the floor all around the barrel. Then, continuing to pour out the powder, he started backing down the hallway.

"What's that for?" Lucy asked.

"This is how I'll set it off," Ulin said. "Let me know when we reach the end of the corridor. I can't see where I'm going."

"We're here," Lucy announced after a moment.

"Good thing," Ulin grunted. He had nearly emptied the barrel. He straightened, grimacing from cramped back muscles.

"Grab one of those torches." He indicated the torches set in sconces on the walls. "We'll need it."

"You want to light a torch!" Lucy stared at him. She held up her blackened hands. "We're covered in this stuff!"

"It won't hurt you," he said patiently. "It needs to be contained, remember? Just be sure not to set off that trail of powder. Not yet."

There came the sound of yelling, triumphant, terrible.

"They're through the gate," said Lucy, her face livid. "Hurry, Ulin!"

He reached up to grasp hold of one of the iron sconces made in the shape of a gargoyle that lined the walls. Removing the flaming torch from the sconce, Ulin heard the small click of a hidden mechanism. He handed the torch to Lucy to hold. Reaching up his right hand, he grasped hold of the sconce and turned it to the right until he heard another click. He then turned the sconce back to its original position and there came a third click. After a pause, during which Ulin nervously chewed on his lip, certain his invention had failed, there came a grinding sound. He sighed in relief and, grasping Lucy's hand, darted into the opening created by a sliding panel in the wall.

"That's remarkable!" she said, impressed. "I didn't know this wall did that!"

"Only my father and I know about it," Ulin returned. "It was designed for just such an occurrence. It was my idea," he added with a touch of pride that not even his fear could obviate. "Hand me the torch. Now get out of here, Lucy. Start running." He pointed down the long narrow corridor that disappeared into the darkness. "The tunnel comes out in the woods near my father's house."

"I'm waiting for you."

"Lucy, damn it!" Ulin glared at her, but she simply glared right back. He didn't have time to argue.

There came a shattering crash, as of wood splintering and breaking. Fearful shrieks of glee split the air. That was the entrance door.

Ulin touched the end of the torch to the trail of lightning powder. It sparked and caught fire. The flame began to eat up the powder, moving relentlessly across the stone floor to the barrels. Ulin watched a moment to see the flame racing along the trail of powder. Then he grasped hold of a length of rope that hung from the ceiling and gave it a sharp tug. The sliding panel reversed its movement, closed off the opening.

"Run!" he shouted. "Don't worry about being modest, girl! Gather up your skirts and run like dragons were after you."

"Very funny!" Lucy grunted, and did as she was told, hiking up the skirts of her robes practically to her waist and haring off down the long tunnel with Ulin pounding along at her side.

They ran and ran and listened with stretched ears, waiting for the explosion. Time passed and there was nothing. Nothing except the echoes of their own footfalls.

"Shouldn't . . . it . . . have . . . happened . . . by now?" Lucy gasped with what breath she had left.

"Yes," said Ulin, his own voice tight with despair. "It should have. We've failed."

****

After a night spent lying wrapped in his blanket on the cold, damp ground, broad awake, staring at the stars, trying to put a name to his fears, Palin had just managed to fall asleep near dawn when a hand shook him.

"Sorry to wake you, Master Mage," said a voice. The face

was lost in the darkness. "Lord Warren would like to speak to you. He says it's urgent."

Palin tossed off his blanket, followed the lord's aide back to the Knights' command tent. The camp was an uproar, officers shouting, waking the men, calling for their horses or their squires. Palin wondered that he'd been able to sleep through it.

"Here's something damn odd, Majere," said Lord Warren, his face grim. "My scouts have just come to tell me that the enemy's gone."

"Gone, my lord?" Palin repeated, still stupid with sleepiness.

"Gone. Vanished. The whole lot of them. Melted into the night. Do you know what this means?" Lord Warren didn't give him time to answer. "It means that this was a feint. We've been hoodwinked! It means that while we're lollygagging like a bunch of idiots down here, they're attacking Solace!"

Fear twisted inside Palin and now his fear had a name. Lord Warren was wrong. Beryl didn't want Solace. She wanted something much more valuable to her than Solace.

Drawing a ring from out a pouch, Palin slipped it onto his finger and vanished.

"We're turning back," Lord Warren began, but he found himself talking to empty air. He blinked, stared. "Majere?"

No response.

"Mages," Lord Warren muttered and left his tent that was already, by his command, being taken down around him. "Strange chaps. Even the best of 'em."

****

"This is the mage-ware room," said Izztmel, staring intently at the closed door and comparing it to a crude map he'd drawn from the description that he'd wrung out of the tormented mage. The four draconians who had accompanied him bunched up behind him to get a look. He glanced around. Yes, this fit with the description. On the lowest level in a narrow corridor down from the laboratory. Several large columns lined the corridor. The only thing that was out of place was a wooden barrel standing beneath one of the columns near the door. The barrel was covered with a black powdery substance that had been spilled all over the floor

"What is this filthy stuff?" Izztmel demanded, suspicious. "Second! Come forward."

"Yes, sir." The bozak approached warily.

"Go examine that stuff more closely," Izztmel ordered. "Tell me what it is."

The bozak crept forward, his eyes fixed on the powder, ready to bolt the moment it seemed inclined to do something alarming. The powder appeared innocent enough. He bent down, stared hard at the substance, taking care not to step in it.

"There's a track of the stuff that leads off down the corridor, sir," he reported.

"Well, go investigate it!" Izztmel ordered, seething at the loss of time. He was so near the magic. The feel of it made his scales click in anticipation.

The bozak tramped down the hall. "It looks like someone tried to use this to start a fire, sir," he reported. "Part of it's burned at this end."

"Humans! Just like their tomfoolery," Izztmel muttered. He reached down a claw, dipped it in the black substance and brought it to his nose. "Charcoal." He sniffed again. "Rotten eggs and horse piss. Some sort of magic, perhaps. Whatever is was meant to do, it obviously fizzled."

"Now there's the magic," he said. "I can smell it!" He pointed toward the iron padlock. His tongue slid out between his teeth in his eagerness. "Their precious artifacts! Wizard lock, iron padlock. A child could break through these."

Izztmel wove a spell with his hands. The wizard lock shivered, but held. He strengthened the spell and at last felt the magical barrier give way. Now there remained only the iron padlock. He called the words to the lightning spell to mind, pointed his finger at the door lock.

The magic flashed from his clawed finger, sizzled near the barrel . . .

****

Ulin and Lucy stood at the edge of the woods, their hands clasped together, watching fearfully the two enormous red dragons flying in lazy circles above the Academy of Sorcery. Outside the smoldering gate, a draconian patrol walked, keeping a look-out for anyone who might disturb their looting and ransacking. They obviously did not expect to be interrupted, for they grumbled and swore in their uncouth language, complaining about being left out here while their comrades were scooping up all the treasure.

From inside the Academy, Ulin could hear raucous laughter, the sounds of furniture being smashed, desks hacked to pieces, glass shattering. Every blow seemed to strike him deep inside himself. The fiends were wrecking the place. Anything valuable they found they tossed out the broken windows to be retrieved later and carried off.

"You did all that you could have done, Ulin," Lucy said softly, her voice shaking. "You did all that you could."

"It wasn't good enough," he returned bitterly. "That's the story of my life. Nothing I did was ever good enough! Not for the magic. Not for my wife ..."

Lucy gasped, dug her nails into his flesh. "Who's that?"

A figure had suddenly materialized in the courtyard; a figure that for a moment seemed to Ulin's startled vision to have been spun out of starlight and moonglow. And then, in the next horrified instance, he recognized it.

"Father!" he shouted.

But the draconian patrol had also seen the figure and they were much closer.

"Father!" Ulin shouted again. "Behind you!"

Palin turned. Seeing the draconians, he raised his hand, prepared to cast his spell . . .

A tongue of flame shot up from the Academy of Sorcery. The flame flared higher than the tallest Tower. The light of the flame was so bright that it blinded all who looked at it. And then came the thunder—a concussive blast that rolled out of the Tower, rumbled over the ground that shivered and shook with the shock wave. The blast knocked Palin flat and sent the draconians reeling backward. The dragons flying above the Academy flailed about, enormous wings beating frantically to carry them out of harm's way. The blast tore the heart out of the Academy of Sorcery.

Rubble and debris flew high into the air, and then crashed down to the ground in a deadly hail storm that snapped off tree limbs and sent huge chunks of stone bounding over the ground like pebbles.

Oblivious to the danger, Palin jumped to his feet. He screamed something, words Ulin could not hear for the awful rumbling of the Academy walls collapsing. The great Tower teetered and then it fell with a deafening crash. Flames leapt up, lighting the darkness, changing night to terrible day in an instant. Smoke roiled into the air.

The draconians, stunned, stared in baffled amazement at the flaming building. One of them pointed up at the red dragons and shook his fist.

"Blundering idiots! What'd you have to go and blow it up for?" he screamed. "Some of our boys were still in there!"

"Not to mention the loot!" another shrieked.

The reds ignored them. Their night's work was finished, albeit in an unexpected manner. Singed and battered from the blast, they took flight, heading for home. In their report to Beryl, they would place the blame for the explosion on the aurak Izztmel.

"We won't go back empty-handed," said a draconian. "We'll take this human scum with us at least. One of their filthy wizards is better than nothing."

"Father! Look out!" Ulin shouted.

Palin stood staring at the end of his dream. He neither saw nor heard anything else.

Ulin started to race toward him. Lucy flung her arms around him, held him fast.

"You can't help him, Ulin!" she said. "They'll only capture you, too. We'll tell your Grandfather! He'll send out a rescue party. The draconians' trail will be easy to follow. Ulin, don't do this! Don't!"

The draconians seized hold of Palin. Still dazed from the blast and, perhaps more, from the sight of his beloved Academy going up in flames, his dream going up in smoke, he didn't fight or struggle. He did not look at them, as they chained his arms behind him. He did not speak. He watched the fire until the draconians hustled him off, and even then he twisted in their grasp to stare behind him.

"You can let go now," Ulin said, his voice ragged from the smoke.

Slowly, she released her grip.

He looked weary to the point of dropping. Tears streaked his charcoal-blackened face. The gleam of madness had died out of his eyes, leaving them dark and empty. Lucy's own tears slid unchecked down her cheeks. In the distance, they could hear the bells in Solace ringing again, calling out those left in the town to come fight the fire.

"Much good it will do them," Ulin said bitterly.

Reaching into his pocket, he took out a sheaf of notes. He ripped them in half, ripped the halves in half, ripped those into fourths and continued ripping until the ground was covered with small bits of paper no larger than the ashes and cinders falling down on top of them.

"My notes on the thunder powder," said Ulin. "And the formula." The notes shredded, he put his hands to his head. "I wish I could tear them out of my brain the same way!"

"Magic could have done that," Lucy said, thinking to comfort him.

"Magic is a skill, a discipline, an art. The use of magic requires study, sacrifice, concentration. The thunder powder"—Ulin glanced back at the blazing building and shuddered—"any thug with half a brain could use it, Lucy. What have I done? What dreadful power have I brought into the world? I wish I had never conceived of it."

"At least no one will know," she said, soothing him and calming him. "We will say it was the dragons that destroyed the Academy."

Ulin crushed the shreds of paper with the heel of his boot. "No one will know," he repeated. "No one will *ever* know!"

Growing Up Dragonlance

A flashback by Jamie Chambers

It all started, quite literally, as a game for me. My father had been playing Dungeons & Dragons for less than a year, and had just started a new campaign. He was excited about it and showed me the photocopied material for the first game session. I was ten years old.

The sheets were messy photocopies on thermal paper, but as I looked them over my heart started beating faster. First was the character sheet of Sturm Brightblade, with a full-body illustration by Larry Elmore. Next was the story "How the Companions Met," which was given out to the players to understand the backstory of the characters they were playing. I must have read it three of four times that first evening.

I don't remember asking Dad to buy me anything, but one day he came home with two shrink-wrapped packets. They were the first two modules in the Dragonlance adventure series. He knew that I occasionally played D&D with other kids in the neighborhood, but suggested that I start my own game. I began to read over them and started to get more familiar with my hardcover rulebooks. I had a mission!

Something about the world drew me in, even from the early game material. Perhaps it was the vivid art from Elmore, Caldwell, Easley, and Parkinson. Possibly it was the characters, as this was the first time in my gaming experience that a character wasn't just a bunch of numbers written on a piece of notebook paper—these people were *real* to me. It certainly could have been the story, which was huge and epic. The world was changing, good battling evil, and no one was safe. Ultimately, I think it was all of these things, and something more.

Even as I began planning my DRAGONLANCE campaign and inviting players to my first gaming group, my father brought another shrink-wrapped present for me. It was a boxed set of paperback novels, the DRAGONLANCE Chronicles by Margaret Weis and Tracy Hickman. I don't know if I even thanked my Dad before I retreated to my room and opened the first book to read Michael Williams's "Canticle of the Dragon."

Reading *Dragons of Autumn Twilight* was a life-changing experience for me. I already knew the characters and basic story from the game materials, but while reading those books I felt like I was actually there! I understood Tasslehoff's curiosity and optimism, related to Tanis' inner doubt, and even saw a bit of myself in Raistlin's jealousy and ambition. After reading the book to myself, my friend Blake asked if I would read them out aloud to him. He was severely dyslexic, and reading was difficult for him, but he really wanted to experience the books for himself. Some of my fondest early memories of DRAGONLANCE were our "reading parties," where Blake would spend the night and lay on the top bunk, while I would read for hours from below.

My DRAGONLANCE campaign went well, and my players are still my friends after nearly two decades. Writing and role-playing games were passions for me that sometimes overshadowed schoolwork and other responsibilities. After graduating from high school in 1993, I discovered an online service that was the official electronic home of TSR, Inc. In no time at all, I was running games online and becoming an active member of the message boards. Dave Gross was in charge of TSR Online at the time, and saw some sort of potential in me. After about a month of so of being part of the community, I found myself a staff member and president of one of the first online gaming clubs.

One of my main responsibilities as a staff member was to host "Tuesday Night Chats." Dave would recruit an author or game designer as a guest, and we would have a question-and-answer session with myself as the moderator. Those Tuesdays led to my acquaintance with a number of people I had long admired: Christi Golden, Jeff Grubb, Colin McComb, Douglas Niles, and others. But one night stands out: the night that Margaret Weis and Tracy Hickman were our guests in the chat room.

Since page one of *Dragons of Autumn Twilight*, Margaret Weis and Tracy Hickman have been my favorite authors. I had long felt a connection with the authors. Perhaps only imaginary, or maybe through the special link between author and reader, these seemed like people I already knew. The chat seemed to confirm this idea, for it was like talking with old friends. Margaret and Tracy were funny and gracious, answered fans' questions as best they could, and then stayed around after the official time for more casual conversation. I thanked them for giving our online group a special treat, but I don't know if anyone could have been more pleased than myself.

My chance to meet the authors in person came at the summer conventions, DragonCon and GenCon of 1994. To my utter amazement, Margaret and Tracy remembered me from the online chat. They had new projects, and they asked me to be involved. Soon I was helping to shape the galaxy of Starshield, later helping to sculpt the rules and world of Sovereign Stone. All of these were great settings and fantastic experiences, but Dragonlance was my first love.

I worked with Margaret and Tracy on various projects through most of college and my first real job. Term papers and productivity reports were things I wanted out of the way so I could read, write, and play games. Each year I visited Lake Geneva in the summer and had the most amazing times. In addition to politics, world events, and casual chit-chat, we also talked about DRAGONLANCE.

Shortly after New Year's in 2001, I received a phone call from Margaret, who was hopeful that her company, Sovereign Press, would be able to finalize a licensing agreement that would allow the company to publish new game material for DRAGONLANCE. I was asked to move my family from Georgia to Wisconsin so that I could be in charge of the Dragonlance game line. A big decision to be sure, and Sovereign Press was willing to give me time to think it over.

The decision was made before I ever hung up the phone.

****

I'm very lucky, and I'm smart enough to know it. I live and work with DRAGONLANCE every day. It's analogous to someone who marries a childhood sweetheart. I've been with DRAGONLANCE for twenty years, and it's been very good to me.

Thank you Tracy, for your vision, support, and encouragement. Thank you Margaret, for inspiring me, for believing in me, and for giving me a new place to call home. And thank you, Dad, for opening a doorway for me into a new world. I'm very happy here.

Jamie Chambers, the Vice President of Sovereign Press, Inc., publisher of the DRAGONLANCE and Sovereign Stone roleplaying game lines, wrote his first DRAGONLANCE short story, "At the Water's Edge," for the *Search for Power: Dragons of the War of Souls* anthology. He is currently working hard on the *War of the Lance* sourcebook, a gaming resource he is coauthoring with Margaret Weis and Tracy Hickman.

The Traveling Players of Gilean

Margaret Weis and Aron Eisenberg
Originally published in *The Best of Tales, Volume One*

The elf was tired and footsore. He had traveled a long distance to reach his destination, although if this was his destination, it was very shabby and disappointing.

Not unlike himself, he muttered caustically.

He wrapped his meager cloak around his slender body and kept his hood pulled low over his face, hoping to be taken for a human in this human village, although any human who noticed his grace of movement and his delicate hands would have known him for exactly what he was. Known him and likely beat him and harried him, if not worse. This was in the Fourth Age, prior to the War of the Lance, and elves were viewed with suspicion and most times with downright hostility in human communities.

The elf found that which he sought easily enough without having to ask directions. The village was small. The time was nighttime and the only patch of bright light in the area must be the place where the troupe of players was said to be performing. The elf turned his footsteps in that direction.

The village street—there was only one—was empty. The

tavern was shuttered, the door closed. Every inhabitant of the village was here for the play, an event in their lives. Rows of benches had been set up in a clearing at the edge of the village, probably where they held summer fairs and revels. People filled the benches, gossiping and chattering and exchanging greetings. Small children escaped their parents and played at kender-catch-me, tripping up their elders, squealing and laughing.

Firelight and torchlight shone on gaily colored wagons, maybe twenty in all, drawn up in a semi-circle. A large stage stood in the center of the semicircle. The stage was bare—nothing but a raised wooden platform built about five feet up off the ground. It appeared wobbly and insubstantial, was built so that it could be broken down and hauled away for the next performance.

The elf looked at the stage and shook his head. Bare boards. No curtains. No backdrops. No scenery of any sort. But then, what had he expected?

"Gone ten miles out of my way to come to this," he said to himself bitterly as he found a seat in the very back row next to a broad-shouldered human male, who glared at him suspiciously and edged as far away from him as possible.

The elf had found the playbill posted on a signpost at a crossroads. The fact that it had been at a crossroads had struck the elf as significant, for he had come to a crossroads in his life and was wondering what path to take. The answer had seemed easy. One path led to thievery, knavery, knives in the back in the dark, hands slipping unbidden in stranger's pockets. The other led to starvation and ruin.

In a world where most elves lived safe and isolated in their own homelands and where humans lived safe and isolated in theirs, a lone elf walking in human lands had few choices for the means to earn a livelihood. The Thieves Guild was one organization that never discriminated against anyone. All who were willing to accept its dark precepts were welcome to join.

He had to decide: Did his road lead to the lord-city of

Palanthas and the Thieves Guild? Or did it lead to this little village and a play? The elf had started down the road to Palanthas. He'd only taken a few steps, when he had turned and, ripping off the playbill from the signpost, he had rolled it up and thrust it into his pack and taken the other path. He could always return to Palanthas.

The play had not yet started. Lights burned in the windows of the wagons, which were rolling homes, apparently, for the elf could see that the wagons were furnished as the taste of the occupier of the wagon dictated. Some had lacy curtains covering the windows, some had no curtains at all revealing interior walls painted bright colors. The wagons were made of wood, ornately carved with scrollwork and curlicues and gewgaws. Some of the wagons were short and squat, others were enormous affairs, more like supply wagons for an army. The elf could hear voices coming from the wagons. Actors practicing vocal exercises by the sounds of it; a woman's light laughter. The audience coughed and shifted restlessly. The elf took out the playbill, smoothed it on his knee, read it again.

CAST FROM THE LIGHT
A Play in Three Acts
Performed by the
Traveling Players of Gilean
Under the direction of Sebatius
Written by Sebatius
Costumes, Sets, Backdrops
Designed by Sebatius
All Rights Owned by Sebatius

The rest of the playbill listed the dates of the tour of the play, the locations where it would be performed. This village was the last stop on the tour, apparently. The last night the performance would be given. The elf couldn't imagine why he had come.

The doors to the wagons banged open simultaneously.

Light streamed out of the wagons, illuminating the actors, who left their wagons and gathered around the stage. Four of the actors mounted onto the stage. The audience gave a collective gasp.

Two of the actors were elves. One of the actors was a human wearing the black robes of Dark Magic. One of the actors was an ogre, with a leering face and slavering jaw.

The audience was astounded and alarmed. There were growls and boos. Mothers called their children in panicked voices to come to their sides and gathered them safely in their arms. Those men who were armed put their hands on their weapons. Several stood up and demanded their money back. The elf in the audience pulled his hood even lower, so low over his slanted eyes he had difficulty seeing the stage.

A large man, a human, climbed the stairs that led to the stage. He took his place in the center of the bare platform and raised his hands for quiet. He was a large man, rotund, with a face that might have been made of bread dough, for it looked as if it could be prodded and poked and worked to portray any and every expression known to man. He was smiling and beneficent.

"Gentle folk," he said in sweet and placating tones, "calm yourselves. Yes, you see elves among us. Our play is about elves and thus we bring you elves to perform in it. Not only elves, but ogres, goblins, hobgoblins, dwarves, kender, gnomes, *and* humans. The Traveling Players of Gilean are not"—here he grew very stern, his bushy eyebrows drawing together—"one of those cheap tramping gypsy troupes that advertises elves and gives you humans with pointy ears made of clay! We do not slap hideous masks on the faces of humans and proclaim to you that they are ogres! We do not send in humans walking upon their knees and try to convince you that they are dwarves.

"No, the Traveling Players of Gilean, directed by myself, Sebatius"—he took a deep bow—"would not stoop so low. We have the real thing! We have elves to play elves, we have ogres to play ogres, we have kender to play kender and all brought here at great expense especially for you here tonight. You will not see the like anywhere else in Krynn, not even in the finest theaters in Palanthas. And we charge you no more than what you pay to see one of those cheap productions."

Flattered and curious, the mollified audience settled back down, though they kept an eye on the elves and on the ogre. Sebastius, his red and golden robes flowing, descended from the stage with dignity. A dwarf member of the troupe clambered up the stairs. He carried a scraggly and half-dead looking stick of a tree in a tub, which he placed in the center of the stage.

Advancing to the front of the stage, the dwarf announced in a sonorous voice: "The lovely and forbidden forest of Silvanesti."

Some in the audience tittered. The elf gave an inward groan. He would have left, but he feared drawing attention to himself. The man seated next to him kept looking at the elf's hands.

The dwarf stumped off the stage. The actors took their places, ignoring the catcalls and the insults and an overripe tomato that splattered against the tub containing the lovely and forbidden forest of Silvanesti. The actors began to speak, and the catcalls faded away into soft gasps of pleasure and amazement.

The elf blinked his eyes. He looked no longer at a tree in a tub. He looked upon the forest of Silvanesti. He was from Qualinesti himself and had never seen the wondrous, magical forest of his cousins, but he had heard of it in story and in song for all the many years of his life and he knew that this was it. Trees with silver bark and leaves of sparkling emerald, roses of shimmering rainbow hues, lush grasses and gently clinging vines.

The play commenced. The audience was quiet as a winter's snowfall.

The story was of a young elf, talented in the art of magic, but who was of low caste and therefore could never be allowed to advance in his art. He argued and pleaded with his elders, but elven law was strict and rigid. The magic burned in his blood. He could no more throw it aside than he could have cut off and thrown aside his hands. He began to practice forbidden magic, dark magic. He was discovered, tried and convicted. He was sentenced to the most terrible sentence that could be placed upon an elf. He was brought to trial before the Heads of Household.

A female elf of rare beauty, so lovely that every person in the audience stared in dumb admiration, came forth to accuse the young elf of lusting after power.

"What is power? Nothing more than the ability to control others. Something no elf wants or needs. We have our leaders, but they govern. They do not dictate. Every elf is free—"

"Free to what?" the young elf demanded passionately. "Free to think so long as you think the same as the Heads of Household! Free to be what you will so long as you will be what they say you will be!

"You are right. I do seek power," said the elven actor in conclusion. "I will not deny it. But I seek more than power. I seek that which I will never have here in this land. I seek freedom. Freedom to dream the dreams that are my own. Freedom to pursue goals that are my own. Freedom to make mistakes. Freedom to repent and freedom to forgive."

The elf in the audience began to weep.

He sobbed uncontrollably, wracking sobs that came from deep inside him and hurt him as if he were sobbing up his heart. The human next to him reached out a hand and gingerly patted him on the back.

The play ended with the elf being bound hand and foot, thrown in a cart, which had been hauled up on stage by the ogre, and driven to the center of the stage. Here, he was thrown bodily out of the cart.

The shimmering silver forest of Silvanesti vanished. The elf lay on bare boards of the wooden stage, huddled beneath the scraggly tree. He lay long moments, his face pressed to the boards. No one in the audience moved, no one breathed.

At the last, he raised his head. He looked upon the shabby tree, so different from the lush beauty of his homeland. He spoke no word. Men in the audience who would have thought it shameful to cry if they had taken an arrow in the gut wiped away the coursing tears. Women held their children close, dabbed their eyes with the corners of babies' blankets. The elf rose unsteadily to his feet. He stood and looked beyond the tree in the tub, looked into the forests of his homeland, which could be seen only now in the imagination. Turning his back, without a word, he lifted his head and walked steadfastly off the stage.

The stage was empty for a moment, and then actors came to take their bows.

The audience leapt to its feet, cheering and stomping and roaring its approval. They surged around the stage to shake the hands of the actors, to take a little part of them away with them. The innkeeper invited the entire troupe, elves and ogres and all, back to his tavern for a drink. The actors politely declined. They needed their rest. They would camp here for the night and then move on in the morrow.

The villagers drifted away, talking in excited, wondrous tones of all they had seen. "You know," said one, "elves don't seem much different from us. I remember saying almost the very same thing to my father when I was but a lad."

"I know how he felt, poor thing," said a woman. "So did I feel when I left my home for the first time."

The elf sat huddled on his bench until all had gone, his mind in turmoil. Eventually, when the benches were empty and the ogre and the dwarf were expertly and swiftly dismantling the stage, the elf rose to his feet. He could not bring himself to talk to the ogre, but he thought he might speak to the dwarf, although he had never even seen one before in his life.

"Where . . . where might I find . . . the director?" he asked nervously.

The dwarf looked up. He had bright black eyes and a long beard and he didn't seem the least bit astonished at the question. He pointed with his hammer.

"First wagon. No need to knock. He's hoping you would come."

"He is?" The elf was astonished.

The dwarf went back to his work, knocking boards loose and yanking out nails, which he stuffed into a pouch to be hammered straight and used again. The elf headed for the lead wagon, passing the tree in the tub on his way. He eyed it closely. It was just a tree in a tub.

He walked to the first wagon, one side of which was painted to resemble a night sky, with stars set in all the constellations sacred to the vanished gods and the three moons: silver Solinari, red Lunitari, and even the black moon, Nuitari. The opposite side of the wagon was painted to look like day, lit by a jovial sun whose face was that of Sebastius himself.

"Not much of an ego," the elf muttered.

He mounted the steps to the wagon and was lifting his hand to knock—he did not truly believe the dwarf, thought he was making sport of him—when a voice called out to him.

"Enter, friend. I have been waiting for you."

The elf entered, wary, his hand on the hilt of his sword. The interior of the wagon was dark; he could not see his host.

"Sit down. Let me light this candle. Now, much better."

The jovial sun-and-bread-dough face of Sebastius leapt into being and it was his face that seemed to fill the wagon with light, not the single candle. The elf sat down on the edge of his chair. He left the door open behind him.

"You have traveled long and far," said Sebastius. "But then all roads are long and far that have no end in sight. Especially those roads which lead away from home. For home is barred to you, is it not, friend? You are one of those who is not welcome among his kind. What is termed a dark elf, one who is cast from the light.

"Nay, sheathe your weapon!" Sebastius waved his hand. "Here are no sheriffs. Here are no bounty hunters. Here you are safe."

"How did you know?" the elf asked in a low voice.

"I saw you leaving your homeland. I saw you come to the crossroads," Sebastius replied complacently. "That was why I posted the theater bill there. That and the hope that I might snag a few coppers from the locals, of course."

"You saw me?" The elf was incredulous. "That is impossible! How could you see me? How could you know I was coming? You are a mountebank, a charlatan." The elf rose to his feet.

"How did I know what play to put on this night?" Sebastius asked slyly. "I put on this play for you. You don't believe me? Answer me this. Would you have come to see 'Magius and the Goblin King?' Would have you have come to see 'The Life and Tragic Death of Sir Rogar of Mooria'? Would you have come to see 'The Magical Sword of Kith-Kanan'? Or how about 'Uncle Trapspringer and the Three Gully Dwarves Gruff'? Oh, I have thousands of them. Right here." Sebastius tapped his forehead. "One for every person who has ever lived upon Krynn. As I said, tonight's performance was for you."

The elf sat back down. He sat down slowly, as if the chair were pulling him and he was reluctant to obey.

"Who are you?" he asked, half believing the human and half irritated at himself for believing.

The human rose to his feet and made a theatrical bow.

"I am Sebatius, son of Gilean," he said with a flourish.

"Son of Gilean!" The elf snorted. "The god Gilean had no sons. Only a daughter. Lunitari."

"Well, there are those who say that," said Sebatius, resuming his seat. He leaned back in his chair, extended his portly legs and entwined the fingers of his hands over his broad belly. "And then there are those who say that Gilean has two sons. One called Astinus—perhaps you've heard of him? He runs the Great Library in Palanthas. The other is myself." He smiled with becoming modesty. "Astinus chronicles all life on Krynn in his great book. I chronicle life, as well, only in my own way."

"Since the god is not here to denounce you, I guess you may call yourself his son and no one will dispute you," the elf said sourly. "Yes, I came to the crossroads. Yes, I took the playbill. All that is true. But I acted of my own volition. No hocus-pocus made me come." He looked very hard at Sebastius as he said this.

"Certainly not!" Sebastius said firmly. "Free will. A precept of my father's. We believe in it most strongly here, as perhaps you noticed from tonight's play. 'Freedom to repent and freedom to forgive'. Some of my best lines. Of your own free will, you could have followed the road to Palanthas. You can still follow it of your own free will. Of your own free will you could have left before the play started. You could have left after it was finished of your own free will. Yet, here you are. Of your own free will. You have come not to where you intended to go but to where you need to be. Such is often the way of life. Your heart brought you here."

"Then why *have* I come?" the elf asked in a tone that was both challenging and questioning, as if he himself was hoping to find out the answer.

"You want to join our troupe, of course," said Sebastius. "You want to be an actor."

The elf looked as if he would deny it.

Sebastius did not give him a chance. "Tell me what you thought of our play?"

The elf's stern and defensive expression softened.

"It was wonderful," he said softly. "The elf who played Dalamar . . . He moved me to my very soul. I have not been able to cry, not since they cast me out. I was filled with anger and resentment. Those terrible flames burned up all the tears I had. But . . . tonight. The tears came."

"He is gifted, that one," said Sebastius, nodding. "Tonight was his best performance. It was also his last performance."

The elf looked up quickly, warily, thinking he heard something behind the words, as one dozing hears voices but has no sense of what they are saying.

Sebastius continued on, however, with what might have been mundane pleasantries. "And where are you bound, friend?"

"Palanthas," the elf said and shifted his gaze away.

"Palanthas," Sebastius repeated. "A good choice. A city in which one can lose oneself in the crowd. Even an elf, though that might be more difficult. What will you do in Palanthas, friend? There are not many humans even in that enlightened city who will hire elves to work for them. How will you earn your bread and bed?"

"What concern is that of yours?" The elf thought he should leave this old busybody, and wondered why he didn't.

"I have connections in Palanthas," Sebastius said smoothly. "My brother, you know. Astinus."

"Yes, right." The elf rolled his eyes.

"Here, read this for me. Let me hear your voice."

"Why?" The elf was suspicious.

"No reason. Call it curiosity."

Sebastius slid over a sheet of paper.

The elf looked at it, saw that it was a portion of a play, for there were the actor's names in the margins and there the lines they were to speak. He cast yet another suspicious glance at Sebastius, but the man's face was smooth and innocent of guile as that of a pan of milk.

"Take the speech there," Sebastius said, leaning over to point.

Curious himself to hear how he would sound reading these lines, the elf began to read. Only when he was begun did he realize that the lines he was speaking were those which Dalamar had spoken at his trial.

"'I seek that which I will never have here in this land. I seek freedom. Freedom to dream the dreams that are my own. Freedom to pursue goals that are my own. Freedom to make mistakes. Freedom to repent and freedom to forgive.'"

At first, the elf was stiff and self-conscious in front of Sebastius, sadly aware that his voice could never imbue these words with the feeling that the actor had given them. But then he forgot that he spoke before an audience. When he came to the last line, he said it from his heart.

Sebastius tapped his fingers lightly on the arm of his chair by way of applause.

"Did I do well?" the elf asked, his face flushing in pleasure.

"No," Sebastius said. "You were stilted at the beginning and sadly over-dramatic at the end. You need training. No shame in that. Your voice is quite good, however. A wonderful instrument. Wasted on a thief."

The elf's flush deepened to an ugly crimson.

"And why not?" he demanded defiantly. "What do I care what happens to me? No one else does. And why should I care about anyone else? I must look out for myself."

Angrily, he shoved the speech back toward Sebastius. But his gaze lingered on it, as did his fingers.

"I believe I mentioned that the elf who gave the performance this night is leaving our troupe."

"You said something about that, yes," the elf replied in surly tones. "Why? Has he received a better offer?"

"Ah, that would not be possible. I offer my players what no one else on Krynn can offer. He always said that he would leave once he gave what he considered to be a perfect performance. His work this night was the one. He can never equal it, or so he believes. He has done what he set out to do, he has achieved what he has worked toward for long years, and this night he moves on. You will take his place."

Sebastius sighed heavily. "I will miss him, though. He was the one who gave me the idea for the story of Kith-Kanan and the magical sword. He knew Kith-Kanan, you see."

"Bah! If he said so, he lied!" the elf replied with a scornful laugh. "Kith-Kanan has been dead for hundreds and hundreds of years. Not even the longest lived among our kind could begin to remember him."

"Ah, but he does. He joined me shortly after Kith-Kanan

ascended the throne. He's been with me the longest of any of the troupe and now it is his time to go on with his life. When he leaves here, he will start to age again normally."

"I believe that you are serious!" the elf said, astounded.

"Oh, I am. Quite serious. You see this glyph?" Sebastius turned his forearm to the light. "The black lotus. If you join us, if you commit yourself to us, you will have this glyph stamped upon your skin. This glyph means that you will never be killed, you will never go hungry, you will never fall sick, you will never age, you will never die. So long as you are with us."

"You are saying that I will be immortal?" The elf was skeptical.

"Ah, that seems a great gift, doesn't it? But I demand a price in return."

"I have no money," the elf began.

"Not money," Sebastius said. "Your soul. Your soul can never more be your own. Your soul is taken away and in exchange you receive the souls of others, countless others. You will feel their pain, their joy, their sorrow, their triumph. You will be a kender, an ogre, a goblin. You will be a king and know what it is to live in a palace. You will be a gully dwarf and know what it is to live in the meanest squalor.

"Did I say you would never die? Your body will never die. The souls who inhabit that body will die a hundred deaths and yet you will live. You will love a hundred loves and never be true to any of them and yet you will be faithful to all of them."

The elf was shaking his head. "I don't understand."

"No, but you will. Our life is a good life and we do good work. I chronicle Krynn in my own way, you see. My actors and I take our book from place to place and open it for all to read. We have played in the steam-filled halls of Mt. Nevermind. We have played in the foul-smelling lairs of the hobgoblins. We have played for ogres who tossed the bones of their victims at us by way of applause. We have played for the dwarves of Thorbardin and for their cousins who live in the hills. We tell our stories and if we do not change minds, sometimes we may change a heart.

"A strange life, but a rich one. Will you join us, friend?"

The elf hesitated. "I don't really believe any of this," he said. "Not about being immortal and all that."

"You didn't believe a tree in a tub could be the forest of Silvanesti, did you?" Sebastius asked gently.

The elf was discomfited. "Well, I have nothing else to do. Nowhere else to go. I guess I could stay . . . just for awhile, mind you. Maybe help with the scenery."

Yet, as he spoke, his fingers touched the speech.

"Take that with you, if you like," Sebastius said mildly. "Take the entire play. Study it. We will begin your training in the morning."

"I have not said—"

"Take it!" Sebastius rose to his feet. "No harm in that. Your wagon is the fifteenth in line, the one that is painted green with yellow trimmings. You will find it vacant, I believe. Its previous owner has probably traveled on by now."

The elf walked back along the row of wagons, counting them as he went. He was confused and dubious. His head didn't believe in any of it and his heart believed every word. Like the play. He knew it was a play. He knew it wasn't real. And yet the reality of it had brought him to tears.

He arrived at number fifteen, looked up to see a wagon that was green with yellow trimmings.

The actor who had played Dalamar stood in the doorway. He looked out into the world and he smiled to himself in anticipation. His gaze shifted to his fellow elf, who stood staring at the actor in abashment and awe.

"Yours now, I believe," the actor said politely, indicating the wagon. "You'll find it quite comfortable. The right front wheel squeaks. Tell Rorg about it. He's the goblin. He takes care of the maintenance. Don't mention it to Quince the gnome, however. Not if you want to still have wheels in the morning."

"Where will you go?" the elf asked.

"To reclaim my soul and keep it for my own," the elf replied with a smile.

"Then . . . what *he* said." The elf looked back over his shoulder to the very front wagon. "Sebastius. Then it's . . . true?"

"Ours is a world of make-believe. Make-believe that is truer than truth." The actor held his bare forearm to the moonlight.

Lunitari's red light shone on the actor's slender arm and by that light the elf saw a black lotus, the same as he had seen on the arm of Sebastius. As the elf watched in astonishment, the black lotus on the actor's arm faded away and slowly disappeared.

The actor made a bow, as if taking his leave at the final curtain. "What have you there?" he asked. "The play?"

"Your speech in the last act," the elf said, awash in embarrassment. "I was . . . was only going to . . ."

"Let's hear how you sound," the actor said encouragingly.

The elf looked down at the speech of Dalamar he held in his hand. Lunitari's light was bright. He could read the words with ease.

"No, really, I . . . You were so wonderful . . . I couldn't . . ."

He tried to get out of it, but the actor stood there and looked as if meant to keep standing there and finally, not knowing what else to do, the elf began to read. As he stumbled over the words, he caught a glimpse of movement out of the corner of his eye and looked at his arm. A large black splotch appeared on his skin. A splotch that was shapeless at first but which slowly, slowly began to take shape and form.

The elf felt his soul slip away. He had not lost it. His soul was being held somewhere, on account, until he should come back to retrieve it. He was frightened, however, at the terrible emptiness left by the loss. His voice faltered.

"No," said the actor. "Feel it like this."

The actor who had played Dalamar put his hand in the hand of the elf who would come to play Dalamar.

The elf was empty no longer. He drew something of the actor's reclaimed soul into the empty place where his own had been. He experienced the wrenching sorrow the actor knew at leaving his home, at parting with dear friends. He experienced the wild joy of freedom, of returning to the world, of starting down a new path.

"Better," said the actor, approving. "Now make your bow."

The elf bowed to applause only he could hear. For the time being, at least. Someday, he knew, someday they would weep for him as he had wept. Someday they would cheer for him as he had cheered.

When he straightened, he found his audience gone. But there on his arm, crisp and clear, was a black lotus.

The newest member of Gilean's troupe entered the green wagon with the yellow trimmings and made it his own.

Through the Dragonlance Years with Weis & Hickman

Margaret Weis and Tracy Hickman are the co-authors of the best-selling Chronicles and Legends trilogies, *Dragons of Summer Flame*, The War of Souls trilogy, and several volumes of short stories and novellas. Originally based on the roleplaying campaign world, their books have sold upwards of thirteen million copies worldwide and have been translated into a dozen foreign languages. They write prolifically, alone, together, and with other collaborators.

Weis and Hickman were interviewed separately in 1998, for the Winter issue of *Legends of the Lance*.

Tracy, at what point did you stop thinking of the Dragonlance setting as a game system and begin to think of yourself as a prospective novelist?

HICKMAN: Becoming a novelist crept up on me and took me by surprise. You'll notice that Margaret's name comes first on all of our work. Primarily that is because Margaret was the writer; I was always going to be a game designer, forever. I had never really seen myself as a writer.

In fact, there are still mornings when I wake up and I have to question if I really am a writer, or if people are being faked out. DRAGONLANCE novels have been out for years, and it's literally only been recently that I've begun to think of myself as a novelist and writer.

What actually spurred your decision to write the novels together?

HICKMAN: I'd been working hard on the DRAGONLANCE setting for a number of months. Margaret was originally hired as a book editor for TSR, and then her first assignment was to edit the DRAGONLANCE books, as I recall. Margaret and I were both unhappy with the direction the manuscript had been taking thus far. A writer had been designated by the company to produce the book, and he did not have the vision of it that we did.

Actually I had come to Arizona for Christmas, that winter of '82, I think it was. While on vacation, I read a Star Trek book by Diane Duane that I found extremely clever. For some reason, reading that book at that time sparked something inside of me. I told myself I had to find some way to write the DRAGONLANCE books. Interestingly enough, Margaret had come to the same conclusion, independently. When we got together after Christmas break, I came into her office and frankly was delighted to hear her tell me that we were really the ones to write the books. It all jelled in that moment.

Why you two? Her status was new, and you weren't a senior game designer, were you?

HICKMAN: No, by no stretch of the imagination. As a matter of fact, that was a saving grace for us. It was the fact that we were not the seniors, or considered to be the most prized on staff, that allowed it to happen. I'm actually grateful to the more prized designers, because they ran interference for us. Whenever management had a game they wanted produced, they always went to these lead designers first. So much of their time was occupied in trying to satisfy management demands. The rest of us were considered the grunt workers and not terribly stellar, and we were quietly left to do brilliant work. It was from those of us who were not the front-runners—not the heads of departments and so forth—that the DRAGONLANCE setting came together and was created.

Initially, the DRAGONLANCE project came from a game proposal that I submitted. There were of course many other people who became involved very quickly. But I think no one understood how story-driven the DRAGONLANCE line would be, how character-driven it would become. Characters and stories were the province of Margaret and me, and to a certain extent, very early on, Michael Williams, who assisted us tremendously in crafting the plot.

How do the two of you work together?

HICKMAN: I think our partnership is unique as all partnerships are unique. One of the wonderful things I appreciate about our partnership is that it has evolved. I don't think that people can work together, without evolving, to allow each other to grow and to allow for all the changes that life brings. Life has changed our thinking and tremendously influenced the partnership, and its evolution is what has kept it so vibrant. In terms of how we actually work together on any one book, that too has evolved. Initially I was the background creator and evolved from there into the storyteller. I was the guy who came up with the basic ideas for plots and themes for books, and then was left to craft the background, while Margaret did the first draft. We'd often exchange texts and ask for changes or more description of characters or incidents.

One of my favorite stories is that, early on in DRAGONLANCE novels, Margaret had the tendency to write the most vibrant battle scenes, while the one really hot love scene—in the second book, between Silvara and Gilthanas—was the one that I wrote. Everyone thought that it was the other way around.

As the years have gone by, I have learned a great deal more about the craft of writing and have begun writing on my own. Margaret has grown tremendously in her ability to tell a story as well. Therefore, the clear-cut lines between what each of us does within a story have actually become blurred, and we each contribute what best we can, depending on the schedule.

People worry that you're done collaborating in the world of Krynn.

HICKMAN: People don't understand the nature of our relationship to begin with, or its evolution. I've moved out West, primarily to be close to my family. Margaret has stayed in Wisconsin. Despite all this, I still get mail that says, "I love the books that you and your wife write together. . . ." Of course I also still get mail addressed to "Ms. Hickman"—and that's even after we started putting my picture in books! Don't worry, we expect to write more DRAGONLANCE novels together, and we expect to write some additional DRAGONLANCE novels separately as well.

****

Also in *Legends of the Lance* Margaret Weis reminisced about the origins and evolution two of the Dragonlance setting's most popular characters.

Where did the name "Raistlin" come from?

WEIS: Harold Johnson, I think. As I remember, Raistlin was originally something like "Waistman" and Caramon was supposed to be "Caring-Man." By the time I came to work at TSR in '83, however, everyone had been named and they all had their game stats. I was just given the names of these people and their stats, and told to make flesh-and-blood characters of them. The stat of Raistlin said his nickname was "The Sly One." He was thin and in not very good health, in contrast to his warrior brother. And he had golden skin and hourglass eyes. I remember asking, "Well, why does he have golden skin and hourglass eyes?" and people said, "The artists just thought that would look cool." I had to come up with a reason why he had golden skin and hourglass eyes, and that led to the whole business about the Test in the Tower. I wrote that short story ["The Test of the Twins"], the first one we ever published, in an '84 issue of *DRAGON* magazine, I believe. That is what gave me a lot of insight into Raistlin's character.

In his foreword to your 1998 book The Soulforge, *Tracy Hickman also gives a lot of credit to his friend Terry Phillips.*

WEIS: Terry was the one who kind of set Raistlin's character in a game-testing session Tracy writes about in his foreword. Terry was a professional actor, and he did decide to play Raistlin with a whispering voice, based on his character description as being sort of weak. What we noticed in the playtest is that everybody was yelling and shouting, like you do, and then all of a sudden Terry would start to say something and everybody would shut up and listen. I thought that was pretty cool, definitely something Raistlin would use even if he didn't need to. Speaking softly sometimes gets you more attention than a shout.

Why do you think people connect so strongly with Raistlin?

WEIS: Power is sexy, and Raistlin has a lot of power. It's mysterious power. We find that women in particular really like Raistlin. He's the dark hero; they think, if only he'd respond to love, he would turn to good. Men identify with him because, unless they're bodybuilders, they've also felt weak and vulnerable in their lives. Everyone wishes they had a magic power that would get them over this feeling. Too, I think the sibling rivalry catches a lot of people. Everybody has felt jealous of a brother or sister, and can really identify with Raistlin on that score.

We know that Caramon is Raistlin's twin. Is he his equal?

WEIS: Yes, but he doesn't realize it. That's what's interesting about Caramon's character and what really comes out in *Legends*. It's a very codependent relationship. Caramon is bigger and stronger than Raistlin, more handsome; the women love him. But he's always living in Raistlin's shadow, because he has to take care of him, but also because he's living his life through Raistlin. That's what leads him into alcoholism, when Raistlin finally leaves and breaks the tie.

Why did it take you so long to write the story behind The Soulforge*?*

WEIS: I had always thought the Test in the Tower should remain mysterious. Also, to be quite honest, I didn't know what happened during the Test. I didn't know until I actually sat down and wrote it and got to that point in the book. Which is kind of an odd experience, because usually when I wrote a book I have everything mapped out in my mind and I know exactly what the ending is going to be. In this case, I did know what the ending was going to be, but I didn't quite know how I was going to get there. I didn't really know what happened between Raistlin and Fistandantilus.

Did you ask Tracy about his opinion on what happened during the Test?

WEIS: Over the years we talked about Raistlin many times. Raistlin was always sort of "my character." I don't think Tracy ever really liked him. Tracy always took Caramon's part, which was good, because it gave me a nice balance.

****

In 2000, preceding the publication of *Dragons of a Fallen Sun*, the first book in the War of Souls trilogy, Weis and Hickman were interviewed for the Wizards of the Coast website.

How and why did the War of Souls project originate?

HICKMAN: It actually began when TSR was acquired by Wizards of the Coast. Margaret and I had been concerned for a while about the direction DRAGONLANCE was taking. There was a definite schism between fans of the Fifth Age stories and the fans of the earlier Fourth Age tales, each side proclaiming that their view was the "true" view of DRAGONLANCE. We very much wanted to bring everyone together again, uniting the best of both, and bring them to a common ground in a new and unique way. With the change in ownership, Margaret and I both saw an opportunity to come in and make a difference where Dragonlance was concerned. Peter Adkison, then president of Wizards of the Coast, personally had a great deal to do with making this possible, and I am grateful to him for it.

WEIS: TSR, Inc. had been in financial trouble for many months until they were sold. We were all of worried that this would be the end of everything—DRAGONLANCE included. When Peter bought the company, it was as if a new day dawned. The idea of starting a new day in DRAGONLANCE seemed perfect timing.

How close did the trilogy come to the original plans for it? What were the major ways in which the storyline changed and evolved during the writing?

HICKMAN: Margaret and I flew out to Wizards headquarters in Renton, Washington, for a series of meetings on DRAGONLANCE and its future direction. I had been contemplating the ending of *Dragons of Summer Flame* and how the seeds of everything that had happened in the Fifth Age—good and bad—were as a direct result of that ending. We were scheduled to meet on the first morning with the design staff. I remember everyone seemed pretty tense about the meeting. I had insisted on not only using my own agendas for all the meetings, but on running the meetings as well. Margaret, Don [Perrin], Laura [Hickman] and I met for breakfast before the meetings. I remember telling Margaret that I wasn't sure but that I had an idea about what we should do.

Peter Adkison was at the morning meetings—I think mostly to make sure that a fistfight didn't break out between all the different parties involved. We listened to presentations by the game design and book departments as well as others. I guess it was about eleven in the morning when the presentations were finished (I like my meetings to run by the clock), and it was my turn. I remember all the different hopes, dreams and visions of DRAGONLANCE that I had heard that morning. Then I stood up, took a deep breath and said, "I'm going to tell you a story." The story I told at that meeting is essentially the same story that you find in the War of Souls books. The course of the plot is essentially the same and the ending is the same.

Have the books and story evolved? Absolutely. You cannot write a book properly without allowing it to "breathe" a little in the telling. There were changes in plotting and in characters, all along the way . . . but the story itself remains true in all important aspects to the tale I told in that first meeting on that first day.

WEIS: Yes, the story has evolved. In the beginning, we really didn't know many of the characters and those we did know (Palin, Tasslehoff, Laurana) were destined to undergo changes. It is important for an author to listen to the characters. They tell you the tales of their own destiny. But as Tracy says, we never deviated from his original plot idea.

I do have to say that, on that day, hearing Tracy reveal what had truly happened to the world literally took my breath away. And I do want to thank the Fifth Age Game Group and Jean Rabe, who came up with some fantastic ideas that were fun to work with as the story evolved.

Who did you plan to kill, who stayed alive? (Or vice versa.) And why?

HICKMAN: No character's death is taken lightly, and we never kill a character without a purpose or reason behind it. There were some deaths that were foreseen from the outset: the most important of which is found near the end of the book. Life and death in Krynn are very much at the center of the War of Souls.

WEIS: Every character's death has a meaning to the story. As I say, we listen to the characters. They tell us how they want to live their lives. They tell us what they want to say with their deaths.

How and why did Tasselhoff become so central to DRAGONLANCE *from the outset of the books?*

WEIS: Tasslehoff is innocence. He has no agenda. He has no allegiance or nationality. He acknowledges that there are reasons for these things, but he understands that there are more important things in life—the small things. He sees through sham and charades to the truth. He punctures pomposity. He laughs at pride. He is loyal to his friends to the death and beyond. He is the wisest person in the books.

HICKMAN: Tasselhoff is simply a great deal of fun. He's the sidekick that we always wanted: a guy who is essentially fun to have around and yet is so annoying to others that he makes us look good. We never planned to make him a central figure, but I think his evolution over time has been one of the most interesting aspects of DRAGONLANCE on the whole.

How did you come up with the idea of Mina?

HICKMAN: Mina was not originally our invention. The character itself had its seeds planted by the creators and designers working with the Fifth Age. Margaret and I simply took that great seed of a character and evolved her into a character of our own: an "anti-Joan of Arc," as I described her in the first telling of the story. As the trilogy comes to a close, I think she is by far our most fascinating character.

WEIS: I wanted Mina to be a dark Joan of Arc. I did research on Joan, including reading Mark Twain's book about her life. I always enjoy working with the darker characters of DRAGONLANCE and Mina was no exception. The really tricky part was that she has secrets which we couldn't reveal to the reader, so the reader was never permitted to see inside Mina, thus making her a very mysterious figure.

In the older DRAGONLANCE tales, with the Kingpriest—and in the new DRAGONLANCE stories, with Mina—you have characters that are evil but with good intentions. Why is that an ongoing theme in the DRAGONLANCE world?

HICKMAN: Actually, I see the Kingpriest and Mina as opposite sides of the same coin. The Kingpriest did evil things with good intentions while Mina, in my eye, seems to do good things with evil intentions. In both cases, however, they thought themselves the purveyors of ultimate truth and right. Much of this goes to the question of the definition of good and evil—the very theme of defining those intangibles being much at the heart of DRAGONLANCE stories. Both the Kingpriest and Mina are obviously "evil." In one case the end does not justify the means and in the other case the means do not justify the ends. Taken together, I think these two characters have a lot to say about the nature and definition of evil—and the exploration of that question is very much a continuing theme in DRAGONLANCE.

WEIS: Tracy said that perfectly. Not much I can add, except that such themes will continue to be explored in the future of DRAGONLANCE.

One of the most enigmatic characters of the DRAGONLANCE storyline is Lord Soth. How did he develop—and where is he now?

HICKMAN: Lord Soth sprang to life—if that is the proper word for him—one day in my game designer cubicle at TSR. I was working up the design for a game module called *Dragons of War* when his character just exploded into being in my mind. I was so excited about it that I ran over to Margaret's cubicle and told her his tragic history. The problem was that the character was just so fascinating and powerful. Whenever we allowed him into a book, he just sort of hijacked it! He always wanted a bigger role and kept dragging the story off in directions that we really didn't want to go. I think I know where Lord Soth is these days but that really should wait until after *Dragons of a Vanished Moon* (the concluding volume of the War of Souls trilogy) is widely read. His fate is heavily implied in that book and probably best discussed at a later time.

WEIS: Lord Soth is a tragic antihero. He is a great character because of his dark romantic past. He is a great villain because he is a sympathetic villain. We can understand and identify with his motives.

How did you come up with the new DRAGONLANCE covers by artist Matt Stawicki? And how in your opinion does Stowicki's style fit into the tradition of DRAGONLANCE?

HICKMAN: I personally love Matt's covers. I think they bring a very epic feel to our books. I love the way the art looks and could only wish to have one of those painting hanging on the wall of my home somewhere. Before the first book cover was designed, Margaret, Matt, [company executive] Mary Kirchoff, myself and several others got together at GenCon and discussed the look we wanted for this series. Everyone thought that "cinematic" was the feel we wanted to see. Someone suggested that a "letterbox" format, with the picture looking "widescreen," was a great approach. Someone also suggested that the front should feature characters from the books, but the back should be used to show something of the world. I think Matt's paintings convey all of those feelings beautifully. He has been a great part in making these books a success.

WEIS: I think Matt has done a wonderful job with DRAGONLANCE. He's picked up the mantle handed down by the other great artists of DRAGONLANCE. Long may he paint!

****

We asked Weis and Hickman, for this special anniversary edition of their collected short stories and novellas, to bring us up to date on their activities. What lies in their respective futures—and the future of DRAGONLANCE?

HICKMAN: A break in my writing schedule has allowed me to do something I've wanted to do for a long time now; write with my wife again. Laura [Hickman] and I started our married life publishing our own game adventures. It was while we were both driving across the country to take a new job with TSR that we came up with the foundations of what would become DRAGONLANCE. Down the years, raising our family and other commitments has left us without time to pursue working together. Now Laura and I are overjoyed to discover that not only can we still write together but we truly enjoy doing so. Our first new fantasy series together is The Bronze Canticles trilogy for Time-Warner books and we are looking forward to many and diverse project in the future—including, we hope, a Dragonlance novel of our own.

WEIS: In other worlds, the second book in the Dragonvarld series, published by Tor Books, will be out in July 2004. The book is called *Dragon's Son* and tells the story of Ven, who is half-human and half-dragon, and his twin brother, Marcus. Both young men have the dragon magic in their blood and both must learn not only how to use it, but to hide it from both humans and dragons. Only the dragon turned human, Draconas, can protect the boys from his own kind, as well as from humans, and he has his own dilemma. He must decide whose side he is on—humans or dragons? For it is becoming increasingly clear that war between the two is inevitable. I am currently working on the final book of that series—*Master of Dragons.*

And I have just finished the first volume in the Dark Disciple series, my new Dragonlance trilogy. Called *Amber and Ashes*, the book picks up the story of Mina after the War of Souls books, telling her tale against the backdrop of a world trying to come to grips with the return of the gods and the ensuing power struggles, both on earth and in heaven. It's important to note that even if you've never read the War of Souls books—or any other Dragonlance book—you will be able to read and enjoy the story of Mina, whose life takes a new and completely unexpected turn in this novel.

Legends Trilogy

Margaret Weis & Tracy Hickman

Each volume available for the first time ever in hardcover!

TIME OF THE TWINS
Volume I

Caramon Majere vows to protect Crysania, a devout cleric, in her quest to save Raistlin from himself. But both are soon caught in the dark mage's deadly designs, and their one hope is a frivolous kender.

WAR OF THE TWINS
Volume II

Catapulted through time by Raistlin's dark magics, Caramon and Crysania are forced to aid the mage in his quest to defeat the Queen of Darkness.

TEST OF THE TWINS
Volume III

As Raistlin's plans come to fruition, Caramon comes face to face with his destiny. Old friends and strange allies come to aid him, but Caramon must take the final step alone.

November 2004

Strife and warfare tear at the land of Ansalon

FLIGHT OF THE FALLEN

The Linsha Trilogy, Volume Two

Mary H. Herbert

As the Plains of Dust are torn asunder by invading barbarian forces, Rose Knight Linsha Majere is torn between two vows—her pledge to the Knighthood, and her pledge to guard the eggs of the dragon overlord Iyesta. To keep her honor, Linsha will have to make the ultimate sacrifice.

CITY OF THE LOST

The Linsha Trilogy, Volume One

Available Now!

LORD OF THE ROSE

Rise of Solamnia, Volume One

Douglas Niles

In the wake of the War of Souls, the realms of Solamnia are wracked by strife and internecine warfare, and dire external threats lurk on its borders. A young lord, marked by courage and fateful flaws, emerges from the hinterlands. His vow: he will unite the fractious reaches of the ancient knighthood—or die in the attempt.

November 2004

Follow Mina from the War of Souls into the chaos of post-war Krynn.

AMBER AND ASHES

The Dark Disciple, Volume I

Margaret Weis

With Paladine and Takhisis gone, the lesser gods vie for primacy over Krynn. Recruited to a new faith by a god of evil, Mina leads a religion of the dead, and kender and a holy monk are all that stand in the way of the dark stain spreading across Ansalon.

First in a new series from *New York Times* best-selling author Margaret Weis.

August 2004